TAMAR

TAMAR

Woman Behind the Veil

Barbara Kuhn

VANTAGE PRESS
New York

This is a work of fiction. Any similarity between the names and characters in this book and any real persons, living or dead (other than those cited in the Bible), is purely coincidental.

FIRST EDITION

Published by Vantage Press, Inc.
419 Park Ave. South, New York, NY 10016

Manufactured in the United States of America
ISBN: 978-0-533-15794-5

Library of Congress Catalog Card No.: 2007903126

0 9 8 7 6 5 4 3 2 1

To my son, Glen: Your memory will never die.

Author's Note

In the Bible, Chapter 38 of Genesis mentions an obscure woman named Tamar. Evidently, Tamar did not wish to remain obscure. She confounded the men in her male-dominated society by becoming her world's first liberated woman. She had an objective—to carve her own place in history, to be remembered for all time. Even to this day, Tamar's name appears in the genealogy of the Messiah, the Lion of the Tribe of Judah. To obtain her share in the covenant blessing that God promised to Israel, Tamar resorted to dirty tricks. Using her ample brains and womanly wiles upon Judah, the man who had wronged her, she played the harlot and played the man for a fool. She wore the veil of a temptress and veils of a bride and a widow. She used shrewdness and seduction before she learned submission. She got what she wanted. She lost much more than she might have had.

The Genealogy of Jesus Christ

Tamar and Judah had a son, Pharez. Pharez begat Esrom who begat Aram who begat Aminadab who begat Naasson who begat Salmon who begat Boaz who begat Obed who begat Jesse who begat King David. From David's seed, God raised unto Israel a Savior, Jesus.

—Genesis 38:27–30; Matthew 1:3–6; Acts 13:22–23

TAMAR

One

Tamar's pace quickened as she neared the end of a journey she called her *new beginning*. The walk from her father's tents to the groves of Mamre was not as long and as tiring as she remembered when, three years before, she had trudged with a reluctant pace and a heavy heart in the opposite direction.

Today a smile all but parted her round, full lips. She was not only relieved to be distancing herself from her cold, domineering father, but also excited to be approaching the place she felt she really belonged—Hebron.

Tamar could see Judah's tents in the distance. The red and white dots were actually striped, berry-juice-dyed dwellings fashioned from animal skins and situated in a circular pattern, but from where she stood, they resembled droplets of color spattered unintentionally from a paint brush onto a green landscape. It was the camp belonging to her father-in-law. It was her former and adopted home. She had been sent away from Judah's household, but, in Tamar's mind, her return today was to be permanent.

She stood on tiptoe and shielded her eyes from the waning sun for a better view. Her face was tanned and nearly hidden by the *kufiyeh* she wore over her head for protection from the elements. Beneath it lay thick, cascading, dark red hair that was her most distinguishing feature. In the sunlight or lamplight, it took on a tawny glow that framed her face and highlighted large, expressive, probing eyes that were difficult to describe. Their color was something akin to a deep purple. They resembled velvet tapestries with tiny, golden flecks that danced in reflected light and that shifted the color's hue to match her environment or moods. Most of her people had black hair and dark eyes, but Tamar was unlike her kinsmen—both in feature and demeanor.

She loved the outdoors with its changing ocean and desert

1

climates struggling against each other for mastery. It was not yet the rainy season, but signs of an early rainfall seemed evident. Farmers looked forward to such rains to soften the sun-baked ground for plowing and sowing.

Tamar's thoughts were not on the promise of an early rain. They focused on the familiar sights that caused a flutter to rise from her ample breast. Hebron, the high country, was the sacred land of promise. Its altars to the true God, Jehovah, and its numerous man-made wells were the identifiable marks of great-grandfather, Abraham. His memory was everywhere. There was the holy landmark of the Great Oak. It was said Abraham entertained angelic visitors there, and the patriarch's descendants continued to revere it as a monument to their faith. There were the hallowed caves, formed by subterranean channels to honeycomb the fertile land, which were the burial places for the honored dead. Tamar's feet were now on holy ground.

Hebron was very different from Tamar's birthplace, a land of pagan altars and heathen rituals. She felt the familiar thrill of walking upon what was called the Land of the Covenant, the promised land God gave all Abraham's descendants who were assured they would inherit his same blessings from God. Judah's father, Jacob, had told her many stories about the chosen people who came to this beloved land and the prophecies of future generations who would inhabit it.

Her favorite stories were those about heavenly visitations, angelic visions, and divine revelations directly from God. She especially was intrigued with prophecies of miraculous births—Father Abraham's son, Isaac, born to him in his old age, and Isaac's twin sons, Esau and Jacob, who fought each other in their mother's womb as a sign of two warring nations they would establish. But most precious of all was the prophecy of the promised Messiah, destined to come from the lineage of Jacob's son, Judah. She had returned to claim her part in that particular blessing.

Tamar's fingers automatically drifted down gently to touch her abdomen. She was determined that her barren womb's curse would be broken when she returned to Judah's camp. Had not Father Jacob prophesied her destiny? To claim her pledge would not be easy, but three years of waiting and planning had prepared her to confront all possible obstacles Judah would be certain to place in the path toward her goal. Laughing and almost skipping now, Tamar imagined herself reading Judah's face at their reunion. Surprise? Shock? Astonishment? Anger? All of these certainly would be expressed, but she had numerous strategies in mind to conquer each one and to turn them to her advantage.

Behind her now was the steppe land with its expansive grasses and treeless landscape. It lay between the desert and the agricultural lands. Ahead were the dense woods of evergreen oaks and a profusion of colorful flowers—anemones, alpine violets, iris, and all the other floral magnificence typical of a forest climate with abundant winter rainfall. Tamar denied herself the pleasure of stopping to pick a bouquet of the fragrant blossoms. She paused only long enough to snatch one perfect bloom for her hair, then she moved on. Each step brought her nearer to the yellow-brown wheat and barley fields, the plenteous olive orchards, and the vineyards of grapes. Her mouth watered at the thought of those plump, luscious grapes with plentiful juice for the wineskins.

Such thoughts forced Tamar to pause long enough to drink from the skin water jug she carried over one shoulder. Then she was on her way again, until, at last, the paint dots transformed themselves into dwelling places. There was the familiar well. She could identify several figures busying themselves around the encampment. She searched the faces of the servant women as they sat cross-legged on the ground, weaving willow baskets and platters from close-woven fibers of palms and rushes. As she approached, the low buzzing of the women's voices indicated that Tamar had become the topic of their conversation.

At last, Tamar caught sight of the face for which she had been searching. A dark-haired servant girl of barely sixteen summers squatted before the outdoor oven, baking the evening bread on a smooth, flat baking stone. Tamar clasped her bundles to her breast and ran, sandaled feet barely touching the ground, earrings dancing with the movement of her graceful, slender body, her fiery hair flying with her *kufiyeh* like a lustrous, metallic banner in the breeze.

Even before the servant girl could possibly hear, Tamar was shouting her name with every quick step: "Cumi! Cumi! Cumi!"

Upon hearing her name, the girl looked up from her work to see the approaching figure. Before her eyes verified the identity, she murmured what her instincts told her: *Tamar returns.*

Running to embrace the friend of her youth, Tamar exhaled breathlessly, "Peace unto you, Cumi. Did I not tell you I would be back?"

They exchanged customary greetings, right arms over the other's shoulder, the left about the side, and then touched first the left and then the right cheeks. Wide-eyed with surprise, Cumi nodded without responding as she stooped to pick up the bundles which had fallen in the moment of excitement. Cumi simply had no words, not even the traditional welcoming phrases extended to a visitor. Hers were mixed emotions—delight at seeing an old friend after a three-year separation, and anxiety—the fearful dread of what Tamar's presence within her master's household surely would mean.

Tamar took no notice of Cumi's reluctance to speak, for the girl was shy, and Tamar was too caught up in the exhilarating awareness of being—at long last—at her journey's end.

"Oh, Cumi, how good to see you again!" Tamar said, still gasping for her breath. "And how the young bud has blossomed!"

Cumi's eyes fell self-consciously at the allusion to her rounding figure, suddenly transformed into womanhood.

At last, Cumi spoke: "I think time changes us all. You do not appear the same, Tamar."

Tamar laughed. It was the same vibrant, rippling laughter Cumi remembered. "Ah, you expected to see me still in my mourning robes, did you, Little One?" Tamar asked, tossing her head so defiantly that her earrings sang out a tinkling protest. "Dark colors are most unbecoming, do you not agree?"

Cumi flushed and fumbled with the bundles. It was expected that a widow should remain in mourning until she remarried, but Cumi did not wish to stress the point. Instead, she moved toward the main tent, Judah's living quarters, and called over her shoulder to Tamar, "Come inside. You must be tired."

Tamar followed Cumi into the sprawling dwelling in the midst of the smaller tents occupied by the women and servants. The lingering sunlight cast a glowing haze upon everything in sight, making Tamar even more aware of the beauty about her. Nothing was more pleasurable to her eyes than the comforts and luxury with which Judah surrounded himself. Immediately, Tamar stretched herself out, full form, upon the heavy, sheepskin rug to touch its softness with her fingertips, to feel the numbness of a day's journey drain from her limbs as she lay there, her eager eyes taking in the magnificence. It was not just that her father's tent was poorer and sparser by comparison. It also was darker, forbidding, and unwelcoming. Judah's home was full of beauty and light. Perhaps it was the heavenly blessing that rested there, unseen but felt all the same.

"I had almost forgotten how restful it is here," Tamar murmured. "And how lovely—the golden vessels, the fine linen tapestries . . ."

Bringing water in a basin and setting it before her guest, Cumi said, "Master Judah is almost as wealthy now as Father Jacob. So many great flocks and herds has he that many had to be sent to Adullam for pasture."

Tamar nodded as she sat up to remove her sandals and place her hot, road-weary feet into the basin of cool water. She removed her head covering and shook her hair as she brushed the fine film of dust from the yellow fringe and embroidery on her *aba*. Then she took the damp cloth Cumi offered her and began to bathe her hands and face.

"In truth, Cumi, I saw the bounty of Judah's flocks grazing on the hillside. And the vast vineyards were never more abundant with fruit. It was a sight to behold."

The reference to the vineyards reminded Cumi of her manners. She asked, "May I serve you some refreshment?" as she moved toward the long serving table laden with dried fruit, smoked mutton, sweetmeats, loaves of fresh bread, and gurglets of wine.

Tamar reclined again and spread her arms wide, both in pro-

5

test and as if to gather all the totality of Judah's possessions unto herself.

"Not now," she said. "Just let me drink in the wonder of this place for a while."

Tamar patted a spot beside her on the sheepskin and said, "Sit here with me, Cumi, and tell me all that has come to pass since I left. It is so good to be home."

"Home?" Cumi repeated too quickly with eyebrows raised. It never occurred to Cumi that Tamar planned more than a short visit. In haste, she began to wipe Tamar's refreshed feet with the soft, linen napkin she had thrown over one shoulder. Trying to force her voice to a natural-sounding pitch, she asked, as off-handedly as she could, "You plan to be living here?"

With her feet now cooled and clean, Tamar clutched her legs under her and curled her toes into the warmth of the rug. "Do I not belong to this household?" she asked. "Am I not Judah's daughter-in-law?"

"But . . ."

"Where is the mighty lion?" Tamar asked without heeding Cumi's attempt to protest.

Cumi sensed an anxiousness in Tamar's voice and then replied, "He and Shelah will be in from inspecting the fields soon. It is nearly the hour of the evening meal."

Tamar probed for more information. "And Shuah? Where is the mistress of the house?"

Cumi's mouth drew into a straight line at the mention of Judah's wife. Once again she seemed unable to speak.

Tamar knew Cumi's expression meant something was amiss. "What is the trouble, Cumi? I shall find out sooner or later, so you may as well tell me now."

The girl's bowed head and slumped shoulders gave certainty to Tamar's suspicions. Without raising her eyes, Cumi spoke with quivering lips, more evidence of her gentle, tenderhearted nature. "This has become a house of sadness, Tamar. Many cross words are spoken. That is, when long days of silence finally come to an end. Mistress Shuah stays confined to her tent of late."

Rather than words of consolation or comfort which Cumi ex-

6

pected from Tamar's lips, a low hum of delight began to rise until it filled the room and fell harshly upon Cumi's astonished ears.

"Hmmm," mused Tamar with a hopeful note in her voice. "Judah and Shuah disagreeing? I cannot say that brings sadness to my heart. Perhaps now Judah will put her away and . . ."

"Tamar!" Cumi interrupted, amazed at the force with which she spoke the name. "Mistress Shuah is very ill. She lies abed with some dark, unspeakable malady that constantly tortures her."

The expression on Tamar's face changed, the brightness fading to wonderment. "The incorruptible one, ill? I never knew her to have a sick day ever before."

"Her illness is mostly in her mind. Partly from Master Judah's anger and avoidance, partly from her own deep grief. She still mourns the death of her sons. Master Judah's rage and neglect, I suspect, are also from grief, but he seems to raise his voice and blame the mistress for things she has no part in. That only makes Mistress Shuah more disheartened and ill."

Tamar lifted her chin defiantly. "Shuah and Judah should learn to bear their grief more bravely, I would say. They lost no more than I. Their sons were my husbands, but do you see me lying sick with maudlin sorrow or stomping about in anger?"

"Oh, Tamar," Cumi said in a quieter tone, "I know you must still grieve also. To lose *one* husband so soon after marriage is tragedy enough, but to bury the second in so short a time . . ."

Cumi wiped her eyes with a corner of her apron and muffled a sob.

"Stop that, Cumi! Do not waste pity on me. You know very well I loved neither of Judah's sons. My three years of widowhood were more pleasurable to me than a single moment I spent as a wife."

Cumi's mouth was open but she did not speak.

Tamar stood up abruptly. "The past is forgotten, Cumi. My life is before me, not buried in a tomb. I married Judah's firstborn because Father Jacob and Judah arranged it. I married the second because it was required of him to take his brother's widow to wife. Neither Judah's sons nor I had much to say about the

7

duty thrust upon us. I am here now to claim my pledge and to start over again."

"Pledge?" Cumi held back her tears as Tamar commanded and searched her memory for a vague recollection of a conversation she had overheard before Tamar was sent away. Then it came to her: "Oh, yes. Now I remember. Master Judah promised to give you Shelah for a husband when he came of age."

"Indeed." There was a strangeness in Tamar's voice. She seemed a mingling of fire and ice, her hot determination tempered with a cool, confident, and resolute air. Observing the confusion in Cumi's eyes, she explained further: "I shall admit, Judah's heart was not in his promise. He meant to put me off, thinking I would return to my people and there forget his words in time. But Judah did not reckon with my infinite patience and determination."

"But . . . Tamar?"

"What a face! Why does your countenance darken, Cumi?"

After a long hesitation, Cumi finally responded: "It is only that I cannot see why you should wish for yourself a husband of such tender years. Shelah is still more of a boy than a man. He's weak and sickly and you . . . you are a beautiful, strong, and . . . experienced woman."

"He is now of nineteen years, is he not?"

"Yes, but very . . ."

"Pampered? Spoiled? Backward?" Tamar suggested. "I know all of those things, dear Cumi. Well I know how Shuah always coddled her youngest. Now that he's the last she has, she's probably made him totally unbearable."

Cumi crossed to the doorway and peered out to be certain her next words would not be overheard. "Not only Mistress Shuah," she said in a low tone, "but also Master Judah. He's become very possessive and protective. He often mothers Shelah more than Shuah does."

Worry lines crossed Tamar's brow. Such protective smothering could pose an unexpected obstacle to her plans. Then Tamar threw back her head and laughed scornfully as she said, "Well, dear friend, if mothering and protecting is what young Shelah is used to, he will feel most secure with me for a wife. A ripe old woman of twenty-six, twice married, should be able to pamper him and teach him the ways of . . ." She stopped herself in time.

Cumi crossed her arms and cast an inquiring look toward Tamar, asking, "But why do you wish it to be so? Your wit and beauty make you most desirable, and you could be the choice of many fine husbands. Never have you seemed to me to be . . ."

"The motherly type?" Tamar seemed to know what Cumi wished to say before the girl could find her own words. "In truth, I am not anticipating the love match of my dreams. I would much prefer a man of strength to care for me rather than a sickly whelp to nuzzle at my breast."

"Then why . . . ?"

"Sometimes one must place value on things other than maturity and manly strength."

Cumi shook her head. "I do not understand your meaning."

"Do you not remember the covenant promise, Cumi?" Tamar's eyes grew wide, and her voice softened to a whisper. "Judah's heir is destined to receive the blessing of Father Jacob, the blessing that one day will bring forth Messiah to the tribe of Israel."

Cumi looked even more puzzled. "But Master Judah is not Father Jacob's firstborn. How is it you say he shall be the heir to the special blessing? Is he not fourth in line?"

"Reuben, Simeon, and Levi have all been disavowed. You know how Father Jacob prizes virtue. The elder brothers' sinful acts have removed them from his favor. He told me the covenant blessing falls to Judah now."

Still perplexed, Cumi asked, "But what has it to do with your wish to marry Shelah?"

Tamar sucked in her breath. "Do you not see? I wish to share in the covenant promise. The fruit of my womb shall be blessed unto Jehovah. Father Jacob so prophesied."

Cumi's thoughts were racing. Yes, Tamar had been brought up in Father Jacob's household before she married, and she could have been told about the blessing. Yet Cumi could not believe Tamar was destined for such a high and sacred honor. Rather than question that matter, which would appear rude, Cumi asked instead, "For this only you would marry a sickly lad whom you do not love?"

Walking across to strike the table for emphasis, Tamar all but shouted, "What is love when a holy destiny is in question?"

"Destiny?"

"Must I explain further? I will not remain a barren widow, Cumi. Neither will I give sons to the stupid Baal worshipers of my homeland. God brought me to this place for this very purpose. I know it! I feel it! I have well marked the blessings that come to those who serve the God of Father Jacob. He is my God now. I will . . . no, I *must* be part of that divine destiny."

Cumi stood transfixed. "With such assurance you speak, Tamar. And you—a Canaanite!"

Too involved with her own thoughts to hear the last remark, Tamar continued to express the feelings welling up inside her. "My name shall be established for generations to come. All the earth one day will know the place I shall claim for myself in history."

The upturned face, the piercing eyes, the rigid stance, the audacity of her boasts were too much for Cumi. Forgetting her usual reserve, Cumi doubled over and giggled uncontrollably.

"Pardon me, Tamar," Cumi laughed, "but it's just . . . just that you speak not as a wife or mother—nor even as a woman. You sounded just now like a *man!*"

The spell was broken. Tamar was displeased that Cumi was laughing at something that should be taken with utmost seriousness. Nevertheless, that bit of reality brought Tamar down, both emotionally and physically, as she dropped once more to the rug.

"Oh, I know," Tamar said through her teeth. "Women are as slaves and cattle—to men." She raised a finger in protest. "Ah, but Father Jacob says this will not always be so. One day women will take an equal place beside their men."

Cumi gasped. What Tamar was saying was unthinkable. "How can that be?" she asked.

"Father Jacob says it is man's pride that makes him wish to rule a wife as little more than a slave. Consider his wife, Rachel. She was Father Jacob's beloved, not merely his possession. And he says God's instrument for the holy blessing shall be a *woman,* not a man. Thus it was ordained in the *seed of woman promise* given in Eden. It says so in the holy writings and sacred legends in Father Jacob's library. Man's part is completely unimportant in the procreation of the promised Messiah." The last sentence, she knew, was not included in the writings. Tamar added it for effect and to prove her point.

Quite dismayed, Cumi studied Tamar for a long moment. Such interest in prophecies and religious teachings was uncommon among women. Cumi had to inquire further. "Why do you say man will be unimportant, Tamar?"

"I am not an ignorant woman, good Cumi. Have I not sat at the feet of Father Jacob for instruction—even as his beloved sons have done?"

Tamar stood to her full height, turned her back abruptly, and ran her tense fingers along the edge of her fringed *aba*. How could she expect one as unlearned as Cumi to understand such secret and lofty ideas? She felt pity for the servant girl who obviously had the intelligence and capacity to understand, but who was relegated to ignorance because of man's dominance.

Cumi also was lost in her own thoughts. To her remembrance came the vision of the same defiant Tamar years before, a teenage girl with hair like the red of an evening sunset, a rebel who sat cross-legged beneath the tree of wisdom, listening attentively to the instruction of an old and bearded man. The other servant girls had whispered about it. Why was Tamar allowed a favored place to sit with Father Jacob when she should be carrying water and grinding meal? Cumi had been a little girl at the time, holding onto her mother's skirts and following Shuah's other handmaidens as they busied themselves about the duties that fell to women. That was before Judah moved his family and servants away from Father Jacob's and made his own encampment.

Even after the move, gossip continued to travel from Father Jacob's tents to those of Judah and Shuah. Cumi had heard discussions of how Tamar's father had exchanged his daughter for two of Father Jacob's prized bulls. When it was noised abroad that Jacob declared himself the better bargainer in the exchange, everyone said it was Tamar's comeliness—not her quickness to learn—that gave Tamar an honored place held by no other woman. Knowledge was considered necessary for the men, but by what right did Tamar claim a need for schooling? She was belittled for her haughtiness and looked down upon for claiming to hunger for man's wisdom. Cumi's mother had said the other women were jealous, and so they were. None among them would have turned down the opportunities given solely to Tamar.

When Father Jacob's wives and his sons' wives became envious of attentions given to Tamar, the old man decided, although it broke his heart to do so, it was time to put distance between Tamar and the other women in his camp. It pained him to see Tamar ill treated. So for her sake and to put an end to the jealousy and unfounded gossip, he arranged her marriage to Judah's eldest. Tamar's reluctance to become his bride was made tolerable only because of what Father Jacob revealed to her about the covenant promise that accompanied the bargain.

In spite of all Cumi's questions and concerns, she could not help but admire Tamar's boldness. Looking at her now, Cumi was certain there was no other woman like her. But who could fathom her sayings?

Cumi asked, "Did Father Jacob really say man was unimportant?"

Caught in her own trap, Tamar gave an evasive reply: "Well, not precisely in those words. But he did stress the importance of the woman's role in fulfilling the Messiah prophecy."

Cumi went once more to the doorway to see if anyone stood within earshot. The other servants were busy within or near their own tents, and Cumi alone had access to the dwellings of her master and mistress. Yet, she needed reassurance that she and Tamar were quite alone while discussing such a controversial topic.

"I hope Master Judah never hears you speak of the greatness of women," Cumi mused. "He rules his household with a strong hand and would not take your words kindly, Tamar."

Tamar almost smiled as she nodded knowingly. "You speak truth. I could never speak in such a manner to Judah."

There was another question Cumi longed to ask, but she was unsure of its propriety. Tamar was so mysterious, a simple

Canaanite native and yet so austere and full of spiritual strivings. She seemed a mingling of the wickedness of Ashtaroth and the holiness of Jehovah she now professed. Cumi was a little afraid of her, but Tamar's frankness and willingness to open her heart to share confidences prodded curiosity and gave courage. Cumi dared to ask, "Tamar, are you still in love with Master Judah?"

Cumi regretted her inquiry when she observed Tamar's eyes flash in response. After a long silence, Tamar's eyes began to sparkle with amusement. Playfully, she teased, "Such an impudent calf you are!" With that, Tamar gave Cumi a swat to her backside.

Relief came with Tamar's good-natured reaction, but Cumi was even more curious. Her own eyes silently repeated the question.

Tamar rested her chin on her knees as she held her legs with firmly clasped fingers to say, "Oh, little Cumi, I have gone much too far in bearing my soul to you. Three years of imposed mourning and lonely hours of silence have loosened my tongue, I fear."

Cumi stepped nearer and said, "You can trust your secrets with me, Tamar. Often I have wished for a friend to . . . to . . ."

"You have a secret too, Cumi?" It was more of a statement than a question. Tamar could tell she had again read Cumi's thoughts. Without waiting for a reply, Tamar continued, "You long for a friend to share your confidences, so I would be honored should you think me worthy of them."

Despite the friendliness of Tamar's voice, Cumi turned away with embarrassment, regretting her hasty words to one so all-knowing and unknowable. Tamar was so unpredictable that trusting her completely was a definite risk. With a wave of her hand, Cumi said casually, "It is nothing."

Tamar grasped the girl, gently forcing her to face forward. Softly, she said, "Our bond of friendship is sealed if we speak our hearts. I will answer your question if you will answer mine."

Cumi knew Tamar did not have to give voice to a confession of love for Judah. It always had been evident in her face, in the change of her voice when she spoke his name. It was surely confirmed by the fact that she risked her own peril in coming back to Judah's household.

For some unknown reason—her own loneliness for companionship perhaps—Cumi needed to share her secret thoughts. A common spirit seemed to envelop the two as they stood in the rosy haze of dusk at the door of Judah's tent. A dammed-up flood within Cumi's young heart was about to burst, and she found herself yielding to the impulse to confide.

"My secret is nothing more than a hopeless love," Cumi said with her lashes hiding the child eyes from Tamar's gaze. She swallowed hard and placed a trembling hand to her mouth as if to hold back any further words which might slip out.

In motherly fashion, Tamar took Cumi's arm and led her to sit down upon a stuffed pillow which lay in the corner with the sleeping mats. She continued to hold the trembling hand as she said, "Nothing is ever hopeless. As long as you live and draw breath, there always is hope."

Cumi's tears came quickly and unbidden, warm and stinging in her dark eyes. "There can be no hope for me, Tamar," she said, "for I . . . I love Benjamin."

Tamar's expression changed abruptly from resolution to dismay, but only momentarily. She held the small hand more tightly and forced a lightness into her voice to say, "Oh, so the maiden aims for the stars. You desire the beloved one, the youngest and favorite of Father Jacob."

Cumi was visibly annoyed at the comment. "It is not as you think!" she cried. "It is not for his father's honor that I love Benjamin, but for himself alone."

Cumi wanted to rise and turn away, but Tamar held to her hand.

"I have tried to put him out of my thoughts, Tamar, but it has been difficult because . . . because I believe he cares for me as well. He comes here whenever he can—and gives me much to hope for."

Tamar was quick to interrupt. "There. You have spoken it. It cannot be hopeless, for you, yourself, have just said hope remains."

Cumi shook her head. "But Father Jacob clings to Benjamin,

14

the child of his old age, as he calls him. Since the death of Joseph, Father Jacob never lets Benjamin from his sight for long. It has become increasingly more difficult for Benjamin to come here to see me."

Tamar released the hand and allowed Cumi to rise. The girl's cheeks were still moist with tears as she continued. "Besides, Father Jacob would never permit Benjamin to marry a servant girl. He will select a suitable bride for him from among his kinsmen—if he ever gives Benjamin leave to marry at all."

"Gives him leave?"

"Did I not tell you how he does cling to Benjamin? Just as Master Judah clings to Shelah."

"Hmmm . . ." Tamar pondered before saying more. "I can now see your plight. Both the plague of being a servant and the obstacle of the possessive father as well. I shall have to think of a plan . . ."

Cumi was awestruck. "A plan?" she echoed. "You think you can do something? How?"

Tamar waved off the questions to clear her mind for strategy. "The first problem we shall solve easily. You are not as the common women of these parts. Father Jacob will have to admit to that much. You were brought to Judah's household as a babe, were you not?"

"Yes. My mother was Mistress Shuah's personal handmaid and companion after my father's sudden death. We joined ourselves to Master Judah's tribe when he came to Adullam to marry her and bring her here. My mother and I were part of the dowry. What has that to do . . ."

Tamar held up her palm for silence. "Very well," she said. "You have been raised, from infancy, almost as one of Judah's own family. You are not even a lowly bondmaid. Why, you are—at your tender years—in complete charge of the household, correct?"

"Yes, Mistress Shuah required me to take Mother's place when she died two years ago."

"And you are a worthy administrator already proven capable of caring for the needs of an Israelite family."

15

Cumi shook her head to disagree. "Tamar, you put too much value upon my services. The head servant is . . ."

"A man who oversees the fields and flocks. We are not discussing such matters. You are in charge of household affairs, so it is plain you are worthy and able. As to the second problem, prying Benjamin from his father's bosom, that will require more effort. But I think I can make the aged one's feeble eyes see aright."

Cumi knew Tamar could obtain the old patriarch's ear. They were closer than many blood relatives. After the loss of Jacob's favorite son, Joseph, Tamar had filled the void. Jacob always needed to single out one person for the special place at his side, someone upon whom he could bestow all his attention and favors. Tamar had been that someone as a devotee and pupil in the knowledge of the world and of God.

In the past, Tamar always had hung upon each word from Jacob's lips and looked up in wonder at his solemn face. She was sincere in her interest, and her reverent attention caused the old man to open himself to her utterly in return. Some even said he was in love with her, for she was always capable of reasoning with him. Few men could make such a claim, for reasoning with stalwart Jacob was no easy task.

When Tamar left Jacob's protection to marry, the favored position fell to Benjamin, and the nearer Jacob came to death, the tighter his hold upon his favorite. Such favoritism always created jealousy and strife among those not so honored. Yet, each new favorite was held more closely than the last. This made Cumi wonder whether or not Tamar still had full sway with Jacob. Three years was a long time, but Tamar did not seem to think the separation nor her successor, Benjamin, would matter in the slightest. She expressed every confidence in herself.

Cumi sighed. "I wish I could be as you are, Tamar. Albeit you could do all you propose, I am not certain Master Judah would give me up to marry Benjamin. He depends upon me for many things now that Mistress Shuah is too ill to manage his household."

"Leave both men to me," Tamar commanded. "It seems we have virtually the same problem, you and I. Possessive fathers who cling to the sons we wish to marry."

16

"And," Cumi added, "both of the fathers are willful, determined ones."

"No matter. We shall not despair, for I shall prove to you that women are more than cattle. I shall demonstrate the importance of what men think to be inferior creatures—women! They all shall stand amazed when the stubborn wills of our adversaries are broken, and we prevail."

Cumi did not know whether to scoff at the boastful one or to put faith in the extraordinary powers which Tamar claimed to possess. She asked, "Do you really believe what you say?"

Tamar's next words provided a window into her very soul: "If we do not obtain what we want most, we shall choose the next best thing. I have learned, my girl, that when you do not obtain what you like, you can learn to like what you *can* obtain."

Mentally adding up Tamar's remark, Cumi came to understand her friend better than she ever had before: "You wish to marry Shelah because you cannot obtain Master Judah. Shelah is your *next best thing*!"

Tamar perched herself upon a carved chest in the corner and knit her velvet brows in feigned anger. "Do not put words in my mouth, you silly imp!" she cried, pointing an accusing finger as a sovereign upon a throne might reprimand a wayward subject. "If you do not watch your tongue, I shall not bother myself to help you with this impossible love affair of yours!"

The ridiculous sight of Tamar posed atop the chest and her playfulness brought Cumi to squeals of laughter and delight. Following Tamar's lead, Cumi bowed before her and said, "At your command, I shall place my hand upon my mouth and say no more. But I humbly ask, before I do, that you honor your vow. Will you now tell me your secret? Do you love my master?"

Tamar nodded. "Cumi, I loved Judah before, during, and after the time I became wife to his sons. I shall never stop loving him—whether or not he ever loves me, or keeps his promise to give Shelah to me, or sends me away again. I can't stop loving him. I have tried."

"What will you do next?" Cumi inquired.

"I will have to take my cues from Judah. I can plead and persuade, but he must decide. My fate rests in his hands."

"That does not sound like the determined conqueror you were a moment ago," Cumi said.

"Do not mistake my meaning, Cumi. Judah's response to me can determine only our future relationship. If there is to be one. He has no control over my part in the holy covenant promise. God has decided that already. I pray that I will find favor in Judah's eyes, but if not, it will not hinder me from fulfilling my covenant destiny. If I cannot be Judah's second wife, I shall be Shelah's first."

Cumi believed her. When Tamar spoke like that, she made the impossible seem entirely possible.

All fears about Tamar's return were completely gone now. Cumi truly was glad Tamar had come back to bring some life into what had become a morbid and miserable household. And she fully expected Tamar would succeed in whatever plans she devised.

It was out of character, but Cumi responded to an impulse by embracing Tamar and saying, "If anyone can change things—for either of us—it shall be you, Tamar!"

Two

It was not yet dusk. Yet, it was pitch black within the tent where Judah's wife, Shuah, dwelled. It always was kept dark there—no drapes opened by day, no lamps lit by night.

Any form of light hurt Shuah's eyes and repulsed her. The brightness intensified the agonizing pain in her head. Sunlight and firelight were for days gone by when she was actively involved in life, when she knew joy and laughter. Now she preferred the soothing comfort and obscurity of her only friend, the darkness. It hid her from mean, hurtful things outside. It allowed her to remain unseen and to cry softly into her pillow without arousing her husband's wrath.

On the rare occasions when Judah would visit, the kindly darkness hid the red puffiness of Shuah's eyes, the premature age lines and crevices in a once lovely face, and the coarse, gray forelocks and faded luster that came, unbidden and too soon, to her thinning hair.

At first, Shuah thought it all was a bad dream. Many nightmares came to haunt her with ghosts and groans of her dead sons mingling in an unholy chant to echo those of her own making. Grotesque figures loomed before her in the darkness—pallid, hollow-cheeked faces, white as the burial clothes which touched them; thin, dry lips that never smiled or kissed; unmoving eyes that never opened because they slept the never-ending sleep of death. Shuah longed for such restful, unmolested sleep. She yearned for peace that would set her free from the misery of just being.

But it was no dream. Shuah had heard voices—not the voices of her visions and nightmares, not the eerie voices in her aching head that droned and tormented her. She heard the servants' voices, whispering at first, then loudly angry and taunting. What was it they were saying? Shuah tried to remember

19

what had jolted her from a half-conscious state induced by herbs and medicines, her only brief respites from pain. She pushed hard against her moist brow and forced herself to remember. At last, it came to her. It was a word, a name, a terrifying name that struck horror and loathing in every nerve and fiber of her thin shell of body. The cursed name: *Tamar*!

Screaming and clutching her head, Shuah bolted up from the couch, violently shaking and jerking, bubbles of white foam at the corners of her mouth. There were no words, no lucid, discernible words. Only the shrieks and piercing cries of panic and torment.

In response to the reverberating screams, the first to appear at Shuah's tent door was Bella, an old and toothless servant whose days of usefulness—as anything other than an occasional midwife—had long since passed. Jumping on one leg, Bella began to grunt and howl, unable to decide whether to go to her mistress or to run for help.

"Cumi! Cumi, come quickly!" Bella shouted when babbling finally sustained words.

Shuah's hysterics petrified the most senior of the women servants, so she remained at the doorway, unable to move in any direction except up and down in a dance of fright. Seeing the gathering crowd of handmaidens coming to surround her—as curious and as frightened as Bella herself—she poked a bony finger at the nearest one and sharply commanded, "Quickly, make haste to fetch Cumi! Mistress Shuah needs her. Now! Begone!"

No one moved. The dumbfounded maidservants stood wide-eyed, gaping at Bella as if they were all frozen to the spot. Bella's hand was raised to strike the nearest one into movement when Cumi, who had heard the commotion and Bella's first cries, came running in their direction. Tamar was close behind as Cumi ran straight to Bella, now crouched on her heels with her finger still pointing into the darkness within Shuah's tent.

Shuah could be heard shrieking wildly: "No! No! Burn the devil! Away! Away!"

Cumi darted into the tent, but she was barely able to see anything until her eyes adjusted to the dark. Then she saw the shadowy movement of a quaking form, shifting forward and back. Shuah's hands were over her face to muffle her sobs.

"Wait out there!" Cumi called to Tamar. "I can handle her best alone."

After Cumi disappeared into the tent, the servants all turned their gaze upon Tamar. There were silent messages of disdain and reproof coming from every pair of eyes. Tamar read the messages in silence for a while; then she stomped her foot.

"Go on about your tasks!" Tamar said sharply to them, annoyed more with their stupidity than their scorn. Bella's squinting eyes vexed her most of all. The others took their orders from her, so Tamar looked straight at the old woman and instructed, "Cumi will call if she needs you. Well, go on with you. Be off!"

Reluctantly, Bella nudged one of the others and grumbled. She ground her toothless gums in an inaudible protest against Tamar's air of superiority, but, finally, she led them all back to the far side of Shuah's tent. They all continued to cast sideways glances in Tamar's direction and to whisper behind their hands. Tamar pretended not to notice. Then, when her annoyance with them reached its limit, Tamar made a face at them and spat upon the ground in their direction. They did not look her way again.

Tamar sighed with relief when Shuah's screams ceased. The only sounds she could hear now were the low, deep-throated groans of Judah's wife and the soft coaxing of Cumi's efforts to calm and comfort. At last, Cumi had the situation under control.

"I'll attend to it, Mistress. I give you my vow," Cumi promised in a tone loud enough for Tamar to hear. The remainder of the conversation inside the tent made no sense at all to Tamar. Something about a devil and curses and death.

When Cumi reappeared, Tamar could see that the girl was greatly concerned about her mistress. Cumi bit her lip and wiped beads of perspiration from worried lines on her forehead.

"Is she like that often?" asked Tamar, extending a hand to steady Cumi. It occurred to Tamar that Cumi might faint. Cumi accepted Tamar's arm, but waved away any concern.

"No, she is seldom so overwrought," Cumi said. "She often

goes for days without speaking at all—to anyone. Oh, she cries a great deal, but never have I seen her so upset."

"What was the trouble?" Tamar wanted to know.

Cumi hesitated, not wishing to tell Tamar the whole truth. "She is not herself. Severe headaches. I rubbed her forehead and placed a cool cloth on her brow. I gave her a double dose of calming herbs, so she should rest quietly for a while. Bella will hear her if she should waken."

Gesturing toward Bella and the other servants, Cumi indicated that they should keep watch and listen for any further outbursts.

Without looking in the direction of the servants as she and Cumi walked away, Tamar opined, "I think Shuah has taken leave of her reason, Cumi. That well could be the trouble in her head." Tamar tapped her own brow for emphasis.

Cumi stopped walking. "It is not as you think. My mistress is disturbed, afraid. That's all."

"Afraid of death?" Tamar prompted. "Afraid of going down to Sheol to the devil?"

"What makes you say that?"

"I heard her mumbling something about being cursed by the devil."

Cumi heaved with relief. She started to respond by explaining Shuah's weird dreams and visions that brought on restless days and sleepless nights, but she stopped herself when she caught sight of Judah, Shelah, and the menservants moving homeward, trudging down a nearby hill. Hurriedly, she grasped Tamar's hand and led her in the direction of her own tent.

Pointing toward the hill, Cumi said, "The men are returning. Come. You may stay in my tent until . . ."

Tamar broke the hold and whirled around to peer at the oncoming men. "Why should I go to your dwelling? It is Judah I wish to see."

"Tamar, let me first tell Master Judah you are here. Then . . ."

"No! Why are you trying to prevent me from waiting here for Judah?"

"I pray you," Cumi implored, "let me tell Master Judah you

have returned—in my own way—before you confront him. He is so prone to fits of pique lately, and he will be tired and hungry when he arrives. He will not be in the best frame of mind for your meeting. I think I should prepare him beforehand."

"I thank you, but I do not require your help," Tamar announced coolly.

Cumi's eyes pleaded so intently that Tamar sensed greater gravity than offhanded words had conveyed. As Tamar turned in her mind reasons for Cumi's obvious apprehension and lack of candor, Cumi was trying desperately to think of a way to convince Tamar to postpone her intentions. Then she hit upon a better approach.

"But, Tamar, will you not want to freshen up and make yourself more presentable?"

Tamar glanced down at her traveling attire and placed a hand to her hair. Her fingers told her, when she touched the limp bloom she had placed there, that she must look quite as wilted as the flower. It would be prudent, for the sake of her plan, to change and look her best for Judah.

At length, Tamar allowed herself to be moved toward Cumi's tent, saying, "Very well, but I do not expect to be kept waiting for long!"

After Cumi settled her guest comfortably, she went to fetch a huge platter of tidbits from the lavish spread on Judah's table. To them she added goat cheese, dates, honey and an entire loaf of warm bread she brought in, fresh and steaming from the outdoor oven. As she poured Tamar a goblet of wine from the wineskin, she was aware that Tamar's eyes were observing every move.

Accepting the silver goblet of deep purple liquid, Tamar said, "All your attentions and this enormous amount of food, which I cannot possibly consume in one sitting, are nothing more than delaying tactics. I do not know why, but you are trying to put me off. It will not take me nearly as long to sup and freshen myself as you may think. So stop being so obvious, and make haste to announce me to Judah!"

Cumi hurried to meet the incoming men, now approaching the camp's well. Cumi knew what her master's reaction would be when she brought him unwelcome news. She also feared for herself. It was likely she would be punished for extending hospitality to Tamar. When Judah sent her home to her kinsmen, there had been an unmistakable note of finality in his voice. He clearly did not want to see her again.

Cumi chided herself for not turning Tamar away. It was not deep friendship that prevented her, for they had been only casual friends, not intimates—before today. But there was something about Tamar that compelled Cumi's admiration. Not just her poise and self-assurance—qualities the girl felt lacking in herself—but something more wondrously mysterious. Perhaps because Cumi had no kin since her parents' deaths, not even a close friend for that matter, perhaps that loneliness in dismal surroundings had created a need that drew her to Tamar's magnetism.

The men were unloading their shoulder packs and pausing to drink at the well as Cumi approached. The servants were beginning to scatter in various directions to attend to last-minute duties before partaking of their evening meal.

Judah and his only living son, Shelah, remained at the well, intent in conversation. They were complimenting themselves on the fat flesh of their herds and flocks, smiling, and touching each other as they talked. Cumi was reluctant to interrupt their levity, for it was uncommon to see either of them in high spirits of late.

She especially regretted bringing news that, she knew, would change the smile upon her master's lips to a frown. Cumi always was a little afraid of Judah, but never more than at this moment. His height alone was intimidating, for he was a man of admirable proportions, tall and powerfully built. To tiny Cumi, he resembled a giant.

Cumi studied Judah's countenance before drawing nearer. He was loosening the silken rope which held the *kufiyeh* on his head and brushing back the folds to bare his face with its broad forehead, straight nose, and sun-baked cheeks the color of coffee berries. He had a profusion of jet black hair which showed little signs of gray despite his forty-odd years. His was a rugged handsomeness with the windswept look of an outdoorsman and farmer, one whose large, strong hands bore the marks of toughness that accompanied toil. Yet, Judah's face seemed a mask for a kinder, holier one underneath. Cumi remembered a sensitive, tender man who used to be gentle and jolly with her when she was a child. She liked him much better then.

The lion, as he was called, sat weary, but content, leaning against the well, his dark beard still glistening with droplets of drinking water, one muscular arm still draped about the shoulder of his son sitting at his side. The son, in contrast to his towering father, was thin and more the image of his mother's frailty than his father's strength. He looked younger than his years. His form, voice, and manner belonged to the transition period from boyhood. His face was oval, and his complexion was more pale than fair, a burden which prevented him from taking many such trips in the heat of the day with his father. His delicate physical condition was indicated by drooping lids that almost hid almond-shaped eyes, by hollow cheeks, and by a bluish tinge to his lips. His chest heaved to reveal the difficulty of shallow breathing which seemed to come from his throat.

Judah's eyes widened, and he knit his bushy brows in surprise when he saw Cumi standing before him. She had come quietly, and she was too timid to come unbidden unless she brought news of importance.

"What is it, Cumi?" Judah asked. "Why, you're trembling like an aspen tree in the wind."

Judah stood up, his towering height only making matters worse for Cumi. She felt as though she were standing in a hole beside a mountain, a dark and awesome mountain that might smoke and fume at any moment.

"It is . . . It is . . ." Cumi could not bring herself to say it. Perhaps some other message first to pave the way for the news about Tamar. "Mistress Shuah was very ill today," she began through her chattering teeth.

The boy was on his feet immediately, the almond eyes wide with alarm. "Is anyone tending my mother?" he asked anxiously. "What is being done for her? Why are you not with her?"

Cumi quickly responded to allay Shelah's fears: "She is resting and better now. Bella is outside her tent if your mother should need anything."

25

Cumi's hands were trembling, so to gain control of herself, she clasped them behind her back and hid them from Judah's discerning eyes.

With no further word, Shelah was bounding off, in all his lankiness, heading for his mother's side. Judah was turning to follow when Cumi found the courage to speak again.

"Master," she began cautiously, "there is another matter."

"What is it, Child?"

"I hope I have not gone against your wishes . . . and may Jehovah forgive me if I offend my lord in any way." Cumi gulped for air and began again. "Have you not always instructed me to extend our hospitality to strangers who pass by our way?"

"Yes. You know that is our custom." Judah's deep, booming voice was tempered with the old gentleness at the sight of Cumi's obvious anxiety. "Have we a visitor within our tents?"

"Yes . . . No . . . That is, not a stranger exactly."

"My father or one of my brothers?"

"No."

Judah reached out and lifted her to a large, flat rock. Then, taking her small, shaking hand in his massive one, he patted her fingers in a fatherly way. It had been a long time since he had spoken to Cumi. She was so efficient in her duties, he rarely needed to speak or even notice her.

Judah easily could have loved Cumi as the daughter he never had, if it were not for the fact that she was a servant and he was master of the house. Seeing her now in such a pathetic state, he realized she feared him. He was appalled at the thought. This small, frightened person revived in Judah a tender compassion that had lain dormant much too long.

"Come, come, little Cumi," Judah said when she still did not speak. "Whatever is troubling you cannot be as bad as you would make it appear. I cannot possibly help if you refuse to speak to me. First you say we have a stranger visiting us; then you say we do not. Which is it?"

Cumi took new strength from the comforting words. Gulping once more, she blurted it all out in one stream of breath: "Tamar returned today, and she said she had come for her pledge, and she said that you promised to give Shelah unto her and that she

26

still was a member of your household . . . and she's waiting for you, even now, yonder in my tent."

There was a grave silence as Cumi's last words broke off in a frantic gasp for air. The expected outburst did not come. Judah did not speak, but his jaw grew rigid with tightly-drawn flesh surrounding his clenched teeth. His knuckles whitened as he formed a fist, and his eyes faded into indefinable slits beneath furrowed brows. Mutely, with no chastisement for Cumi, Judah pulled himself to his full height, and, with militant strides, looking neither right nor left, head bent slightly forward, he marched to the circle of tents as a war captain ready for invasion.

A perplexed Cumi trailed after him. "I . . . I hope I did the right thing, Master. I could not send her away when she insisted on seeing you. And to ask her to return home when it was almost nightfall seemed most dangerous. Master . . . ?" Cumi continued to call after him, but she was unable to keep up with his longer strides. The giant man, now far ahead of her, either did not hear or ignored Cumi's words.

It was Judah's intention to go directly to Cumi's tent, there to face the daughter-in-law whose unexpected visit was causing blood to rush to his face. Before reaching his destination, however, Shelah's head poked through the doorway of his mother's tent.

"Father!" Shelah called. "I pray you, come here."

Judah turned to see his son's drawn and troubled face peering out from the folds of the tent flaps. There was only momentary indecision before Judah retraced his steps to face his son.

"What is it?" Judah bellowed.

Shelah cringed, not knowing why his father, so jovial before, was speaking so harshly. "Mother is calling for you. I have never seen her so distraught. Come in and see about her. You must!" Tears were running down the lad's cheeks as he pleaded.

Hateful as it was to see his son weeping like a woman, Judah allowed his anger an interval of abatement. He ducked his head to enter Shuah's tent just as Cumi caught up to him. The girl was trembling worse than before as she stood at the tent entrance in case she was needed.

"Judah, is that you?" It was a weak and pitiful voice that called out as Shuah extended a thin, gaunt arm.

Almost reluctantly, Judah moved closer. He was glad for the darkness. It pained him to look upon her face, a face once so pleasing to him, but now drained of all its former glory. Why was it that he, who valued strength and vitality in himself, almost to the point of vanity, was afflicted with a family prone to weakness, sickness, and death? He forced himself to take Shuah's hand as he said, "I am here."

Shuah grasped for him and tried to raise herself from the couch. Her mouth strained to form each word: "Judah, you must find her. Tamar is here. I know it. Heard servants saying so."

Shelah threw a desperate glance at his father and whined, "Mother thinks Tamar has returned to . . . to get me." He sounded much like a frightened child awaiting impending doom.

Mustering all her strength, Shuah implored, "Burn her! Burn the devil whose curse brought death to my sons! She must not take my third!" Her final words trailed off, overtaken by a fit of racking coughs. Shuah struggled, pushing against Judah to rise to her feet.

Judah held her as she struggled. In a husky voice, he said, "You must lie back down and be still. Shelah, help me quiet your mother."

Before Shelah could say or do anything, Shuah was flailing both arms in the air and wailing, "No! No! I will find her myself. I will kill her if you will not!"

Shuah was on her feet only briefly before her withered form collapsed in Judah's arms. She could not stand—too weakened from the sickness, from the little nourishment she could be forced to take, and now from the utter exhaustion of her tirade.

"Father?" Shelah questioned, beseeching with his eyes and feeling more than a little ill himself.

"She will be herself again. She just needs to rest," Judah said as he laid the limp figure back upon the couch and pulled the coverlet over her. For an instant, Judah's hands touched her shoulders, and he felt bones protruding through the thinness of her tunic. He winced at the clamminess of her flesh as his fingers passed her neck. He felt himself going through motions he had made just before his sons died. Did his nostrils actually sense the stench of coagulated blood and dried sputum—or was it his imagination? Was the plague that had taken his sons back to claim his wife as the next victim? It could not be. Unless Shuah spoke truth when she called Tamar the devil of the plague. Had she brought the death curse back with her to heap more sorrows on his head?

Forgetting all else, Judah bounded toward the doorway, calling back to his son, "Stay with her, Shelah. Give her the medicine. I shall return later."

"Father," Shelah cried fearfully, "I do not have to marry her, do I? Mother kept saying Tamar would put the death curse on me. You will not let her do that, will you?"

"Stop talking nonsense, and tend your mother," Judah replied scornfully.

Judah was both touched by his son's fears and repelled by the want of fortitude the boy showed in a moment of stress. Shelah's lack of manliness was the sickness Judah hated most of all. Manly courage could not be spoon-fed to the lad with his evening broth, nor could Judah expect Shelah to change his nature as he would change a garment. He was his mother's mirror image, and all Judah's futile efforts—hunting trips and vineyard inspection tours—could not transform the lad into a son in whom his father could take pride.

"No, my son," Judah said without looking at Shelah. "You will remain here within my tents for many years to come. Fear not, for I go to rid this place of Tamar's presence even now!"

Judah almost stumbled over Cumi, still crouched at the doorway, as he rushed past her toward his confrontation with Tamar. He strode briskly into the evening shadows, leaving Cumi feeling guilty and responsible—for Judah's anger, Shuah's hysterical illness, and Shelah's childish fears. She wondered if she had asked Tamar to leave before all the day's events happened if things would have turned out differently. No, Tamar would have remained despite anything Cumi could have said or done. Tamar always did what she set out to do.

Judah was completely unprepared for the vision before him as he threw back the door flaps and gazed into the dim and flick-

29

ering lamplight within Cumi's tent. Tamar, well aware that Judah would be coming eventually, had sprawled herself in a provocative pose which best showed her slender body to advantage. She had changed into a filmy gown under a mantle pulled and draped at the sides to reveal the garment beneath. She had carried both pieces of attire in her bundles for just this occasion, although she had not been quite certain whether or not she would need to wear them. She had decided that the desperate conditions of Judah's camp required equally desperate actions on her part.

Each garment and accessory had been selected especially for a dramatic effect upon Judah. Fabrics of fine silk and gauze veiling were chosen for their softness and sheerness. They were to send Judah the message: *Tamar is soft, gentle, delicate, feminine, and transparent—not coarse, harsh, abrasive, or deceptive.* A monochromatic color scheme, ranging from deepest purple to palest violet, brought out the color of her eyes and suggested *royalty, richness, honor, and consistency—nothing vulgar, common, debased, or gaudy.* Although her head was covered to indicate *modesty, chastity, and faithfulness,* the fullness of her tawny-red hair was visible, falling naturally and loosely about her shoulders and down her back, unadorned except for the thin, golden band holding her veil. It resembled an *angelic halo* encircling her brow. This meant that the enchanting seductiveness of her fiery, passionate nature was held in check by a band of *purity, goodness, reverence, and sanctity associated with the holy symbol of the wedding ring.* An armlet and neckchain of gold matched the head band and echoed the same theme. The simple, gold hoops in her ears enlarged upon that theme and carried additional symbolism—the mark of a bond slave, bound forever to be *obedient in servitude and submissive to her master.*

Naturally, Tamar did not expect Judah to make all of these associations consciously or overtly. But because *she* knew the meanings her wardrobe was to convey, she was certain the message would be reflected in her behavior. Judah would be able to read that message most clearly, and it would appeal to his masculinity. All items chosen had been wedding gifts from wealthy Father Jacob. He had purchased them from traveling merchants, and he had explained to her the subliminal meanings that were intended to captivate her first husband. Unfortunately, her time as a bride was short-lived, and the beautiful adornments were packed away and exchanged for drab robes to mourn first one and then another husband in rapid succession.

Upon seeing Judah, Tamar flashed a broad smile and rose to glide slowly across the room to bow demurely before him. "Greetings, Lord Judah, and peace unto you," she whispered sweetly with her head still bowed. Then she stood, extended the cup of wine she held in her hand, and said, "If you have not dined, Cumi has prepared a feast on the table there. I am sure the walk from your fields has made you thirsty and hungry."

"Cease!" Judah's command cut through the perfumed air like a dagger. "How dare you barge in and take charge in this manner!" With his wrath ascending, he grasped her with biting fingers that dug into her shoulders with such force that the wine goblet went flying.

Judah took a step back from her and bellowed, "I have come here for one purpose only—to tell you how odious your presence in my camp is to everyone here, and to make certain you understand you must leave and never return!"

With no sign of notice of the spilled wine goblet on the floor or of Judah's rage, Tamar stood firm and placed one perfumed hand to Judah's chest as she asked, "Is that a proper greeting for your daughter-in-law? I had expected a more hospitable welcome after I traveled most of the day in the hot sun to visit you, Judah. Do you really expect me to believe you wish to turn me out? Now? Into the night?"

Judah pushed her hand away. Ignoring the question because it was absurd and beside the point he wished to make, he decided to change the subject instead. "Look at you!" he jeered. "Where are your robes of mourning? Or do you not have decency enough in that black heart of yours to honor the dead?"

Tamar's voice was calm. "I mourned your sons the required time of three full years. But now the time of mourning is ended." She could see that the lion, the masterful man of strength, was visibly shaken by her presence. Despite his harsh words, his eyes

31

had not failed to show the response she had intended and expected.

Judah walked away from Tamar and stood with his back to her, finding it increasingly difficult to think clearly with her so close. He had not missed much of Tamar's scripted scenario.

The lamplight was catching the shine of Tamar's hair and eyes. Her close-fitting garments fell in line with the fullness of her breasts and accented the tiny, girded waist, down, down to the drape over the rounded curve of her hips to end in soft folds at her ankles. She smelled of myrrh and fragrant oils. Judah knew she had chosen each prop for the drama of their meeting. After coming from the stench of Shuah's putrid illness, the contrast was even more enticing.

He dared not look at her again, for he felt himself aroused. That part of himself had been sealed away and tightly guarded because of his ailing wife. He hated Tamar for reminding him of desires and pleasures his religion excluded outside of marriage. He thought Tamar meant to play the temptress of Ashtaroth, the forbidden goddess of pagan love, and he was meant to play her human sacrifice. When she had looked at him with her great, penetrating, wide-open eyes, she stood so approachable and motionless that her glistening gold earrings hung down unswaying. He could have taken her then—with no request or consent even necessary.

Since Shuah had become bedridden, Judah had not held a woman. He had busied himself with his orchards and flocks and with his attempts to instruct his son—a thankless task with one so immature and slow to learn. Judah's spirit groaned against his lust as Tamar stood mutely waiting for him to speak. She was so near that he could touch her. He knew she'd be willing if he did.

Tamar watched the conflict welling up within him. How well she knew his nature—his conscience and his willingness to deny his urges, to suffer rather than yield to sin. She had met the cruel spear of his virtue in the past. Always before, it had cut her asunder. Always before, she knew when he desired her, but his thirst for purity would rise above his thirst for the love she yearned to offer him. Would it be tonight as it was when she was the wife of

32

his sons, when civil and religious laws of propriety stood between them? Would the burden of a wife who could not satisfy him make him forget his wedding vows and bring him into her arms?

In frustration and desperation, Judah lashed out at her: "Why did you have to come back?"

"I come to claim that which is mine." Tamar's evasive answer could be taken to mean either the pledge of her marriage to Shelah or the gift of Judah himself. Tamar wondered, for she could not possibly know for sure, how Judah would interpret her response.

"Could you not find a husband from among your own people?" he asked, feeling a lump in his throat that made it difficult to swallow.

Tamar's voice remained a silken contrast to Judah's coarseness. "I probably could," she said lightly, "but I did not choose to do so."

He forced himself to face her. "Why? Why must you . . ." Judah found no more words when he looked into the depths of those unbelievable violet eyes.

"Have you forgotten your promise?" Tamar asked, never taking her gaze from his.

"Tamar," Judah began, trying to approach the matter rationally, trying not to look directly into the velvet eyes that seemed to have a spellbinding, hypnotic effect on his own reason. He thought Shuah must have been right to call Tamar a devil, for never had he seen the like of those eyes on any earthly woman. He began to pace, unwilling to stand before her, unwilling that she should know how her presence unnerved him. But she knew. And Judah knew she knew.

"Tamar," he spoke her name again, letting the sound roll as he accented the last syllable. Hers was the name that had become both a blessing and a curse to him. He sat down on a nearby cushion to see if words would come more easily there, and they did. "Much has changed since I promised my youngest to you in marriage. Shuah lies gravely ill—sinking toward death, I believe. To take away her only child would be the end of her. Of that, I am certain."

Tamar knelt at his knee and spoke honestly when she said,

"I wish no harm to come to your wife, Judah. Do not think that of me." Her eyes remained fixed upon him. She marveled at the sinewy firmness of his arms and the broad expanse of his shoulders. She felt his body tense, and, for an instant, she thought he would move away again. So she rose herself to cross the room.

Like a merchant ship in full sail, she glided toward the fallen wine goblet. After replacing it on Cumi's table, she deftly refilled it along with another which stood ready nearby. She moved slowly, for she was aware of Judah's eyes upon her, as she hung the wineskin on a peg which was wedged into a post supporting the tent. Judah sat, silently watching her graceful movements, as she returned and extended one cup in his direction. Tamar hoped the wine would relax him, give him something to busy his hands, and keep him still long enough for a real conversation.

Judah accepted the wine without protest or thanks. Then he waited for her to speak.

Kneeling beside him again, Tamar said, "Since Shuah cannot bear to part with Shelah, could we not live here within your tents, so Shelah could visit his mother as often as he desired?"

Judah set down his wine goblet with such force that the liquid cascaded over the rim and dripped on the carpeted, earthern floor. He uttered an oath under his breath and then raised his voice: "No! That cannot be!"

"And, pray, why not? Father Jacob's sons bring their families to live within his tents after marriage."

Judah clenched his fist to reply, "But I am not Father Jacob!" Tamar had struck a nerve. Her face showed dismay, so Judah tried to control his temper long enough to explain: "If and when Shelah marries, he will be master of his own household, even as I am master of mine."

"I meant only to suggest . . ."

"Shelah will be ruled by me no longer when he takes a wife. A married man must be strong, stand upon his own feet, and make his own decisions when he takes responsibility for a family."

Tamar heard the catch in Judah's voice and read its meaning. They both knew the picture of Shelah as a strong, self-sufficient, and responsible decision-maker was the height of

34

irony. She was unwilling to appear argumentative, so Tamar posed a question: "Why do you always strain against the customs of your forefathers, Judah? What is your need that makes you take the role of an independent rebel?"

Judah was uncomfortable when Tamar edged toward things he pushed down to hide deep inside himself. She could not possibly know why Judah, who loved his beloved father so much, punished and denied himself the pleasure of Jacob's company. His response was a lie: "I need no one. Not my father, not my brothers. No one!"

"We all need someone, Judah," she whispered, inching closer to him. "Could there be another reason you do not want Shelah to marry me and live here? Could it be that you could not bear to have me so close to you?" Her voice floated into to his ears, and it took on a sultry quality, low and inviting from her sun-browned throat.

"Do not flatter yourself, Prideful One," he replied as he stood up and walked away from her. He surprised himself with his resistance, but he still evaded her eyes. "You are right. I cannot bear to have you close by me. But it is only because I despise you!"

"If that be true, why will you not look at me? Why do your eyes keep turning away? Are you afraid of me—or of yourself?"

"Afraid? Afraid? You think you have the power to instill fear in me?" He reached down for her and lifted her up as if to do some harm to her. But once she was in his arms, he silenced her in a way he had not intended. He pressed his sun-parched lips hard upon her cool, welcoming mouth. He no longer was aware of anything else. He no longer cared about the circumstances of her coming. He could not be rational or distant, and he was not thinking of the consequences. He wanted only to feel her softness against the firmness of his own body and to yield to the delicious excitement she engendered.

Judah felt Tamar's smooth hands wrap themselves around his neck, and then his own hands were exploring her body, flowing through her hair, sliding down the arched curve of her back, and pulling her closer until every part of her touched and merged with every part of him.

Judah realized he had been ensnared in Tamar's trap. It was plain that she meant to weaken him and use her wiles to get her own way. But there was more to it than that. Holding her, he believed he meant much more to her than merely a means to some end. And even if he did not, he was lost in the warmth of her embrace, the passionate kiss, the filmy down of her veil against his calloused fingertips, her provocative fragrance floating up to his nostrils to intoxicate his mind and quicken the beat of his heart next to hers. He was reveling in the tremulous sensation of awakened emotions, deeper feelings than he had ever known before. Temptress or not, he gladly would have surrendered his lion's strength to her and exchanged love offerings—if only she had not spoken as she did:

"Oh, Judah," she breathed against his cheek. "It is you I have always loved. I do not want to marry Shelah. I want only to be your wife. I will bear you sons to replace those which you have lost. I will bring you joys of love Shuah never can offer you."

She spoke Shuah's name, reminding Judah of his wife and his vow to rid her of Tamar's presence. In health or sickness, he was obligated to care for Shuah and to do nothing that would bring her greater pain. He reached to unclasp Tamar's hands at his neck, but she would not let go. He grasped her hair once more, but now it was to tear her from him, to send her sprawling in a blur of purple froth and flashing gold. So powerful was Judah's force that Tamar's feet left the floor, and she struck her head on the table corner. Blood oozed instantly from her forehead onto her fingers as she touched the wound. Tamar did not cry out, but she looked up questioning him with her eyes as he towered over her.

"This is insane!" Judah cried out. "Now I come to myself, you heathen she-devil! Begone!"

Tamar leaned forward, dazed and puzzled by the unexpected outburst. "What is it, Judah? What is my sin that you should speak so unkindly to me?"

Judah's face flushed. The veins stood out in blue lines on his temples. "First you take the lives of my elder sons, then you want my youngest. My wife approaches death because of you. And just now you wanted me in your snare as well. You are an Ishtar, de-

36

vouring men so that they die of your lusting. Shuah said you were a devil, and so you are!"

"No! You cannot mean what you are saying! Are you mad, Judah?"

"No more! Not another soul of this household will you destroy as a vampire. I'll see you dead first!" Judah's ravings were words he did not mean, but he had to make her leave. For the sake of Shuah's and Shelah's fears, and for the guilt he felt for allowing his passions to become unleashed, he had to be cruel. Even if she hated him for it.

Tamar jumped to her feet. Her anger rose to match that of the raging lion beside her. She placed her hands at her hips, leaned toward him, and shouted, "Vampire? Ishtar? You think I am responsible for the deaths of your sons? Not so, Judah! They were sick and nigh unto death when I married them. If anything, my care prolonged their lives. You speak slanderous lies!"

Even though Judah knew she spoke truth—and how he hated it when she was right and he was wrong—there was no defense against her now but to spew forth more venom: "You are a heathen Canaanite, beneath contempt for wanting to bring my family death and destruction!"

"Say what lies you will, Judah, but you will speak them before the city council. You will not get out of your pledge so easily when I plead my case there. Father Jacob will testify on my behalf if you try to send me away without the husband you are bound—by law—to give me. Everyone knows I am no heathen, for I have been raised as one of Father Jacob's own daughters. I worship the same God you do, and you will know Jehovah's wrath if justice is not done."

Judah was outraged to be challenged by a mere woman. "My father will not defend a murderer. You caused my sons to die," he said flatly, expecting that to close the argument.

Tamar almost smiled as she shook her head and taunted, "You will not like my version of that story. You will be shamed when I tell the judges about the abuse I endured from the sons you claim were my victims. First Er, your eldest, the wicked, wayward one who . . ."

"Speak no evil against the dead, Tamar. You go too far."

37

"But did he not make sport of me? He never treated me as a wife. He preferred . . ."

"Enough! You never acted the part of wife," Judah retorted. "You wished to be his equal, not the kind of woman he could rule with the respect that was his due."

"I wished to be more to him than a slave or a plaything. Is it so wrong for a woman to wish to share her husband's life? He tired of me within a week and bounded off to seek others to fulfill his needs. When I refused to be numbered among his prostitutes, for fear of diseases they are known to carry, he tried to beat me into submission. Then he fell ill, and the rest of the marriage I spent as his nursemaid."

Judah winced at the picture Tamar painted of his son. No other women spoke so boldly to a man, even when there was just cause. Secretly, he felt she was right in much that she said. How often had he longed to open his heart to Shuah, only to find her aloof and unconcerned? She had given him the rights of the marriage bed, she had given him three sons, but never had she given him the gift of herself. He did not wish to hear more, so he raised a hand to silence her.

Tamar took no notice of Judah's raised hand. She began to pace as Judah had moments before. Gone was the sultry voice. He no longer heard her tender words of love. Now Judah would listen to a scorned and angry woman's list of complaints.

"What was even worse," Tamar continued, "I was doubly wronged in my second marriage. When Onan was given to me after Er's death, as is the custom, he also made a fool of me."

Judah found himself defending a position he felt he might have taken had he stood in his son's place. "It was only that Onan was unhappy that he had to be a surrogate husband, to raise up seed unto his brother and not unto himself."

"How typical of you to take his part!" Tamar exclaimed. "Oh, he was very like his independent father—to curse my womb, decreeing that I should be forever barren, spilling his seed upon the ground rather than raising up an heir in his brother's name!"

"That," Judah had to admit, "was one injustice I will grant you. But I more than repaid you by sending you back to your fa-

38

ther with heaping measures of silver—enough dowry to entice any number of husbands."

"Do you honestly believe that silver was an adequate replacement for a child? You may be bereft of two sons, but I was never given any! My womb cries out against such robbery, Judah. I am the one sinned against." She crossed her arms to accentuate her determination. "And besides, I do not want a heathen husband from my father's horrid neighbors. I want your son."

"One instant ago you said you wanted me."

"But you reject me! Why, I would be willing to be your concubine, Judah. A bondslave to do your bidding when Shuah cannot perform her duty to you. I would be content with any crumb of kindness from you. But since you turn from me, I have no recourse but to claim my right."

"You shall not have Shelah. He is still a boy. He is not ripe enough to marry anyone, least of all a woman such as you. He is no more ready . . ."

"Than you are?" Tamar prompted. She was goading him for his restraint and his ridiculous methods of resisting her. All of his arguments seemed flimsy and invalid.

Judah bristled at the insult to his manhood. "I am a married man," he reminded her.

"You make a pretense of being manly and strong. But beneath the guise is a heart of fear."

He raised his hand to strike her, but the blow never fell. "No wonder my son wanted to beat you. You are the most infuriating woman, Tamar! I will not listen to more of your babbling."

Judah lifted Tamar in his arms and marched out the doorway. She struggled and fought him with every step. Beating her fists against his chest, she cried, "Put me down! You shall pay for this when I have the council force you to give me Shelah—according to your sacred bond."

"Bond?" he repeated, setting her on her feet and holding her at arm's length in a vice-like grip. "There is no bond but word of mouth. The word of a Canaanite woman against mine. And I can be just as persuasive before the judges, Tamar. I shall convince them that you are an Ishtar with the curse of Ashtaroth and Baal and every other heathen god in the territory. You will burn before I am forced to hand over another son to your death clutches."

Tamar calmed herself and said tartly, "We shall see, Judah. Like thunder and lightning we are, but my flame will not be quenched by your loud noises. I will get my God-inheritance!"

Judah released his hold. "What is your meaning in that?"

"I know that the covenant of Jehovah promises to bring forth, from your loins, the Messiah. It has been prophesied that I also shall have part in that holy promise. The fruit of my womb shall be blessed unto the Lord."

Judah threw back his head and laughed. "You? You think the Lord God wants you to mother the Child of the Covenant?"

His scorn was unbearable, but Tamar did not let him know how much he could hurt her. She wanted to hurt back, so she said, "If God can use sinful flesh such as yours, Judah, son of Jacob, then He can bring forth greatness from any lowly being."

Judah's head went to his chest as he replied, "Your reproof is warranted. God's promise cannot be accomplished through me. The covenant of which my father speaks—if it is true—must find fulfillment in righteous flesh. I carry the guilt of sins you know nothing of, so you must see that your foolish notions about bearing a son into my family would do you no good whatever."

She was touched by the sudden change in Judah when the subject of the covenant arose. She knew how precious it had always been to him, and to see his dreams shattered became as painful to her as it was for him. Regardless of his words to the contrary, she knew him to be a godly man. The rebel spirit and iron will were only armor he chose to wear for protection. What evil had estranged this man from his God?

The moon was coming over the Hebron hills. Servants had long since retired. Cumi and Shelah were still at Shuah's bedside waiting for her to pass into quiet sleep. Only Judah and Tamar stood in the cool evening air, their robes blowing gently in the breeze. Judah was too weary to quarrel, so he lowered his voice and said, "Tamar, speak no more of this matter now. You may remain here in Cumi's tent tonight. Then tomorrow, I pray, you, be on your way."

Again she was hurt. First humiliated at his rejection of her

40

advances; then angered by his unbending will; now no further toward her goal than before she came. Nevertheless, she remained determined. She dug a sandal into the soft earth and raised her resolute eyes upward.

"Judah, tonight you have shown me my place . . ."

"Your place is within the tents of your kinsmen."

"I meant you have reproved me well for speaking of my love for you. It was wicked of me to think I could part you from your wife. I promise you, never again will I be so brazen."

"It is of no importance." He was anxious to be away from her. With her quietly beside him, it was difficult to stay on even keel. He wanted rest from the uneasiness of her presence.

"Hear me out, please," Tamar said, acutely aware of that uneasiness. "I know now you will never give your love to me, but this one thing you must know. I will not be sent away as an outcast. I am no longer a child of Baal. I am, through your own father's instruction and personal conviction, a child of the true and living God. I admit my actions tonight give you cause to doubt that, but I had to be sure . . . I had to know if there could be any chance for us at all . . ."

Judah gently touched the gash on Tamar's forehead and wiped the dried blood from her wound with the flowing sleeve of his tunic. This was all he could do, for he could not bring himself to ask her forgiveness.

Aware of Judah's tenderness, albeit outdistanced by his stubborn pride, Tamar loved him all the more. She had to plead one last time: "You must listen to me, Judah. I thought our son—yours and mine—would be the Lord's anointed one. But now that I know you will never share my dream, you must agree to give me Shelah. For the sake of the covenant, you must!"

"You would take my last lamb from me when he fears you so?"

"But he must marry someone. Why can it not be one who would strive to allay his fears?"

"Because you deserve better. He could never make you a happy, contented wife. You know you are too much woman for young Shelah. It would be a mockery, not a marriage, and I must prevent such a union—in order to save both of you misery." To

41

himself, he thought, *"And because I love you, Tamar, and I do not wish to be jealous of my own son."*

"Do you still think me an Ishtar, a slayer of those I take to my marriage bed?"

He could not answer. If he denied it, there would be no reason to withhold Shelah from her. To confirm it would be an untruth. Somehow, he could not add another falsehood to his sins against her. He did not wish to hurt her any more.

At length, Judah said, "Do not look for something a sickly boy could never give you. Dear Tamar, find yourself a man, a healthy, strong and loving man, to care for you. That is my prayer."

"For the covenant promise, I gladly would exchange all romantic notions of nuptial bliss. I am willing to make any sacrifice."

"Not the sacrifice of my only living son. I told you Shuah would die if I gave you Shelah."

"Then she need not be told. After we marry, you could pitch a tent for Shelah and me nearby. Or I could live with Father Jacob, and Shelah could visit me from time to time. Or give me to him as a concubine. Anything—only do not deny me your pledge! My God-inheritance!"

"I cannot, Tamar. I will not. Neither I nor my son will ever have a concubine. It is a poor excuse for adultery; it breeds jealousy; and it is contrary to God's sacred design for marriage. As for the covenant blessing, I have told you it will not be passed on through me. So forget your foolish obsession for something that cannot be. If I allowed you back into this family, it would hurt too many people, complicate too many lives. You ask too much."

She fell to her knees and grasped him about the legs. "On bended knee, I beg you."

Rigid and unmoving, Judah spoke with finality: "Go home to your people. Remain a widow and mourn the two husbands I already have given you. Or marry anyone you please, but leave me and my loved ones alone!"

Before he disappeared into the darkness, he flung these parting words over his shoulder: "If you are not gone from here by morning, then by my oath, I'll see you burned for the dev—, for the evil, exasperating woman you are."

He was gone, and she was completely alone, still upon her knees. She dug her fingernails hard into the earth and cursed him under her breath. Then she collapsed prostrate, her filmy garments blowing all about her, and cried aloud to her unseen enemy: "A devil, am I? We shall see what devilish schemes I can match against your stubbornness, Master Judah! The lion will be tamed! I shall have my inheritance! You will live to see it! I shall have what is mine!"

Her words trailed off into uncontrollable sobs as she lay with her cheek to the dew-soaked ground and pounded the earth beside her head.

Three

Before the pale glow of daybreak, Tamar was once again preparing for a journey. Judah had instructed Cumi to attend to Tamar's needs and then see their visitor on her way. But there was something in Tamar's manner that gave Cumi the decided feeling that the resolute one had no intention of changing her mind about anything they discussed the day before.

When Tamar opened her eyes, she forgot for a moment that she was bedded down next to Cumi on the sleeping mats. Then she had made a decision. She had no course left open to her other than going to Father Jacob. She would enlist his help in pleading her case against Judah. Jacob was, after all, the tribal prince, the patriarch and titular ruler of the territory, despite all of Judah's independence and claims for himself to the contrary.

Cumi was surprised to see Tamar wide awake so early, especially after the events of the night before. It had been with difficulty she had brought in a limp Tamar, too exhausted even to remove her clothing before retiring for a restless, fitful sleep. Now she was bathed and dressed in her traveling robes—a simple white under tunic and the decorative outer *aba*. She already had refilled her water skin and was busy repacking her bundles.

There was a lightness to Tamar's step as she moved about, nibbling a hurried breakfast and selecting a travel lunch of choice tidbits from Cumi's table. She appeared refreshed and none the worse for last night's tumult.

Cumi rubbed her eyes sleepily and yawned, "Why did you not call me? I should be up, helping you prepare for your journey."

"You have done quite enough for me already," said Tamar. "I thought I should start out before daybreak."

"In truth. It will be a tiring walk in the sun." Cumi cut her eyes toward Tamar. "I am sad you are going."

"Do not be. I shall return soon enough."

44

Cumi had stopped expressing surprise at anything Tamar said, however outrageous. She simply asked, "You expect to return?"

"Indeed. I shall not have to return, actually, for I shall never leave." Tamar knew her riddle was too much for the sleepy Cumi, so she added, "I am not going home, but unto Father Jacob. He will see to it that my pledge is fulfilled."

Cumi rose. "Oh, Tamar, you must not! You have made Master Judah angry enough. Do not cause him to be more displeased with you."

Tamar tossed her head and stated flatly, "Judah's displeasure is the least of my concerns."

Cumi shrugged, for to argue with Tamar was fruitless. Instead, she helped her guest gather her belongings and then stood, holding back ever-present tears, as Tamar prepared to leave.

At the last minute before departing, Tamar asked, "Cumi, where might I find Shelah at this hour?"

"Shelah?" Cumi echoed in surprise.

"Yes, Shelah."

"Within his mother's tent, I venture, since her distressing illness yesterday. Usually, he breakfasts with Master Judah and the men before they leave for the fields, but I heard him say last night that he wished to stay close by Mistress Shuah today."

"My thanks for your every kindness unto me," Tamar said, kissing Cumi on both cheeks.

Without further mention of Shelah or any explanation for her inquiry, she departed, waving her farewells and not wanting to look back at Cumi, who was choking back her tears. Tamar heard Cumi say, "God go with you," and then the small, dark head disappeared back into the tent.

Tamar was glad the early morning hour kept servants' inquisitive eyes away from her. She hoped to speak to Shelah alone without Judah's knowledge. She had another plan, one that did not involve her father-in-law. He would be certain to interfere.

She was relieved to see Shelah, standing alone, at the well. He splashed water onto his face with awkward jerks of his bony arms, spilling the liquid down his short, brown tunic and allowing it to drip from his nose and chin. Then he shook his head from side-to-side like a puppy who had put his face too far into a drinking bowl.

Watching him, Tamar thought how simple and childish he still was. Aloud, she said, "Peace unto you, Shelah," as she walked up to him. "How is your mother today?"

Startled, the lad stumbled backward and would have fallen into the open well's mouth had he not been steadied by Tamar's hand. He grimaced at the sight of her hold upon his arm and pulled away from her. His eyes widened in fright.

"Father said you would be gone today," Shelah said, trying to keep his voice even and his chin from quivering. "How is it you are still here?"

"I wanted to see you before I left," she replied, setting down her bundles to move nearer.

"Stand back!" The words were both a command and a frightened plea.

Tamar went straight to the point: "Why do you dislike me so, Shelah? Do you really believe your mother's ravings about my being a devil?"

"You are a devil! You killed my brothers!"

Tamar gracefully floated down to sit upon her bundles and lifted the velvet eyes up to him. He would be less fearful if she did not communicate from a position of dominance, she reasoned. "Dear Shelah," she drawled, "you know that is untrue. You remember how sick your brothers were before we wed. You also know Father Jacob and Judah would never have agreed to my marrying either of them had they believed I was anything but a true follower of Jehovah."

He considered her argument briefly before he moved away from her, heading toward his mother's tent. "Even so, you are not welcome here. Before my mother becomes upset again, you must be on your way."

Tamar was on her feet and after him. She caught his hand and stood deliberately close as she said sweetly, "Do not speak so harshly to me, Shelah. I have not wronged you. Nor do I intend you any harm. I could never do anything to hurt you."

The first glimmer of the rising sun was playing in her hair, causing highlights to dart like arrows into Shelah's eyes. Her round, full mouth was still opened slightly even after the honeyed words faded away, and her face was so close to his that it caused him to swallow long and hard, several times. The outline of his Adam's apple was visibly moving.

"Will . . ." Shelah cleared his throat and began again, trying to lower his voice from a child-like squeak. "Will you be off soon? Now, if you please?"

"Not if you would have me to stay," she whispered. "You have been pledged to me."

Shelah ran a hand through a shock of wispy hair and coughed. "I . . . I do not understand," he said. "Why should you wish to marry me?"

Tamar smiled. It was the opening she had hoped for, and she had a ready reply: "Because I know I could find no better husband in all Hebron, yea, in all the kingdoms of Canaan and Edom."

His face drained of the little color it possessed and then reddened at the compliment. Never had anyone spoken to him in such a manner. He hesitated for a moment, studying her face, before saying, "You speak to me like this only because . . . because . . ." He truly did not know why.

"Because I want to destroy you?" she suggested. "How can you think evil of me, when I have endured such pain for you?" Her full lips formed a sad pout.

"Pain?" He raised his brows in question.

Tamar sighed. "Have I not waited three long, lonely years for you? There have been many men wishing to have me to wife, Shelah. Why do you think I refused them and kept waiting?"

"I do not know." He really was dumbfounded. He only knew what he had heard from others about Tamar. He had little firsthand knowledge of her at all.

"Because," she said, moving her hands up along his arms to his shoulders, "I will have you for my husband, or no one! You must give me your love, or I will surely die of the rejection."

Tamar was surprised at the sound of her own voice, the artificial ring which she knew Shelah would never detect. She closed her eyes, trying not to hear the wheezing sound from the sunken place in Shelah's throat, and kissed him briefly on one hollow cheek. His lips seemed bluer than before, and for one dreadful moment, she was afraid he would fall upon her.

"I must go attend to my mother," he said lamely.

"Can you not spend one moment with me?" she asked, allowing her hair to brush against his face. His arms fell limp at his sides, and the slight tremble of his body told her that he never had been so close to even a girl, much less a woman, before.

Shelah wanted desperately to run, but something compelled him to stand there and allow her to touch him. A new and pleasant feeling came over him, a warmth to match the warmth of her breath upon his face. She must be a devil, he thought. Else why was he under her power and unable to make his feet move to flee from her?

Tamar knew the camp soon would be stirring, and the open space in which they stood was not suitable for carrying out the next part of her plan. She pointed to her bundles and said, "I have food packed for my journey. Come with me to the hidden brook over against the hillside, and have breakfast with me. Surely you should get to know me better before you decide whether or not I am worthy to be your wife."

"No!" he said at once. "I cannot."

"Cannot or will not? Are you not man enough to do as you please?"

"What is your meaning?"

"I think you fear your father. You know he wants to keep you close to himself and opposes our union. He thinks you too young and immature for me. He would not want to find you even speaking to me." She wondered if he would take the bait.

Shelah pushed his drooping shoulders back to say, "I do not fear my father. I cannot go with you, I mean, I *will* not go with you, because I must see to my mother."

Tamar encircled her arm in his. "The servants will tend to her needs. Can you not spend one last farewell moment with me—before I am sent away forever? Is it too much to ask for one hour before we must part?"

He shrugged helplessly and almost without realizing it, he allowed her to lead him to the stalls where the donkeys were bedded down. The old animal keeper was still asleep in the straw, his gray beard rising and falling on his chest with his heavy breathing. Tamar put her finger to her lips and silently unloosed the colts she remembered as sure-footed and swift.

Shelah wanted to protest, for he knew the missing animals would cause a stir when the old man awakened, but Tamar moved more swiftly than he could think or speak. She tied her bundles onto the colt she had selected for herself and then led the other into his hand. Before he could think of any further protest, he was riding beside her in the direction of the hidden brook.

The uncertainty of it all caused an uneasy feeling in the pit of Shelah's stomach. He felt both fear and boldness as he was caught up in the pleasant adventure of something forbidden and exciting. His spirit seemed to soar in spite of the dread he still had for Tamar, riding straight and tall at his side. Somehow, Shelah likewise felt taller and stronger than ever before. His father would be furious. His mother would be distraught. Both reactions, he knew, were inevitable.

Shelah pushed aside all thoughts of what would ensue. Suddenly, he felt himself much older and wiser. He liked that. He could take care of himself. After all, what could a woman do to him? She could not really be a devil, could she? Well, on that count, he was not completely certain. But he needed to decide for himself. Others his age, even the younger servants, often took actions on their own without asking permission of their elders. He would give Tamar her breakfast picnic and a courteous farewell. What harm in that? It was exhilarating to think of himself making a choice independently, without his father's consent. It was the first indication that, at long last, he was being initiated into manhood.

As he rode along, he could not but wonder at Tamar's words to him. One moment she had spoken as though she still wished to be his wife. Then she spoke of her departure and of being sent away forever. What did she really intend to do? He dared not ask, for he was afraid to know. Mingled with his qualms about her was an unshakable feeling that whatever Tamar did, leave or stay, he would be deeply affected. It was frightening to think of marrying her, but if she left, he'd be his mother's pampered boy again, perhaps never to know any other woman's touch.

When they arrived at the appointed place, Shelah's spirit of adventure reverted to his unrelenting anxiety. He watched the awesome goddess alight swiftly and silently from her beast and begin to unload the supplies for their repast. In his head, he could hear his father's question: *Why did you ride off with Tamar for a secluded meeting*? He had no appropriate answer. Oh, why had he come indeed! He only could stand, still clinging to the milk-white donkey, and pray silently that all would be well and that he would survive long enough to return home again.

The stillness of the morning lay upon the vineyards and the rocky plots which bordered the region from which they had just traveled. But nowhere was the silence more acute than where they stood. A calm, little wind played carelessly in the shining foliage of the trees overhead, but even that gentle, swaying motion was as a hushed whisper.

The landscape of green touched the ever-bright blue of the sky in a tableau of lush, tropical beauty. A touch of mortal beauty was added to the scene as Tamar knelt beneath a crutched mulberry tree to prepare their feast. She removed the veil with which she had covered her head for the donkey ride. Her reddish hair hung down as she bent over to lay out a circular piece of leather, sewn at the edges with metal rings, which served as a traveler's tablecloth and table as well. It was a Bedouin invention, particularly used by desert folk because it served a double purpose. When a string ran through the rings, it was hung from the pack animal's back as a carrying bag. Tamar had removed it from the animal shed for just that purpose and used it to transport her bundles and napkins of food from Cumi's table.

"Come," Tamar called to Shelah, who still was standing with the donkey between himself and his hostess. She opened her arms to him and then gestured to indicate the fine feast she had laid out upon the leather cloth. "I have brought fruit and cakes, parched corn, cheeses, and a goatskin of fresh milk. Is this not a meal fit for a city prince and his bride?"

Tamar had chosen her words carefully, all to implant in Shelah's mind the idea of marriage. She also sought to tempt him with the breakfast, but that part of her plan was far from successful. Shelah's delicate stomach was queasy with uncertainty, and he kept his eyes from even looking toward the food.

"I'm not hungry," Shelah said truthfully. "I don't know why I even came."

The brightness faded from Tamar's face as she rose and slowly approached him. She reached across the donkey's back for Shelah's hand. He was still clinging to the bridle strap for support. There was genuine compassion in her voice for the pitiful figure quaking before her:

"Shelah, I thought you had put away your foolish fears concerning me. I thought your manliness in coming here alone with me proved that you no longer believed your mother's wild tales about me. What possible reason would I have to do you any harm?"

Shelah was moved by the hurt in Tamar's eyes. Nobody would enjoy being likened to a devil, he thought. When he could speak aloud he said, "My mother is very sick in her mind. She often does not know what she is saying."

Tamar pressed her hand harder upon his. "Then—if you do not fear me any longer—why do you stand here, afar off?"

"I do not know. I wish I had not come."

"But I thought you were beginning to like me. To trust me. I thought that we might become friends. You wanted to come, did you not?" The hurt in the pleading eyes intensified.

Mutely, Shelah nodded. He did, and he did not. He was too confused to explain.

Tamar, taking note of the distaste with which Shelah had eyed the food, decided to forego the picnic and to continue to play the part of the sad and wounded one. She sensed a hint of sympathy in Shelah's expression. Gently, she coaxed him to the brook's grassy bank. It was a deep, clear stream with bubbles dancing lightly over smooth rocks under and above its surface.

It had been named *hidden* brook because it was virtually unknown and untouched in the sanctuary of its secluded location. Other streams and springs of the city folk and wandering tribes of sheepherders were for public use in watering flocks. People thronged to such public watering places, not only for their thirsty animals, but also to catch up on the news of the day. It was at such places the women would do the washing, beating clothes with broad sticks upon the rocks. They also were places for gossip about neighbors' faults, rumors, and secrets better left unsaid. That was why Tamar avoided the public watering places. She often had been the topic of conversation among hateful women—and even, at times, among bearded menfolk who found her both charming and annoying in her nonconformity. Tamar preferred hidden brook's solitude with its restful, gurgling, welcoming waters to keep her company.

She spread her mantle upon the grass and quietly pulled Shelah down to sit with her on it. He obliged, but announced as soon as he was seated, "I must not stay long. I shall be missed, and they will come looking for me."

"I shall miss you also," Tamar said with the great eyes uplifted. Then she added, "When I must leave."

"Then . . . then you really are going away? Back to your people?"

Tamar sighed deliberately. "I shall have to if your father does not relent in his decision concerning you."

Shelah's curiosity about Tamar's future caused him to relax a little. Tamar, aware of his every move and any slight indication about how to proceed, took full advantage of his cue. She took his chin in her hands and eased him down until his head lay in her lap. She stroked his hair as a mother would quiet a frightened child, and spoke in a whispered tone:

"I tried last night to convince Judah that you are now ready for marriage, but he thinks you still unripe." Her tone made it seem like a misdeed.

"Many marry at an age earlier than mine," Shelah said defensively.

"I know. I know," Tamar cooed her agreement, still stroking his tousled hair. "I tried to tell him that, but he thinks your mother needs you close at her side . . . *always*. Oh, I could take him before the council and force him to fulfill his promise to me. By law, you are bound to marry me to honor your brothers' memory. But I do not wish to bring trouble to anyone."

Shelah tried to rise to look at Tamar, but she held him still,

52

her smooth hand gliding upon his boyish face in a hypnotic rhythm which caused him to lie quiet once more without speaking.

"I suppose," Tamar continued, "with your mother so ill and with your being his only child now, Judah begins to cling to you as Father Jacob does to his Benjamin. I can understand his wishing you to remain *forever* his unmarried son, even if I must suffer from such overprotection."

Shelah's mind was dancing. From his reclining position, he was unable to search Tamar's face for sincerity, but her words gave him much to ponder. It was mildly pleasant to think of his father defending him when Tamar demanded her pledge. Still, he had no great desire to be overprotected, especially if it meant being compared to the way his grandfather, Jacob, held to Shelah's young uncle, Benjamin. People poked fun at the way Benjamin was babied and coddled, tied to his father's skirts. Shelah considered the possibility that people were, likewise, making crude jokes about him as well.

With words that were more wishful thinking than fact-based conviction, Shelah declared, "My father does not cling to me as you say. I am allowed great freedom."

"Oh? Great freedom to do what? When has Judah ever treated you as the adult man that you are? Or even as his equal? You're of an age to marry, but he told me *he* refuses to allow it."

"He is just waiting for *me* to make the decision," Shelah lied. "He puts great stock in independent thinking, and such matters should be determined only with my approval."

"How marvelous!" Tamar exclaimed, trying not to laugh aloud. "If the marriage decision is yours to make, as you say, then there is no reason why we should not be wed. That is, unless you will not have me. Tell me, Shelah, do you have eyes for another more worthy to be your wife?"

Shelah squirmed in the trap. He could not admit to her that he had never even thought of courtship or marriage. "It is not that you are not worthy—or beautiful, Tamar. I am sure you would be a fine wife. It is just . . . just . . ."

Tamar had to interrupt before he thought of reasons against their union, so she said, "I was not denied to your brothers. Judah thought me an adequate match for them. I wonder why Judah considers you so differently. Are you not as good as your brothers?"

"Of course I am."

"And would you be unwilling to honor them by raising up children in their names?"

Shelah could not answer. Tamar knew he could not, so she bent her head down to him with the fullness of her mouth almost touching his. She breathed her next words with as much alluring appeal as she could: "I would indeed make you a good wife, Shelah. And you always could have your choice of others, if I should ever displease you. But I will not displease you."

Tamar lifted Shelah's head toward her, one hand behind each of his red ears, to plant a willowy kiss upon the boy's thin line of a mouth. It was a brief, chaste kiss, for Tamar needed to proceed slowly and cautiously. She knew it was the first romantic kiss he had ever received.

Whether from fright or awakened emotion, Tamar could not tell, but suddenly he was clutching her as a starving babe hungers for nourishment. His scrawny arms were fast about her neck, his face buried in the softness of her bosom. He did not speak, but she heard his labored breathing coming rapidly from his throat as though he were choking back a sob. She recalled words she had spoken to Cumi about taking the sickly lad to her breast.

Tamar encircled Shelah in her arms and swayed to and fro in a comforting rocking motion. Instinctively, she began to hum to him in rhythm with the rocking. She patted and rubbed his heaving shoulders until his hold upon her became less frantic. She planted soft kisses on his forehead and continued to hum her lullaby of love. At last, he lay still, cradled in her arms, and his heavy breathing died to a placid wheeze.

Tamar tried not to think of how absurd they must look. She suppressed loathsome and unnatural feelings that infected her mind. She refused to compare this scene to the one last night when Judah's strong arms enfolded her in the thrill of mature passion. She willed away all thoughts that bordered on something akin to incest that came from embracing her only true love's son. She denied that she was betraying both Judah and herself by a pretense that prostituted genuine, holy love. She forced herself to focus on obtaining her heart's desire, not on having to endure the grotesque caricature and charade she was scripting.

Intrusive thoughts kept coming, no matter how hard Tamar tried to fend them off. How could she hold this boy-man throughout her entire life? Could she endure his constant fears and whimperings? What if he escaped his brothers' fates and lived a long and healthy life in spite of his frailty, so similar to theirs? Certainly, she could wish Shelah no ill, even at her own expense.

If Shelah would but perform for her the one essential task, if he got her with child, and if that child were a boy, then—oh, then—it all was worthwhile! So many conditions to be met, so many odds against the probabilities of everything going her way. Nevertheless, she had to capture the moment of opportunity and make the attempt. This might well be her only chance, and she was driven to take it.

For one startling moment she wondered if he were capable of performing the rites of love. She doubted if Shelah even had knowledge of the secrets of his physical abilities, for it was most unlikely Judah had spoken at length to the lad on the subject. Judah had said he placed his son's prospects of marriage in the distant future, if at all. But far surpassing all these obstacles was the overriding obsession with her perceived destiny. That alone urged her on.

Tamar hushed her song and whispered, "Shelah, I can show you pleasures of love you know not of—unbelievable joys God has ordained between woman and man."

He moved his head up to look at her, not understanding her meaning entirely, yet feeling that the magnitude of her words held some dark and awesome motive.

"You mean . . . Now?" He was shocked. He was both enticed and repulsed by the thought.

"If you so desire."

"But, Tamar," Shelah blushed, "I have not . . ."

". . . Been with a woman before? I know. It does not matter. It is, in fact, a rare treasure you would offer me—the gift of your

55

manhood for the very first time, unblemished by any other before me."

"But we are not wed."

"And we may never be if you allow me to be sent away. You said yourself the decision concerning our betrothal was *yours* to make. How shall you know if you desire me as your wife if you do not taste of the love offerings I can bring to you?"

"But it is wrong. I have been taught that our religion forbids it to those unmarried."

His words were like scorpion stings, for Tamar knew he was right. How could she defend an unlawful proposal in the name of obtaining a godly blessing? She searched for a loophole to rationalize the proposition, as much for herself as for him: "Shelah, have you heard Father Jacob's teachings of the promised Messiah? The prophecy of the Anointed One of God?"

Shelah searched his memory. "My father used to speak of it, I think. To my brothers. But that was long ago. I do not think he believes it or gives it importance any more."

"How sad for him!" Tamar exclaimed. "Whether or not Judah believes it does not change one word of the sacred writings. His disbelief cannot alter God's purposes. It is ordained that the Messiah will be born from Judah's lineage. You are the last of that lineage. It is your holy responsibility to fulfill the promise. Since Judah opposes our marriage, it is necessary for you to act now, before inaction thwarts the will of God and you are forever denied the blessing."

"Denied the blessing?" Shelah mused. To become part of a supernatural moment in history made him gasp with wonder. "But would our God wish me to . . . here, in this place . . . with *you*?"

"Father Jacob has prophesied that I should be the woman to bear this holy child through whom God's anointed will come. Unless we act now, you deny us both our holy inheritance. Rather than a blessing, you will bring a curse upon us. Can you not see that your brothers were unworthy, and God meant them to die so *you* could become His chosen one? With me?"

Shelah's head was reeling. It was unthinkable. "I cannot understand all you say, Tamar."

"Are you still afraid of me?" she asked as she felt him tremble again. "Do you really believe I would risk Judah's wrath and God's punishment to come here with you if I were not convinced it was God's will?" She almost choked on the words, for she knew she was risking both.

"I do not think I still fear you any longer . . . exactly. I do not know. I do not know . . ."

Tamar decided there had been too many words, words she might come to regret later when she allowed herself to reflect on them. So rather than speaking, she began to stroke Shelah's body again. At first she touched him through the barrier of his clothing, her deft hands moving down from his chest to his thighs. Then one hand was under his short tunic and against bare flesh.

At first, Shelah was startled. He sucked in his breath and tried to move away. But Tamar's embrace was tight and firm as she murmured, "Today, Shelah, you shall become a man."

Shelah no longer wanted to move. He felt himself carried upon a strange, new flood of impulses rising from within him, warm and unbelievably delightful. Tamar's last words had placed her in full control. Shelah wanted, more than anything else, to be a man. To gain the respect of his domineering father, to know the pleasure of a woman's closeness—other than that of his mother. Most of all, he wished to respect himself as a grown person doing grown-up things.

He surrendered himself to Tamar's invitation to leap beyond the insecurity and clumsiness of the sheltered, protected existence of his youth and the unbearable burden of a weak and unattractive body. Shelah believed he was approaching his adult moment of conquest, just as Tamar felt seducing Shelah was hers. He might never again have such a knowledgeable woman offer to teach him the secrets he only had heard whispered among the older men around an evening campfire.

Shelah knew his father would never permit him to marry Tamar. That was definite, despite anything Tamar or anyone else might say to Judah. Shelah was not even sure he wanted to marry her. In fact, he was certain he did not. She was so overpowering that old tinges of fear of her still remained. But his initiation into manhood was the only thing that seemed to matter now.

Tamar read the signs—Shelah's quickened breathing, the low moans and sighs of his utter contentment, now coming in rapid succession. She sensed that the time was almost right for her initiate's next lesson. She kissed him deeply on the mouth as she continued to caress and stroke him with greater intensity. Then quickly she rose and stood, unashamed, to unloose her robes.

Still breathing heavily, Shelah remained seated on the mantle, his eyes fixed straight ahead as one entranced. He was conscious of the dramatic changes in his own body that had occurred in response to Tamar's inducements. Then he saw first Tamar's *aba* and then her white tunic fall to the ground. He watched the sandaled feet step lightly over the fallen garments. Then slowly, slowly, he allowed his curious eyes to rise up from her slender ankles, up the well-formed legs to the curve of her hips, up to the round hanging fullness of her bosom. There his eyes stopped and widened. It was the first time he had ever seen a woman's bare breast, except for the half-hidden views of the servants suckling their nursing young.

Shelah's mouth dropped open. He let out a yelp of alarm, and, without a word, he turned to race for the waiting donkeys. He barely was on the beast's back before he dug his heels hard into her fleshy sides and gave an unintelligible whoop which instructed the animal to move at topmost speed. He fled away, holding to the bridle strap of the other donkey, the one Tamar had ridden. He never once looked back in her direction.

Clad only in her sandals, Tamar stood watching after the dust of his unexpected retreat. For a moment, anger flashed from her eyes and played upon the lines of her forehead. Rejected again! First by the father. Now by the son. Slowly, her anger turned to amusement at the absurdity of it all. She threw back her head to laugh. *The frightened, silly calf,* she thought. She had scared Shelah out of his wits. She chided herself for not taking a more lingering path to his seduction. Now he'd taken off with her donkey, and she would have to walk back.

Tamar decided there was no hurry now. Standing naked as

she was in the morning sunlight, she thought the most logical thing to do was remove her sandals and wade into the brook for a leisurely bath. With the coolness of the waters flowing over her, she rested her head upon a large rock in the midst of the bubbling stream to think.

The original plan had to be followed. The detour with Shelah had not provided the shortcut she anticipated, so she would press on toward Father Jacob's tents and arrive there long before nightfall. He lived but a few hours away in convenient dwellings within the village walls, the protective walls made of loose, baked loam and dung. It would be good to spend some time, finally, with a man who would not reject her, someone whose unconditional acceptance and love allowed her to be herself.

Jacob was not reclusive as was his fourth son, Judah. Within Jacob's camp, Tamar knew she could rest herself and spend enjoyable and peaceful times with her old, respected friend, the bearer of the blessing. He was more of a father to her than her own. Like Tamar, Jacob enjoyed ease and comforts in contrast to the half-Bedouin kind of life that surrounding tribes led. She would have her bath, eat some food to sustain her on the road, and then be on her way.

The breakfast was still spread under the mulberry tree, a haunting reminder of another fruitless failure. Tamar told herself she should have gone directly to Father Jacob in the first place. There was nothing but wasted time to show for her efforts to sway the patriarch's stubborn son or his weak-kneed grandson.

Upon reflection, Tamar decided that the events of the past two days had not been totally in vain. Judah now knew Tamar was back, and he would have time to think of the trouble she could cause him if she brought him before the city judges to hear her case. And Shelah, poor, shy, frightened Shelah. He, at least, had been exposed to her. She wondered if he still thought her to be a devil. Probably now more than ever. But it had proven that they could communicate with each other.

There still was the barrier of the invalid mother, but Tamar would not worry about that for now. For this moment, she would think only of what she would say to Father Jacob, what could move him to reverse the decision of his most independent son, Judah of Hebron. Judah, the only man who could both stir her heart and dash her dreams, the only man she would ever love so willingly, completely, and painfully.

Two defeats had slowed her progress, but the episodes with Judah and Shelah had served to revive her determined spirit, to spur Tamar on toward the undeniable victory she felt would be hers when she gained Father Jacob's ear.

Tamar closed her eyes and told herself all would be well. Jehovah would bring it to pass, in spite of her clumsy efforts to help Him. Oh, please bring it to pass! It *must* come to pass!

Four

Within Hebron's city walls lay the expansive settlement belonging to Jacob. The noble patriarch occupied the largest of the tents—a beautifully-woven felting of black goat hair stretched over stout poles and fastened by strong ropes to pegs driven into the ground. Scattered about it were the separate dwellings of Jacob's wives and servants and his sons' families who resided with him for convenience and mutual protection in the compound.

Not all of his sons remained with him at one time. His great herds and flocks needed vast pasture lands, so various sons and servants would take turns moving their tents on to Shechem, a four-day journey to the north. Sometimes they traveled even farther to Dothan's green plains to the northwest.

Jacob was really a stranger in the land, a highly respected guest who had established himself as a citizen, a rich member of the city's ruling class. He was honored for his wisdom and virtue by both the cattle-keeping peasantry and the wealthier townsfolk. His rented plough lands harvested crops of corn and barley, but Jacob's true riches came from his teeming, movable property, the flocks. He exchanged all they produced for plentiful supplies and luxuries he had accumulated over the years. Jacob had accustomed himself to the comforts of extravagant living.

Although Jacob lived alone in his great, sprawling house of hair, his youngest son was never far from his side. Benjamin did his utmost to make his aged father's declining years as pleasant as possible with entertainments. Together they would sit on cushions by a low taboret at the tent entrance joking, telling stories, singing psalms of praise, or playing games. Benjamin's attentions and indulgences of his father's childish whims came with the price of having to endure his elder brothers' mockery and his neighbors' gossip. But because he loved his father dearly,

61

Benjamin sacrificed other valued interests for the honored position of being the favorite son.

It was almost dusk as the two sat in their accustomed place playing a game with stones spread upon an engraved, bronze playing board. Benjamin let his father win by purposely putting himself at a disadvantage, and Jacob was extremely pleased with himself in the victory.

"Ah, my son," the bearded one chuckled, "it is a good thing indeed that I defeated you so quickly, for my thoughts are prone to wander of late. A prolonged game would have brought many blunders and misplays."

"Not so, Father," Benjamin said good-naturedly as he rose and stretched his arms high behind his head. "Your wisdom is so exceeding great that even in your sleep I would find you a worthy opponent."

The saying pleased Jacob. He stroked the gray-white strands of his beard which hung down with the hairs of his head, clearly visible even from under the looped and fringed head covering he wore. His figure was stout and stately, and it was accentuated by the huge scarlet, scarf-like girdle which circumscribed his expansive waist. His moustache ran like white streams from the corners of an almost invisible mouth to lay upon the beard. His cheeks, with hundreds of little wrinkles embedded in them, stood out above the line of the beard and just below two swollen eyes which resembled flabby carbuncles. His forehead, although wrinkled with age lines, was serene with a paradoxical smoothness. It characterized a freedom from anxiety and a complete reliance upon God, both of which gave the old man an air of tranquility, not only in his nature, but also in his appearance.

Drawing his son to his side, Jacob said, "It is blessed I am in having a son like you to comfort me in my last days. So like your blessed mother you are."

Benjamin always cringed at the comparison. Jacob never seemed aware of either his son's discomfort or his own frequent repetition of references to his beloved Rachel who had died at Benjamin's birth.

Even though Jacob's other wife—Rachel's older sister, Leah—and two concubines had given Jacob ten of his twelve sons, it was Rachel and her two offspring—Joseph and Benjamin—that Jacob always regarded as his true family. With Rachel and Joseph gone, Benjamin was all the old man had left to dote upon. The dead mother's ghostly memory lived on and seemed to be personified in the youngest son, much to the boy's dismay. Benjamin hated the constant memory, for he could not help but feel that his father held him somehow responsible for his mother's death in childbirth.

There never was anything voiced by Jacob to give Benjamin that feeling. Only words of love and kindness were spoken. Nevertheless, the message came by way of wistful expressions in the father's faded eyes, the sighs, the turn of the lips, the gray eyebrows fusing together in melancholy meditation at the sound of Rachel's name. Before Jacob could say anything more on the subject, Benjamin mentioned the lateness of the hour and proposed that evening prayers be offered so they both could get some needed rest.

The dark brown, close-cropped head of the son was bowed with that of the gray-haired father. Benjamin soon forgot his uneasiness. Prayer time at the close of the day was a deeply moving experience that always made the lad forget everything else. When prayers or hymn psalms were offered, Heaven's windows seemed opened to receive the praises and supplications, and those same windows poured down an unexplainable spiritual blessing of such magnitude that his young heart was not large enough to receive it all. To Benjamin, the earth grew quieter, and even the trees seemed to draw their branches close about them, lest they disturb the silence of the sacred moment.

Benjamin had been well-schooled in things spiritual. Man is more than body and mind, his father had taught him. The spirit was that part of one's being which could be likened to God, the part that could even bring itself to conceive the thought of a Creator. It was what brought one to an understanding of inadequacy and a need for strength outside the self. Worship was spiritual nourishment for the soul, just as food was required to strengthen the body. It allowed one to achieve wholeness, peace, and hope for any semblance of happiness in life.

As Jacob prayed, it occurred to Benjamin that his father had a wondrous—no, *miraculous* and very *personal*—relationship with his God. The thought rocked the imagination with awe—a mortal actually communing with the divine. He longed for such a closeness, but he doubted that he ever would achieve anything close to it. After all, he had never seen angels as his father had. He listened in rapt attention as Jacob lifted his arms and trembling voice to sing the words:

O Lord, our souls humbly bow before You in offering our
    worship.
You make clouds Your chariot and ride the wings of the wind.
You have laid the world's foundations and created every good
    thing.
We thank You for all abundant blessings of our earth's rich
    bounty.
We live only to serve You and to bless Your magnificent, holy
    name.
We will honor You with adoration as long as we have breath.
Forgive our secret sins, and remove all our iniquities.
Make us to walk in Your ways, and free us from all
    wickedness.
May we always sing Your praises, O Worthy, Blessed Lord,
And rejoice in Your love now and forever more. Amen.

She appeared as the praise psalm ended. The swaying motion of the incense burner was still sending scented clouds of smoke, heavy with the fragrant offerings of cinnamon, styrax, and galbanum. Through the smoke she materialized—silent, garbed in white, head bowed, hands folded in honor of the rites of worship she did not wish to interrupt or disturb.

At first glance, Jacob, whose dull eyes could play tricks on him, thought she was a figment of his imagination. But when she continued to stand there with the glistening whiteness of her robe creating a halo effect from the smokey firelight and the dimming shadows of twilight, he began to think a heavenly visitor had been sent to him as in days long ago.

"Speak," Jacob said reverently. "Your servant hears to obey your every command."

"Father!" Benjamin cried. "It is Tamar!"

Jacob was not disappointed that the vision turned out to be mortal. To him, Tamar was very like an angel of good tidings. Her presence always lifted his spirits. He opened his arms wide in a welcoming greeting. "Merciful Jehovah be praised for your safe return," he chortled.

Tamar dropped her bundles and the folded *aba*, the outer garment she had removed because of the heat of the sun, and ran to embrace him. Her enthusiasm at their reunion matched his. She was laughing at Jacob's mistaking her for something supernatural and for the sheer joy of seeing his face again. Suddenly, all three of them were laughing and creating such a stir that two nearby servants came running to investigate the commotion.

Jacob waved the servants away and said, "Go back to your tents. It is only Tamar—come home."

"*Only* Tamar?" she teased. "That sounds like the handmaiden holds a lowly place in the eyes of her lord. Not at all a proper greeting for one who travels so far in the blistering sun to partake of your company." She nudged Jacob gently in his ample side, remembering how the old man enjoyed a jest.

"I meant no disrespect to our most honored guest," Jacob replied, bowing in feigned humility. "A thousand pardons, Mistress, I beg you."

Benjamin was no longer laughing with them. To see his aged father cavorting with a young woman was unseemly. The absurdity of his bowing to her—even in sport—was beneath the dignity owed to one of Jacob's high rank. His father demanded respect from everyone else, but with Tamar he seemed to step out of character and become childish. Neither of them paid the slightest attention to him or noted his pique of distaste. Being ignored made him even more annoyed, so Benjamin announced that he was going to retire. He suggested that his father follow his example, knowing full well that his words were also being ignored.

"Something displeases young Benjamin," Tamar said when he stomped off toward his tent.

"It is nothing more than silly, changing moods of youth," Jacob told her. He was glad to have Tamar to himself. He had missed her presence more than he realized until her return stirred within him the old, reawakened feelings, something which mildly reminded him of his youth and his deep love for his Rachel. Benjamin made him feel it too—but to a much lesser degree. It was Tamar who caused a strange happiness to soar and make his spirits lift to unbelievable heights.

"He is not so young as you believe," Tamar began, cautiously approaching the matter she promised to manage for Cumi. "He will be seeking a bride for himself soon, no doubt."

"Not so!" Jacob exclaimed abruptly.

His tone was definite enough to cause Tamar to withhold any further mention of marriage for Benjamin until a more suitable time. Instead, she changed the subject: "It is good to be here with you again. Forgive me if I spoke out of turn."

Jacob's momentary outburst melted into forgetfulness as he drank in her beauty and listened to the lilt of her voice. "I am an old man, Tamar. I hold fast to that which gives me pleasure, for I know it will not be mine much longer."

Tamar lifted his hand to her cheek and held it there as she said softly, "May Jehovah grant that I also may give you pleasure in your last years."

Jacob smiled. How good to hear her cheerful voice again. He had begged her to remain with him after the deaths of her husbands. It was with reluctance he saw the wisdom in her decision to do as Judah commanded her and return to her people until Shelah was of age. So Jacob had sent her on her way with his blessing. They both knew it was the best way to ensure Judah's good pleasure when she returned for her God-inheritance. Judah could be such a stubborn man! But Jacob was certain, beyond doubt, that Tamar eventually would have part in the promised blessing. Had he not planted the notion in her mind himself? From the beginning, he had felt she was the chosen one, the different one, the one to lay claim to the holy promise. And now the time of mourning was over. He smiled broadly, rejoicing in her safe return.

"Have you been to see Judah?" Jacob asked as they sat at the tent door.

"It is a long and unhappy story I must tell you," she said

slowly. "But, please, not tonight. Tonight we must have only pleasant thoughts and happy talk to celebrate my return."

Jacob nodded. He had anticipated trouble with Judah. He had heard of Shuah's illness and of Judah's close ties to Shelah, something he could understand when a wife was no longer there for company and comfort. But, as Tamar proposed, they could speak of the problem tomorrow.

"Come inside," Jacob said, rising with difficulty. "I will give you some refreshment, and we can talk of only the pleasant things you wish before you retire to your tent."

Tamar's small but comfortable tent was not far from Jacob's. It had been made especially for her alone, even though all the other women were housed together in larger dwellings some distance away. That Tamar had such a nearby and lovely tent all to herself had aroused the displeasure of the eldest wife, Leah, and the jealousy of the concubines and their handmaidens. Jacob paid no attention to Leah's questions or complaints from his sons. Even after Tamar married and moved away, the tent remained unoccupied. He wanted the dwelling untouched by others and kept only for Tamar. Whether or not she returned, it was her property. Her shrine.

As Tamar entered Jacob's tent, she recalled his words, words that stirred her heart: "It is only Tamar--*come home.*" Indeed, she did feel more at home here than she had ever felt among her kinsmen or living with her husbands. She knew a welcome awaited her here, but to hear Jacob say so gave her secret delight, especially after all the turmoil of the past two days.

For a long moment, Tamar stood gazing about Jacob's dwelling place, remembering the similar feeling that came to her earlier within Judah's tent. But how different were the homes of father and son! Where Judah's was lavish and resplendent with a shining newness and freshness to its beauty, Jacob's tent was more lived-in, more useful somehow. It was just as richly ornate, but there was something comfortable about the luxury. A great curtain hung from the middle posts to separate Jacob's storeroom and supply chamber from his living quarters. He insisted on keeping the donkey and camel saddles and other supplies near at hand, and the heavy smell of leather hung in the air.

There also was the smell of the hanging skins for food-stuffs—grain, butter, and palm wine made of soaked dates.

Tamar loved the living chamber with the warm, carpeted floor coverings and the gaily-colored, smaller rugs. Some of the more decorative ones adorned the heavy tent walls. By far, her favorite furnishing was the huge, cedar-wood bedstead with its shining bronze feet. Coverlets and cushions were strewn carelessly upon the bed for added comfort. No sleeping mat for Father Jacob! Some day Tamar would have such a bedstead, Jacob had promised her. She immediately went to sit upon the multi-colored coverlet as she continued to move her eyes from the tall coffer beside the bed to the earthen lamps, the ornamental vases and bowls, and the flickering glow of the shallow lamps with their wicks forever giving light.

"The lamps are still glowing," she remarked in remembrance.

"Of course, my daughter," Jacob said, pouring her some wine and placing slices of cheese upon bread left over from the evening meal. "It would be unfitting and poverty-stricken for it to be said that Jacob's lamp is out."

Jacob's lamps were lighted even in the day, in keeping with the custom, and such a man as he never would stoop to sleeping in the dark.

Tamar took the wine and food in her hands and crossed the room to the carved chests in the corner. They were decorated with texts in several languages upon their magnificent, vaulted lids. The other furnishings were low stools, a table, a glowing brazier for removing the chill of dewy evenings, a flat gold basin on a stand, several wardrobe and storage chests, hand mills, and other gear in corners or upon pegs in wall posts. But the most prized possession of all was Jacob's valuable specimen of Phoenician art. Tamar fixed her eyes upon it and sucked in her breath.

"You appreciate great beauty," Jacob said, watching her admire the masterpiece. "It takes a sensitive nature to show such regard for artistic creations. My sons think it was foolish of me to spend my gold upon something that cannot serve a useful purpose."

"Beauty does not have to be useful, does it, Father Jacob?" Tamar murmured.

"Certainly not. We agree on many things, Tamar. Our natures are amazingly similar."

"I take that as a great compliment," she said, turning to him. "I could wish for nothing better to be said of me than that my nature can be likened to that of Father Jacob."

Smiling, Jacob indicated a plump cushion near the warmth of the brazier. "Sit here, and rest yourself. You must be weary. I do not like the thought of you traveling so far unattended."

"I am quite used to it. There is little danger in the daytime," she said carelessly. She dropped to the cushion to finish her meal. She started to relate the account of the added distance of her longer walk from hidden brook, but that would bring Shelah's name into the conversation. She was determined to refrain from any mention of that subject. Tonight she wanted only to relax and to listen to the sound of Jacob's voice.

"How are your father and your kinsmen?" Jacob asked, seating himself beside her.

"My so-called father is the same. My relatives are always the same." There was a hint of sarcasm in her words. She did not have to say more, for Jacob knew how ungodly they were.

"You still feel great resentment, my dear child. That should not be."

"And why not, I pray you? Have I not cause for resentment?" she sneered.

"You must honor your family, no matter how undeserving."

"Even those who are evil?"

"Especially those who are evil. They have the greatest need to be shown God's love and understanding."

"I have no father but you. When I left my people this time, it was to return no more."

"I rejoice in having you here again with me, but my heart is saddened that you were not able to teach your kinsmen the ways of Jehovah God."

"It would have been of no use to try. Their minds are too shallow to receive the truth."

"No, it is their hearts that are too full."

69

"What is your meaning?"

"They have filled their hearts with love of strange gods, gluttonous sacrifice feasts to Baal and Ishtar, and the unspeakable rituals of whoredom. There is little room for righteousness in hearts so full of wickedness."

"I am sickened every time I go there," Tamar said, nodding her agreement with Jacob's evaluation. "It is more than the fertility rites performed with the temple women now. It is a daily occurrence to see men with their manhood bared running around in rank frenzy, whoring after the Baals of the land. Or dirty, crazed oracles mutilating themselves, eating polluted food, and shouting wild, demonic prophesies with erotic meanings."

Jacob shook his head and said sorrowfully, "And all this in the name of religion."

"The cults of Ishtar and Sheol are not religion," Tamar protested angrily. "It is but filthy, wanton lust. Every woman takes her turn as a temple prostitute."

It was getting worse than Jacob had known before. His eyes widened anxiously to ask, "You mean *every* woman? Even those married? Surely they have not taken God's sacred rite of married love to profane and make mockery of it? And you . . . you were not compelled, were you?"

Tamar laughed lightly. "Of course not. My father thinks me too stupid and unworthy since I have forsaken his religion for yours. I barely talked to him while I lived there alone, counting off the days of my mourning in an eternity of waiting. The only reason he tolerated me was that he knew I would not stay permanently."

"I praise Jehovah that you were not harmed and that He sent you back here before you were lured into their depraved way of life."

"That is another reason for my burning anger."

"That you have returned to my household?"

"No. That my father was so eager to be rid of me. Two bulls were of more value to him than his own daughter. He was afraid my return meant I had displeased you and you wanted the bulls returned that you traded for me."

Jacob reached for Tamar's hand and stroked it as he spoke

70

reassuringly: "Those under the influence of false gods have no sense of value. Do not despise your father, but rather rejoice that you came here to learn the ways of the true God."

Tamar's expression softened. "Truly, you speak gems of wisdom. And we have broken our pledge to speak only of pleasant things this night. Was that not our agreement?"

"So it was. And what topic shall it be?"

Tamar drew her legs under her in a half-reclining position. "Tell me a tale as you used to do when I was a silly girl sitting at your feet."

"What would you hear? The tale of the great flood? Or the journey of my grandfather Abraham from Ur? Or the sacrifice of my father Isaac? Which will you have?"

"I would have the tale of Isaac's son," she replied with a witty gleam in her eyes.

"Ah," Jacob played along with her. "A most worthy and noble man. You could not select a greater hero for your bedtime story. And which famous exploit of his illustrious life would it please you to hear?"

"All of them. From the day he was born until this night."

Jacob roared with laughter, his scarlet girdle rising and falling with the movement of his heaving belly. "Such a girl you are, Tamar! In one evening I am to tell all the events of my entire life? We shall be here until the next new moon!"

Tamar thought for a moment. "You need not give every detail. Just about receiving the birthright blessing intended for your brother . . . and how you worked for your uncle to obtain the hand of Rachel . . . and how your uncle tricked you into marrying Leah, the eldest, first . . . and about the heavenly vision with angels on the ladder . . . and . . ." Tamar stopped short. Jacob was looking at her through squinting eyes. "What is the matter?" she asked him.

"It seems you remember all the tales quite well yourself. There is no need to repeat what you obviously know already."

Tamar chose her words carefully, lest she should offend the father figure at her side. "The stories are old, but each time you tell them they become new again. There is no teller of tales like unto Father Jacob."

71

The flattery satisfied him, so in response to her urging, Jacob began to relate the events of his life in a style grand and forceful, much like the man himself. Long into the night, the old man reminisced, and the young woman listened eagerly to every word.

Tamar heard once more about Jacob's brother, Esau, the Red One, the wild and hairy hunter who was such a contrast to Jacob, the home-loving shepherd, and of the scheme which gained for the younger son the father's blessing and the powerful right to pass it on through descendants.

Seldom did Tamar interrupt Jacob as he presented his narratives, but a question formed itself in her mind and compelled her to ask, "Father Jacob, if the blessing is sacred unto the Lord, and if Jehovah demands righteousness from the bearer of the blessing, how is it He allowed you to take the blessing under false pretenses?"

Stunned at the question, Jacob cleared his throat and stroked his beard. Usually, the story of the great deception of his father was toned down to save face. Here and there, the narrator was accustomed to going delicately. For instance, when speaking of Rachel's loveliness and his affection for her, Jacob tried to spare Tamar, just, as in the other instance, he tried to spare himself. With his knowledge of human nature—especially feminine human nature—Jacob knew one did not praise too highly the charms of one woman while in the presence of another. The question put to him now showed a greater maturity in Tamar. She had moved beyond girlish desires to be entertained. Now she wanted adult answers about God's purposes and human motives of people who sought to fulfill them. His answer could not be glossed over nor handled with delicacy this time. He had to answer with total honesty.

"Tamar, in youth and inexperience, one often tries to take into his own hands the Lord's will. I knew my twin brother, Esau, was unfit for the blessing, and in my heart I knew Jehovah had chosen me to be bearer of the covenant promise. Do not ask how or why I knew. I just knew. It was a sense of destiny—of being chosen, of being used to further God's purposes."

"I know the feeling," she mused, thinking of her own striving

72

and of the unexplainable certainty of God's hand upon her own life. She also felt convicted of plotting and scheming to force circumstances and people to conform to God's will as she understood it.

Jacob continued, "But instead of waiting upon the Lord's proper timing, I became impatient as my father's last days drew near. And when my mother proposed I disguise myself as Esau and fool my blind father into giving the blessing to me, I seized the opportunity. I did not consult God or my conscience. I acted without considering the dire consequences or the price I would pay."

"But I still do not understand Jehovah allowing the blessing to fall to . . ."

"A thief. That is what you are thinking—and rightly so, for that is what I was. I believe God was not hindered from His purposes in spite of my self-will and sinfulness. God is never limited by man's opposition, failures, or lack of faith. But, oh, how much better if I had been patient!"

"But if you had not acted, Isaac would have blessed Esau, the brother born first!"

"Can you be certain of that?"

"But he was the rightful heir."

"Nowhere in God's law has it been written that the eldest must rule over his brothers. Only in man's tradition has the custom been established."

"Is that the reason Reuben, although eldest, will not receive the God-inheritance?"

"I think birth order a poor reason for giving or denying such a destiny. If Reuben's sinful incest had not occurred, he might still be the chosen heir. I am not opposed to traditions of our fathers. But of greater importance is following God's leadership in such a weighty matter."

"You seek the most righteous son." It was more a question than a statement.

"No. I seek God's will and direction. That lesson came to me through hard experience."

"And Judah is the chosen one?" She tried to keep the eagerness from her voice.

"As of this moment, that is what I believe, Tamar."

"I needed to hear you say you had not changed your mind about him."

Jacob's face darkened. "Judah is a willful, stubborn man, not unlike myself. But, at least, his righteousness exceeds that of his older, married brothers. He has kept himself to one wife. He reverences the Lord. I must confess, I have my doubts about him at times, but we shall see."

"You said Judah's righteousness exceeds that of *older, married* brothers. You are not thinking of giving the blessing to Benjamin, are you?" The thought was a stab to Tamar's heart.

"He is yet too young for me to determine the matter. Who knows what the future may bring or what the Lord has predestined?"

Tamar rose to her feet, her pulse racing, to protest: "It would be unwise to elevate the youngest above all his brothers! It would bring their displeasure—and would break the age-old traditions of your neighbors. Would you not be mocked to shame for such a breach?"

A twinkle played in Jacob's eyes. "Do you imagine that I have forgotten, Tamar? I know how much the covenant promise means to you—and how you wish to take part in it."

"I do not understand. One moment you speak of giving the blessing to Judah, then to Benjamin. Tell me straight, Father Jacob. Does the blessing fall to Judah and his descendants or not?" Tamar was anxious and distraught, knowing how her future depended on Jacob's answer.

Jacob sighed with disappointment at Tamar's lack of understanding. "I feel that Judah is God's choice. Regardless of my personal feelings, or my great love for young Benjamin, I must seek only to follow God's leading. When I desired to give the blessing to Joseph—out of God's will—the lad was taken from me. Another bitter lesson I learned from the corrective hand of the Almighty. I will not make that same mistake again, I assure you."

Tamar was still confused. "But if God's choice *should* be Benjamin, what becomes of me? Surely, you do not intend me to wed one even younger than Shelah! That is preposterous!"

Jacob took her hand to calm her. "Tamar, God's will for you

cannot be determined by what seems logical to human reason. Do not seek to reduce the glory of the covenant blessing to something you selfishly desire for yourself." Then, seeing the hurt and fear in her eyes at his rebuke, he added, "If Judah should turn aside from God, that would be the sign that I must choose another. But as long as Judah remains faithful and walks uprightly, he shall receive the promise. It must be God's choice—not yours or mine."

Tamar was somewhat relieved, but still uneasy. "I am glad for that much," she said.

Jacob was lost in his painful memories. "I had only one son who was truly righteous before the Lord. I wanted so much for Joseph to be the chosen one, but then . . ." His words broke off at the agonizing remembrance of a coat of many colors, torn and blood-stained, delivered into his hands by ten of his other sons.

Now it was Tamar's turn to console the old man. She stroked his shoulder and whispered, "Always your thoughts turn to your Joseph, the one who was killed. It still pains you deeply?"

Jacob nodded mutely as tears filled his eyes. "He had visions from the Lord, Tamar. He could interpret dreams. So talented and wise and gifted was he that I believed he surely would serve God in a mighty way. But who am I to presume to have more knowledge than the Lord? He gives and takes away. Bless His name, for He needs no human help to run this world. Our duty is to forego self-indulgent, ambitious pride, to comply, and never to think *we* are in control."

Taking note of the emotions stirred with memories of his lost son, Tamar tried to put lightness in her voice: "Once more we fail to keep our pledge to speak of only agreeable things. It would be pleasant if you would tell me the story of the great dream and the ladder of angels."

Jacob shared Tamar's desire to turn the subject away from Joseph. The two dearest people on earth to him—Rachel and her firstborn, Joseph—had been taken away, as if God were saying, "Let go. Do not love so completely and exclusively, for that is idolatry." He had tried never to love in such a way again—but to no avail. Jacob always needed a favorite as an object for the abundance of his passion. Benjamin had become his Joseph, and, while he would not admit it even to himself, Tamar had become his Rachel.

"Will you tell me of the ladder?" Tamar repeated when she saw Jacob's mind had lapsed into his own thoughts.

Jacob told the tale better than all others, for it was his favorite. He began with his flight to save his life from his enraged, disinherited brother and the journey to his Uncle Laban's home.

Jacob spoke with uplifted head and plentiful gestures to describe the place of his vision, Bethel, the place where he rested while on his journey of escape: "I beheld shining steps leading to Heaven, as angels ascended and descended the ladder. The voice of the Almighty spoke to me. Like thunder it was, so overpowering that I covered my ears at the hearing."

Tamar sat upright, barely breathing, as she said, "Speak again to me the words. The words from the mouth of the Lord." To her, this was the most thrilling part.

Jacob made his voice as strong as he could and strained to keep it from shaking: "I am the Lord God of Abraham and Isaac. The land whereon you are lying, to you will I give it, and to your seed. And your seed shall be as the dust of the earth, and you shall spread abroad east, west, north, and south. In you and your seed shall all families of the earth be blessed. And I am with you and will keep you wherever you go, to bring you again to this land. For I will not leave you until I have done that which I have spoken to you."

Sighing in wonderment, Tamar said, "Every word. You remember every last word."

"One does not forget such a moment. Many things fail to come to my feeble remembrance, but these words of my God are locked forever in my heart."

"Was there a special meaning to the dream?" Tamar asked. "I mean, did the ladder and the angels have some message of significance?"

Jacob nodded approval. "Tamar no longer merely listens to my tales for their own sake. Now it is significant meanings and interpretations she desires. That is good, very good."

"Ah, there is a meaning!" she cried, delighted with her insightful discovery.

"The ladder was to show me the connection between the created world and Heaven and that communication was possible between God and man. Despite teachings of my youth and having been brought up to honor my father's God, never before did I have a *personal* relationship with Him myself—until that moment. He was actually there with me. I knew He loved me and would never leave me, in spite of the sinful deeds I had committed. I realized, that with God by my side, I could endure the loneliness of separation from my family . . . the guilty remorse I felt for my evil deceptions . . . even the uncertainty of the future as I journeyed to an unknown land. In one instant, I knew all this because I found communion with a Strength outside of myself."

After a long silence, Tamar probed further. "May I ask yet another question?"

"Always you have questions. What troubles you now?"

"I wish to know the meaning of the promise, 'from your seed all the families of the earth will be blessed.' What, precisely, did that mean?"

"Why, Tamar, I am sore amazed. I thought you knew well that particular meaning."

"It was the blessing of Messiah, God's Son, was it not?"

"Indeed. Shiloh—the Holy Prince of Peace, the Anointed One—who will reign from sea to sea and bring God's kingdom to earth, the One to whom every knee will bow."

Clasping her hands to her breast, Tamar said with joyful delight, "I thought it must be so! Oh, Father Jacob, I just wanted to hear the promise again. I wanted to be reassured."

Jacob eyed her closely to ask, "Are you now reassured—beyond all doubt? Do you truly believe in the promised blessing?"

"Oh, yes! Now more than ever. I do not know why I even had to ask, forasmuch as so many other of the promises already have come to pass. God promised to bring you back to this land and to protect you from harm. Are you not here now, safe and bountifully blessed? And did He not protect you from Esau's fierce anger when you returned?"

Once again Jacob's face expressed his approval. "Well said, my daughter. Your eyes are opened, while others remain closed to these sacred revelations."

Tamar sat quietly pondering Jacob's sayings and the mysterious ways God accomplished His will through mortal man, while still allowing man's free will to choose his own course of action.

She did not fully understand such a mystery of God, but the fact that she believed in it was, in itself, an indication of her growing faith. She wanted to delve deeper into the philosophical and theological implications, but to do so would delay the completion of the story. She could see Jacob's fleshy lids were drooping with the approach of sleep. His head was bent to his chest and rolled to one side. She knew he would not be awake much longer, so she pulled at his sleeve.

"Father Jacob, I know the hour is late, and you need your rest, but . . ."

He jumped with a start at her words. "Rest? I am not tired in the least," he said, yawning.

"Then could you finish the tale before I leave you to retire?" she asked, rising to fetch a tray of fruit on Jacob's table and setting it before him. Perhaps refreshments would keep him awake. Then she placed a pillow behind his back, not so much for comfort as to shift his position, thereby making him more alert. She reminded him where he had left off: "You had just explained to me the meaning of the ladder from Heaven."

Jacob chewed a slice of dried fruit with the few teeth he had remaining and continued the tale. He spoke of waking from his vision-dream and of taking stones to build an altar, a pillar of remembrance to memorialize the spot: "I changed the name of the place from Luz to Bethel, which means 'House of God' because it was there Heaven's gates were opened to me. It was to be a sacred shrine, a sanctuary where intimate fellowship with God was established forever."

Then he spoke of the vow he had made at the holy place: "I told the Lord that if He would go with me and guide me on my journey, that if He would give me food and raiment so I might live and one day return to my homeland, then I would serve Him all my days. The Lord would be my only God, and I would return unto Him a tenth of all He gave unto me. I have kept my word, to this day, even as the Lord has kept His. It has been an unbroken covenant between us."

Jacob smiled, quite pleased with himself and his pious promises. Then he noticed a frown had formed itself upon Tamar's face.

"Father Jacob, was it not presumptuous of you to dictate to God the conditions by which you would serve Him, especially after He already had vowed to care for you? I mean, should you not have offered Him reverence and tithes without first requiring protection, food, and raiment? Often you have told me the Lord knows our needs and provides them before we ask."

It took Jacob a moment to get over Tamar's mild rebuke and perceptive reasoning. It was, indeed, a changed woman he saw before him now. Three years alone to meditate upon his teachings must have produced a great deal of spiritual growth. He groped for words to satisfy her inquiry: "You must remember I was very young, and my spiritual life was immature. It was my very first encounter with God."

"I see," said Tamar, still reluctant to accept Jacob's rationalization, but anxious to complete the story before Jacob succumbed to sleep. "After that you went on to the land of your mother's brother, there to labor for him and to marry his two daughters. Let us dispense with that part and move on to your return to Canaan. I would hear how you wrestled with the angel. Never have I fully understood that encounter. Are you too tired for just that much more?"

"I see that you prefer to hear legends of God and angels rather than stories of men and women." Jacob chuckled in amusement. "You are still child-like, Tamar, for all your wisdom. One last story before bedtime, is it?"

"You are good to indulge me. It has been so long since I have been at your feet, and I have missed these sessions so much. I suppose I want to recapture all the past in this one moment."

Jacob was quick to comply with Tamar's request. He proceeded from the point in the story where he was returning from Laban's home, back to Canaan, rich with possessions acquired in a foreign land. He attributed his wealth not only to God's blessing, but also to his own shrewdness as he worked for Laban as a

79

shepherd. He returned with his wives, Leah and Rachel, and their handmaids who became his concubines, Zilpah and Bilha, and all the children they had borne him.

The old man was relieved to bypass the events preceding his marriages. It was unpleasant to dwell upon his uncle's trickery which forced him to marry the elder daughter, Leah, and then have to work seven more years before he finally could take his first choice, Rachel, to wife. To satisfy Tamar and to save his own reputation, he let the story take a different focus: "I returned rich in flocks and oxen and servants. Angels visited me as I departed, and they, likewise, greeted me on the way back, assuring me of God's continuing love."

"Always there were angels. Was it then you wrestled the heavenly messenger?"

"It was the night before I was to meet Esau. I sent my family and servants to a safe place across the brook at the ford, Jabok, and I waited alone on the other side. Although I had sent elaborate gifts to secure my brother's favor, I was troubled, lest Esau should not be reconciled to me. After all, he had threatened to kill me before I left. I had heard of the wild man of Edom, as he was called, and I feared my company was no match for the followers of mighty Esau."

"Did you doubt God's word?" Tamar asked.

Startled, Jacob asked, "What say you?"

"God had promised to be with you and bring you back here safely. Angels assured you of divine protection. If you feared Esau, it seems you doubted God would fulfill His promise."

Jacob squirmed uncomfortably. Once again Tamar had pointed a finger at Jacob's lack of faith. Others never dared to question his motives or behavior, but Tamar had become Jacob's mirror, forcing him to see himself as he really was in earlier days.

Without looking at her penetrating eyes, Jacob said, "I was not afraid . . . exactly. I just needed time to myself to think. And to pray for guidance before meeting Esau."

"Oh," Tamar said without conviction. "And then?"

"Then, as I sat alone, the angel messenger appeared. He grasped me and threw me to the ground. All night we wrestled. I tried every hold I could lay upon him, but I was no match for such supernatural strength. He saw, however, that I was determined to hold onto him. I refused to let go until he blessed me. Perhaps I could not win; nevertheless, I would not let him go."

"Were you not exhausted?"

"More than you could imagine! As day was breaking and I felt I could stand it no more, he suddenly gouged the hollow of my thigh and wrenched it out of joint. I know not how I endured the pain, but still I would not let go!"

Tamar's eyes moved to the corner of Jacob's tent where his walking staff stood. Seldom did Jacob go far without leaning upon it for support. The leg which the angel had maimed was a constant reminder of the struggle, and Jacob had limped with every step thereafter.

"Then," Jacob continued, "the angel asked my name. I told him it was Jacob. He said I no longer would be Jacob, which means *Supplanter,* but Israel— *a Prince who strived with God.* He said I had fought as a prince and prevailed."

Tamar shook her head in wonder. "You prevailed against the angel of the Lord!"

"Yes," Jacob replied, relieved finally to touch on part of the story which drew Tamar's admiration rather than her condemnation. "And the angel blessed me there. I called the place Peniel, which means *I have seen God face-to-face."*

Rather than the expected admiring glance from Tamar, Jacob saw a pout form on the fullness of her mouth. "Why should angels appear to you only, Father Jacob? Why have I never seen one?"

"I have never received the gift of interpreting dreams as my Joseph did. God works through mortal beings in many different ways to serve His purposes. One may see visions, one may interpret dreams, one may utter prophetic words from God. Another may bring forth sons to be used by the Lord to bless others."

Tamar knew the last inference was meant for her, and she was both amused and satisfied. She let the remark go and asked another question: "But why did you have to wrestle with the angel? The meaning of that experience completely escapes me."

"It was symbolic of my struggle within myself. As you have

been quick to point out this night, my life up until that time was not always as it should have been. I used my wits, through trickery and deception, to further my own selfish desires. But when I was forced to engage in a titanic contest of strength, I realized my inadequate weakness was unequal to the superiority of the living God. I could not overpower God. It was all I could do just to hold on. When that realization of inadequacy came, that is when I prevailed and came out stronger for the victory over my baser, prideful self. I had to bow, yield, and submit to stand on my feet as a man. Humbling myself, I became a new person with a new name and a new purpose."

"And that purpose was . . . ?"

"To walk with God and to seek His will above my own."

Tamar was still confused, but, she told herself, she could not be expected to understand all the ways of God. She only could catch glimmers of light along dark paths of life. She rose to leave, knowing the gossip that would be forthcoming if she were seen leaving Jacob's tent at such an hour. Always she was suspected and forced to bear ridicule. Only Jacob, Prince Israel, was her faithful friend. She needed to express that thought aloud, in appreciation for the time he had spent with her, easing her loneliness, entertaining her, teaching and inspiring her.

"Of all people of the earth, you are my dearest, truest friend," she said.

"No, my daughter. God is your truest friend. You are His beloved child, and you can never be separated from His love. You must never put a mortal in that place of honor."

She smiled and kissed him lightly on his forehead, saying, "Always you speak truth. I will leave you to your rest now."

"Tamar," Jacob said, rising with her and taking her arm for support. "I hope you have learned a lesson from my history this night."

"Many lessons, most honorable father."

"But one in particular. Although Jehovah God has blessed me and used me as a channel of His promise to all generations, I have reaped a sad harvest for the evil seeds I have sown."

"What harvest of evil have you ever reaped? You are so wondrously blessed that it is apparent God has forgiven you the sins of your youth."

"One may be forgiven, the wounds may heal, but the scars remain forever. The bird never soars as high again, regardless of the love with which a broken wing is mended."

"This is my lesson for tonight's instruction?"

"Yes, but I must explain it, specifically as it applies to you." He motioned for her to be seated again as he went on. "Because of my fraud in taking my father's blessing by theft, I was repaid in like coin. Leah, a wife I never wanted, was thrust upon me by Laban's deceit. Her presence in my household has caused jealousy and strife. Moreover, my sons are often deceitful in their dealings with me. I suffer to this day for evil deeds perpetuated into the present."

"Never have I heard you speak of suffering before."

"Indeed, I prefer to speak of my many blessings. But I must make you understand."

"Understand what? I shall try to heed your instruction, but I still miss your point."

"The point comes directly. But first you must see that much of my pain was needless. We learn to follow God's path one of two ways—through obedience or through suffering. I chose the harder way before God broke my prideful spirit. I suffered at the hands of my uncle. I still suffer the loss of Rachel and Joseph."

Jacob's eyes became misty, and Tamar wanted to avoid any more unpleasant memories for him, so she said, "Please, Father Jacob, I pray you, do not speak more of this now."

"But I must. Attend to me, Tamar. I am not saying that God *caused* my sufferings, but that He *used* them to enlighten me and turn me from evil. I pray you will take the path of obedience, so you will escape the suffering that accompanies disobedience."

"Why do you tell me this?" Tamar asked, suddenly afraid God has revealed to Jacob the sins she had committed at Judah's encampment. Jacob seemed suspicious. She felt guilty. Could he know she had tried to seduce his son and grandson within the space of two days?

"I tell you because I know you wish to have part in the covenant promise. You yearn for it, even as I did when I was your age and younger. Take a lesson from my suffering, dear Tamar. If God will use you—and I truly feel that He will—then He will bring it to pass in due season. All things are possible with God, so you must not impose your will over His. Nor must you try to force His hand to move before His appointed time. To do so would bring you only misery."

Tamar wondered how Jacob could see into her heart so well. Just as she saw him stripped of all pretense, he saw her as she was beneath all outward appearance. She dared not tell him of the past two days—not now. Would he not call her attempted conquests "imposing her own will over God's"? He would indeed!

Breaking into Tamar's thoughts, Jacob continued: "Even after I returned to the land of God's promise, I was to suffer for shameful deeds committed by my sons. I was disgraced in my neighbors' eyes and forced to move here to Hebron. Only then did I realize how I had neglected the ethical and spiritual instruction of my children. Like their father, they needed a *personal* relationship with the Almighty. They could not depend upon my righteousness any more than I could claim the righteousness of Isaac and Abraham."

"Again I am confused," Tamar said. "What do the sins of Reuben, Simeon, Levi, and the others have to do with this?"

"I am trying to show you *your* need to return to Bethel. After their shameful sins, I took my sons there to cleanse and purify themselves and to worship at the altar I made to Jehovah."

"You think I am in need of cleansing?" Tamar asked with trembling in her voice.

"Everyone does. I want you to find that sweet relationship of personal communion with God. That alone will keep you attuned to His will and make you a fit vessel for His use. To be cleansed from sin is the first step toward your own private Bethel."

Tamar dropped her head and nodded. "Tomorrow we shall worship together at the altar. Will you pray for me and let me purchase a lamb from your flocks as my sin offering to God?"

"I shall indeed." He patted her shoulder. "I know how difficult it is to wait, especially when circumstances seem hopeless. But make no foolish mistakes, Tamar. Wait upon the Lord."

No foolish mistakes, Tamar thought. She felt miserably

cheap and debased. Her behavior with Judah and Shelah had no purpose but to further her own desires. She had been no better than the heathen Baal worshipers and temple prostitutes she condemned so quickly. The evil influence of her kinsmen must have affected her, for she had imitated them without awareness of it. She had not considered how Judah and Shelah must have felt, nor had she thought of the hurt she could cause to poor, ailing Shuah. It had taken only an hour in the company of this prophet of the one, true God to show her what she had become. How easy to drift away from the path of righteousness! She lowered her eyes in shame.

"I perceive," Tamar said, "that it is possible to do the wrong thing for what may seem the right reason."

She did not look at Jacob, but she knew his face expressed total understanding, even without an explanation from her. Jacob's final words rang in her ears long after she left him to walk silently to her tent: *Wait patiently; walk uprightly before the Lord, and He will give you the desires of your heart.* Jacob had touched her greatest need—a return to Bethel for cleansing from sin, for prayer, for forgiveness, and—most of all—for patience to wait for the desires of her heart.

Five

Benjamin burst into his father's tent without the customary request for permission to enter. He did not bow nor kiss his father. Rather, he moved directly to Jacob's bedside and to the point.

"Father!" Benjamin called, breathless from running. "You must cease this disgraceful folly! Tamar's presence here is causing a commotion. You have become the subject of ridicule!"

Jacob did not answer at once. He rose from bed, embraced his son, and said cheerfully, "Good morning, my heart's beloved. I trust you had a restful night." It was Jacob's way of reminding his son of the importance of keeping first things first.

"I did not rest well at all," Benjamin responded, greatly annoyed at his father's evasion of the point. "How could I sleep when the entire household is laughing behind your back?"

"Laughing at me, is it? Well, a merry laugh is good medicine for the spirit. Do not be concerned if our household is laughing, dear Benjamin. You should be distressed only if everyone begins to weep."

"Father," Benjamin said, stepping in front of Jacob as the lame old man limped toward his walking staff. "Father, I do wish you would listen to me. This is a grave matter, and you will not be serious enough to hear me out."

Jacob seated himself once more upon his bed. "Very well, Benjamin. Though it is too early, and you are too rude to deserve my attention, I shall listen. Say on."

Benjamin turned away with embarrassment. "Forgive me for speaking to you without respect, Father. It is just that I cannot bear to hear your wives and servants saying . . ." Benjamin grimaced. ". . . saying what they are saying. Soon it will spread throughout the land. And you will cease to be honored by the townspeople."

With a twinkle in his eye and cocking his head, Jacob

86

feigned great alarm: "Just what terrible thing have I done to make myself a laughingstock to the entire community?"

"It is . . . your relationship with Tamar."

"My relationship? Hmmm. I would categorize it as that of a father to an adopted daughter."

"That is not what everyone is saying."

"Everyone? And what do *you* say, Benjamin?"

"What?" Benjamin heard the question, but it caught him off guard, without a ready reply.

"Do you say that my relationship with Tamar is inappropriate? I do not pay attention to gossip, but I do honor the opinion of my son, for he is just and honest in his judgments."

Benjamin lowered his eyes. "I know you to be upright and beyond reproach, Father. But I cannot say I approve of Tamar visiting in your tent last night. It did not go unnoticed. I also disapprove of your allowing her to return here at all."

"What is your reason? Has Tamar done something amiss?"

"She is not well thought of. She is an evil, scheming woman."

"And what proof of that have you? Or are you simply repeating slander you overheard whispered among the womenfolk?"

"Well, I . . ."

"My son," Jacob said tenderly, drawing Benjamin to sit with him and placing a hand on the lad's shoulder. "What people are saying is of little importance. The truth is the important issue."

"The truth is that you are blind to her faults. She beguiles you with her charms, and you lap up the honey of her every word. You set her above the other women—with a tent all her own—and you give her an exalted place which is unfitting for a woman to hold."

"I suspect those are more words you overheard and not your own conclusions. It is wrong for you to think I abuse myself by honoring another—even a woman. It is a good thing to learn humility, and Tamar has a rare gift for teaching me that virtue."

Benjamin stood to his feet. "But you are head of the family. I do not want you to lose the respect of those you rule."

"If showing kindness to Tamar costs me the respect of my household, then my place of honor is on very unsure ground indeed!"

"Father, if it is more companionship you require . . ."

"Benjamin, attend unto my words. The displeasure of the womenfolk is understandable, for they always have been jealous of Tamar. Jehovah has given Tamar the gift of wisdom beyond that of other women. She has a deep, abiding desire to learn—especially the things of God—and she soaks up my teachings as the thirsty ground receives the summer rain."

"I think your instruction to a lowly woman is a waste of your time. What need has a woman for wisdom?" Benjamin sneered and rolled his eyes in derision.

"Would you deny the lowliest ewe lamb a morsel of food when hungry? Tamar hungers to learn, and God has appointed me, her teacher, to feed her. Is not woman God's creation, the same as man? I see no difference between the two in the eyes of God, and I do not understand why men make such a fuss about distinctions. Unless they are afraid of the rivalry . . . or jealous. Could it be that *you* are jealous of the affection and attention I show to the maid?"

Benjamin's concern for his father's reputation suddenly changed to hot anger: "If I am jealous to hold onto the place I have close to your heart, it is your own fault! Always you show favoritism—and always it causes trouble!"

Jacob's conscience was pricked, but he could not tolerate his son's scorn. "Rail not upon me, Benjamin! You speak of the respect which is my due, but you fail to show it in this moment!"

"How can I now respect you, Father? Your singleness of affection for my mother caused Leah and your other wives to feel rejected and unworthy. Their ill will continues to this day. Your exclusive affection for Joseph turned my other brothers against you. Now, if your need to dote upon Tamar severs the closeness you and I have shared, so be it!"

Benjamin tried to walk from his father's presence, but Jacob's arms were quick to grasp the hard-breathing, red-faced lad. Holding him still, Jacob forced Benjamin's eyes to meet his as he said, "Benjamin, I said Tamar had taught me the lesson of humility. I now see that youth, likewise, can instruct the aged. If my favoritism has turned my loved ones from me, then it is a regrettable sin indeed. I stand correctly admonished."

"Father, I . . . I am sorry. Forgive me. I spoke in haste."

"And in truth, but be assured that no one can take the special place you hold in my heart."

Benjamin flung his arms about Jacob's neck. He buried his head in the flowing softness of a beard as it received a tear, rolling slowly down a wrinkled cheek from one squinting eye. The lad felt ashamed and small, like a child again. His own eyes were wet when he lifted his head to cry, "Who am I to judge my righteous father? It was foolish of me to speak in such a manner."

Then the realization of what he was doing descended upon Benjamin in full force. He saw himself clinging to his father's neck when he should be standing tall, like a man. Had he not been pampered and spoiled long enough? Had he not been chided for allowing himself to be babied? He should be glad his father took interest in Tamar, for that could free him to seek other interests. His thoughts flew to Cumi and his desire to see her. Why should he rebel at the thought of losing his father's constant company? Aloud, he said, "What a stupid goose I am!"

Jacob, believing Benjamin's remark was self-inflicted chastisement for disrespect, said, "It is now all forgiven and forgotten."

Benjamin pulled away from Jacob to say, "Father, forget all I said about you and Tamar. If she pleases you, I shall be pleased as well."

Jacob laughed and slapped Benjamin upon the back. "The entire matter is absurd, really. Neither you nor my wives should fret, for Tamar will not remain with us for very long."

Wide-eyed, Benjamin asked, "Tamar will not be here long?" Suddenly the idea was as distasteful as it was pleasing an instant before.

"No," Jacob said, still smiling. "I journey to Judah's tents to persuade him to give Shelah in marriage to Tamar, as is the custom and as is Judah's solemn duty. When Tamar is married, there will be no more cause for jealousy or hard feelings among any of my household."

"Oh," Benjamin said lamely. His face drained of its color. "Well, then, if Tamar is to be married . . ." He could not finish the sentence, for he did not know whether to rejoice or despair.

"When Tamar is gone, it will be just the two of us again, and you can have me all to yourself," Jacob continued. He saw the confusion in Benjamin's face. "Well, does not that saying please you?"

"Oh, verily," Benjamin replied without expression in his voice or face. He cleared his throat. "Father, while we are on the subject of marriage, might we discuss mine?"

"Yours?" Jacob bellowed.

"Indeed. You do plan for me to marry, do you not?"

"In the fullness of time, we shall find a suitable bride for you."

"And have you thought who might be your choice for me?" Benjamin prompted.

"Oh, perhaps Mahalia, daughter of Aran. Or it might be that Arbath, daughter of Simron, would be more suitable. I will match you with a worthy damsel from among a God-fearing tribe, never fear." Jacob was anxious to end such a discussion.

"Father, what would you say to Cumi?"

"Cumi? The handmaiden in Judah's household? Surely you are not serious!"

"But I am, Father. I find her—most pleasing."

Jacob's expression had a look of finality. "Cumi might be acceptable as a house servant or concubine, but never as a wife for the honored son of Jacob!"

Benjamin decided to say no more. He did not want to arouse his father's ire again, and it was a touchy subject. Then another idea came to mind: "Very well, Father, for you know best. I will go and see if your breakfast is being prepared as you favor it." He shrugged indifferently as his alternative plan began to form.

"You are a good and dutiful son. I am glad we had our talk this morning, but, please, reserve any such further discussions until I have satisfied my belly with breakfast."

"I will," Benjamin vowed. Then, as casually as he could, he called over his shoulder a question he hoped would seem an afterthought: "Might I travel with you to Judah's tents? I have not seen my brother in many moons—and I should like to be at your side in case you need me."

Jacob's face broadened with a wide smile. "Your concern for

90

your aged father touches my heart. Of course you may go. I would not think of leaving you behind."

Benjamin's step quickened with joy as he left his father's tent. He would see Cumi again! And his father, for all his wisdom, had not suspected the son's true motive behind the desire to visit Judah. Or had he? It was difficult for Benjamin to know who was outsmarting whom. As he had allowed himself to lose at their board game, was Jacob playing games now?

"Good morning," called a cheerful voice as Benjamin stepped outdoors. The youth turned in surprise to see Tamar seated on the ground, preparing breakfast in a pot over an open fire. He looked again to assure himself that it was really Tamar. She appeared out of character attending to domestic chores. He imagined that haughty Tamar considered herself more to be waited upon than one to do a servant's duties.

"Well," Benjamin began icily, "you are up and busy at an early hour. Dressed, cooking your own breakfast, and getting a head start on everyone else."

"I like to rise early—before noise of the day breaks the blessed silence. But I've eaten already. This is not for me, but for your father. He likes the way I prepare this savory porridge."

"His servants will not like your taking over their duties," Benjamin snapped. "You are here one day and already trying to run my father's house?"

"No, Benjamin. I merely am trying to be of help." She began to hum as she worked.

"The most help you can render is to leave my father alone. Have you considered the evil that can come, the gossip that results, from an old man spending time with . . . a younger woman?"

Tamar smiled as she stirred the porridge. "Oh, yes. Much evil can come—into the minds of those who look for wrongdoing in others when they have nothing more worthy to do."

Benjamin squatted beside her and looked directly into her eyes. "Tamar, please think of my father's reputation. I do not like to hear him mocked. You no sooner arrived than rumors spread through the camp. I despise hearing my father's name spoken in tones of disrespect."

"You also do not like favors given to me instead of to you, is that not also the truth?"

It irked Benjamin that she sounded so like his father. "Of course not!" he frowned. "I should be happy to have another occupy his time. It would relieve me of great inconvenience. But I do not want my father slandered."

"And you think I am capable of causing that? You flatter me. I could not cause the downfall of the great and mighty Jacob!" Tamar set aside her wooden spoon. "I love him as you do, Benjamin. As a father."

"He has a daughter of his own."

"Now married and moved far from him."

"But every time you come near him . . ."

"There is trouble." Tamar sighed deeply. "Yes, it seems I find favor with very few. Why is it the other women always hate me so, Benjamin?"

He avoided her eyes. "I . . . I suppose it is because you act so very superior. Father says your wisdom surpasses that of all the other women."

Tamar smiled and heaped a large spoonful of the steaming porridge into an earthen bowl. She extended the bowl to Benjamin, who refused it with a strong shake of his head.

"Go on," Tamar encouraged him. "You will find it better than Hannah's."

The aroma of the unusual mixture was too great a temptation for the hungry Benjamin to resist. Slowly, he accepted the peace offering from Tamar's hand.

Eating greedily, Benjamin mumbled, "Ummm. Perhaps Father is right. You are wiser than the other women—at least when it comes to making porridge."

Tamar watched him from the corner of her eye as she began preparing a tray to take to Jacob. "It is just that I dare to be different. I accept tradition only when it pleases me. Take that porridge, for instance. Hannah and the other handmaidens would prepare it in the usual way—the same way women before them made it for generations—only some grain with goat's milk blended in. Tasteless! I put in cinnamon, ginger, and other spices. And honey for sweet flavoring."

"Perhaps that is why the others envy you," Benjamin noted. "You have honey and spice in your life, while their lives are tasteless and dull."

"Such a lad—speaking with the wisdom of your father!" She knew the comparison was taken as a high compliment. "Yes, I enjoy being different, but I pay for it. I am lonely and shunned by those who do not understand I cannot help being me. Why is being different considered a curse or a sin?"

Benjamin thought about it. "I would say being different is not wrong. It is just—different. People do not trust those who have strange, unfamiliar ways."

Tamar nodded. "There is but one woman who accepts and trusts me, for all our differences. She is the only one I can call a true friend in all the world. She is not a woman, really. She is but a girl. A lovely young girl named Cumi."

Benjamin almost dropped the porridge at the mention of the familiar name.

"Cumi is your friend?" he asked with eyebrows raised.

"Indeed. We became friends when I was married to Judah's sons. She was the only one in Judah's household who did not resent and shun me."

"Cumi is too kind and gentle to be cruel to anyone. Tamar, perhaps if you tried taking an interest in the things the other women do . . ." For some reason, he wanted to help her.

Tamar scowled her disapproval at the suggestion. "Spinning flax and drawing water? Gossiping? What great contribution to the world are such meaningless occupations? Tasteless! I prefer to improve my mind—to learn about the world and the wonders of Jehovah-God."

"And Cumi does not think it queer that you wish to take a man's role?"

"As you said, Cumi is too kind to pass judgment. She values the importance of improving the mind. That is as noble as any work with the hands. And who, pray tell me, decided that learning is reserved for men only? Cumi works hard at her tasks, but she also has a discerning mind. Someday soon she will make someone a very good and wise wife."

93

Benjamin rose to his feet to protest, "You mean Cumi wishes to be like you? Impossible!"

Tamar threw her head back to laugh, "No, I doubt that. But what would be so terrible about it, Benjamin? After all, if Cumi were like me, then perhaps Father Jacob would favor her as he favors me. Would that not open the door for you and Cumi to be wed?"

Benjamin stood dumbfounded. "Our marriage? How could you know? You . . . you were listening at my father's tent door this morning when I spoke to him of Cumi!"

"No, no," Tamar said, still laughing at Benjamin's expression. "Cumi told me herself. She wants me to encourage Father Jacob to see the wisdom in such a union."

Benjamin was pacing about, confused and angry. "She dared to speak of our love to you? How could she reveal such a secret to a . . . a stranger?"

"Oh, I am no stranger. I told you I am her friend. I shall be yours too, if you will but let me. Does not Father Jacob attend unto me? Think you not that I can help you win your love?"

"I need no help from the likes of you!"

"Oh? Very well then. I will not even bother . . ." She rose with the breakfast tray.

"Wait! Perhaps I speak in haste. It is a bad habit with me. Do you really think you might have influence with my father in this matter? He seemed most opposed when I suggested it."

"It will do no harm to try."

"What shall you say? When shall you say it?" Benjamin's voice grew loud and excited.

"Shhh," Tamar warned with a finger to her lips. "Have you forgotten your father is nearby, within his tent even now? He would be displeased to overhear us plotting behind his back. I shall have a chance to speak with him before you leave to visit Judah."

"You know of that also? You *were* listening outside the tent's door!"

"Benjamin, there are some things I know without even speaking of them to Father Jacob. He knew when I returned last night that Judah would need persuading before he will give

Shelah unto me. I did not have to tell him so. Likewise, I know Father Jacob will go to plead my cause to Judah—even though I have not heard him say so in words."

"You and my father can read each other's thoughts?"

"Let us say we are close enough to sense things. Our common feelings come from an understanding of each other."

Benjamin scratched his short-cropped mop of hair and looked at her with a questioning glance. "I do not see how that is possible."

"Neither do I, but it is true all the same. Some things we must learn to accept without understanding."

Benjamin smiled at Tamar for the first time. "Yes, I did not accept you without having a better understanding of you."

"You play upon my words, Benjamin. Do you mean that now that we have reached an understanding, you will accept me?"

He stretched forth his hand to her. "Even without complete understanding, for I doubt that ever is achieved with someone like you. But, like Cumi, I wish to accept you—as my friend."

Shifting the tray to her hip, she took his hand. "I am glad. Very, very glad."

"The trouble is, I did not bother to get to know you. I was too young to notice you long ago when you lived here in my father's household. After you left, I let others determine my opinion of you. I have learned better this morning."

"Do they . . . do they speak ill of me always?" Tamar asked, trying desperately not to care.

"It is Leah mostly. She despises anyone who spends time with Father. She even resents me, though she dares not say so. She gets gossip started—and then the others always follow her lead."

"I shall have to have a talk with Leah," Tamar said. "She is Judah's mother. I will need to win her friendship."

"I would not if I were you, Tamar. Better not disturb a hornet's nest."

"I'll not fear her sting. Besides, you said I was not so terrible once you got to know me better. Perhaps it will be the same with Leah."

Benjamin shook his head but protested no further. There

was a matter of greater importance he wished to talk to Tamar about.

"Tamar, what will you say to Father? I mean, to change his mind about Cumi?"

"Oh, I shall tell him of her beauty—how she has filled out and become a fair flower now."

"Indeed she has," Benjamin said, almost to himself.

"And," Tamar continued, "I shall tell him of Cumi's quick mind. Unlike you, your father admires intelligence in a woman."

"I suppose that is why he has so little use for Leah and the others. It is said my mother was very wise. Why, Tamar! You must remind my father of her. That is why . . ."

Tamar's lips parted, but for a while she did not speak. "Father Jacob has compared us at times. I always was complimented, for he held her in highest esteem."

"He loved my mother with all his heart," Benjamin said, trying to push from his mind her death and the guilt he always felt when he thought of her. Quickly, he changed the subject back: "I do not think mentioning Cumi's beauty or her quickness of mind will cause Father to forget she is a Canaanite servant and not a true believer by birth."

"No, but I shall tell him of her faith in God. She is more devout than many kinsmen, and no more a heathen Canaanite than am I. And I shall praise her ability in caring for Judah's entire family. She has been in complete charge of his household since Shuah's illness."

Benjamin continued to scowl. "I still do not think . . ."

"You are right. It will not be enough. I will lay a foundation, but Cumi, herself, must build upon it. While you are visiting Judah, you must get Cumi to come before your father, serve him, smile at him, hang upon his every word, and flatter him."

"The way you do?" Benjamin asked. He had watched Tamar carefully prepare the breakfast tray—everything orderly, clean, and prepared as Tamar was scrubbed and bedecked herself. A flower upon the tray for Jacob; a flower in Tamar's hair. The sweet smell of the porridge; the perfumed sweetness of Tamar. None of this escaped Benjamin's notice.

Tamar nodded. "A man—even one the age of Father Ja-

96

cob—likes beautiful things, little kindnesses, special attentions. A man must feel he is admired by a woman."

"But Cumi is very shy," Benjamin lamented.

"A woman often changes her nature—for love! I shall give you further instructions for Cumi later. Now I must go and serve your father before the breakfast turns cold." Tamar thought to herself that she would have to do some changing before she encountered Judah again.

Tamar had gone but a few steps when Benjamin called after her. She stopped as he reached her side to say, "I just wanted to let you know I appreciate what you have pledged to do for Cumi and me. My most humble thanks."

Tamar did not respond, but, instead, she bent toward Benjamin and lightly placed a kiss upon his cheek.

After she had disappeared into his father's tent, Benjamin stood rooted to the same spot for a long while, rubbing the place of the kiss. He was thinking about the strange mixture of emotions he had felt since the night before. And every one of those feelings—jealousy, rage, hate, resentment, friendship, and, finally, affection—all were set in motion and evoked by the same force, the unusual creature called Tamar.

Six

Jacob and Benjamin set out on their donkeys toward the tents of Judah's camp. Trailing behind them were men servants and pack animals laden with supplies and gifts. The gifts were included as an inducement for Judah's good will, but Jacob knew it would take more than gifts or words—a miracle perhaps?—to pry Shelah from his father's tight grasp.

As they rode, Jacob and Benjamin talked, and the conversation turned to the subject of Tamar. She was left behind, but her presence seemed very real as they spoke of her.

"God speaks out of Tamar's mouth," Jacob said.

"How can that be, Father? Tamar, a Canaanite, comes from people who do not worship our God." Benjamin still was confused and somewhat uncertain of his exact feelings about Tamar. He may have accepted her as a friend, but he questioned her abilities as an oracle of God.

Jacob replied solemnly, "The Lord sent her to me, that I might acquaint her with Him, and that He might speak out of her."

Benjamin shook his head to say, "Well, if she is God's instrument, why do people dislike her? She, herself, has said she has few friends and endures great ridicule."

Jacob looked at Benjamin in silence until the son's eyes met the father's. "I will tell you a strange truth," Jacob began. "Those who seek God are seldom sought by humankind."

"Why is that, Father?"

"Many reasons. Envy enters into it, but it is mostly because seeing someone walk close to God is an unwelcome reminder of distant and contrary paths other have chosen. Few like their sinfulness pointed out by another's holiness."

Benjamin's head was still shaking in disbelief: "I do not know Tamar as well as you do, but my opinion is that holiness is not her most outstanding virtue. She seems to take on haughty airs, as if she thinks herself superior to other people. She is so distant and . . . different."

"Perhaps that is because her head is above the clouds and set on heavenly things, while others' eyes are looking down at mundane things of this earth."

A spark of understanding came to Benjamin to make him ask, "Is that why there was such strife between my half-brothers and Joseph, my true brother? You always have spoken of Joseph's closeness to God, but I remember only contempt for him was expressed by the others."

"Except for Judah. All the others are examples of exactly what I mean. Joseph's goodness and prophetic gifts were hard for the wayward ones to bear. They were jealous and cruel to him."

"Did they not repent of such evil after Joseph's death?" Benjamin asked. The memory of his true brother's tragic accident was vague in his memory. Seldom did Jacob speak of it.

"They appeared to mourn his death—outwardly if not from within sincere hearts. But only Judah was, in truth, deeply sorrowful. I believe he somehow felt responsible for Joseph's accident. I know for certain that is why he moved away from me. When our eyes meet, it is a painful reminder of my lost Joseph . . . and some secret guilt he cannot hide when we are together."

"Why would Judah be the only one to feel responsible? Reuben, as eldest, should have seen to Joseph's welfare. And surely all the others could have protected him as well."

"Reuben was not with the other brothers when . . . when the animal attacked Joseph." Jacob's voice became husky. Despite the healing of time, the memory was still difficult and painful.

"Strange," mused Benjamin. "Nine brethren tending your flocks with Joseph, and not one able to save him?"

"That very question has plagued me through the years. Your brothers brought me only Joseph's blood-stained coat and the story of a wild beast. No explanations. There is no logical answer to solve the mystery, so it is best to avoid thinking or talking of it."

Benjamin now shared his father's doubts. "Father, do you suppose . . . ?"

Jacob's upraised hand and voice indicated closure of the subject: "We will speak of this no more! Pray for your brethren!"

Benjamin grew silent. In the ensuing stillness, his mind turned to instructions Tamar had given him for Cumi. How would he see her alone when they arrived? Perhaps when Jacob was involved in private conversation with Judah? A messenger had been sent ahead, so Judah was expecting them. Benjamin hoped that meant Cumi had made all necessary arrangements and, with her duties completed, she would be free to slip away with him to a place Tamar had given him directions to find. The place was near Judah's tents and called Hidden Brook.

Suddenly, another thought entered Benjamin's mind: "Father, do you think it was wise to leave Tamar behind?"

"Eh?" The rhythmic jogging of his donkey had rocked Jacob into a half-sleep.

"Should Tamar have been left home alone, unprotected from the other women and servants? If their anger is half what they expressed on the night she arrived, it could mean disaster for Tamar." Silently, he was comparing Tamar to Joseph and envious ones relating an *accident*.

Jacob said, "Fear not on that account. Were we not just speaking of mistreatment that often befalls God's chosen ones? Having learned that lesson at a dear price, I did not leave Tamar unprotected. Eliezer is sleeping at her tent door and guarding her with his life."

As pleasant as it might have been to bring Tamar with them, Jacob knew it would have been more dangerous to bring Tamar into Judah's presence. She had given him only a sketchy account of Judah's reaction to her last visit, but Jacob well could fill in the omitted details.

Benjamin was not convinced. "Father, I know Eliezer's your oldest and most trusted servant, but, even so, I fear for Tamar's safety."

"No harm will come to Tamar," Jacob said with conviction. "Those of my household know I would hold them responsible if such should come to pass during my absence. I told them so."

"Still, I would prefer it if there were more distance between Leah and Tamar."

Jacob cast a sideways glance at his son. "When did you obtain such a strong concern for Tamar's welfare? Was it not a short time ago you were taking the side against her?"

Benjamin's face flushed. "Er, yes, but that was before . . . I mean . . ."

"Before you tasted her porridge, all sweet and savory?" Jacob smiled.

"She told you?"

"Yes, she told me." Jacob was glad to see his son's attitude change. It was a sign of independent thinking, forming his own conclusions, ignoring others' opinions, and growing up. As distasteful as that thought was—his youngest approaching manhood—it was needful and right. Then to put his son's qualms totally away, Jacob added, "I spoke directly to Leah before I left. And I gave her a gift. All will be well with Tamar, I promise you."

"I should have known," said Benjamin. "Always my father attends to things in the best way possible, and always he acts in wisdom to care for his loved ones."

The words struck Jacob with greater force than Benjamin could know. "My protection and care of loved ones is the very reason I keep you at my right hand at all times, my son. You must not fall in with the evil ones."

Benjamin pondered the words as they rode along. He wondered if the evil ones were all the rest of the family or only certain ones. He did not pursue the matter. He was taking in the beauty of the landscape and enjoying the morning ride as he sat with his brown legs stretched out and his body leaning gallantly back upon his beast. They were passing villages of the hilly country now.

Glancing back at the pack animals, Benjamin saw each one laden with baskets of food and gifts for his half-brother, Judah. It reminded the lad of the gift he had for Cumi—brightly colored, glass beads which, he was sure, would delight her eyes. He carried them well hidden in his girdle sash, away from his father's probing eyes.

Neighbors on the road and in the fields immediately recognized the passing travelers and joyfully called out to them and shouted blessings as they passed by.

101

"Health to you, noble Jacob!" one shouted. "Blessed is the fruit of your loins, even your heart's delight, young Benjamin!"

"And all health and blessings to you," Jacob called in return. "May Jehovah prosper you and give your sons dominion and wealth!"

Benjamin's heart swelled with pride at the ready recognition and honor given his father. A wide smile was visible as he waved to those they encountered. It was a glorious day as they rode in good cheer up the roads and mountain paths, a smooth journey unmarred by unforeseen mishap. Best of all, it was soon to be Benjamin's happy reunion with Cumi.

In contrast, the arrival of Jacob's caravan was met without great ceremony. Judah was most displeased with his father's coming, not only because it meant he had to stay home from his fields, but also because he knew the purpose of the mission and his father's intent. Judah already had decided no words, threats, compromises, or bribes would change his mind from his decision. Under no circumstances, would Shelah ever marry Tamar!

The welcoming party was composed of only three—Judah, Shelah, and Cumi. Others in Judah's camp had been sent to their tasks in fields or within their tents. Shuah was still bedridden, and Judah wanted no commotion to disturb her—least of all, talk of Tamar.

Judah went through the motions of the customary greetings. Helping his lame and feeble father to alight from his beast, Judah held the traveler in a firm, if not somewhat distant, embrace and murmured traditional blessings. Jacob's eyes brimmed with tears as they often did when he was moved to emotion. How he had prayed for God to melt the icy heart of his stubborn son, and how cold that heart seemed at their meeting. Jacob reached into his pack and took an amulet from its wrapping in a silk scarf. He hung it around Judah's neck and pressed him close.

"Peace unto you, my beloved son. My heart rejoices to see you in good health."

Judah tried to avoid his father's eyes, for they made him most uncomfortable. As sincerely as he could, Judah said, "I likewise rejoice in seeing my father in good health. Thank you for the generosity of your gift." He wanted to add, "But it will do you no

102

good, for it will not purchase my son." Instead, he commanded Shelah to greet his uncle, Benjamin, and to entertain the young guest while he withdrew to his tent to speak with Jacob.

Prepared for such an arrangement, Benjamin immediately spoke up: "Shelah, I know a new game we might play, but it calls for three players. Judah, might Cumi join us in the game?"

Judah playfully tousled the hair of his young brother and said, "A new game, is it? After Cumi serves you refreshments, and providing her other duties are completed, I see no reason to forbid her. Cumi?"

Cumi lowered her eyes. "The preparations for mealtime are attended to, Master. And our guests' quarters are readied. I should like to learn the game, if I may."

Jacob wanted to protest. It was not considered socially proper for his son and grandson to share entertainments with a serving girl, but Benjamin was calling the others away before Jacob could frame words of opposition. Jacob had more weighty matters on his mind than a slight breach of etiquette, so, in spite of misgivings about Benjamin's interest in Cumi and Tamar's thinly veiled praises on the girl's behalf, the matter was dropped. For now.

While Jacob's servants led their donkeys to shelter and the company of Judah's staff, Jacob allowed Judah to lead him toward the master tent. At the same time, Benjamin was leading Shelah into a well-planned trap.

"What is this game?" inquired Shelah. While games, sports, and music were regular parts of life within his grandfather's household, Shelah's life within Judah's was dull by comparison. His mother's illness and his father's proneness to anger made Shelah more than ready for diversion.

"We play with this," replied Benjamin, drawing from the hanging pouch at his waist a gift he had brought his nephew. It was a round, metal object, with a tipped point at the top and bottom. Benjamin squatted on his ankles and set the object in motion. Around it went, like a spinning top.

"What is it?" Shelah gasped, his eyes bright with excitement. "Listen! It sings!"

The hum of the spinner delighted Shelah, who knelt beside Benjamin for a closer look.

"It is a rare and valuable gift I received from Father's servant, Eliezer. It shall be yours after we have finished using it in our game," Benjamin announced.

"Where did Eliezer get it?" Cumi asked. Her shyness was giving way to curiosity equal to Shelah's.

"From a tradesman who brought it from Egypt. See the inscription on it? Eliezar says the words are a prayer," Benjamin said, feeling quite full of himself as he enlightened the other two.

"Such a treasure! Thank you," Shelah said politely. "Later I will show it to Mother. Perhaps it will cheer her in her illness."

Benjamin took charge again, anxious to get started. "It will indeed. Now for the rules of the game. Shelah, you set the spinner in motion on that smooth piece of firewood over by yonder tree. Cumi and I will go to the other side of the animal stalls and hide ourselves. When the spinner ceases to hum its song and becomes completely still, you must come to find us. The one you find first must then take a turn with the spinner while the others hide."

"That sounds like a fine game," Shelah said without taking his eyes from his new toy.

Cumi looked apprehensive. "But Master Benjamin, I have not yet served you refreshment, nor have I brought water to cleanse your hands and feet."

Benjamin took her hand and commanded, "Come. I am not hungry, and we must hurry before the spinner's song is ended." He forced Cumi's reluctant feet into motion and made her run with him to the stalls where servants were unloading the donkeys.

"Do not unsaddle those two donkeys. We need them—for our game," Benjamin told them. "If Shelah comes looking for us, you must not tell in which direction we are heading."

As Cumi and Benjamin rode hastily away, two of the servants looked at each other and laughed. Pointing after them, one said loudly enough for Benjamin to hear, "I think I know the game our young master plays. I have played the very game myself in younger days."

104

Benjamin ignored the remark and tried to remember Tamar's directions to Hidden Brook. It was not hard to find once he came to the secret pathway which lay hidden behind some foliage and a large boulder. He smiled triumphantly at discovering the path and at tricking Shelah and his elders. He noticed that Cumi was both silent and quaking with fear.

At their destination now, Benjamin dismounted and then reached up to help Cumi from her donkey. Puzzled at her pained expression, he asked, "Why do you tremble so, Cumi?"

"Because I am afraid. I do not mind a beating for myself if we are found out. But *you* may be punished also. We never should have come here."

"Oh, put away your fears," Benjamin scolded with an offhanded shrug. "Shelah will never find us. The simpleton is too fascinated with his new spinner even to care that we are gone."

"I do not fear Shelah. It is your father and my master. They will be most angry with us."

"Well," Benjamin said, walking Cumi to the mulberry tree which Tamar said he would find on the bank of the brook, "either we can spend our few moments here worrying in dread and fear, or we can enjoy this rare time alone. Which shall it be?"

Cumi's frown slowly changed to a weak smile. "As long as we already are here, I suppose we should enjoy the moment. But I must not be away for very long."

They sat with their backs against the sprawling trunk of the tree and looked at the softly flowing waters playing over the rocks. The lush green surroundings, the quiet peace of that place, and the sweet smell of flowers that filled the air all merged to provide a backdrop of contentment.

"It is lovely here," Cumi said softly as she allowed herself to relax as much as she could under the circumstances. "How is it you know this place?"

"A friend of yours told me ot it. Her name is Tamar."

"Really? Tamar has spoken to you? How is she?"

"Well content. Or, at least, *well*. She's back within the tent my father gave unto her."

"She is a strange one, that Tamar. I've become fascinated by her."

Benjamin turned away from Cumi and blurted, "I did not bring you here to discuss your fascination for Tamar. I should much prefer to hear you say how you feel about me."

Cumi caught her breath and lowered her eyes. "So bold so young, Master Benjamin?"

Benjamin snapped a twig from a nearby branch to indicate his displeasure. "I fail to see why everyone always must refer to my age! Being the youngest in the family has sentenced me to a lifetime of being thought of as a baby!"

Cumi touched his arm lightly and tried to think of a way to undo the blunder: "I meant only that our time of courtship is young."

He turned to face her and say, "I think you change your meaning just to please me." He gazed into her eyes. Such sad, innocent eyes uplifted to him, pleading for a better start to the conversation. He could not help but smile at her and relent. "And it is pleased I shall be," he said.

Benjamin took Cumi's hand and felt a tremble. Was it hers or his own? He held it tighter and groped for something to say. "Tamar has sent instructions for you—ways for you to behave while Father is here. She says following her methods will win favor for you in Father's eyes."

She drew back a little. "Oh, I doubt that I ever could do anything the way Tamar does or follow any plan she has devised. I would be too frightened! I surely would falter and ruin things."

He waved off further protests. "We can speak of that matter later. First, I want to show you something I have brought you." He took his gift from its hiding place and held the glass beads up to catch the sparkle of the sunlight.

"How beautiful!" Cumi breathed. "But I cannot accept such a gift!"

"I knew you would say that. I knew you would have to explain where you got them. So I think it better if you wear them under your robes. No one can admire them that way, but the beads will be close to your heart to remind you of me while we are apart."

Cumi was breathing with difficulty as Benjamin leaned nearer and nearer. He place the beads over her head, and, as the

106

ringlet encircled her slender neck, his face was almost against hers. The magnitude of Cumi's young emotions overwhelmed the girl. Quickly, she stood up and moved away from him. Without looking at him, she said bashfully, "I . . . I have no gift for you."

Benjamin scrambled to his feet to pursue her. "Do not turn away from me in fear, Cumi. I will not harm you. Never could I harm you!"

Slowly she turned back to face him. "I am not afraid of you, Master Benjamin. I suppose I am afraid of . . . of myself."

He clasped both of his hands to her shoulders. "I want you never to be afraid—of anything! I will protect you always. I will . . . love you always." Then he cupped her chin in his palms to lift her face toward his again. As their lips neared, Cumi ducked under his arms and once more darted from him. She looked for a hiding place, a barrier to conceal herself behind until she could stop the fierce beating of her heart. Finding none, she unthinkingly sat down in a flower bed and began to pick the blossoms. Fast and furiously her fingers flew, grasping one bloom after another.

"I . . . I shall make for you a necklace also," she said nervously. "It will not be as beautiful as the one you gave me, but it will be a fragrant garland of myrtle."

Pounding a fist into his other hand, Benjamin moaned, "I want no garland of myrtle!" He began to pace about, greatly annoyed that both of this attempts to kiss Cumi had been thwarted. Then, in frustration, he flung himself down beside her among the flowers.

More keenly aware than ever before of Cumi's delicate nature, Benjamin resolved to lower his voice and take a gentler approach. There was no time for a lingering courtship, but he could not rush her, lest she run from him again. He whispered softly, "Cumi, my beloved, just now did you not . . . did you not feel something inside?"

She stopped plaiting the garland. "I felt . . . I felt . . ."

"What?" He eased his body down to lean on one elbow. Then slowly he inched forward to approach his targeted point of contact for the third time.

"I felt . . ." Cumi could stand it no longer. She could not

breathe. She could not even think with him so close. She lurched away as he neared her, causing him to lose his balance. He landed with a thud as his mouth emitted a shriek and his face disappeared into the flowers.

"Oh, Master Benjamin!" Cumi cried in alarm. "I am so sorry! Forgive me! What have I done?" Without taking time to consider what she was about, she grabbed him up, clasped him to her heart, and began to stroke his head. She was crying and murmuring words of comfort for him and contempt for herself for causing his fall. "May Jehovah forgive me! Oh, my dear one!"

Benjamin, quite enjoying the gestures of concern, did not move. Nor did he bother to tell her he was unhurt. When she finally loosed her tight hold upon him to look for bruises or some sign of life from his unmoving body, Benjamin seized the opportunity. He lunged to plant the long- awaited kiss firmly upon her soft lips. Startled, she struggled at first, then relaxed, gave way to her pent-up yearnings, and kissed him back. She was dizzy with emotion when he released her.

"Now?" Benjamin demanded when he mastered the conquest. "This time, did you feel anything inside?"

Tears streaming down her cheeks, Cumi sobbed, "Oh, Master Benjamin, I feel the terrible hopelessness of all this. You are a wealthy man's son. I am but a humble servant. We cannot . . ."

He hushed her mouth with another kiss, softer and less passionate than before. Then he began tenderly to kiss each tear from her eyes and cheeks as he comforted her, held her closer, and said, "Do not cry, Cumi. Dear, dear, blessed Cumi, you are more than a servant. You are as a near kinsman in my brother's household. And if I but knew you did love me, then the servant's role would be mine. I would serve you and care for you all the days of my life."

Cumi looked at him in disbelief. "But I cannot be your wife. I have no dowry."

"Do not think of that," Benjamin told her. He placed her head snugly to his shoulder and felt a surge of self-importance. "We shall work this out. After all, Tamar is on our side, and she has a plan. If anyone can change Father's mind about a suitable wife for me, Tamar can."

An idea popped into Cumi's bewildered mind. She lifted her head slightly from Benjamin's shoulder to suggest it: "Even if I cannot be your wife, I could be a servant in your household when you do marry. Perhaps Master Judah would give me to you on your wedding day."

"No!" Benjamin uttered emphatically, drawing her back beneath his chin. "You most certainly would be a most welcome wedding gift from my brother, but only if you were the bride. It will come to pass. Believe me, Cumi, it will. It must!"

"Speak no more of it now. This is a time of sadness in Master Judah's household with my mistress so ill and sinking slowly toward death. Let us leave it all in God's hands. For if the Lord has ordained that we should be wed, then He alone can direct our feet to the right path."

"I shall pray day and night for nothing else. My love, you will be in my thoughts and prayers every moment until you can be in my arms for all time to come." Benjamin thought his wooing ended in a most impressive speech. He smiled to himself, very pleased with his first attempt at love-making and at finding the object of his affection finally conquered.

Cumi was more overcome than impressed, but she eagerly hung upon each endearing word that came from his lips. What had she done to deserve this glorious moment? If another never came, she felt she could live her whole life in the joyous rapture of this, her first and only love.

For a while, neither of them spoke. They were drifting away from time and space on the age-old clouds that elevate all who taste the luscious fruit of first love. Cumi no longer trembled. She buried her head deeper into the crevice of Benjamin's shoulder and closed her eyes to revel in the warmth of his embrace and the smell of his body. All her senses were awakened as she closed her eyes in blissful, contented serenity.

Benjamin sat erect, feeling older and more important than ever before in his life. He stroked Cumi's shoulder and patted her as one would give unspoken affection for a beloved pet, a very small and weak little creature that needed his tenderest care.

"Cumi?" Benjamin called softly to assure himself that her

quiet breathing and lack of movement did not mean that she had fallen asleep.

"Yes, Master Benjamin?"

"Must you keep calling me *master*? I should think you might have a more affectionate name to call one who has pledged himself to be your husband."

"Very well," she complied. "What says my dearest one, *Benjamin*?"

"You have not yet told me that you love me. Do you?" There was a hint of desperation in his voice. He needed to hear the words.

His question gave Cumi the courage to speak a truth she had kept as a hidden treasure laid up for such a time as this. "Benjamin, I have loved you since I first saw you. I shall always love you, whether we ever can be wed or not."

"Do you still have doubts about that?" In his mind, it was all quite settled.

"I have doubts about your father and my master. Father Jacob will part with you no more easily than your brother will part with me. Master Judah depends upon me more than ever before, especially now that Mistress Shuah is so ill."

"What is the illness that plagues my brother's wife?"

"It is a terrible sickness of her mind. It began when Er and Onan died, and it has become much worse recently. She is consumed by grief and languishes upon her bed day and night."

"Is there no cure?"

"I think she might improve if . . . if Master Judah showed her more kindness."

"What do you mean? Is he cruel to her?"

"No, not exactly. Perhaps I speak out of turn. I should say nothing against my master."

"We shall have no secrets, Cumi. You may trust me to keep your confidence."

"It is just that he avoids her. I think it pains him to see her so weak and frail. When he does enter her tent, he shows her no affection. He accuses her of bringing disaster and sorrow to him."

"I thought he and Shuah both blamed Tamar for the death

110

plague. Father says because Tamar is a Canaanite, they falsely accused her of putting a curse of Baal upon their house."

"Have you forgotten? Mistress Shuah is, likewise, a Canaanite. Master Judah has said anyone who takes a Canaanite wife will suffer great evil." Cumi sat up abruptly and let out a low moan. "Oh, Benjamin! My mother also was from Canaan. If what Master Judah says is true, I might very well bring the same curse upon you!"

"Nonsense! Many of my brothers have married Canaanite women and suffered no ill. If the mighty lion has trouble, I think it is of his own making. Judah is trying to find someone else to blame so he will not have to accuse himself. Father says he bears some strange, unspoken guilt."

Still alarmed, Cumi asked, "But how can you be sure? Benjamin, you take such risks in giving your love to me. Your father's disapproval and now—the danger of a terrible curse!"

He kissed her forehead. "Little Cumi, I gladly will take all risks to obtain your love."

She closed her eyes and allowed him to enfold her again in his arms, this time with all resistance giving way to submission. Her own arms encircled his neck, and she willingly received the fullness of his kisses. She felt herself succumbing as his passion became more intense.

All at once, Cumi pulled away from Benjamin and tugged at his tunic. "Oh, we must go back At once! The others surely will have missed us by now."

Trying to recapture the moment, Benjamin held on to her. "Not yet," he pleaded. "We are playing a game, remember?"

"Please! We must not take the chance of being found out. It would mean punishment, and we might never be allowed to see each other again."

Reluctantly, Benjamin nodded and released his hold. "You are right, of course. But first, we must speak of the way you are to behave before my father. Tamar says you are to be attentive to his every word and wish, showing sincere interest, commenting on his profound wisdom, and flattering him at every opportunity."

Cumi was not listening. She was moving toward the donkeys

111

and calling to him, "Come! Make haste! You can tell me Tamar's plan as we ride back. We dare not stay a moment longer."

Benjamin arose unwillingly. His eyes fell upon the half-finished garland upon the ground. He picked it up and held it high as he approached Cumi. "Here, you must finish this."

"I thought you said you did not want a ringlet of flowers."

"Not for me. For Father. Tamar says you also should wear a blossom in your hair because he is most partial to the fragrance and beauty of flowers. Whatsmore, she said you are to enhance your body with perfumed oils. She sent you some, and they are with my belongings on the pack animals."

"Oh, Benjamin," Cumi cried as she waited to be helped onto her donkey. "Do hurry! I will try to do as Tamar bids, but I am not schooled in such enticements. That is not my nature."

Now upon his own donkey, Benjamin leaned over toward Cumi to tease, "Oh, I do not know if that is true or not. You were most enticing to me a moment ago. Besides, Tamar says a girl can change anything—for love."

"Then Jehovah grant me courage. I'm starting to tremble again."

Benjamin tossed the flowers to Cumi and bent toward her for a final kiss. "This for courage," he said, and they sped away.

Seven

Judah and Jacob did not notice that Cumi and Benjamin were gone. Nor were they aware that a bewildered Shelah was wandering the camp, looking and inquiring about the missing pair. The amused servants at the stalls heeded Benjamin's command to give no hints, so Shelah gave up his search and went to his mother's tent, there to show her his new spinning treasure. Judah and his father were intent on just one thing—settling the issue of Shelah's marriage to Tamar.

"No, I tell you. Never!" Judah's deep, bass voice bellowed to assault his father's ears.

"Lower your voice, Judah," the old man said with his hand raised. "We need no shouting to discuss this matter intelligently."

"What is intelligent about your request? Do you wish my son, the only one I have left, to die as did his brothers—in the arms of that Ishtar, the devourer of youth?"

"Guard your tongue!" Jacob commanded, raising his voice. Then, heeding his own advice, he began to speak more reasonably: "Tamar is not what you say, and well you know it, Judah. She is obedient unto our religion, a devout convert who abhors false gods and heathen practices. Jehovah speaks truth through her mouth."

Judah pointed a finger to say, "You are a foolish old man, Israel, if you believe that. She will say any words, profess any religion, do anything to get what she wants. I have seen her trickery. You should be ashamed of yourself for being charmed and beguiled by her scheming and cajoling."

"You also, Judah? I overlook wild babblings against Tamar from my jealous wives because the women are unlearned. I forgave Benjamin's false accusations because he lacks the experience of years. But you are neither woman nor boy. There is no excuse for you, a wise, grown man, to spout such hateful words without proof. You are wrong on two counts. Tamar is no Ishtar, and your father is no beguiled old fool. Shame upon you for speaking such evil slander about your aged father!"

Jacob's face indicated feelings of betrayal and disappointment. But his sharp scolding was mingled with a secret pride in the way Judah still chose to address his father. Jacob thought to himself, *"Judah continues to call me 'Israel'—not Father or Father Jacob as the others do. He calls me by the holy name given me by the Lord. That proves that Judah still believes in the covenant promise and knows the heavenly blessing shall be passed on through Israel's seed."*

Judah's next words lacked the former harshness, but not the former determination. "Forgive me if I wrong you. But I know my judgment of Tamar is free from error."

In a gesture of rejection, Jacob pushed away the food tray Judah had offered him. Then he said sarcastically, "How marvelous that the Lord has given you such discernment to judge another's intentions—totally free from any human error. With this rare gift, you should join the council fathers. Those men cannot reach a verdict as quickly as you, for they must consider evidence and hear both sides of a case many days before passing judgment."

"You need say no more," Judah grumbled, noting his father's sarcasm. It stung Judah all the more for its ring of truth. "Even if Tamar were as righteous before the Lord as you say—and I do not for an instant believe it—and even if she possessed every godly virtue of womanhood, I could not give Shelah to her now."

Raising his brow, Jacob asked, "Pray, what is your reason for such words?"

"My wife leans every day nearer to death. Shall I take away her only son and thereby speed her to her grave?"

Jacob shook his head to disagree: "I think it is not for Shuah's sake, but for your own that you will not release Shelah. They call you the lion, but you are really a lioness, a mother standing guard to protect your last cub from leaving your den."

Judah sneered, "If I were a lioness, I should roar with laughter at that remark from you!"

114

As was his habit when angry, Judah began to pace about the room. The rapid flow of his words began to match the quickness of his steps: "You, Israel—who hold so tightly your youngest son—you condemn me for your self-same indulgence? Does that not make you a hypocrite?"

"Benjamin is all I have in my old age. It is quite a different matter with me . . ."

"The only difference is that you have many sons and three wives. I have but one son and one wife. If Shuah dies, Shelah will be all I have left of a family. All I have left!"

Pangs of sympathy that Jacob felt for his son's misfortunes were set aside to keep the argument free of emotion and focused on logical reasoning: "Judah, you are still young enough to marry again, to raise up other sons. My time of fatherhood is passed. It is an unjust comparison."

Judah pounded a fist upon his table to give his next words both emphasis and finality: "Unjust or not, I still resist. Everything in me rises against yielding up my only son to Tamar."

"You push me too far, willful one. I shall have no alternative but to bring you before the council. You are bound, by law, to fulfill your obligation to Tamar."

"And how far would you go, Israel, to protect your Benjamin? Shelah is my Benjamin!"

"Protect Shelah from harm, but not from marriage!"

"In this case," Judah said, thrusting out his jaw, "they are one and the same! Can you not find another husband to satisfy the demands of the red-haired temptress?"

"You speak again with unguarded tongue in defaming your daughter-in-law. Of course, I could find any number of husbands for Tamar. That is not the question. The issue that requires you to comply in this matter is the holy covenant's promise."

Judah sat down to cover his face with his hands and mutter under his breath, "I was afraid we were coming to that." Then he raised his head, looked directly at Jacob, and said, "It is beyond me to understand why you still believe she is the intended one. Of all women I know, she seems the most unlikely to be foremother of the Messiah!"

"God often chooses unusual people for His unique purposes."

"Oh, say no more!" Judah rose and threw his hands up is desperation. "I am not even certain I still believe in your tales of visions and promises from Heaven. If they are true, then the blessing should be bestowed upon another of your sons, but not me. Give the birthright to another—and, while you are about it, give him Tamar as well! I want only to be left alone."

Jacob leaned on his walking staff and looked with unbelieving eyes at Judah. The lion, the mighty one, was spilling tears. Never before had Jacob seen the sight, and it so amazed him that for a long while he could not move or speak words of comfort. He saw Judah bite into his lip to hold back the flood of emotion. Blood began to run with the tears.

"My son, my son," Jacob said at last, limping over to place an arm about Judah's shoulders. "What is this terrible grief that makes you speak things you do not mean?"

Judah shrugged away from his father's hand. "Do not touch me! Do not look upon me. I am shamed by my tears!"

Jacob's voice told Judah that his father also was weeping: "It is no shame to shed tears when there is good reason. Has not God given us this gift, this outlet for sorrows too great to hold inside the heart?"

"It is a woman's outlet. Not a man's!"

"Always you feel you must be a paragon of strength. Sometimes the greater strength comes from admitting to weakness. It is a good thing to know you have tender feelings beneath your outward appearance of harshness. God has taught me, through sorrows of my own, that He wants to harden what is soft, but He also wants to soften what is hard. Do you not see I am right?"

Moving away from Jacob, Judah moaned, "Question me no more about what is right or good. I have no ability to know either. And I wish to hear no more of your self-righteous preaching of platitudes. They are wasted on me, Israel!"

"Judah, please tell me what troubles you. Why do you choose to live here, out of sight from me and your brethren? Why do you defy my just commands and loving council?"

"Ask me no more questions. Just go home, Israel. Go home!"

Jacob had to ask another question, the one he never before

116

dared to mention: "Judah, is it your own love for Tamar that prevents you from giving her to Shelah?"

Judah turned his face away from Jacob. The fire in his eyes evidenced the intense rage and pain welling up within him. He strained to put disgust into his reply: "How can you say such an outrageous thing?"

"Because I have seen the way you have looked upon her. I, too, have looked upon a woman in just such a way." Jacob's thoughts turned to memories of his beloved Rachel.

"You are wrong, and everything you say is false!" Judah railed in anguish, knowing neither he nor his father believed the words.

"Judah, for some reason unknown to me, you feel you must punish yourself. You deny anything which might give you pleasure. You separate yourself from loved ones. You take no other wife, even when Shuah is unable to fulfill her duties to you. You will not allow Shelah to marry so you may have the joy of grandchildren. You will not yield to God's will in the covenant and thereby prevent His blessings upon you. How can Messiah come, if neither you nor Shelah will be wed to Tamar?"

"Ask me nothing further, for I have no answers for you. If I choose to do all you say, that is my affair, and I am not required to account to you for my actions. Leave me alone. Go home, Israel, and do not come back!"

Judah was gone. In his haste to flee, he charged past his father, almost causing Jacob to stumble at the impact of a strong body meeting the feebleness of the old man.

Jacob was left alone in the tent, leaning heavily on his staff, not only for support, but also for strength in his anguish. He bowed his head to pray for his son and the secret torment that seemed to portend Judah's chosen destiny of self-destruction. He prayed for a yielding spirit to overtake Judah's stubborn will. Jacob also prayed for guidance, for he had no idea what to do next. He did not want to bring Judah before the council to force a decision, but what other alternative did he have? His most fervent request was that he might follow the advice he had so freely given to Tamar—*Have faith, be patient, and wait upon the Lord.*

Judah was heading straight for Shuah's tent. His moment of

weakness was over; yet, the force of dammed-up emotions sent him seeking a channel, an outlet for releasing overpowering feelings ready to burst forth. He was angry with Tamar and Jacob, for he knew they had plotted against him. He was angry with himself for breaking down in front of his father. Most of all, he was angry with Shuah, and he had to tell her so.

Finding his son with Shuah only intensified Judah's fury. "Leave us!" he shouted to Shelah before any word of greeting prefaced his command.

"What is the trouble, Father?" Shelah asked, arising from his mother's couch.

"The trouble will belong to a disobedient son if he does not heed my request!"

"Very well, Father. I shall go."

Shuah did not speak, but she knew, even in the darkness, that Judah's demeanor meant that he had come to upbraid her. She wondered what she had done to cause his displeasure this time.

As Shelah pushed back the door flap to depart, it occurred to Judah that Benjamin and Cumi were not with his son.

"Shelah!" Judah called after him. "Were you not instructed to entertain Benjamin? Why have you left off playing his game to come here to your mother?"

"I did not leave Benjamin and Cumi, Father. They left me. It was for me to try and find them as part of the game. But I grew tired of seeking them in vain."

Judah pointed outside and said, "Well, go and find them now. Tell Benjamin that his father has decided to return home immediately. You and Cumi help them pack their belongings and see them on their way."

"Will you not come to bid them farewell?" Shelah asked, puzzled at the abrupt departure.

"No! Now, stop gawking and asking foolish questions. I have matters of importance to attend to, so be off!"

Shelah hardly had stepped outside before Judah cast the fullness of his rage upon Shuah: "Woman, you are the cause of all my troubles this day. Do not look away from me! You, daughter of Canaan, have brought me nothing but grief and sorrows!"

118

Shuah's whisper of a voice was a conspicuous contrast to Judah's ravings. "What have I done to deserve my husband's reproach?" she asked, wanting to add words she dared not speak, something like, *What could I possibly do from here on this bed?*

"You became my wife, and that is the reproach and shame I am forced to bear!"

Shuah held back the sob. She knew Judah despised her tears, and to cry only would make matters worse. When he was in such an unexplainable rage, he always made her responsible, so she had learned to grit her teeth and wait out the storm.

Judah threw back the door flap to let in some sunlight. "Always you lie here in the accursed darkness. Daughter of darkness and evil, that is what you are!"

"I still do not know what troubles you. Have I committed some sin?"

"You are too evil to know sin when it surrounds you! Why did I take unto myself a heathen daughter of Baal?"

With both hands, Shuah covered her eyes to shield them from the unwelcome light. Then she said, "Judah, I renounced the gods of my fathers when we married . . ."

"But the curse remains—the death curse. You accused Tamar of bringing death to our sons when you, yourself, bear much of the blame. They were sick from childhood, nursing poison from your Canaanite breast! Where are our sons, Shuah? Dead! Dead because of your sins!"

Shuah drew her knees up in pain and let out a low moan. "Please, please stop. I can bear no more. I shall be sick to my stomach from the torture!"

"You speak of torture, when it is I who have endured more pain than you will ever know. You have wronged me, Shuah! I wanted my father's blessing, the promise to Israel, to be fulfilled in me. Did you bear me strong sons? No, only sickly whelps who barely reached manhood before they died . . . without leaving a single heir to carry on my name. My entire family is blotted out when I die. It is God's punishment for my guilt in marrying you!"

Shuah tried to rise from her pillow, but she fell back in agony and exhaustion. A second effort brought her to one elbow, and she leaned forward toward Judah to say as forcefully as she could: "My husband, if it eases your mind to take out your anger upon me, so be it. But, I beg you, do not speak of our dead sons. I can bear anything else, but please, not that."

"Why should I spare your feelings? You do not spare mine! You are not even a wife to me any more."

"Oh, Judah, I have loved you with all my heart. It is you who turned away from me—long before I became ill. I believe you stopped loving me the day Tamar became part of this family. First, she took away my sons; then she robbed me of my husband's love."

"You speak in riddles. You are mad!"

"Yes, I am nearly mad—with grief. You might have leaned upon me when our boys died. We might have comforted each other. Instead, you left me to grieve alone. I almost wish I had not begged you to send Tamar away, for that was the day I knew whatever love you might have had for me left with her. Now you do not come to me except to place your own sins upon my head. I shall welcome the sweet escape of death, for only then will I be free from this misery."

Judah was stunned. Never until now had Shuah spoken to him in such a way. Always before, she listened in silence and accepted all his verbal abuse without complaint. He gazed at her and heard her cough as she lowered her head back upon the pillow. Suddenly, he felt ashamed and blurted out the words, "Do not speak of dying!"

"And pray, why not? We both know it is coming. But before I die, my last wish is to find the strength to say what is heavy upon my heart. You must hear me out—just this once."

Judah drew a low stool from the corner and placed it beside Shuah's couch. He had no more words to say, no more accusations or fury to release upon this poor creature wasting away before his eyes. He felt empty and strangely numb.

"Judah," she said with a deep sigh. "You must realize what you've been doing and stop it before it is too late for you, as it is for me. You seldom smile or show love any more. Over time, something has changed you. Whatever bedevils you will kill you if it is not conquered soon."

"Hush now," Judah said in the first civil tone he had uttered since coming in.

"You must let me finish. You accuse me of being sinful, of shirking my responsibilities of the marriage bed, of harming this family, of carrying guilt and shame worthy of God's retribution. Are not all those things what you feel about yourself?"

The question punctuated the stillness of the room. He did not want to hear it, much less answer it. How could he respond? A hundred answers raced through his mind. Should he deny it, admit it, rationalize his behavior, explain feelings he did not understand himself, or keep silent? At last, he answered her question with one of his own: "Is that what you think I have been doing?"

Shuah reached up a frail hand to touch the black, thick mane of hair resting on his broad shoulders before she continued: "Always there has been some dark cloud—some great wickedness of your past—hanging over you. You have never spoken of it, but it drives everyone away from you. It pushes me away. It keeps you from being close with your father, your brothers, even Shelah who longs to know you as he knows me. This evil monster eats away at you and makes you so enraged that you become almost inhuman—even to those you love."

"You have known this for long?"

"Almost from the first time I met you. Your dark moods came less frequently then, but they came. I have prayed that you would share the secret cause with me and let me help you confront it. But I waited in vain. It worsens every day, and I fear now may be too late for its healing."

She coughed again and reached her shaking hand for a goblet of water on her bedside table. Judah rose and took the goblet in one hand. With the other, he held Shuah's head and helped her to drink. Shuah's eyes spoke her mute thanks for the kindness, the first in so long, as Judah said to her, "I never knew you wished to know my past. I thought it best to forget and build a future."

"But you do not forget. I have not wished to pry or upset you. A woman's place is to wait for her husband's readiness to share a

121

confidence. I felt you should unlock your heart willingly, not at my insistence, but now I chide myself for waiting too long."

Judah shook his head. "It does not seem possible that two people could live together so long and not know each other. I thought you wished to remain unburdened and withdrawn from my troubles. I thought it would be unmanly to speak of my shame to you. I never realized . . ."

"Perhaps I should have spoken long ago, but the matter was of such pain to you, I was afraid I might enflame the wound. You say you feel you never really knew me, but I know you, Judah. I know how proud you are and how you hate to admit the least sign of weakness."

Judah kept getting the same messages. His father had admonished him for covering up his weakness with false strength. Tamar had said a woman desired to be more to a husband than Judah had trained his sons to understand. Why had he held Shuah at arm's length when he longed for closeness? Why had he never gotten to know this person of insight and wisdom that he saw so clearly now? How could he, in this one moment, atone for years and years of his failures?

The only thing Judah could think to do was to apologize, something he always had thought of as a sign of weakness. He made himself do it for Shuah's sake: "You are right, Shuah. I have been accusing you of my own sins. Can you ever forgive all my unkindness to you?"

A weak smile came to Shuah's mouth as she said, "Oh, Judah, of course you are forgiven. I knew you did not mean to speak and act as you did, else I never could have endured it. I felt it was helping you somehow—when you were able to turn your anger at yourself upon me."

Judah was humbled, touched in the deepest part of his being. "How could you abide it?"

"I love you with such love that I gladly would bear any suffering for you. But the time is approaching when I no longer can be here to do that. I have been fearful that you might turn your rage upon Shelah. He is so fragile, so young—and he cannot understand these things."

"Oh, God! What have I done?" Judah wailed, burying his face beside Shuah on the couch.

"My husband, I say all this, not to add to your sorrows, but only that you might take care to treat our son gently. Give unto him the love you could not find in your heart for me."

Judah's fist clenched. He wanted to scream or run or fight or throw something. He felt helpless as he asked Shuah the question he was asking himself: "What can I do?"

"Do you not think now is the time to unburden yourself? Perhaps to speak of what troubles you will ease the pain and drive the demon out."

"No," Judah protested, "I can tell no one. It is too unspeakable."

"When I said it would ease the pain, I was speaking of mine as well as yours. My only remaining wish is that we may have this one moment of closeness. One moment when you take me completely into your heart of hearts." Shuah seemed to gasp for air, just for strength enough to get the words out: "Could you do that for me, Judah?"

Judah wanted to take her into his arms as well as his heart. He wanted to make up to her for all he had done to hurt her. But she looked so pale and weak. He feared to put a hand upon her, lest she should crumble at his touch. He said, "I cannot afflict you any more. Do not ask that of me. I cannot take you down to the depths of my wicked soul to dredge up something that would make you hate me. It sickens me even to think of it."

"I could never hate you, Judah. This unseen thing has been my enemy for too long. I beg you, allow me to help you face and slay the enemy, so that I may draw my last breaths in peace."

Judah touched her brow, wet with droplets from exhaustion. Her irregular breathing was labored as it came deep from her heaving breast. He thought of how much of her pain he had caused and how bravely she had endured his wrath. She, a Canaanite, had been more godly than he, a true believer. But how could he find the words to fulfill her awful request?

Shuah jerked forward, choking and clasping her hand to her throat. "Judah! Judah!" she cried. "I haven't long. The death angel hovers near!"

123

He took her hand from her throat and held it in his own. "Fear not, my wife. My father wrestled with an angel, and I stand ready to do battle with any who come this way."

She tried to smile as she said, "I am foolish to be afraid." For a moment, she rested easier. Then the agony of the pain in her chest seized her again, and the racking cough became more intense than ever before. She gasped, "Speak quickly, Judah. Tell me all your heart."

Judah sensed the urgency in her words. His guilt seemed magnified a hundred times in the presence of this woman who had forgiven him for every harsh word and rebuff when she had cried out in pain or groaned with melancholy. Why was it he never knew he had caused so much of her unnecessary suffering? He no longer blamed Shuah or Tamar or anyone else for all the wretched miseries of his own making.

Never before had Shuah placed demands upon him, and to deny her last request seemed utterly cruel. So he forced himself to agree, promising himself he would not gloss over the truth nor save his pride in the telling. He had spared himself too much for too long.

Judah began the account with an honest evaluation of himself: "The source of my guilt was burning jealousy. While we still were living with my father, I went with my brothers to tend our sheep in the grazing areas of Shechem. I just had learned that my three elder brothers were denied the covenant blessing. I was next in line. But I knew my father favored our younger brother, Joseph. I feared I also would be denied, and Joseph would be the one blessed."

"Joseph?" Shuah repeated the name that struck a chord of recognition. "The one killed by a wild animal?"

"That is the lie we brought to my father. When I realized Joseph and I were rivals for the blessing, I despised him—as did my other brothers. Reuben convinced me that to spill Joseph's blood would be unthinkable, but still I wanted Joseph out of the way."

"I always wondered why you and your brothers hated Joseph so."

"It was because he was more godly than any of us, and be-

124

cause we knew he was our father's favorite. He was given a colorful, prince's coat. He acted so superior, bragging about his gift of interpreting dreams, claiming one day to rule over us, and saying we all would bow before him."

Judah caught himself. The old resentment was returning. The same feelings of jealousy and rivalry and hatred came over Judah as he pictured Joseph showing off his beautiful coat and running to his father with tales of the brothers' evil deeds.

"No," Judah corrected himself. "I do Joseph an injustice. He was upright and pure before the Lord. His righteousness made my own wickedness and unworthiness for the blessing become clearly evident to me. That is why I hated him."

"I can understand that," Shuah said. Her words made it easier for Judah to continue.

"Seeds of fierce anger grew into a crop of conspiracy—evil plots to do harm to Joseph when he came to join us in Shechem. Then . . ."

Judah stopped when he heard Shuah moan. Her eyes winced into tight lines, and her face was drawn with pain. Judah reached for her medicine and gave her more than the usual dose. He could not bear to see her like this. He did not wish to continue talking and adding his own source of torment to hers.

Shuah, guessing Judah's thoughts and fearing he might not finish, forced herself to say, "I am better now. Pray, go on. I shall just close my eyes and listen."

Judah began to speak more rapidly, both to be done with the distasteful subject and to allow Shuah to rest: "I was determined to wrest the blessing from Joseph. I convinced my brothers to . . . to *sell* Joseph to a band of Ishmaelites—Midianite merchants who came passing by in a caravan bound for Egypt."

Shuah's eyes flew open momentarily, but her voice showed no alarm. "You sold your brother into slavery?" It was more of a confirmation than a question.

For a long interval of silence, Judah could not say anything. It was agonizing to face the truth he had buried for so long. But, at last, he nodded. "I thought, at the time, that my plan was less drastic than killing him—the plan some of my brothers kept suggesting."

Judah waited for Shuah to comment, but, when she did not, he made himself continue. He was no longer speaking to Shuah, but to himself and to God. It was a confession long, long overdue.

"Once Joseph rode off in chains, bound for Egypt, sins of endless deceptions accumulated. Telling our father an animal attacked Joseph . . . Showing him the bloody coat to confirm the lie . . . Watching our father's face writhe in pain and sorrow as unbelievable explanations were given to his endless questions. I could not bear to look at Israel or my brothers any more. It seemed the intrigue would never end. I had sold my own flesh and blood—and for what? A blessing! How could I have imagined God would bless me after such a horrible deed? That is when I moved us away from there—to escape my father's agony and his weeping, disbelieving eyes."

Judah looked down at Shuah. He was glad the medicine must have taken effect, for she was resting peacefully, and her face was no longer contorted in pain. That encouraged him to open the floodgates and to exchange his former reluctance to speak for relief in a torrent of flowing words:

"Since we left my father's house, I have continued to run ever since—from my sin and from myself. This moment now is the first time I ever have stopped running and trying to escape the horror of facing up to my guilt. I have tried pushing the deed from my memory, blaming others, even blaming God for the retribution of punishments I so justly deserved. Thank you, Shuah, for showing me that I cannot run any longer. Thank you for helping me to face myself and to admit that I, alone, am responsible for the cursed evil that has plagued this family. Shuah, do you think God will forgive me? Do you think I now can be free and make amends so I can pick up the pieces of my shattered life and become a whole person again? Shuah . . . Shuah?"

At first, Judah thought she had fallen asleep. But the stillness of her body, the contentment on her face now devoid of pain, the silence that replaced the sounds of her gasps and coughs in a struggle to take the next breath—all these clues sent alarm signals Judah wished fervently to deny.

He grabbed her limp body and shook her by the shoulders until her head rolled back as through it were something detached. Her eyes did not open. He cried her name over and over again. Still she did not respond. His fear and denial gave way to acceptance of what he wanted most to prevent. Shuah was dead.

Judah released his hold and collapsed upon her lifeless body to pour out agonizing cries: "Now you too! Everything I touch sickens and dies! Oh, God, will I never cease paying for my guilty sins?"

Judah's anguished shouting dissolved into silence. He was unaware when his father's hand touched his shoulder and a crowd of faces began to stare at him from outside Shuah's tent. All had come running at his loud cries, but no one had dared move near him except Jacob. Shelah stood with the others for only a moment before he ran, screaming, to his own tent, there to fling himself upon the floor.

"Come, Judah," Father Jacob said, tugging gently at Judah's tunic. "You must think of Shelah now and go to comfort him."

Glassy-eyed and dazed, Judah rose to face his father. "Shelah," he repeated. "He will be next. Everything I love dies before my eyes. I must get away from here! I must go before it is too late—before Shelah is taken too!"

"You are making no sense," Jacob admonished. "Here, let us help you back to your tent. Perhaps you need to lie down a while."

"Not before you promise me. Promise me you will look after Shelah."

"Yes, yes, I promise. Anything you ask. Now, come away."

Jacob's quickness to promise might have been withheld, had he realized what Judah was asking. It was not until later that night, sitting by the campfire with Benjamin, that Jacob came to understand Judah's meaning.

"I do not know, Benjamin, whether we should leave for home tomorrow or stay and offer what assistance and comfort we can. This sad turn of events makes it difficult for me to leave, even though Judah said he wished me to go," said Jacob with a forlorn and puzzled expression.

"I think we should stay, Father," Benjamin stated emphatically. "Shelah and Judah need us."

"I know, my son, but Judah is in such a strange state of mind that I fear my presence here may have a disturbing influence on him. We must pray about this matter."

Then Cumi stood before them. Her message settled the question.

"Father Jacob," Cumi said with alarm in her voice, "Master Judah is gone!"

"Gone?" Jacob repeated. "Where has he gone?"

"He has ridden off for Adullam. He said for me to ask you to remain here for Shelah's sake."

Benjamin jumped to his feet. "Oh, Father," he cried. "How could Judah leave now? His wife's body has just been laid to rest in her place of burial!"

Jacob's face darkened as he said, "Gone to Adullam, the city of sin! This is not good."

Cumi continued, "My master said he dared not stay here for fear the death curse would pass on to his son. He said he had to leave before harm befell Shelah and every servant of his household. He was most distraught. He seemed to be in a panic to gather his belongings and ride away without telling anyone except me. I fear for him—traveling at this dark hour."

Jacob stroked his beard in concern. "Judah feels the weight of Shuah's death very deeply. He always wants to blame himself for every misfortune that befalls."

"Is that why he has fled? He blames himself that Shuah is dead?" asked Benjamin.

Jacob nodded. "I fear so. That seems to be Judah's pattern—to run away when any disaster comes. We should not have left him alone in his tent. I thought he needed rest and solitude to deal with his grief. I suppose his rash action determines our decision, Benjamin. We must remain here to care for Shelah until his father's return."

"But what if Judah does not return?" Benjamin proposed.

"We must not think such a thing," Jacob replied. "Judah will not be happy among the heathen for long. We will give him time. Time is a healer for all those who grieve."

"Father Jacob, may I speak?" Cumi asked.

"What is it, Cumi?"

"I think we should send someone after my master. He was so

upset and beside himself. Should I get servants to follow him and see that no harm overtakes him upon the road?"

Jacob paused to consider the suggestion. "No, Judah would not appreciate interference with his decision. If he is bound for Adullam, he will visit Hirah, who is not only Judah's head shepherd, but also his friend. Judah is in need of friendship at this dark hour. He has rejected mine, so I am thankful he seeks comfort from another. I only pray that the visit will be brief and that my son does not fall prey to Hirah's intemperate and disgusting habits."

Benjamin nudged his father to say, "Shelah also will be needing a friend in this time of grieving. I shall try to befriend him. With both his mother and father gone, he will be all alone now." Benjamin knew what it meant to be motherless. He saw Cumi smiling her approval.

"You are a good son," Jacob said, patting Benjamin's shoulder. "Tomorrow I will send a messenger home to tell our household of Shuah's death and our decision to stay on."

"This will be a great disappointment to Tamar," Benjamin said to his father.

"We must not think of our mission for Tamar now, Benjamin. Shelah needs time to mourn before he could take on the responsibilities of marriage. Tamar will understand we all must wait. Once she hears of this tragedy and Judah's flight to Adullam, she will have no choice but to wait."

Jacob limped away on his staff toward the servants' quarters to instruct his messenger to be ready for an early morning journey home. He left behind Benjamin and Cumi standing together.

"You have been crying," Benjamin said, looking at Cumi's swollen eyes.

"I loved my mistress very much," she said with a catch in her voice.

Benjamin slipped his arm about her. "Do not grieve. There is a bright side. With Father and me remaining here, you and I shall see each other often, and Father will come to love you."

"Oh, Benjamin, how can you even think of our happiness in

this time of sorrow? Dear, frightened Shelah lies even now upon his sleeping mat, hiding his head and weeping."

"I did not mean to take the tragedy lightly, Cumi. I only meant to cheer you."

Cumi wiped her eyes. "I know. I know."

Benjamin thought of another cause for concern. "Tamar will be most grieved of all, for now she never may have Shelah and obtain her heart's desire for the covenant blessing."

Cumi sighed, "Everything seems to go wrong for us all. We must pray as never before!"

Eight

Judah's evening ride through the hilly paths to Adullam was evidence of his disturbed state of mind. No clear-thinking traveler ventured out upon lonely roads after dark. Bands of robbers and wild animals lurked in the bushes, ready to pounce upon passers-by. But Judah was not thinking of safety when he grabbed a few changes of clothing and his money pouch to speed away.

The journey allowed him to escape his father's watchful, accusing eyes, and it seemed the only action he could think of to protect Shelah from being the next to join his mother and brothers in the family burial tomb. After Shuah's horrid death, Judah paced for hours in his tent, barely able to cope with making preparations for her burial, dreading to face all the mourners—especially his poor, devastated son. It was repulsive to think of having to speak to anyone at all. Getting away seemed all he could do—for others and, certainly, for himself.

The journey was both liberation and imprisonment. He could not escape thoughts that rode with him and held him captive. He tried not to think. Remembrance caused only more discomfort. But Judah had come to accept mental anguish as part of the payment for his regrettable sins. His brothers might lead normal lives, unscathed, unconcerned about past sins, but his strangely arrogant conscience kept him the one tormented for their common crime against Joseph.

Judah was certain all his sufferings bore the sign of Ashtaroth, the wicked folk goddess of sexual love. Oh, he did not sacrifice to her, but he was her slave anyway. She had tempted him to play the fool with strange women in his youth and to choose a Baal-born wife. He had met Shuah through his Adullamite friend, the lusty Hirah. Now he was being goaded down the path that led to Hirah's tents of wickedness once more.

Ashtaroth seemed to mock and plague him as he rode. When

131

he found strength to fight the urgings of her temptations, restricting himself to one wife, Ashtaroth did not leave him to find peace. Instead, she reaped her evil reward through human sacrifices of his family, one by one.

The weaknesses of Judah's oldest sons he had laid upon Shuah—the price he was doomed to pay for the folly of marrying a heathen. His sons' deaths he tried to lay upon Tamar, another Canaanite. Only now, after Shuah's death, could he see how unfair he had been to both of them. The heathen women turned from their strange gods to follow Jehovah, while he still strayed far from paths of righteousness. Even now, in a time of loss and sorrow, he was not turning to God nor seeking solace from his God-fearing father. Rather, he was on his way back to the pleasure-seeking, foul-mouthed Hirah. He imagined Ashtaroth must be having a hearty laugh about now.

He remembered telling Shuah in her dying moments that he could run from himself no longer. He had asked if she thought God would forgive his sin. His return to Adullam answered that question for him. Here he was—unworthy of forgiveness, still trying to escape a guilty conscience, and making the ironic choice of returning to the place of his sinful youth. If he had no prospects of being forgiven or finding peace of mind, so be it. At least, he would be damned in a place where he no longer would need to struggle against the ways of evil any more. If Ashtaroth were stronger than any of his puny efforts to fight her, then he would submit and laugh with her. He tried. He strained to bring a carefree laugh from his soul, but he emitted only low groans and stifled sobs.

Hirah was overjoyed to see Judah, even though his old friend's arrival at that late hour meant delaying plans with his selected bed mate. After initial greetings and embraces, Hirah immediately was aware that something greatly troubled Judah.

"What brings you so far from home at this wretched hour?" Hirah asked, offering Judah a cup of wine. "You came charging in here like you were being chased by a thousand devils!"

Judah did not bother to comment upon Hirah's apt word choice to describe the journey. Instead, he drank the wine in a long gulp and extended the cup for a refill before he said, "I had to get away. May I stay here with you? For quite an extended visit, I mean?"

Hirah howled in mock derision: "That is most amusing, Judah. I am your hireling, and you think you must ask *my* permission to stay here? Of course you can! My tent is your home for as long as you may wish!" He opened his arms wide in a welcoming gesture.

A rugged lover of the outdoors with features to match his lifestyle, Hirah was a man completely absorbed in two things, his vocation and his avocation. The former—tending Judah's vast flocks and overseeing the duties of the other shepherds—Hirah performed with aptitude, vigor, and dedication. The latter—the enjoyment of himself with wine, women, and all sensual and excessive pleasures of hedonism—he executed with exuberant flourish and complete abandon.

Judah nodded his thanks for Hirah's hospitality. He did not wish to talk, but neither did he wish to be rude. He searched for something casual to say: "You look well, Hirah."

"You do not!" Hirah responded bluntly. "Do you want to tell me what troubles you?"

There was no escaping it, so Judah decided to say it and have it over: "Shuah is dead."

Hirah winced and let out his rancid breath: "Shuah dead? That is indeed sad tidings. Does her family here know?"

"No, not yet. It just happened. Would you see them for me, Hirah? I do not think I can."

"Of course, my friend. I will attend to it tomorrow. Now, what you need is someone to take your mind from your troubles. I know just the one! She is the daughter of one of the shepherds. Not very bright, but young and a delight to the eyes. Her breasts are as round and full as plump melons, and her . . ." In the midst of a grotesque gesture, Hirah stopped abruptly, seeing Judah's expression and his upraised hand.

"Cease, Hirah!" Judah shouted as he stood to his feet and turned away.

"What a stupid ass I am!" Hirah cried, slapping his knee. "It is too soon, too soon. But when you are ready, just say the word.

There are many lovely maidens from which to choose when you feel your mood more inclined."

Judah nodded mutely and sat back down.

"Of what did Shuah die?" Hirah asked. "The same illness which claimed your sons?"

"Shuah died of grief. She had much to weep about and grieve for . . . much to forgive."

Hirah frowned. "I see you are depressed. But take heart, Judah! You still have another son. And you will have many more, eh?" He poked Judah in the side and grinned devilishly. "There is still time left for you to sire a hundred sons!"

Judah wiped his forehead, knowing Hirah did not, could not, understand. They spoke entirely different languages and came from totally different worlds. Judah decided to turn the conversation from himself to his host: "How many sons have you now, Hirah?"

"I have lost count! I cannot tell mine from the other shepherds' offspring."

"Have you never wished for just *one* wife?"

"A wife?" Hirah feigned outrage. "Now, what would I do with a wife? I have no need of a woman to think she owns me, someone to nag and whine with jealousy whenever I slept with anyone else. I have women enough to cook my meals and spin wool for my garments. I have observed the unfortunate men who have taken wives, and I have concluded that a wife is nothing but trouble!" Hirah caught himself and said no more. Momentarily, he had forgotten about Shuah.

A few days before, Judah might have agreed. But since his last visit to Shuah's tent, he could not see himself holding such a low opinion of marriage. He found Hirah's comments most distasteful, but, rather than argue the point, he said simply, "Marriage is sacred to my people."

"Oh, yes. I had forgotten about your religion. Tell me, Judah, how can your people find any satisfaction in a religion which forbids pleasures of the flesh? If a man must have something to worship—and I am not at all sure that he does—I much prefer to believe in religions like mine. We do not merely build altars and sing prayers. We worship the angel of desire. We do not make forbidden the fruit of love."

Judah knew it would do no good, but he explained what he had been taught to believe: "My people do not forbid love, Hirah. They honor it, as sacred before the Lord—not a casual thing to be thrown before any woman who comes along, street tramp or temple prostitute."

Because he really was curious, Hirah overlooked the obvious contempt in Judah's voice and asked, "Tell me, do you not fear that in worshiping only one deity, you incur the wrath of other gods? How can you honor a being who would restrict you to one wife and a life of self-denial?"

"Jehovah is the only true God," Judah said, amazed at the conviction with which he said it. "Obeying His laws is not considered a punishment, but, rather, a protective blessing."

"I shall never understand such a strange god. But to each his own beliefs. We shall not let our differences over religion come between our friendship, shall we?"

"They never did in the past," Judah replied, "but, back in those days, I was very much like you—lusting after every wench in village or camp. I cannot behave in such a way now, Hirah. So do not try to force your ways upon me."

Hirah shrugged. "You speak like an old, impotent man. But if it pleases you to sleep without a woman to warm your back, I will not urge you to do otherwise. I shall just feel sorry for you on cold, rainy nights!"

In spite of himself, Judah smiled. "Always the same, Hirah. You never change, do you?"

"I certainly hope not. And for the sake of your manhood, I hope that *you* will."

Since his manhood had been brought into question, Judah felt he must say something in defense of it: "Perhaps—in time. But I must make the decision myself. Remember the tale I once told you of my father who wrestled with an angel?"

"Yes, and an exciting fable it was. A way of explaining your father's limp, I believe?"

Because it was beside the point he wished to make, Judah ignored the fact that Hirah did not believe Israel had seen an-

135

gels, much less wrestled with one. "I also am wrestling, Hirah. I fight against myself, looking for the path I will choose to follow, which part of my nature will win or lose. In this moment, I do not pretend to know what is right or wrong. I am so tired of wrestling that I do not much care."

Hirah studied Judah for a while. Then he asked, "Why do you tell me this?"

"Because I may be here for many days, and I do not wish to fight with you. Before I married Shuah and took her home to my people, you and I did not have the barrier of great differences between us. After time, my visits to see you were strictly business-related. Brief visits, that did not provide sufficient time to argue matters such as religion and principles of personal conduct."

"And you think now we might find religious barriers creating problems between us?"

"It is possible."

"No, Judah! I repeat what I said before: Our religious persuasions will not break our bond of friendship nor create a gulf we cannot cross. Just do not try to convert me, that is all I ask!"

Again Judah smiled. Hirah was a rogue, but such a likeable one, so straightforward and devoid of any mask of dissembling. Judah admired that, perhaps because he was so fragmented himself, so uncertain of who he really was and who he only pretended to be.

"You must be weary, Judah, so I will leave you to your rest. You may contemplate your God in solitude tonight, but I have more vigorous religious rites to perform before I sleep." Hirah went to the tent door, gave a signal call, and stood waiting. He rubbed his hands in anticipation. "Tonight is Mai's night, and she will join me in worshiping the love goddess. And a most devout devotee Mai is too!" The playful twinkle in Hirah's eye indicated he was only teasing his master.

Soon a dark-haired girl in her teens appeared before them. She eyed Judah in a way that made him very uncomfortable. "Will your guest be needing me?" she asked hopefully.

"No, Mai. This is Judah, our master. The owner of the flocks."

"Oh," she breathed with obvious and mingled disappointment and admiration.

Judah watched Mai as she bowed to him. Deliberately positioning herself directly in front of him for the act of homage, she made certain his eyes would not overlook the fullness of her bosom. Her naked flesh was clearly visible under her filmy, transparent garment. Slowly, slowly, she descended until she was at Judah's feet. Then, just as slowly, she began to rise with a slight swaying of her body that resembled a rhythmic movement in a dance. She opened her mouth in a wide smile while touching the tip of her tongue to her bottom lip. The well-practiced gestures of seduction had their intended effects, for Judah felt an involuntary response stirring within himself. The entire pantomime was observed by Hirah, who seemed both intrigued by Judah's reaction and pleasantly aroused himself.

Mai's words were liquid and inviting as she purred, "A thousand welcomes, Master."

Hirah, with his gaze still upon Judah, asked him, "Are you sure you do not wish to change your mind? If Mai pleases you, I can call another for myself."

"No!" Judah barked. He felt he was being manipulated by both of them. "I told you, Hirah, I wish you to withhold your interference and to allow me to make my own decisions. Kindly show me to my sleeping quarters."

Mai pouted as Hirah rolled his eyes and grumbled, "Go to bed now, Mai." When she did not move at once, Hirah clapped his palms together and pointed toward the veil that separated his sleeping quarters from the rest of the tent. "When the bed mat is warmed, call unto me." When she was gone, Hirah turned back to Judah: "You may sleep here. I will fetch sheepskins to make you a bed in this room. I could not allow you to go to the inferior dwellings of the shepherds."

Judah pointed a thumb in the direction of the veil where the silhouette of a disrobing girl was clearly visible. He fumbled for appropriate words that would disguise his agitation and still convey his meaning emphatically. Finding none, he stammered, "But, Hirah, I thought . . ."

137

Hirah laughed. "Oh, you will not disturb us. Nothing ever does."

"Never mind. I will sleep outside by the campfire," Judah declared.

Gasping in disbelief, Hirah protested, "I'll not hear of it!"

Judah firmly grasped Hirah's arm and spoke in a tone that left no question of who was master and who was hireling: "Please! I have made my decision. I wish to sleep by the campfire."

Hirah shrugged his shoulders, went into the bed chamber, and returned with sheepskins, blankets, and sleeping mat. Handing them to Judah, he said, "Never will I understand."

Even outside the tent with the noises of nature and the crackling of the fire, Judah could not shut out the sounds from within Hirah's sleeping quarters. Judah groaned and tossed, covered his ears with his hands, and tried to focus his thoughts upon something else. But the flame of passion in his loins was raging with more intensity than the burning campfire. Judah was tired, so very tired. For all of his weariness, he could not rest, much less sleep. He turned from side to side and buried his head into the deep softness of the sheepskins.

Judah thought about his father and great-grandfather. Both of them claimed to have been visited by angels. He was certain his restless body and wicked thoughts would prevent any ministering angels of peace from appearing, but he did imagine demons might be hovering near.

Was he now awake or dreaming? Images of disease and fire kept creeping into his mind. Everywhere—nothing but disease and fire! The disease was the sort that ate away the flesh to devour it. It also was a disease of the mind that destroyed all reason and control. Worst of all, it was a tormenting disease of his grieving spirit which groaned before it shriveled into nothingness, fell silent, and, finally, died. Died in fire! Fire that glowed with a white heat that consumed everything in its path until it burned itself out and then smoldered into an ash heap of nothingness. Everything was nothingness.

Judah opened his eyes, rubbed them, and blinked to peer into the darkness. It was only his mind—playing ugly tricks, painting horrid pictures. He would sleep. How he longed for sleep!

Judah had known Shuah to cry out for sleep when she was in pain and wanted to close out the world. Poor, afflicted Shuah! Was her ghost joining the demons to harass him? No. Sweet, forgiving Shuah would never do that. It was this place. That was it. No. The source of his misery was not to be found in anything external. The source was inside himself.

He was torn between choices—staying with Hirah, which surely meant befouling the covenant and bringing further pangs of his wretched conscience, or returning home, there to face his father, the worst of all reminders of his guilt. Home? There he would be pushed to make a decision about Shelah's marriage. No. He could not return home. He must stay in Adullam where his father could take no action against him for ignoring the demands of the widowed Tamar. Tamar. What would the crafty one do next? She could do nothing without Israel's help. Israel. His father surely would respect a son's sorrow and a grandson's time of mourning. So it was necessary to remain here in this hell hole and do battle with the demons that arose from Hirah's campfire.

Judah turned upon his back and looked up at the stars. "As many descendants as stars in the heavens." That was the promise given first to his great-grandfather, Abraham, and then passed on to his grandfather, Isaac. Now it rested upon Israel. Who would receive it next? He could not think of the covenant. But Tamar was thinking of it. Tamar, with the touch of death. No. He was to blame, not Tamar. But was it wrong to deny Shelah, his only heir, the covenant blessing? Shelah. Would he be next to die? Stay in Adullam where all would be well. Why could he not turn off the thoughts that raced and jumped about to plague and disease his mind?

Plagued, diseased minds cannot be cured. No use to try. Fires of torture! Demons with flaming torches licking the flesh! Never can be quenched. Disease and fire! He was burning!

Hirah rushed to Judah's side. "Awaken, Judah! You have fallen into the fire!"

Judah opened his eyes. His snatched his hand from the em-

139

bers of the campfire. The burn was not severe, but the pain was magnified by the vestiges of his ghoulish nightmare.

Hirah helped to lift a dazed Judah to his feet and began gathering up the sleeping equipment as he said, "Come back into the tent. I have some healing herbs and ointments."

"Foolish thing to do," Judah mumbled as Hirah led him inside.

"You must have been suffering a bad dream. You cried out in your sleep."

Judah saw that they were alone. "Where is . . . ?"

"I sent Mai away so I could get some sleep. That she-devil would consume me if I but let her. Never can she be satisfied."

Judah nodded. "That is the way of all devils which plague us."

"What?" Hirah looked up from wrapping the wound with a clean napkin.

Judah waved the question away. "Never mind."

Hirah was concerned about Judah. He did not seem himself. To make his friend less apt to harm himself again, Hirah said, "Tomorrow we shall have you a tent pitched. A fine one—all your own. But for tonight, please sleep in here." Hirah indicated the sleeping mat vacated by Mai.

Judah was too exhausted to argue. He slumped to the mat, closed his eyes, and wondered which bothered him more—the pain of the burned hand or the lingering fragrance of Mai's perfume. Neither kept him awake for long, for he immediately was gifted with dreamless sleep.

The next morning Judah accompanied Hirah on an inspection tour of his flocks. The sheep stretched as far on the hillsides as the eye could see.

"You have done well," Judah commended Hirah. "I praise your worthy service to me."

"It is I who am fortunate, Judah. The wool will bring a good price. Soon I shall be rich. I am thinking of buying a plot of ground for myself."

"You? You wish to buy land?"

"I have been wanting to start out on my own. I should like to have a head shepherd working for me while I sit back and take in the profits, as you do, Judah."

The morning sun and a good breakfast helped to put Judah in a better mood than he had exhibited the night before. He was almost jovial as he said, "And what would you do with all your spare time, Hirah, once you become a big land owner with your own flocks and vast riches?"

"I might surprise you by following your example and taking a wife. Frankly, Judah, so many women are beginning to tire me."

Before sitting down under a shade tree, Judah shoved Hirah good-naturedly and sneered, "You are impossible! Not for one instant do I believe a word you are saying."

"Well, maybe it is I who am becoming tiresome to the women. I am not the young colt I once was. I am not always able to . . ."

Judah interrupted to ask, "How many shepherds and goatherds have you employed for me?"

"Judah, why is it you always wish to avoid any mention of the ways of men and women?"

"I find it odious to defile the subject by making sport of it."

"Are we back to your religion again? It seems to dominate your whole life and ooze from your every pore! Never have I seen such a hunger for virtue in a man."

Judah picked a stalk of sweet grass and placed it in his mouth. "I am not what you say, Hirah. I am neither virtuous nor religious. I am a sinful man."

"Such a wayward one I should be! By all the gods, I cannot understand you any more."

"That is probably because I do not understand myself lately."

"Your problem is that you take yourself too seriously, Judah. You need to relax. To enjoy yourself. All your troubles and sorrows have turned your mind black and your disposition sour. You are not the cheerful companion I used to know. Soon it will be sheep-shearing time and the feast of the harvest. This time it will be held in the mountains at Timnath. The journey to new sights, new friends, the feasting and drinking and laughing—all that will make a new man of you."

"I hope so, Hirah. I am tired of being the man I am," Judah said wryly.

Hirah slapped Judah on the back. "There! You have not forgotten how to make a jest. Perhaps there is some hope for you after all."

Judah decided to take Hirah's advice. It would do no harm to relieve his stress by going to the festival. He stretched and tried to relax his body. Every muscle seemed knotted and tense.

"Tell me, Judah, whatever became of Tamar, the fiery one who married your sons? Now, there is a woman to excite the senses and speed up the blood! Is she still widowed?"

"Yes. But I would prefer that we not talk of my daughter-in-law."

"Pray, why not? I thought you once found her most attractive."

"Those days are gone, my friend. She has caused me much trouble of late."

"She would be trouble for any man, but I would not mind her troubling me for a night."

"You do not understand. She wants to marry Shelah, my youngest."

"Shelah? The sickly one? I mean no disrespect, Judah, but I do not think Shelah is man enough to handle someone like Tamar. Are you giving your consent to such an uneven match?"

"Of course not! I should rather give my son to a harlot. I told you I did not want to discuss Tamar. The very thought of her fills me with rage!"

"I think you still care for her."

"How can you say such a thing? You sound like my father."

"He has noticed the passion she evokes from you also, eh?"

Judah rose and walked to the edge of the hillside. "I see some strays up the hill yonder. We must send one of the shepherds to fetch them."

"Always you change the subject when it touches on matters of the heart. I think you fear women."

"I do not fear women. I fear myself. I know my weakness, Hirah. To allow myself to taste the fruit would be my first mis-

take. I would not be satisfied until I had made a glutton of myself."

"Well, I should be delighted to see that! I am glad to know
you still could find a woman desirable. The way you acted last
night made me fear for your manhood."

"Put away your fears, and let us go back now," Judah said
walking ahead a few paces.

"How is your hand today?" Hirah asked as they descended
the hill.

"Better. Let us talk of other things." The bandaged hand was
a reminder of a painful night.

"You always wish to talk of other things. We no sooner start
one conversation than you wish to switch to another. By the
gods, Judah, will you please tell me what subject it is safe to discuss with you?"

"Sheep and goats."

"But not matters between the he-goats and she-goats, I presume. Nothing of mating season or times when a billy goat has
the urge to mount the nanny goat or . . ."

"Enough, you ugly oaf!" Judah shoved Hirah ahead of him
down the hill and heard himself laugh for the first time in many
days. The release was good therapy for Judah as the two of them
played at hitting and shoving and running like a couple of young
boys. Hirah was glad to see Judah's spirits higher, for his master's strange behavior had been a nagging worry.

"At the risk of having my hairs pulled out one by one, I wish
to say one thing more concerning Tamar," Hirah said when they
tired of frolicking and resumed a slower pace. "I know of a way
you can avoid giving her to Shelah."

"And what is that?"

"Give her to me."

"What? Do not be absurd, Hirah. You said you were becoming tired of women."

"I might change my mind for that one! With her for a wife, I
might regain the potency of my youth and live in contentment for
the rest of a long and passionate life!"

"You are sick in your mind. Tamar would not have you!"

"Oh? Am I not good enough for her? One moment ago you

said she was worse than a harlot, but now she is too good for me, eh? Well, that just proves the truth of what I said before. You are still in love with her, Judah. Do you dare deny it?"

"Of course I deny it."

"Then I am more convinced than ever that you do want her."

"You are impossible! You have lost your reason!"

Hirah stopped walking, snapped his fingers, and stamped his staff on the ground both for emphasis and to assure himself of Judah's full attention. "That is the solution," he said.

"What are you jabbering about now? What nonsense flows from your perverted brain?"

"If you marry Tamar, Judah, you save Shelah from her. And you do not come out too badly in the bargain yourself. If I cannot have her, I should like to see her bring a little joy into your dismal life. She would snap you out of your depressed state of mind in no time!"

Judah walked on ahead of Hirah, waving him off as he went. "Thank you very much, but I need no matchmaker today. Should I ever decide to take another wife, I will be capable of making a selection without the help of a wanton who has never married and knows nothing about the subject. That would be like seeking counsel on wine making from someone who has never seen a grape."

"Better give it some thought, Judah. You could do worse than Tamar as a replacement for Shuah. As mistress of your house, Tamar would put a smile back on that cheerless face of yours!"

As he continued to walk, Judah called over his shoulder to Hirah, "I am not paying you good wages for worthless advice, you lazy dolt, so busy yourself with the tasks you promised to do for me today. You were going to see Shuah's family and raise a tent for me, remember?"

Hirah's words were not forgotten as Judah walked on alone. The proposal was one Judah had thought of, secretly, himself.

Back at Hirah's encampment, Judah tried to sort out the puzzle that had become his life. He decided to take a clear-headed, logical approach to filling in the puzzle, piece by piece.

His first concern was for Shelah. Judah wanted to save his son from the death curse—if one really existed. To marry Tamar himself certainly would meet that objective. What good father would not sacrifice himself to save his son? If nothing else, it would be an act of charity.

The second consideration was Tamar. He was so conflicted about her. Could she truly be a she-devil with a death curse? Or was that only a foolish superstition that emerged from Shuah's fevered brain, a way to explain or find someone to blame for her sons' deaths? Israel said Tamar was an angel through whom God spoke messages of great wisdom. The truth was she was neither devil nor angel, but a flesh and blood woman. Even if Tamar did bring death to her next husband, the one to die, if they married, would be himself. His life was worthless, so that would be no great loss to the world. The only reason he rejected Tamar's advances was to spare Shuah's feelings. Shuah was dead, so that barrier no longer existed. He did not want to admit to what everyone—from Shuah to Israel to Hirah—suspected: Judah loved Tamar. He had pushed that feeling so far down for so long that he was frightened imagining what would happen if he allowed it to surface. Just thinking of her was to unleash a bittersweet flood of emotions that swept over him, preventing the reasonable objectivity he was trying to apply to solving his problems. Hirah was right. One could do much worse than to have Tamar for a wife. Perhaps marrying her was the perfect way to atone for his sins: A life-long sentence of being her prisoner.

Then there was Israel. His father would be delighted if Tamar were to marry Judah. There would be no need for council fathers to sit in judgment. No distasteful trial or scandal to stain the family honor. It would be good to see his father smile at him again without the suspicious eyes that always pricked Judah's guilty soul. The matter of the covenant blessing would be settled for Tamar, whom Israel claimed to be destined for it.

That was the only remaining impediment—the blessing. Judah knew his secret guilt would continue to prevent him from deserving, much less accepting, the God-inheritance . First, he would have to go to his father and confess his sin. Would the old man be able to forgive him? Even if he did, what effect would a confession have upon the other brothers? They most certainly would be at Judah's throat for revealing their involvement in the secret conspiracy.

Judah wished that he could pray. He needed divine guidance, but he felt too ashamed and unworthy even to try to regain what was lost the day he betrayed Joseph, betrayed his father, and, worst of all, betrayed his holy faith.

There were too many questions to be decided in one moment. He would have to weigh all the possible consequences of any action he might take, for he did not want to make the tragedy he had created even worse for all those concerned. He would have to wait and give himself more time to think and plan the proper strategy.

After the sheep-shearing festival, perhaps he could find the courage to return home.

Nine

While Judah was trying to decide what to do with his life, Tamar was contemplating what to do with hers. Days were painfully slow in passing for Judah's daughter-in-law.

Even the luxury of the tent given to her for a dwelling within Jacob's encampment gave Tamar little pleasure. She grew more and more impatient as she waited to hear how the ambassadors, Jacob and Benjamin, fared in their mission to negotiate on her behalf with Judah.

Her impatience was magnified by loneliness. Her only companion was the old servant and teacher, Eliezer. He was as interesting, wise, and full of tales as Father Jacob himself, but Tamar's mind was more upon obtaining her heart's desire than upon entertainment or instruction.

"Your master's extended absence gives me cause for alarm," Tamar said to Eliezer as they sat beneath the awning in the forefront of her tent.

"The days have not been as many as your anxieties," the old servant replied.

It was said of Eliezer that he was like Jacob's grandfather, Abraham. It was Eliezer's grandfather, who bore the same name, who had served Abraham years before and who had been entrusted with the mission of seeking a wife for Jacob's father, Isaac. The comparison probably came as an indirect compliment because the blessings of tranquility and godliness seemed to pass from father to son, not only among Abraham's descendants, but also among servants' offspring.

Eliezer was a little older than Jacob, similar to him in demeanor, and dressed like him in Bedouin garments accented by a scarf-like girdle where his writing materials were kept. His beard was more yellow than white, and his face all but glowed with serenity. He was Jacob's house steward, friend, and advisor.

He was in complete charge during the absence of the master. Although his position was actually that of a bond slave, he was greatly respected and given higher honor than other servants because he could read and write.

Tamar had passed the time studying with Eliezer. Her lessons included learning to play the harp. She loved strumming the ancient instrument and singing the songs and hymns Eliezer taught her. She even had composed some psalms and folk songs of her own. She first created a story from her imagination or adapted one from Eliezer's library of volumes of legends. Then she wrote down her composition. Finally, she would accompany herself on the harp as she sang or told her tales. She seemed to have a gift for writing. She imagined that one day she would play and sing to her son, tell him the sacred legends, and teach him to be a great musician and scholar. It was for her unborn child that Tamar soaked up all she could learn of history, religion, and arts. She wanted her child to be as honored for his wisdom and talents as were Father Jacob and Eliezer.

"Shall we continue today's lesson?" Eliezar asked her.

Tamar had lapsed into a dream world of her own, far from her studies of the world, the mystic science of numbers, astronomy, or religious laws. These wonders usually fascinated her, but today she was unable to stay focused on anything but events occurring within Judah's tents.

"I am sorry, Eliezer," Tamar apologized. "What did you say unto me?"

"For what three reasons did God create man last, after the beasts and all growing things?"

A probing question always caught Tamar's imagination, as Eliezer well knew.

"I would say," Tamar began slowly, "that one reason was that all things might be ready for man, that he might sit down to enjoy the created things—as a guest for whom the meal had been made ready. It would be unlikely that a loving God would create man and place him in a world with nothing to harvest for food or hunt for his meat."

"Well said," Eliezer declared, nodding his approval. "And another reason?"

"Man was created last, lest someone might say God had man's help with the rest of the work. With all else created first, we can know the greatness of our God, who is able to do what man cannot duplicate."

"And the third?"

Tamar thought in silence for a long moment. At last, with a twinkle in her bright eyes, she said, "Lastly, for the humbling of man, that he would dispose of all his human pride when he realized that the ants and fish were born before he was conceived."

Eliezer held his sides as he laughed at her. "You remind me of Joseph, Jacob's eleventh son. He was apt and quick of wit, even as you, Tamar."

"Did he love his studies, even as I ?" Tamar inquired.

"Far beyond all I have ever seen. Younger than all but one of the other brothers, but exceeding them in all areas of learning. Such memory! He retained all that I taught him of the earth, ancient history, and mysteries of God."

"Was he a better pupil than I?" Tamar probed.

Eliezer caught the note of envy in Tamar's voice. "With diligence, my daughter, I think you soon may rival his commendable knowledge."

The challenge was the very thing Tamar needed to keep her mind diverted from her troubles. Eliezer knew the purpose of his master's mission and Tamar's claim to the covenant destiny. He also knew of the ill will the women throughout the camp felt toward the one they called "the outsider." Tamar was forced to go to the well in the noonday heat, not at morning or evening when the other women went to draw water and to visit. They scorned her, giving her sideways glances or turning their heads away as they passed by with their water jugs on their heads.

Eliezer had tried to ease the pain of Tamar's rejection. Regardless of her attempts to feign unconcern for their ridicule, she was hurt by the gossiping women's unjust rebukes. That was why Eliezer engrossed Tamar in her studies and imparted to her information the other women never could have learned, even if they were interested, which they were not.

Eliezer began to lecture, and Tamar wrote down all he said. Then she read her transcriptions back to him and repeated from memory the lesson. Tamar held on her lap the writing tools, the clay tablet on which she made wedge-shaped signs with a style. She also had writing papers made from leaves and reeds pressed together. Sometimes she wrote on skins, making rows of pot-hooks with a reed sharpened to a point and dipped into the red or black part of her paint saucer.

"Eliezer, do you think I could learn to paint a picture? Something beautiful like one of the pieces from Father Jacob's collection of prized art?"

Secretly, Eliezer knew Tamar hardly was ready for creating a masterpiece, especially since she had never painted anything before. But, knowing that a teacher never discouraged a pupil's desire to explore something new, Eliezer said, "I think that would be a welcome addition to your studies. How came you to this sudden interest in art?"

She pointed her reed in his direction as she responded, "The world is so full of beauty. I would like to see if I could capture it to save as a reminder—for when it no longer exists. You know, flowers in full bloom before they fade and die. I think I should like to make a picture of you to show my grandchildren when I tell them about you."

"That certainly would keep my memory alive after I go to be with my fathers," he mused. "But I think your artwork should be a happy diversion *after* you have completed your lesson for today. Dabble with the paints while I am napping, but, right now, apply yourself to what is unfinished and at hand."

Tamar sat erect with her knees slightly apart and began to write. Sometimes she wrote the ordinary writings of the country, sometimes the sacred writings of God that included the laws, doctrines, and sagas. Eliezer possessed many beautiful models that told about the stars, hymns to the moon and sun, chronological tables, weather records, prayers, and psalms. Some of the writings were fragments of great fables of primitive times. None of them were true, but they captured the reader's imagination all the same. Tamar began to read one of them aloud.

As Tamar read to Eliezer, her voice rose and fell with proper inflection as she followed the script with her index finger. The text was written in the language of Babel. She tired not to make a mistake, so as to impress Eliezer. He had indicated her skill might be inferior to Joseph's. For some reason, she needed to prove she was as capable and proficient as a young boy.

Her teacher was overjoyed with her performance: "Hail to you, lovely one! Your progress is brilliant!" With that he kissed the hem of her garment.

"As brilliant as the reading of young Joseph?"

"I would say you have now equaled his accomplishments."

"Then teach me more, reverend teacher, for I would surpass his knowledge, and then go beyond even that!"

Although well pleased, Eliezer was reluctant to tell Tamar she was far from reaching the intellectual heights of young Joseph's attainments. His capacity of mind often was superior even to Eliezer's. But Joseph had divine gifts that only God could bestow. Some of his prophetic knowledge had no earthly source. But as a woman, Tamar was unique—not only because those of her gender were not expected to pursue formal studies, but also because she had an inquisitive nature, a creative spirit, and an intuitive ability to understand concepts or solve problems without being taught underlying principles or supporting details. That was rare for anyone, man or woman.

The lesson would have continued had it not been interrupted by Bilhah and Zilpah, Jacob's inferior wives, the handmaidens who had borne four of their master's twelve sons. As the two were passing by, they stopped to jeer at Tamar.

"Look, Bilhah, there sits the swaggering, inky-fingered fool!"

"Oh, you mean the one who sits at the feet of old men to kiss their wrinkled faces and to hold their feeble hands?" Bilhah mocked in reply to Zilpah's question.

"Think you she seeks the company of old ones because no younger men will have her?"

"I think it is because old men's eyes are too dim to see her cursed face."

"She thinks herself too good to do a woman's work, so she lazes around all day in front of her lavish tent with her nose in things intended for menfolk. Did you learn anything to make your brain any smarter today, Tamar?"

Tamar was on her feet, ready to do battle. "I learned that it

151

is against God's law to defame and to bear false witness and to waste time in idle, spiteful gossip. Would that the two of you had the capacity to learn such lessons."

Before Tamar could say more, Eliezer cried out to the concubines, "Hence, you daughters of the devil! Close the ivory gates about your tongues, or I'll report you to Master Jacob when he returns! Go on about your business!"

Bilhah and Zilpah were shocked to hear Eliezer's voice from his unseen position behind the fold of the awning, else they never would have dared to speak as they did in his presence. Upon hearing his voice, they turned in fear and quickened their steps back toward the women's quarters.

"Wait!" Tamar called after the women as they were walking away. She caught up to them to say, "You may tell Leah that I shall come today to call upon her."

Zilpah scowled at Tamar in disbelief: "You would dare contaminate the women's quarters with your presence? You should not go where you are unwelcome."

"I will ignore your hateful remarks because they are so typical of an aging, shallow, and ignorant mind, Zilpah. Merely deliver my message," Tamar said coolly.

"Deliver your own messages!" shouted Bilhah. "Do you presume we are your servants, that you think we should do your bidding?"

Tamar did not respond. She walked back to her tent, her head held high, confident in the knowledge that the two women would be most anxious to tattle the news of her coming to Leah.

Eliezer, who had heard Tamar, shook his head in disapproval as she returned to the awning.

Pointing a finger to admonish Tamar, Eliezer said, "You will make a mistake if you go unto Leah. Why should you wish to stir up more trouble with your enemy?"

"Because I wish to make my enemy my friend."

"Pray, explain your meaning."

"Leah has always hated me. She is responsible for the hatred of all the others. She has spread lies about me and defamed my character. I am tired of it. So I plan to get her to change her opinion of me, that is all. Once I win over Leah, the others will follow."

"And how do you plan to accomplish this conquest of Leah?"

"By going to her on bended knee to confess my sins."

"What sins?"

"Any ones she thinks I have committed. As Father Jacob's only remaining true wife, Leah likes to feel superior and lord it over people. I shall indulge her whim in order that I may get some peace to come and go freely. I shall put an end to taking abuse from everyone in the camp."

"I suspect that such action is doomed to failure. Leah is a hard woman and not easily fooled. You are not sincere in your intentions, and she will discern it. Why are you *really* doing this?"

"Because I can use Leah's friendship to my advantage. She is Judah's mother, and she must have secrets about him locked in her heart that I can use against Judah's stubbornness. Who knows a man better than his own mother?"

"Will God be honored by such manipulations derived from deceit and selfish motives?"

Tamar pouted. "I am willing to use any means, sacrifice my pride or my reputation or anything I possess for the sake of the covenant blessing."

Eliezer placed a gentle hand upon her shoulder and spoke prophetic words Tamar would recall when it was too late for anything but regrets: "Only the foolhardy rush ahead of God. You may get what you want only to lose all you could have received."

"You sound like Father Jacob. You mistrust my judgment because you are a man and do not understand women as I do."

"I mistrust one so headstrong and obsessed with an ideal that no judgment is used at all."

Tamar began putting away the tablets and writing materials to indicate that the lesson and the conversation were over. She did not want to hear Eliezer's counsel when it contradicted what she believed was best. She went into her tent to look for a gift suitable as a peace offering for Leah. There was little to choose from among belongings she had carried in her bundles. With only a brief moment of reluctance, she selected armlets and bracelets of gold, her most prized and valuable possessions, and reminded herself she was willing to sacrifice anything for her cause. She tied the ornaments in a silk handkerchief. Then she took the flower from her hair and covered her head with a mantle. It would be best to dress simply and modestly for her audience with Leah.

With the peace offering in hand, Tamar came outside, pausing only long enough to speak a final word to Eliezer, who was still sitting in the same spot. She said, "Do not abandon hope for my finishing my lessons today. I may come flying back sooner than expected."

"I do not doubt it, Tamar. Do you not fear you may make matters worse for yourself?"

"Doing something is better than doing nothing. I am a woman of action, Eliezer."

"I am coming with you," he said, remembering his responsibility was to protect Tamar.

"No. I must fight this battle alone. If you come with me, it will seem to the women that I fear them and bring you with me to intimidate them. If I am accompanied by the head steward, it will throw in their faces another indication that I hold a place of favor. Please, Eliezer, stay here and pray for my mission."

"I cannot force you against your will to submit to me, but I shall pray you will be submissive to the Lord before you open your mouth! If you do not return soon, Tamar, I shall be coming after you."

As Tamar departed, she kissed her palm and waved the kiss toward Eliezer, who still looked perplexed and unhappy. She called to him as she danced off, "Put away your fears, and be thinking what you wish for our evening meal. I'll be back to prepare whatever you desire."

Although Hannah, the cook, and other servants would have brought meals to Eliezer and Tamar, the two ate apart from others, away from gazing eyes and buzzing voices. Tamar loved to cook, and Eliezer preferred her extravagant fare to the plainer meals the others ate. Nothing Tamar did ever was ordinary, and the dishes she concocted were masterpieces of invention. Her behavior, Eliezer noted, was equally unconventional. Risking Leah's wrath proved the point.

As Tamar suspected, the news of her arrival had gone before her. The oldest and most revered of the women in camp, Leah was sitting with her personal servant girls within their separate part of the tent. Her dwelling adjoined ones where the two other wives and unmarried servant girls lived. By virtue of her high standing, Leah had a larger, more private living area. Two handmaidens were spinning flax and humming a tune as Leah lounged on her couch. A third girl stood fanning her mistress. With the approach of Tamar's footsteps, the humming ceased.

"Leave us," Leah commanded with a sweep of one hand in the air. Immediately, the girls scrambled to their feet and hurried to their sleeping quarters behind the center dividing curtain.

"I hope I am not intruding," Tamar said as she stood at the tent door and bowed.

The woman on the high couch tilted her head to look down at Tamar as a queen might give a condescending glance to a lowly servant. "Of course you are intruding," Leah snapped. "I was unaware that such a fault ever stopped you. You intrude when you take my husband's time. You intrude in my life constantly! What is the purpose of your intrusion this time?"

Tamar moved forward slowly to bow again beside the couch. Without lifting her eyes, she said, "I come humbly to beg your forgiveness."

Tamar sensed that Leah was unprepared for such an act of submissiveness. This, however, did not make Leah's scorn any less evident nor any easier to bear. Leah was a tall woman, large boned and awkward. Even in her youth, she had not been attractive like her younger sister. Now, with age lines and gray hair plaited low on her brow to hide the wrinkles, she was homelier still.

"My forgiveness? That is amusing. For which of your crimes?" Leah asked acidly.

"For all of them, Mistress." Tamar knelt and laid the opened handkerchief of jewels at Leah's feet and said softly, "I bring an offering and pray your mercy upon me."

Leah rose to her full height. She was almost six feet tall, as formidable an enemy as Tamar had ever faced. Her voice boomed down upon Tamar's bowed head: "I perceive some foul trick afoot. What is it you are after, scheming one?"

"I come only to seek your favor," Tamar replied meekly.

"Are you not content with my husband's favors?"

Tamar lifted her eyes but remained on her knees. "I look to Father Jacob as a child unto a parent. But now that I know you are displeased with me for sitting at his feet, I shall keep me away in future." Tamar set the first trap, knowing Leah would not know how to respond. If Leah admitted displeasure and banned Tamar from her husband's company, Jacob would take it as interference, an insult to his judgment. Leah did not want to heap Jacob's wrath upon herself.

Leah laughed scornfully. "You actually think I care whether you cling to him or not? My concern is only for him. People ridicule him for playing the part of a young fool, making sport with a Baal-daughter like you!"

"I can see such concern is grounded in love. I do not wish to be the cause of gossip about Father Jacob. I came back here only to ask for Father Jacob's help."

"He has gone to seek another husband for you. Yes, I know of that matter. You wish to marry a young boy, my own grandson, a mere child. What kind of woman seeks pleasure from old men and young sucklings?"

"A very wicked woman, Mistress," Tamar responded. "In days past, I have suffered greatly for my sins, and that is why I have come to repent. I seek your forgiveness."

"As well you should." Leah's words hung like ice in the air.

"Are you pleased with my offerings?" Tamar pointed to the jewelry still lying untouched.

Leah sprawled her huge form upon the couch and picked up an armlet with an air of indifference. "These are hardly gifts enough to pay for the suffering and anguish your presence here has caused."

Tamar rose and turned toward the door. "Then surely I must go away. I will no longer cause you or the others more pain. Tell Father Jacob, when he returns, that you showed me the error of my ways and that I have departed."

The second trap Tamar was setting was a risky one, and she

156

knew it. The walk retracing her steps to the tapestries overhanging the doorway seemed much longer than the distance of her entrance. She already was outside and becoming increasingly more anxious when, at last, Leah's voice called after her, "Tamar! Come back in here!"

Forcing the victory smile from her lips, Tamar returned with head still bowed.

Leah was not going to be responsible for sending Jacob's beloved away. Neither was she going to be swayed so quickly by Tamar's wiles. Leah's curiosity demanded that she ask, "Suppose you tell me what you really are after. Be truthful, for you do not fool me with your beguiling performance and insincere words of flattery, Tamar."

Tamar shifted to her next strategy: "I see that to try and outwit one as wise as Leah was indeed foolish of me. You saw right through my little scheme, did you not?"

"I did indeed," Leah said harshly, asking herself what scheme it was. She had no idea what Tamar was up to nor the meaning she was supposed to have discovered underlying it.

Tamar was quick to give Leah the information: "I should have known you would know how desperately I need your help."

"Naturally, I knew that was your intent," Leah lied.

"You must have known that, without your assistance, my cause is lost, and I may never remarry. I shall have to stay here and be a burden to you, a disturbing influence on this household forever."

"Without my assistance, your cause is lost," Leah repeated. She hoped repeating the gist of what Tamar said somehow would make a clear meaning appear. While she still had absolutely no understanding of what Tamar's words meant, she would not admit the fact for one moment.

Tamar continued, "You know that Father Jacob will not allow me to return again to my wicked homeland of unbelievers now that my mourning time has passed. Unless I marry again, he will insist I stay here under his protection. That will mean I will continue to be a thorn in your flesh." Tamar stopped to observe the effect her words were having on Leah.

Leah's squinting eyes and knitted brows indicated that her

head was spinning in confusion. When Tamar did not offer anything more, Leah said, "Suppose you tell me, just to confirm my suspicions, exactly what it is you expect from me."

Tamar heard, in her imagination, the snap of the shutting door to her third trap as she said the next words: "If you can find it in your heart to aid me, I will be able to bring Judah to release Shelah to marry me. As of now, he stands firmly opposed. You can tell me Judah's weakness, a way by which I may sway him to fulfill his obligation. Once the marriage is arranged, I can be away from here, never more to bring further displeasure to you."

"Oh, so that is it!" Leah bellowed. "You think I would bother myself to help you, you daughter of the devil? You expect me to tell you secrets about my son so you can steal another of my grandsons from him? I will not join you in your plots to destroy what is left of Judah's family! You have done my son enough damage already!"

Burning with anger at Leah's hasty reproach, Tamar fired back, "I thought you might want to help me—in order to restore yourself to the favored position among women in the eyes of your husband."

Tamar bit her tongue, knowing immediately that she had gone too far. In speaking to Leah with such an air of superiority, she completely reversed all her progress. She saw Leah run at her like a lightning bolt, her large arm outstretched, to strike Tamar a blow across the face. It left the imprint of Leah's palm in red streaks down Tamar's cheek.

"You harlot!" Leah screamed. "How dare you insinuate that you have replaced me in my husband's eyes!"

Quickly, Tamar tried to regain her ground. "I ask your forgiveness once more. I spoke in haste. Always I say the wrong thing." Tamar put her hand to the burning flesh on her face. Besides the sting of the slap, the ring Leah was wearing had left a welt that was throbbing in pain.

"Forgiveness, ha!" Leah spit toward Tamar. Lifting the handkerchief of jewelry, Leah threw the offerings back at Tamar, who stood immobile and wide-eyed. "You are just like my Judah, the lusty one! Both of you take and take whatever you can to gratify your own wicked desires, but you give nothing in return. You prey upon my husband with the same curse of Ashtaroth on you that Judah had in his misspent youth. I will not be party to your seductions! Go from my presence before I see you dead!" Leah grasped a bronze statue and began to raise it overhead to strike.

Tamar had played the role of a humble penitent as long as she could stand it. Every nerve in her body was ready to fight back as she knocked the raised statue from Leah's hand and shouted, "No wonder Father Jacob preferred your sister, Rachel, to you! No wonder he prefers my company to yours! You are not a woman! You are too powerful to be feminine, too cruel to be loved . . . too much of a man to be a wife!"

Tamar stooped down to gather her scattered jewelry just as Leah picked the statue up again and let it fly. It missed Tamar's head by inches and landed against the curtained wall. The new offensive aroused in Tamar an even greater desire to do violence, but reason overcame her emotions. She knew she had better leave before she did or said anything further to create trouble while Jacob was away. This incident surely would be reported to him, and anything more from her would be exaggerated beyond what she had done already. She saw the glaring eyes of all Leah's handmaidens. They had come running in response to the noisy argument and had witnessed her outburst. She did not need to fight with them too.

Running back to her own tent, Tamar could still hear Leah's angry shouts. Tamar knew she would be even more of a laughingstock now. Leah would brag to everyone how Tamar came on her knees to beg forgiveness and how, like a coward, she had run away. But Tamar was glad she was getting away. Had she stayed longer, she surely would have even more to regret.

She ran straight into Eliezer's arms. For one awful moment, she was afraid she was going to cry. Never did she allow herself to cry in front of anyone. If she had to break down, she would hide her weakness in a secret place where no one could see her tears.

"Leah struck you!" Eliezer gasped, clasping Tamar's chin and lifting her face for a closer view. "She shall pay for this!"

"No, Eliezer. Do not tell Father Jacob. It was my fault. All

159

was going well, and then I had to throw it in her teeth that Father Jacob preferred my presence to hers."

"Master Jacob prefers the presence of his goats to hers," Eliezer said, trying to cheer Tamar as best he could.

Tamar sat down, exhausted from running. "Oh, Eliezer," she said ruefully, "you warned me not to go to Leah. Never do I listen." Tamar still clutched the golden jewelry, a cruel reminder of her stupidity in causing the scene with Leah. She recalled a saying Father Jacob had taught her about the folly of casting pearls before swine.

"Tamar," Eliezer said softly, "you are the kind of person who always must make a mistake before you learn better. Life is a cruel teacher, but as long as you learn, that is the important thing."

"But how much wiser if I could learn before making a fool of myself." Tamar rubbed the ache on her cheek. "I must get slapped down with reality before I will believe it exists. Do you realize, Eliezer, that by going to Leah I have made matters a thousand times worse for myself? She has more against me now than ever."

Eliezer did not remind Tamar that earlier he had spoken almost those very words. Instead he said, "Do not grieve over this unfortunate incident. There is much more grief I must tell you of when you are recovered and strong enough to bear it."

Tamar jumped up to look him directly in the eyes. "What is it? News from Father Jacob?"

"Yes, but let us dine first. Then, when your mind is more relaxed, I will tell you."

"No! Tell me now!" She tugged anxiously at his sleeve.

"Do not take my arm from my body. Very well, very well. Sit down and calm yourself."

Tamar dropped to the ground and tucked her legs under her. "Tell me quickly, old man, or I shall explode. What news from Father Jacob? Why has he not returned? What has gone wrong?"

Slowly, Eliezer eased himself over to sit beside her. "One question at a time, impatient one. The news came while you were with Leah. A messenger was sent to tell us that Benjamin and Master Jacob will not be returning for a while . . ."

Tamar sprang to her feet again. "Not returning? Pray, why not?"

"Shuah has died." Eliezer waited for Tamar to do the expected and sit down again. "Master Jacob says he and Benjamin are needed there in Judah's household in this time of sadness."

"Shuah is dead? I cannot believe it," Tamar said.

"In truth, it is so. The messenger also said Judah had fled to Adullam, there to nurse his sorrow. He somehow blames himself for Shuah's death. He said he had to escape before the death curse fell upon Shelah as well."

"Poor Judah. Always needing to cast blame on someone for his great misfortunes. Now there is no one left to blame but himself."

"It is, indeed, sad tidings. Judah left right after Shuah's immediate burial. He left all of the administration of his mourning household to Master Jacob. That is the reason for the delay."

Tamar's mind was racing. "Shuah is dead. What now is to become of me? With Judah in Adullam, what did Father Jacob say for me to do?"

Eliezer shook his head slowly. "There was no mention of your name."

"No mention of my name?" Tamar repeated, clenching her fists. "Does not Father Jacob realize how this matter affects me? What am I to do? Remain here to endure Leah's wrath until I am an old and barren widow with gray hair? Was there no news of whether or not my case will be brought before the council? No mention of Judah's decision regarding my marriage to Shelah?"

Eliezer took Tamar's hand and said, "Sometimes Jehovah uses a time of sorrow, that we may learn lessons thereby. This is a time for you to learn patience, dear Tamar. This is a time for you to seek the Lord's face and to wait to find His will."

"A time to wait? For three years I have waited! I shall wait no longer. I shall go to Judah's household and demand what is mine. It is time to have done with waiting!"

Eliezer grasped her wrist. "Tamar, can you, in good conscience, go to a place that is filled with sorrow to demand your claim upon a lad who has just lost his mother? And, with Judah away, a missing father as well? How can you be thinking of your-self and your own desires?"

"Perhaps I can offer Shelah comfort now that he has lost Shuah," she proposed hopefully.

"That would displease Master Jacob. He sent you no such in-structions."

"Oh, Eliezer, I do not know. Everyone tells me the same thing—to wait upon the Lord."

Eliezer nodded. "Then perhaps that is exactly what the Lord is telling you to do."

"Every day that I have waited, the matter looks more and more hopeless. My life looks more hopeless. I tire of constant waiting. Soon I shall be able to wait no longer!"

"There is no other choice, Tamar. You must remain here un-til we receive further word."

"No, no, no!" Tamar's voice rose with each word. "I must travel to speak with Father Jacob. I must come to an under-standing with him, once and for all."

"In time, in time. Give the matter time—for the sake of all those concerned."

"I have no more time to give. I travel at dawn tomorrow," she said flatly.

"Dear one, did you not say a moment ago that you always paid for it when you did not listen and when you refused to heed the wisdom of your advisors?"

Tamar touched her throbbing cheek. "Perhaps it will be so again, Eliezer. But I cannot stay here another day. I cannot take any more. Leah will find more ways to torture me, and I do not wish to fight with her again. I just have to get away from here!"

Eliezer saw the tears burning in the velvet eyes as Tamar blinked to keep them from falling to her swollen cheek. He shrugged and said, "If I cannot constrain you, then go to Father Jacob. Perhaps he will not mind if you go as one concerned for the grief-stricken. But promise me you will not demand Shelah for yourself until the proper time of mourning is over."

Tamar nodded. She was afraid to speak, afraid her voice would give her away. She had no idea what she might say to Father Jacob. She knew only that she was impatient. And ashamed and miserable.

Eliezer embraced her and kissed her forehead. "You became acquainted with grief when death took your husbands. You have suffered, and perhaps remembrance of that suffering will enable you to help bear the burden of those who grieve now."

"Cumi!" Tamar cried. Suddenly the girl's image came to mind. "Cumi was very close to Shuah. Cumi will need me. I can offer my comfort to her and help her with her duties."

Tamar nodded once more to Eliezer and then turned from him to enter her tent. She had to pack her things. Another journey. This time she would not walk. She was too weary to walk, and she had to get to Father Jacob as quickly as possible. She would borrow one of his donkeys and set off at tomorrow's first light. She wondered where this latest journey of hers would lead.

Ten

Tamar's best thinking occurred when she was traveling. Lately, it seemed she was spending more and more time deep in thought.

As the swiftest and most surefooted of Jacob's donkeys bore Tamar toward Judah's camp, Tamar took an inventory of all her recent journeys—and her thinking processes—to assess them. The conclusion she reached was that both were leading her fast down roads to nowhere.

Tamar saw herself covering the same ground, moving in circles, making no progress. She was no closer to her goal now than on the day she first married into Judah's family. The covenant promise, Father Jacob had told her, was assured on her wedding day. Instead of a beginning, her marriages were endings. Like her journeys, they led nowhere too.

Solving a problem required finding a cause. Death, she decided, was causing the roadblocks and detours along her journey through life. She longed to bring forth life, but death kept getting in her path—the deaths of Judah's sons, the death of his wife. Each death turned her back to start over again. Each time she reached out to claim her destiny, the death angel took it from her grasp.

Tamar's heart really was not set upon returning to Judah's household at this time. It surely was a preferable choice to remaining under Leah's thumb, but Tamar knew no progress was made by going. Father Jacob would not give Shelah to her while Judah was absent, so this trip was another dead end. Besides, she dreaded seeing Shelah again after their breakfast meeting at the hidden brook. Shelah probably still was frightened of her. Moreover, she was frightened of him, at least wary of his ability to sire a child—especially a strong, healthy child of the covenant. How could the son of her womb be mighty before the Lord as the offspring of a sickly whelp who ran from her? The entire situation would be laughable if it were not so tragic.

She simply had to think of another plan. Think, Tamar, think. Devise a plan this time that was not going to end in another failure. Then, suddenly, it came to her. It was as though storm clouds lifted to reveal the sunlight of a beautiful dawn of a new idea. She had gone to Leah seeking a weakness in Judah's character, a way by which she could conquer his opposition. Leah had given the answer without either of them knowing it. Why had she not realized it sooner?

Leah had compared Tamar to Judah, the *lusty* one. Of course! Judah's weakness was his *passion*. Tamar remembered sensing it briefly that night in Cumi's tent when Judah's kiss took her breath away and the room seemed to spin and desire dispelled all thoughts of anything else. But then Judah's sudden restraint and his harsh rebukes interrupted to close the door. Judah's restraint had blinded her eyes. She had not realized, until now, that his rejection of her was a defensive cover for his true feelings—just as his rebellious spirit was a disguise he wore to conceal his virtue.

The more Tamar thought about it, the more it all fell into place. Judah's wife scarcely had drawn her last breath before Judah headed for Adullam, the city of sinful ones whose passions ran unbridled. Was this not the time of the wool harvest when sacrifices to the love goddess were as free as the wine, the feasting, the dancing, the music, the idolatries? Yes!

Why should Judah give his love offerings to the heathen women in Adullam when she could, so willingly and gladly, fulfill his desires? She decided it in a moment. She would bypass Judah's tents and go on instead toward Adullam. There she would find Judah. With no loyalty to Shuah any longer hindering him, Judah would be receptive—no, anxious—to make love to her.

But suppose Judah refused her advances again? He might still be angry with her. He might find her boldness in following him to Adullam offensive. Judah was a proud man who resented being dominated by others, especially by a woman. She had to design a plan that allowed Judah to be the aggressor, the one in control who made the first move, the leader in the dance of love.

How could she arrange that without Judah realizing Tamar actually was orchestrating the dance?

Think of another plan, Tamar. Find a way to make Judah the one to seek, to demand, a love offering. Who could do such a thing? The temple prostitutes! The *kedeshe* or daughters of joy as they were called. That was it! If Judah could wear a disguise to mask his true nature, so could Tamar. She would go to the city merchants to purchase the *kedeshe* garb, wrap herself in the shrouding garments of the temptresses, veil her face from Judah's view, cover her recognizable red hair with the prostitute's mantle, and wait for him to approach her. If she could not win his love by her own merit nor by his free will, she would gain his seed by any means at her command. The scheme was entrapment, but she did not care.

For a few moments, doubts forced themselves into her thinking. She remembered the strong admonitions from Father Jacob and Eliezer. She seemed to hear their mocking voices telling her to wait upon the Lord, to be patient, to refrain from trying to take God's will into her own hands. Such thoughts were most disturbing, for it was a drastic thing to presume to be wiser than her mentors. It would be even more drastic to be found guilty of fighting against the Almighty. But Father Jacob had wrestled against God's angel. Had he not prevailed? Come what may, she had to prevail also. Right or wrong, she would not let go until she obtained her blessing!

It would do no good, she told herself, to sit within Judah's tents awaiting his return. She had to go to him in Adullam. Now that he was free of his marriage bonds, the time was right. The deciding factor was Tamar's calculation of the date. Was it not, even now, the beginning of her season of fertility? It was said midway between the cycle of women's menses was the ideal time for conceiving a child. The thrill of that speculation sent a shiver through Tamar's entire body. It was an omen, the first sign of hope she had seen in a long, long time. All past hopes had vanished. All past attempts had ended in failure. But this time she was determined to succeed.

Tamar urged her donkey to speed up the pace. She was on her way to Adullam!

166

While Tamar was riding in his direction, Judah was celebrating with the shepherds and herders in Timnath. After the sheep had been shorn, all thoughts of work gave way to the desires for pleasure. It was a time for making merry in the form of ecstatic singing and dancing, drunken revelry, gluttonous feasting, and wildly savage sex orgies.

For a while, Judah held himself aloof and withdrew from the obscene practices. Then, with the urging of Hirah, who denied himself nothing his eyes beheld, Judah began to relent. At first, he just watched and listened as others drank and sang lewd songs. He remained a passive observer when sacrifices were offered to their gods. His excuse for his reserve was mourning a dead wife.

Then, by degrees, Judah found himself drawn into the activities of the crowd, so as not to stand out as the only one different from everyone else. The first taste of the strong festival wines was warm and invigorating. The second was more enticing and brought him to a third and fourth. These wines were nothing like simple ones brewed by vintners at Judah's own vineyards. Festival wines were strange concoctions of fermentations with additives, herbs said to have supernatural powers to excite the senses and unlock sexual potency. With each subsequent wine cup, Judah found the erotic dancing girls lovelier and the lure of temptation less offensive. It did not take long for him to forget he was supposed to be a man destined for the promised blessing of God.

"Hail, Judah!" Hirah cried, toasting his master and holding his wineskin aloft. A cup was much too shallow for Hirah's insatiable thirst, so the wineskin better suited him. "Come join us in a game of chance."

Judah almost welcomed the lottery game, for it diverted his eyes from Mai. She kept dancing past him at every opportunity. She seemed determined to make him regret having rejected her favors on the night of his arrival.

"The goddess of chance is smiling upon you," said Hirah after Judah's toss of the painted stones won for him a signet ring for his finger and a gold-knobbed walking staff. With a thick tongue, Hirah called for another toast: "Drink to Judah, my master and the son of fortune!"

Judah was ready to stop playing, but Hirah's loud mouth kept encouraging others to keep their full attention focused on Judah's every move. "One more roll of the stones and perhaps Judah will win an even greater prize!" Hirah shouted.

Immediately, Hirah reached out and grabbed Mai by the arm as she danced about the men and lifted her swaying skirts in their direction. He swept her from her feet and into his arms. Then, with drunken, staggering steps, Hirah moved to the center of the game ring and dropped Mai there. He announced, "Here is the grand prize for all you sons of Baal. Cast your stones for a night with this whore if you think you are man enough for her!"

Yelps of approval went up from the gambling crowd. Others standing outside the game ring drew near to see the sport. Judah wanted to walk away, but all eyes were fastened upon him. He dared not leave, lest they think him an unmanly weakling. When it was his turn, he tried to lose the game by barely throwing the stones. Mutely, he begged for a low score. But, once again, his was the highest number. He had won, and all wine cups were raised to him in raucous cheers of approval.

"Claim your prize, Master Judah," called a half-naked shepherd boy. "Or will you let your foreign religion prevent you?"

An older man shouted, "Perhaps Judah's god forbids him to sacrifice to the love goddess. Are you afraid, Judah?"

Another cried, "He hesitates before Mai. He must know the ways of this Ishtar!"

They were beginning to laugh. They jeered and mocked him. Then came Mai's voice as she looked up at him and taunted, "Be not afraid of me, Master Judah. Come, I will not hurt you!"

The challenge to his virility and the jeering crowd were too much for even Judah's strong will to endure. Without a word, Judah lifted Mai into his arms and carried her away to a nearby wooded area. The shouting and clapping of hands still could be heard behind them.

With her face close to Judah's, Mai whispered, "I am glad you won me. Everyone says you are too virtuous to partake of the joys of love. I know better than to believe such nonsense of a man of your great strength."

Judah stood still and opened his arms. Mai fell to the ground with a thud.

"Why did you do that?" she whined, rubbing her backside.

"I thought you women of Adullam liked men to give you rough, animal-like treatment. You did not protest when Hirah dropped you in the game ring a while ago," Judah said tartly.

"You may play rough with me, if that is your desire," Mai said. "Perhaps you wish to begin close to my heart." She placed one hand to her breast and with the other yanked her low-cut robe downward. Then she pulled the hem of her skirts up to her waist to expose her nakedness and lay on her back with her legs widespread apart. She opened her arms wide and writhed like a snake.

At first, Judah felt the surging lust of his youth return to fire his blood. Her invitation urged him to fall upon her, but he could not move. Something about her sickened him. Was it the hollow eyes and cheeks that reminded him of a lifeless skull or the nauseating odor of sweat coming from her unwashed body or the rancidness of regurgitated wine that reeked from her panting breath? It was more that all of that combined. She seemed to personify all that was evil.

"You harlot from hell," he murmured.

"Come, come! Share with me the mystery of the goddess. Why do you wait? Haste to come!" Mai arched her back and tried to entice him with seductive glances that moved from Judah's loins to the unclothed areas of her body.

When he continued to stand over her without moving, Mai rose to her feet in anger. She tore her garments down so that they hung from her waist. She cupped a hand under each bare breast and waved them back and forth as she swayed her hips. Still Judah stood motionless.

"I see that I must play the part of lusting if I am to have your virtue this night," she said.

Mai's bared shoulders and breasts were rubbing against Judah's chest as she panted and groaned into his ear. Her hands pawed wildly at his *aba* to tear it from his body. She seemed crazed, almost demonic. She was ready to devour him in a frenzy of obsessive eagerness.

"Stop this grotesque display!" Judah commanded. "Who am I that you think you can overtake me with your heathen, unholy perversions? I will have no child-woman take my part as lustling!" He pushed her away as he would reject vomited, worm-infested meat.

Mai cocked her head and stood with her hands upon her hips to sneer, "So they were right. You are afraid. Or perhaps you prefer to have a boy to pleasure you? Or are you a eunuch?"

"Think what you will about me. Here is what I perceive about you: You know nothing of the rites of real love. You are but an immature child trying to play the part of a seductive wanton, but you lack the skills for it. You possess no allure of femininity. Your antics are not attractive to a man, a human man. They are repulsive! You are unschooled in acting like a desirable woman."

She blinked her eyes in surprise at the lecture. "You are the first to complain," she snapped.

"That is because you never have learned secrets hidden from the heathens you sport with. The wild men of this place are as ignorant about the art of love making as you are."

"And will my lord teach me the secret ways of which he speaks?"

"Another night. When you come to me with your wits about you and your spirit gentled. And your body washed from its filth! Give me your bracelets."

"My bracelets?"

"I will keep them as a pledge until you come to redeem them. But you must approach me with a submissive spirit, or never will you receive my seed. Only when you act like a human being will I teach you the ways of highest love."

Mai did not know whether to be annoyed or believing. "I think you say all this only to put me off. How do I know you will do what you promise?"

"Come to my tent when we return to Adullam, and you shall see. There is more to love making than displaying raw passion. Think you not that I have seen hundreds of women unclothed? Think you that your silly gyrations are the way to captivate a man's desire? Tonight you are a child, but back in Adullam, I will make of you a woman."

Judah removed the bracelets from Mai's arm and left her standing amazed in the dusky darkness. He had no intention of giving his manhood to such a heathen, but he could not help but pity her. His only hope was that his fast talking and the trickery of taking her bracelets were convincing enough to keep her from belittling him before the others. He was torn between betraying his virtue and making a spectacle of himself. He had no wish to be an object of contempt in the minds of the shepherds in his employ. Then it occurred to Judah that the opinions of these drunken whoremongers should be of little value to him anyway. Why had he felt compelled to pretend? He chided himself for stupidity worse than theirs.

Judah went back to find Hirah to make excuses for leaving the celebration early. He found everyone too drunk to comprehend his words or to insist that he stay. He picked up the walking staff he had won and leaned upon it as he strode off, thankful to be away from the boisterous crowd. He needed quiet and solitude to clear his mind.

Perhaps he should have taken one of the donkeys to ride, but he preferred to walk and enjoy the evening air. It was a distance back to Adullam, but he did not mind. Travel would be safe, he believed, along the hilly paths and village roads which were still familiar to him from earlier days.

He thought of the degenerates he left behind on the hillside. They were to be pitied too. Their lives revolved around nothing but frenzied, erotic idolatry. He had come close to becoming one of them. How easy it might have been to put his conscience to sleep! He was thankful that his father had taught him a religion that did not include such nonsense. He also was glad he had come back here. It made him appreciate a heritage that, before this night, he had taken for granted.

At the foot of the heights on the road leading toward Adullam, Judah passed the mud walls that protected the city. A figure crouched near the gate. At first, he could not make out the shadowy outline, but he believed it to be a woman. If that were so, Judah thought, she was foolish to be out, unescorted, after dark. He also thought he heard faint sounds of singing.

As he drew closer, his eyes confirmed that it was a woman indeed. She was wrapped in the identifiable garments and veil of a temple prostitute. Temptation seemed to confront Judah every place he went. He decided to pass by on the other side before having to do battle with his passion for a second time in one evening.

Judah had no way of knowing that Tamar was the temptress behind the veil. When she arrived in Adullam, Tamar purchased the shrouding robes from merchants and left her donkey to be reclaimed later. She inquired of the merchants which way the shepherds—those who had gone up the hill for the wool harvest festivities—would pass on their way home. Learning that the frolicking men would have to take the road by the wall, she positioned herself there by the gate. She was prepared for a long night's vigil, because she was given no indication of what hour the shepherds might come. It was one time Tamar accepted waiting with willingness and patience. Tamar would have waited, without complaint, for a month, if need be.

Tamar was shocked when she spied Judah, walking alone on the homeward road, long before any other revelers appeared. She took it as another good omen to spur her on. It was as though their meeting alone were planned ahead of time. *Judah has been sent to me,* Tamar thought.

Judah's struggle with his conscience was weakened by Tamar's voice, softly raised in song. She began to hum the tune, lest Judah recognize her singing voice. It was a sweet, lilting love song, very different from the lewd ones roared loudly over the wine cups at the festival.

Judah turned his head to avoid looking her way, but the constant self-denial was becoming increasingly more difficult. He cursed his shameful craving and told himself to have respect for his dead wife until a proper time of mourning had passed. Then his aroused curiosity started to get the better of him. He changed his mind about passing to the other side, just to get a brief look at the singer of the beautiful melody. Even though his youth had been an untamed one, he never had been with a *kedeshe* before. His youthful love affairs had not required payment. What would such a woman say? How would she behave? Why did the unknown hold such acute fascination?

Just as Judah convinced himself to deny both his curiosity and his lust and to leave the woman to the next passer-by, she spoke to him. He stopped and did not walk past her.

"Greetings to you," she whispered. She dared not speak in her natural voice for fear of being found out. The softness of her silken whispers only heightened Judah's desire.

"Greetings to the mistress," Judah heard himself say in reply.

"May you be strengthened and blessed with all pleasant delights." Tamar had heard the temple women use such phrases while she was serving the three-year waiting period in her homeland. Never did she suppose observing such wretches would be useful in any way.

Passion had seized Judah once more, and the second temptation was not as easily turned aside. The wine and half-naked women at the festival had paved the way for Tamar's conquest.

"Whispering wayside one," Judah said with an anxious voice, "for whom do you wait?"

"I wait for one who needs my comfort. With him I will share a brief moment of love."

"And how will you know when your lover passes by?"

"He will bid me come unto him, and I shall be his willing, obedient servant." Tamar had learned by bitter experience that she must not push Judah nor place demands upon him. She was determined to advance slowly, for she knew a bold, domineering woman was not to his liking.

Judah smiled. Soft whispers, submissive will, gentle nature—all so different from the clawing, raging Mai. The shrouded one captivated him. He wanted to hear more from her: "Being a stranger here, I am not as the lusty ones of this place. Mistress, I do not know your customs."

"I am glad of it," Tamar said sincerely. "This is a new experience for me, and I shall be comforted that you will not be as others, to judge my offerings too harshly if I should falter."

"I find you pleasing. Will you allow me to come in unto you?"

Tamar's heart leapt to her throat. She spoke with trembling

lips from the depths of her soul as she said, "To give my love to you would be all my desire. I am honored to be regarded with your kind favor."

The gentle words moved Judah to reach out his hand to touch her. Slowly, he drew her toward him, trying to gaze upon the face behind the veil. Only her eyes were visible. Those penetrating eyes! There was something strangely familiar about them.

Tamar yearned to fall into his arms, but she could not make a single mistake now. Coming this far, she had to guard her every word and deed, lest she be found out. She knew a real temple woman was required to receive payment for her services, so that was the next step to be taken.

Drawing back a little, Tamar said, "What will you give me in return for my humble favors?"

Judah thought for a moment. "To prove to you that I am at least a man of some worthiness, I will give you a he-goat from my flocks. Is that honorable enough for your service to me?"

"But you have it not with you."

"I will send it to you. I am on my way to Adullam. Give me your love gifts tonight, and tomorrow a messenger will return to this place with your reward."

"A man may promise a gift beforehand. Afterwards, he may forget his word. My duty is to take a pledge to hold until the promise is fulfilled."

"Name what it shall be, angel of loveliness."

At those words, Tamar almost forgot what she was about and stepped out of character. She wished Judah's endearing words were not wasted on a harlot of the streets, but that he would think of Tamar as his angel of loveliness. She forced such thoughts away and said, "Give me the signet you wear on your finger. And the bracelets you carry there."

"The signet ring I freely can give, but not the bracelets."

Tamar did not want to sell herself too cheaply, so she said, "Then also give me the gold-knobbed staff in your hand."

"You know how to look out for the mistress," Judah said. "I win these prizes at a game of chance, and you would take them from me in the space of a moment."

"I shall endeavor to be the prize you win at the game of love. If afterward you think the prize unworthy of a high price, I gladly will receive whatever you offer. Is that not a fair bargain?"

Amused at the woman's quickness of wit, Judah was moved to banter back, "One who gambles at the game of love always loses something of himself. Here—take them all. The bracelets too. I shall be relieved to rid myself of these odious mementoes for the greater prize you promise."

At that, Tamar led him by the hand to a concealed area she selected in advance. When they arrived, she spread the ground with a blanket she had removed from her donkey. They sat down, and Judah took her hand.

"Will you not remove the veil?" Judah asked, caressing her and having a sudden urge to stroke her hair, mostly because it was completely concealed beneath the shroud.

"Pray, do not ask that of me. If you knew my face, my office as your servant would be ended, and never could I show my face again."

"Do not think that I would be so cruel as to disclose your identity."

"I prefer to remain unknown . . . to save embarrassment for myself." Tamar was glad both for the head covering and the covering of darkness to protect her anonymity.

Judah's curiosity increased. "How does a woman . . . I mean, why does someone like you . . . ?"

"Do you not know?" she whispered. "All women must take their turn at the office."

"But why?" Judah asked.

"To be a temple woman is to honor Ashtaroth, the goddess of love."

Judah scowled. "My religion honors women, not a false creation of paganism."

Tamar knew she had to move quickly away from the subject of religion: "I do not believe in the goddess, Sir. But I am compelled to do this service, nevertheless. With other passers-by, I might feel even more ashamed and dishonored. But not with you. I discern that you do not give your love to every woman of the streets."

Judah was relieved to hear that she was capable of feeling shame. The others had none. This woman was different. Her modesty was appealing. "How could you discern anything about me when we have just met?"

"I see kindness in your eyes. I hear respect for me in the tone of your speech."

"You are right that I respect your womanhood, but my religion forbids any dealings with a prostitute. Fornication, adultery, or any relationship of love, outside of marriage, are abominations to my God. I defile myself to be here . . ."

Tamar had to interrupt before all was ruined. "Sir, I see that we both suffer because we fall short of higher ideals. It is for that reason only that I offer myself—to help you forget all your cares and shortcomings . . . and sufferings."

"If only you could do that—if you could cause me to forget—then . . . then . . ." He reached out to hold her and to feel the comforting closeness of another human body next to his.

"Only allow me to keep the shroud upon me for a covering, my lord. I could not stand to have my body bared to add to my shame."

Judah did not say more. Her words had driven away all his former restraints. Years of loneliness, guilt, and deception had built a wall of protection to keep Judah distanced from others. Now, with the gentle impress of a soft hand upon his cheek, the wall crumbled away. All Judah's pent-up feelings of rage and confusion found a strange, new release as he lay with the shrouded, unknown woman who seemed to him so knowable. She was, after all, a familiar stranger. She became part of Judah himself. She was his lust, his temptation, his greed—all that was sinful within his soul, that which he fought against with all the strength of his will. She was that part of him to which his better self now surrendered.

Tamar no longer was the one pursuing Judah. She was the pursued. Judah took her in complete and utter abandon, not with the tenderness his words had made her believe would be forthcoming. The old recklessness of his younger days returned to drive him to be harsh and abusive, much in the same ways he had seen the festival shepherds treating the wantons upon their laps. If Ashtaroth wanted him to sacrifice to her, then she would receive the full measure of his carnal nature with all its hidden lechery and lasciviousness. For whatever reason, Judah could not be gentle with a harlot, nor could he copulate with one with the same sensitivity and consideration he always had tried to find within himself for Shuah. He projected one personality upon the sacred marriage bed. He became a different man as he desecrated himself on Ashtaroth's altar.

Tamar murmured against the heaving force of Judah's body, but he was deaf to her pleas. His hands gouged at her flesh, and his mouth spewed out vulgar obscenities to her.

"Cares my lord for nothing but his own gratification?" Tamar questioned with a cry of pain.

"Is that not what you are paid for? You are the child of whoredom, not I!"

For a time, everything went black for Tamar. She seemed to lose consciousness as the earth whirled about her head. What had happened to Judah? Who replaced him to rape her with such violence? It was not the beautiful, romantic moment of Tamar's dreams. She was not the recipient of Judah's love, but the object of his lust. What went wrong to make Judah exchange his sweet words and caresses for harsh oaths and animal brutality? Demons that drove Judah to abuse Shuah with words now drove him to abuse Tamar with his latent, ungodly passion.

Tamar did not let herself cry out again. She endured his cruelty by silently closing her eyes and biting her lip to await the end. At last, he released her, and she turned from him to bury her head in her quivering hands.

When it was over and Judah stood to his feet, he came to himself. He saw the pathetic creature, curled up with pain and trembling from shock, lying dejected upon the donkey blanket. He could not believe what a monstrous thing he had inflicted on her.

"I . . . I did not mean to . . ." Judah tried to apologize, but he could not. The thought of asking forgiveness of a prostitute was as repulsive to him as the acts of violence he had committed. He was disgusted by the sight of her and even more sickened with guilt for what he had done. Even a heathen harlot deserved better than this woman received at his hands.

Once again, Judah felt compelled to escape. Without a word of farewell, he threw his *aba* about him and shuffled down the road toward Adullam. His head was bent down to his chest, and his shoulders were slumped as if they carried a huge and unbearable burden.

Tamar heard Judah's footfalls grow fainter, and, when she was certain he was gone, she breathed a sigh of relief. Always they leave me, she thought. Every man I have ever held in my arms—or even wanted to hold—all of them turn from me. They flee, or they die.

She drew the donkey blanket over her legs. She would spend the night outside in this secluded place. She was too weary and too heartsick even to move, much less to seek lodging. There was much to think about again.

She had seen a side of Judah undisclosed to her before. Somehow, she could not be angry with him. Her instincts told her he was hurting, and he had taken out his hurt upon her. Virtuous Judah could not lie with a prostitute; only an unrighteous lecher could.

In spite of all she had just endured, she knew that she still loved him. It always had been Judah she wanted. Now she had claimed him—crudely and deceitfully, to be sure—but he was hers for one, brief moment in time. She would hold onto that memory and not allow herself to remember anything vulgar or painful about this night.

Even more precious than remembering he had called her an angel of loveliness was the most important of all—she had received his seed! She touched her hand to her abdomen. From this will spring new life, she told herself. A good result will come from a bad start. She would not allow herself to doubt it, not for an instant. This was the moment she had lived for, waited for, prayed for above everything else. She would not remember the pain nor the circumstances of this child's hapless conception. She only would remember that she had succeeded. The blessing of the covenant that was to pass to Judah was now hers to claim as well.

Tamar congratulated herself for overcoming so many obsta-

178

cles to reach her goal. She had not let anything—not even death—defeat her. She brushed a tear away with a swish of the veil she had removed and then crushed it in her hand. She looked at the cursed veil and decided that when she told her son stories and sang to him to the accompaniment of the harp, she would omit the fact that his mother dressed as a harlot and resorted to sinful trickery so that he could be born.

If everything were so marvelously fulfilled and victorious, and if she were to be blessed among women, and if her name would be remembered throughout all history in the lineage of the Messiah, why was she weeping? Why could she not offer up a prayer of thanksgiving? Why did she feel so wretched that she wanted to die?

Eleven

Having accomplished what she set out to do, Tamar had no further reason to remain in the region of Adullam. The next morning, she decided to double back and to complete the mission she originally went to fulfill, consoling the bereaved within Judah's household.

Trudging along on her donkey, Tamar thought of Judah—his moods, his words, his love tokens—the walking staff, signet ring, and bracelets. "Little friend," she said aloud to the donkey, "you are bearing a treasure richer than those golden trifles. You have the honor of transporting Judah's son upon his very first journey."

Although she looked forward to seeing Father Jacob again, Tamar told herself she must not tell him of her wayside tryst and the escapade with Judah. Her hope was that, when Father Jacob was told, he would have to be understanding because he had obtained the covenant blessing by deception also. It was much too soon for such a conversation now. In the fullness of time, everyone would know she would bear Judah's son. For now, she would keep her delicious secret and await the expected results. She was certain, beyond just wishing it so, that she was with child. It simply could not be any other way.

She smiled as she neared the groves of Mamre and almost laughed when she spied Judah's striped tents in the distance. It was the same excitement she had felt before, but now she believed she soon would call this place her permanent home. Any twinges of guilt interrupting her sleep the night before were replaced by this day's thrill of anticipation.

Her happiness was short-lived. There was a heavy silence that pervaded the atmosphere of Judah's camp, a foreboding that had to be attributable to something more than the continued mourning of Shuah's death. She sensed it when she passed the field hands as she neared the crest of the valley. It grew stronger as she entered camp and observed the house servants walking with lifeless strides, their faces devoid of all expression. The inactivity and ominous silence could only mean that some other tragedy must have befallen someone among those of Judah's tribe.

Tamar scarcely alighted from her donkey before Cumi came running to meet her. The young girl's eyes were swollen, almost shut, and she burst into a flood of tears as she threw her arms about Tamar's neck.

"Cumi, what is it? What is wrong?" Tamar asked anxiously.

Before Cumi could respond, they were joined by Father Jacob and Benjamin, who had been notified of Tamar's arrival by the servants.

"Tamar!" called Jacob, approaching her, limping and leaning upon his staff. He embraced Tamar and Cumi together because they were still clinging to each other.

"Father Jacob, peace to you," Tamar said quickly. She wanted to get to the more important matter: "Please tell me what it is that troubles Cumi. She cries so hard, I cannot understand her."

Even though Cumi had not practiced the instructions Tamar designed to obtain Jacob's favor, the servant girl had won the old man's admiration just by being herself. During the days after Shuah's death, Jacob, Benjamin, and Cumi had become close, drawing comfort from each other. Jacob noted well the girl's abilities in managing things and her capacity for loving and serving those about her in a self-sacrificial way. He also knew she was tenderhearted and prone to tears, so he had become quite gentle in his dealings with her.

"There, there, little blossom," Jacob said as he patted Cumi's head. "Benjamin, take Cumi down to the well and let her bathe her eyes in the cooling waters." Jacob did not want to speak of the tragic matter in front of Cumi, lest it bring about an even greater deluge of tears.

Benjamin took Cumi's hand to lead her away. He had a helpless expression on his face, wincing each time she sobbed.

"Please, Cumi," Benjamin pleaded, "you promised you would try not to shed any more tears."

When the young people were out of earshot, Jacob took Tamar inside the guest tent he shared with Benjamin. Gravely, he said, "Young Shelah has gone to join his mother."

"Shelah is dead?" Tamar asked with her mouth agape.

"Yes. A house of sorrow. All my Judah's family gone. All gone."

"Of what did Shelah die? How did this happen? When?"

"Cumi found him earlier today. Whether it was an accident or not, we do not know. Poor Cumi lost all control of herself. We had just gotten her calmed. I venture the emotion of seeing you stirred her up again. Why are you here, Tamar? Why did you not remain with Eliezer?"

"When your message came about Shuah's death and Judah's leaving for Adullam, I thought you might need me here to help. I did not know I was coming to offer comfort for *two* deaths! Tell me about Shelah. What happened?"

"I do not know the whole account myself. Cumi has been too upset to give us many details. All I know is Shelah drowned. It seems there is a hidden brook nearby, a secret place few know about. Cumi had gone there to gather berries from a tree beside the brook. She found Shelah floating face-down in the deepest part of the water." Jacob's last words trailed off in a heavy sigh.

Tamar shook her head in disbelief and took Jacob's hand. "Did . . . Did he fall into the water? Take his own life? Was someone else responsible for this?"

"I wish we had answers to your questions. Benjamin says he ventured that way just after it happened—although I'll never know why Providence brought him there at that moment. He placed the body on his donkey and brought both dead Shelah and hysterical Cumi back here immediately."

Tamar knew at once that Benjamin's arrival at the brook was more than happenstance. It seemed clear that he was there for a tryst with Cumi. Tamar had told Benjamin of the secret place for just such a romantic encounter. But she did not understand why Shelah was there also.

"This is, indeed, a dark mystery," Tamar said.

Jacob's voice choked up as he said, "With the death of Judah's only remaining son and heir, he is completely bereft of all family. I shudder to think of his reaction to this latest news. A messenger will ride to Adullam at tomorrow's dawn to take him word."

"Judah is now free," Tamar whispered, almost to herself.

"What say you?"

"Judah is free of all ties to his past life with Shuah and her sons, all sickness and death and sorrow. Now he can marry again. He can start a new and happier life to raise up sons who will replace those who lie in their graves."

Jacob was shocked at her words: "How can you speak so in this hour of grief?"

"Because Judah *must* marry again. The covenant blessing, Father Jacob! The blessing!"

"Tamar, I am disappointed in you. You are thinking of *your* part in the blessing, not of Judah's. You cannot plan Judah's future for him. Shelah's death may be the sign that I was wrong about bestowing the blessing on Judah. Since he has no heir, I am sure you can plainly see . . ."

"No! I do not see!" Tamar stood up abruptly with a look of terror on her face. "You must not even think of giving the blessing to another of your sons!"

"You forget yourself, Tamar! Who are you to instruct me as to what I must do? I will make the determination as I am guided by the Lord God, not you."

Tamar grasped his arm. "Oh, Father Jacob, forgive my quickness of tongue. I meant only that you should wait, should you not, before arriving at a hasty decision? Perhaps Judah yet may have an heir. You always tell me to be patient and to wait."

"And were you not thinking that you might be the one to give Judah such an heir?"

"If Judah so desires." She placed her hand below her breast and closed her eyes. Then she added quickly, "And if Jehovah wills it."

"It seems most unlikely that Judah will take you to be his wife, Tamar."

With eyebrows raised, Tamar asked, "Why do you say that?"

"Judah has been very angry with you. Have you forgotten his words when he sent you back to your people?"

Tamar grit her teeth. "One does not forget being thought of as a murderer. But back then it was his grief seeking a source to place blame. Judah knows better now."

"Even so, this latest blow, Shelah's death, may put him in the same state of mind. I had hopes of convincing him to give Shelah unto you because Judah was bound by law, but now . . ."

"Is he not still bound? With no more sons, is he not obligated to take me himself?"

Jacob stroked his beard thoughtfully. "That is a decision for the council judges."

"Never has there been a case more deserving of justice than mine! Shelah's death means *three* husbands have been taken from me. Am I not entitled to the fourth—Judah himself?"

"This is not the time to speak of the matter. Turn your thoughts from yourself and think of Judah. He will need a period to grieve. This would not be an appropriate time to bring him before the judges—or even to inquire at his mouth concerning you."

Tamar fell upon the old man's neck. "Oh, Father Jacob, I know you are right. You must pray for the Lord to tame my impatient spirit and give me strength to endure the delay."

"Have you lost the ability to make your own petitions before the Lord?"

Tamar did not respond, but she was certain that, as always, Jacob could see into her secret heart. Because she said pray *for* me, not *with* me, she had revealed a sin barrier between herself and the Almighty. She turned away from him and put her head in her hands.

"I will pray for you," Jacob said, taking her hands down to hold them. "And also for Judah. He should be returning home quickly. There is nothing to keep him away any longer."

"Judah will need all of us to support him in this latest sorrow. May I stay here until he arrives?" Tamar asked hopefully.

"No. I have instructed the messenger to tell Judah that even Benjamin and I have returned home. We will not be here when Judah arrives."

Tamar was appalled. "Why? Why would you leave now of all times?"

"Because I know my son. He will want to be completely alone without people hovering over him. And, with no one here to run his household and to oversee his servants and vineyards, he will be more inclined to return."

"That seems most cruel."

"Think you that I am cruel when I know the best therapy for grief is to stay busy? It will do Judah no good to sit, moping in a sea of self-pity, in wicked Adullam. I find no cruelty in forcing Judah away from that place and giving him good reason to return. He must engross himself in productive work, absorb his thoughts in things outside his troubles, if he ever is to triumph over the multitude of his sorrows."

Slowly, Tamar nodded agreement. "I see the wisdom of your words. This is no time for Judah to remain in Adullam." She was thinking of diversions he might seek in order to forget this latest loss. If he stopped for an unknown prostitute, what more might happen with other women there? He might even *marry* an Adullamite wife! Had not Hirah introduced Judah to Shuah? Tamar felt her face flush with secret thoughts of jealousy, frustration, and fear. Mostly, she feared losing Judah and all hope for any future with him.

"Do you have qualms about Judah's conduct in Adullam?" Jacob asked.

"You have taught Judah to be a virtuous man." That was all Tamar could think to say. She was amazed that Jacob always touched on truths she tried to hide from him. Had God given him the mind and voice of a prophet as well as the soul of a saint?

Jacob looked into Tamar's eyes to say, "I think you defend Judah's virtue only because you do not want him denied the blessing. Always you want to twist destiny around your finger."

"But Father Jacob," Tamar cried, "you, yourself, have told me it was God's will for me to partake of the covenant promise. How can I—unless Judah and I come together in marriage?"

Jacob spoke slowly and deliberately, so Tamar would understand the gravity of a subject he had hoped to postpone: "I told you I am now uncertain about Judah. His strange behavior of

185

late raises great doubts. I am awaiting a further sign from the Lord."

Tamar thought of the irony. She would give him all the sign he needed when Judah's child began to grow large within her body. But it was too soon to speak of that. Aloud, she said, "I must know what you propose to do if you pass over Judah for the blessing. All of your other sons are married. Except . . . except Benjamin." She was aware of the sharp edge to her voice.

With a smile, Jacob nodded. "I can think of nothing better than bringing together my favored ones. Benjamin would make you a fine husband—in the fullness of time, when he has matured."

"Father Jacob!"

"Why do you look so startled?"

"Benjamin is but a youth. I am much too old for him!"

"Age did not matter to you when you considered Shelah—God rest his departed spirit. Benjamin will be more of a man and suitable husband for you than Shelah ever could have been."

"But you forget—I love Judah! You told me you guessed that."

"Would you put your own desire before the will of the Lord, Tamar?"

"No more than *you* in proposing such a mismatch. You want Benjamin to have your blessing because you love him above all your other sons. You do not seek God's will, but your own!"

Jacob lowered his eyes, hearing the Lord's truth in her just rebuke. He said with regret, "We human creatures always see faults in others but remain blind to our own."

"There are other reasons why I cannot marry Benjamin," Tamar continued, thinking of Cumi. Tamar would go to many lengths and use many people to achieve her ends, but she could not imagine taking away the loved one of her only friend. And what would become of her child if it became known she, an unmarried woman, were pregnant? Such a sin carried a death punishment, either by stoning or being burned alive. Was that to be her fate for fornication and harlotry?

Jacob could see further discussion would upset them both

and be to no purpose. He said, "We spend too much time with human words and not enough time at godly prayer. Let us change the subject before we have any more unpleasantness. Tell me why Eliezer allowed you to travel here unattended."

"I have become accustomed to traveling alone."

"But why did you disobey my command to remain in your tent until my return?"

"I could not endure it there any longer. I was lonely for your company."

"Did the women make it unbearable for you? Did Leah forget to keep a civil tongue in her head? Did not Eliezer divert your mind from the gossips by teaching you glorious wonders? Tell me, what new things did you learn sitting at his feet for instruction?"

"Those are too many questions for me to answer on a hungry stomach. If you will feed me a slice of bread, I will feed your curiosity."

"Even in a time of adversity, Tamar knows how to bring a smile to my lips," Jacob said as they prepared to eat and talk of anything except what was foremost on their minds.

Judah, meanwhile, had no knowledge of things taking place at his encampment. That same morning, at the very time Tamar had mounted her donkey to ride toward Hebron, Judah had awakened to find Hirah back with him in Adullam. This came as a surprise, for Hirah was the last person ever expected to leave a festival, especially to dash away long before daybreak.

"Hirah!" Judah exclaimed when he opened his eyes to see his friend entering the tent pitched especially for the visiting master. "I did not expect you back so soon. What have you there?"

"Your breakfast," Hirah replied. "I was greatly concerned about you, Judah. I was too full of wine last night to think clearly, else I never would have permitted you to return alone. And on foot. In a strange place. What were you thinking?"

"I was thinking I am an adult who needs no nursemaid to watch over me. What makes me so deserving of such watchful pampering?"

"You are not only my master. You are my guest. I am responsible for your welfare."

"I hereby relieve you of all such responsibility. Give me no more mothering; instead, give me my breakfast. I did not intend that you give up the enjoyment of the festival on my account."

Hirah placed the heavy tray in front of Judah and said, "I could no longer enjoy myself for wondering about you here alone. You carried many costly prizes with you on the road, and I feared you had been attacked by robbers."

"Well, as you can see, I made it safely back. Something smells delicious."

"Mai insisted on returning with me. She prepared her special oatmeal cakes for you."

Judah shoved the breakfast tray away. "I shall eat later," he said.

"Does it displease you, Judah, that Mai came back early? She said you told her to come to your tent when she returned to Adullam."

"So I did," Judah admitted. "But it was to put her off. I do not like her."

"But she said you took her bracelets as a pledge to reclaim when she came unto you."

"That I did also. I no longer have them. I gave them to a harlot."

"What?" Hirah's mouth dropped in astonishment before he doubled over with roaring laughter. "You, Judah? To a harlot? In truth? You are jesting, just to sport with me!"

Judah was annoyed that Hirah would not stop laughing. "And why not? Do you think you are the only lustling in all the world? The truth is, I preferred a wayside harlot last night to Mai."

Hirah dropped to a floor cushion and slapped his thigh. "Now I have heard everything in the world. Wait until Mai learns this! She will be cut from the quick of her fingertips to her heart!"

"I also gave the wayside one my signet and the staff I won," Judah said offhandedly.

Hirah whistled with admiration. "Why, Judah, you son of a dog-sired wanton! She must have been some whore indeed to demand such treasures!"

"I do not wish to talk of it."

"Now we are back to that again? Just when my faith in you was being restored!"

"Hirah, say nothing of this to Mai."

"But what will you tell her when she comes for her bracelets?"

"You will get them again for me."

"Come now, Judah. What kind of harlot returns the customer's gifts when the love feast has been consumed? Do not tell me she wishes to pay *you*!"

"I promised her a kid . . ."

"That she might receive, in truth!"

"Be serious. I promised her a kid from my flocks—a he-goat. She merely demanded the other things as pledges until I sent it to her."

"And you want me to take the goat unto her?" Hirah ran his hand through his straggling crop of hair and beamed with delight at Judah's tale. "What is this harlot's name?"

"I do not know. She would not say."

"Then how, by all the gods, shall I know her—to take the goat to her?"

"She will be by the mud wall gate at the foot of the hill. You know, on the road leading to Adullam. That is where she waits to perform her services."

"Gladly shall I go! I will take her a fine, big billy-goat, the one with the magnificent ringed horns and long beard. Perhaps she will think it suitable payment for another night of joy with me!"

"No, Hirah! Do not ask it of her."

"Pray, why not? That is her business, is it not?"

"No, she is not a regular temple prostitute. She only pays her due for the sake of your stupid religion. Put not a hand to her, Hirah, for she would not be to your liking."

Hirah nodded slowly as a frown came over his rugged face. "Oh, I understand. A mistress who would be worthy of you would be too high and noble for me. Is that not it?"

"No, no. You mistake my meaning."

189

"Then what is your meaning? Why may I not seek her favors?"

"There was something pitiful about her eyes. They were all I saw of her, for she was too modest even to remove her shroud before me."

"Now I know you jest with me, Judah. A *modest* prostitute? One who refuses to undress so that you may explore her body? That is the most outrageous tale I ever have heard!"

"It is true, nonetheless. She was . . . different . . . special somehow."

"Special? She seemed special to you? You want her reserved for yourself only?"

"No, you miserable buffoon. Ask me no more questions. Just do as I have bidden you."

Hirah scowled in silence before he said, "One last question, I pray you, Judah. If she is so extraordinary and special, as you say, why do you not take the goat unto her yourself?"

"I do not wish to see her again."

"That makes no sense! Judah, I do believe you make up this fantasy. Either that, or you have lost your reason." Hirah scratched his head in confusion. "First, you brag to me of this woman's special charms. Then you say you wish never to see her again. If you want me to carry a goat to seek an unknown woman with no name who pleasures men with only her eyes showing, I think I deserve some sort of an explanation."

"I do not expect you to understand me, Hirah. If you must know, I was an animal last night. That is the fact of it. I hurt her. I do not wish to cause her—or anyone else—any further pain. So please tell Mai to seek another when you return unto her the bracelets."

Hirah let out his breath in a long, noisy stream. "Such a man you are, Judah, son of Jacob! When you arrived, you held yourself up as a paragon of virtue and belittled me for what you called sinful practices of my people's religion. Then you claim to have debased yourself with—of all things—a whore! You called her pitiful—as though a street woman were sacred to you. I must tell you, I was starting to doubt my religion, to feel guilty—until now. Now I am only bewildered."

"So am I, Hirah. No man is more confused than I."

Leaving Judah and the tray of untouched food, Hirah went to fetch the goat from his herds on the hillside. He visited there with the few goatherds and shepherds who had been left with the animals that were too young for shearing or, in this case, rare ones protected at home. Since the men had been denied the pleasure of going to the shearing festival with the others, Hirah felt compelled to tell them all about it. He also needed to attend to several tasks while he was there. He was in no hurry to set out upon his master's unbelievable errand in the heat of the day. When the sun was down far enough and Hirah's bad temper was cooled enough, he began his search to find Judah's anonymous prostitute, carrying his prized he-goat and shaking his head as he went.

It was late when Hirah returned from his errand. He found Judah still within his tent, lying on his back upon a bed mat, and gazing at the ceiling. Judah was surprised to see Hirah enter with the billy-goat in his arms and even more surprised when Hirah dropped it on the floor beside him.

"Many things you are, Master Judah, but the worst of them is a liar! You could have made up the story of your pitiful, eye-blinking, no-name harlot without sending me on a fool's errand carrying this foul-smelling animal from countryside to village and back again!"

Judah raised his head. "What nonsense are you spouting now, Hirah?"

"I am not the one spouting nonsense. No, Judah, *you* are the one who does that. There is no whore in the place where you sent me!"

"What say you?" Judah asked. "The woman was not there by the gate? Perhaps you went too early and should have waited until evening."

"I could have waited there day and night for a week, but your mystery woman would not have appeared. Not by the gate nor by any other place thereabouts! I should have thought something amiss when you sent me to that walled village. Never have I known a temptress to procure in that area."

"Did you ask of the people of that place?"

191

Hirah pointed to a raised welt upon the back of his neck. "Yes, and I paid dearly for it too. I asked within a house nearby, 'Where dwells the whore who sits by the gate?' The good man of the house let fly with stones upon me. 'We have no temple women here,' he cried. 'This is a decent place, so look elsewhere for a she-goat for the he-goat in your arms.' "

"Strange," said Judah, rising to pace about. "Most strange indeed."

"And then I inquired in a merchant's shop. He told me some stranger had purchased a temple woman's robes from him, but she did not even live in the area. Do not try to fool me with false words and surprised looks, Judah. I know you only pretended with Mai last night to save face. If you do not care for the act of joy, that is with you. But to send me to chase a ghost woman who lives only in your mind was most contemptible!"

Judah lunged and grasped Hirah by the throat and shook him fiercely. "Call me not a liar! There was a woman there last night. Who she is or where she is from or where she has gone, I know not. But she was there, I tell you. She was there!"

Hirah gasped for air and began to nod as fast as he could with Judah's hands at his throat. When Judah finally released his hold, Hirah said weakly, "Very well. It is as you say, Judah."

Judah could not tell from Hirah's voice whether the story was believed or whether fear induced the hireling to agree, just to appease the master's wrath. Friends though they were, Hirah was not about to risk losing his job over such a silly incident.

Judah turned away and sat down. He was deep in thought, wondering if last night's episode could have been another nightmare, one more of Ashtaroth's curses to plague his mind. To break the dismal silence and to reduce the tension that still hung in the air, Hirah said wryly, "It does not matter. I needed the exercise. The long walk probably did my health great good."

Judah laughed in spite of himself. "I can see why you would doubt me, Hirah. It was a most bizarre experience, and it must have sounded incredible to you. Such an incident could happen only to me. I am sorry I choked you. Are you recovered?"

Hirah joined in the laughter, relieved that Judah no longer

was angry. "Think nothing of the red imprints of your fingers upon my throat. They match the welt at my neck."

They laughed harder, and Judah clapped Hirah on his back to show that friendship had been restored. "There's another blow to match the others," Judah said. "All souvenirs of a wastrel's wasted day!"

Still rubbing his throat, Hirah asked, "What now of Mai? Her bracelets?"

Judah thought for a moment. "Give her instead the billy-goat."

"Such a fine one as this for Mai?" Hirah gestured to the animal still upon the floor by Judah's sleeping mat. "It is the best of the herd. Could I not give her a little ewe lamb?"

"Give her the goat—anything to rid me of all this folly. I'll not have Mai call me a thief as well as a liar. That big goat will buy her a hundred bracelets."

Hirah hesitated before saying, "I apologize for calling you a liar, Judah. I realize now that you could not have made up such a wild tale. And you obviously do not have the bracelets, ring, or walking staff. There must have been a woman. The likes of her, however, I am happy to say I have never met. I prefer to behold much more than just a pair of eyes!"

Judah was not sure that Hirah was completely convinced, but he no longer cared.

The rest of that day and evening Judah kept wondering about what Hirah called the ghost woman. Judah would have preferred for her to be a ghost rather than real. He was not proud of his conduct with her, for it showed him a dark side of his nature that troubled him greatly. Living here with Hirah and lust-crazed drunkards had done nothing to improve either his disposition or his character. He seemed a stranger, an outsider among people he hired and property he owned.

Besides that, Judah was bored. There was little for him to do because Hirah had business matters well in hand. The hireling was more interested in proving his capabilities to his master than in allowing Judah to be of any assistance whatever. There was no reason to interfere nor to usurp Hirah's authority. That would be an insult to his friend.

To try to fill his time with local diversions and entertainments had proven to be Judah's folly. He tasted the fruit and found it bitter and disgusting. Trying to avoid Mai was going to remain a problem also. Judah began to wish he had never set his foot back in Adullam. It was a constant reminder of his youth and a time when he had been a wanton shepherd like all the rest.

His thoughts turned to the reason he had come. Shelah. Judah wondered what made him hold the ridiculous notion that leaving home would protect his son from harm. Shelah must have felt abandoned by a father who ran away in the midst of sorrow, leaving an aged grandfather and young uncle as overseers and substitutes for departed parents. Judah had not even said goodbye to Shelah. In trying to escape his problems, Judah found he not only brought all of his troubles with him, but also added to them. When he thought of leaving his sickly son to grieve alone, Judah felt himself a coward, a weakling. That filled him with even more self-loathing.

Hirah noticed Judah's restlessness and depression. The next day, Hirah did not go to the fields. He decided to spend the entire day at Judah's side. They took a lingering morning walk after breakfast. They chatted when Judah seemed willing. Part of the time, Hirah just sat in silence in his master's tent to be there. He offered Judah what encouragement and friendship he could.

It was later that day that they were interrupted by Jacob's traveling messenger who arrived at Judah's tent door, jumped quickly from his camel, and ran to bow at the entrance.

"Hail, Master Judah! I bring you an urgent message from your father, Jacob!" the man said.

"Nathan!" cried Judah. He was so glad to see a familiar face from home, he quite forgot that the man was a servant. Raising him to his feet, Judah embraced him. "Hirah, this is my father's steward, Nathan. Hirah here is my head shepherd."

The two men bowed in customary greetings, mumbling words about peace and health and prosperity to each other. Nathan had accompanied Jacob to Judah's tents and remained to serve his master during the visit. He was a tall, dark-skinned camel driver with the swiftest camel in all Canaan. He lowered his voice to speak directly to Judah.

"I have news, Master Judah. It is of a personal nature," Nathan said politely.

Overhearing the remark, Hirah turned to leave, but Judah raised a hand in protest. "Stay, Hirah," Judah ordered. To Nathan, he said, "Hirah is my friend. Any message for me can, likewise, fall upon his ears."

Nathan was certain Judah made a mistake. The news he brought was distasteful enough to bring to Judah alone. Nathan knew the humiliation Judah might feel if he were to break down or show emotion before another man. But it was not a servant's place to question his master's son.

"Very well," Nathan said as Judah motioned for him to be seated under the awning that stretched over the doorway. The three men sat in a semi-circle with their legs crossed Bedouin-fashion. "It is the saddest of tidings," Nathan began.

A lump already had formed in Judah's throat. His fear was grounded in the fact that his father would not send Nathan and his fast-moving camel with an ordinary message. That would have come by those who rode on their donkeys to bring news.

"Never mind condolences, Nathan," Judah said. "The news! Is it Shelah? Is he ill again?"

"It is of Shelah I must speak . . ."

Judah pounded his fist into his palm. "How stupid of me to leave him! I had a premonition that his mother's death surely would make Shelah sick with grief."

"Please, Master Judah," Nathan interrupted. "Shelah is not ill. He is . . . dead."

"Dead?" cried Hirah. He never in his life heard of so much tragedy befalling one man in so short a time. The gods must be terribly angry with Judah, he thought.

Judah did not speak for a time. He searched Nathan's face and turned to Hirah, hoping one of them would say something to correct a misunderstanding of Nathan's words. Surely Shelah could not be taken too. No, there was no misunderstanding. Nathan's face told him so.

195

"How did he die?" Judah asked finally in a voice devoid of all expression.

"He drowned in deep waters of a brook over the hillside near your dwelling. Your brother, Benjamin, fished him out. Your father speculates that Shelah must have fallen or hit his head upon the rocks that lie in the brook."

"No!" Judah roared. Everything in him denied what his ears were hearing. "Oh, would to God I had been there to stay his hand!"

Nathan hurried to say, "There is no reason to believe Shelah did anything intentional to bring about the misfortune. It must have been an accident."

Hirah rose to his knees and placed an arm about Judah's shoulder. He knew Judah was a man who would prefer solitude in such a moment. "I will leave you, Judah. If you should need me—for any service whatever—call unto me."

Judah did not speak as Hirah departed. He could not. Shuah's death he had met with frantic cries of remorse. His reaction to the death of his last remaining heir seemed to go to the opposite extreme. He was numb, beyond all reaction. He had no tears, no anger, no feeling at all. It was like being out of himself and into a dream sequence in which someone else would have to move and speak for him. "Is there anything else you can tell me?" Judah asked at last.

"Your father and brother have departed for home. Master Jacob said he knew you would want to deal with this matter alone and in your own way."

"That is indeed remarkable. He is mistaken, Nathan. Before I left, I told my father I did not want him near me, but now I dread going back to such . . . emptiness."

"My master instructed me to stay with you, to attend you in all possible ways. He said if you should want him after all, I was to ride to his tents and bring him word of your requests."

"Has the burial taken place?"

"Master Jacob thought you might want to take charge of that also, but he instructed your steward to place Shelah's body to rest with his mother and brothers in the tomb if you should not return immediately. He was uncertain what you would want to do—come back or stay here."

Judah stood to his feet. "I shall go home, of course. Straightaway. I shall appreciate your staying on with me, Nathan. My head steward is an incessant-talking magpie. I shall be happier sending him to oversee the fields and vineyards while you stay at my right hand within the camp. The handmaiden in charge of my household is but a child. She could use your assistance also."

"It will please me to serve you in any way I can," said Nathan, who was thinking how well Judah seemed to be taking the news. Almost too well.

"I will gather my belongings for our departure," Judah said as he moved inside his tent.

Nathan followed to assist him. "Master Judah, I do not know if I should speak of this now to you or not . . ."

"There is more? Out with it, Nathan. Withhold nothing from me."

"It is your handmaiden, Cumi. She was the one who first found Shelah. It has never been explained why Shelah was with her at the secluded place where he drowned."

"You do not think . . . ?"

"I do not think anything, Master Judah. I just assumed you might want to question Cumi since she was there. Especially since she was too upset to provide explicit details. Many pieces of the account seem to be still missing."

"Did you speak of those concerns to my father?"

"No. Before I had opportunity, he departed with Benjamin and Tamar."

"Tamar? My daughter-in-law was there?"

"Yes. She came to mourn with the household when she received word of Mistress Shuah's death. She did not know about Shelah until she arrived."

Judah nodded in understanding. His father's hasty departure now had two explanations. Yes, Israel would want to return decisions to his son without interference or interruption of needed solitude. But he also would want to take Tamar away before Judah's return.

Judah knew his father would be concerned about Tamar's

welfare, afraid Judah would turn his wrath upon her as he always had done when death occurred. Judah thought, *Israel does not know I no longer blame Tamar for my sorrows. I only blame myself.* Then aloud to Nathan, he said, "Tell me what pieces of the story you believe to be still missing."

"It is just that Cumi never before ventured so far away from camp. The coincidence of both Cumi and Shelah being at the brook at the same time. Benjamin's arrival there also. No reasons or full explanations. I just think the young people know more than was reported."

"It would seem so."

"And Cumi has been almost frantic since the accident."

"She is an emotional girl and easily moved to tears."

"It appears, to me, to be more than just shock or sorrow. She acted in such a strange, mysterious way. But I go too far."

"No, you are right to tell me your suspicions. I intend to question Cumi when I get home."

"I have said all this, not to give you further alarm, but only because I know how I would feel if there were unanswered questions regarding my own son's death. I would want to know all the truth."

"Yes, Nathan. I wish to know the truth. About many, many things." Inaudibly, Judah added, "Especially about my wretched self."

Twelve

"Father, I think we ought to take Cumi home with us," Benjamin said as preparations were being made for the return trip to Jacob's camp.

Jacob did not hear the statement. He was busy checking the pack animals to assure himself that all their belongings were loaded.

"Secure the baskets of provisions more tightly," Jacob said to a servant. "We want no mishap on the journey homeward."

Benjamin was annoyed at his father's inattention. He repeated his statement.

"Why do you say that?" Jacob asked, half-listening and still engrossed in the packing tasks.

"We should not leave Cumi behind after all that has come to pass," Benjamin said. "She is not herself. She is still so distraught and full of tears, I fear to leave her behind."

"Your brother would not appreciate our taking away his servant. This is Cumi's home. Besides, she will not be alone, Benjamin. Judah's other servants will attend to her needs."

"But Father . . ."

Tamar interrupted. She feared Benjamin's persistence was on the verge of driving Jacob to exasperation. "Father Jacob," she said, "Benjamin's concern may be well-founded. Have you seen Cumi today? Look, yonder she sits by the well. Just wringing her hands and staring at the ground. Perhaps if I stayed with her—just until Judah returns."

"That would be even less to Judah's liking. And you would need to travel the road home alone again, Tamar. Where do the two of you get such ridiculous notions in your heads?"

Benjamin tried another approach. "We do not even stay to mourn Shelah. Why must we rush away before we pay our last respects to him?"

Jacob turned to face Benjamin. "I already have explained that. If Judah wishes any of us to be with him, he will send Nathan to fetch us."

"That would mean making two trips," Benjamin protested. "Would it not be wiser if we remained and asked Judah his wishes to his face?"

Jacob did not want further discussion of the matter. "It would be wiser if *you* were obedient to *my* wishes."

Benjamin whined, "I thought you were beginning to like Cumi very much."

"What has my fondness for the child to do with it? Of course, I like her, and it grieves me to see her upset. But Cumi is Judah's responsibility, not mine. You concern yourself too much with your brother's affairs."

Tamar walked over to stand beside Benjamin and said to him, "Do not fret for Cumi's sake. Judah will be here soon to look after her."

Jacob shook his head and struck the ground with his staff. "I think you have it turned around backwards, Tamar. Cumi is the one to look after Judah. Both you and Benjamin seem to be obsessed with raising a servant girl to the position of mistress of Judah's house."

"Forgive me," Tamar said. "I meant only that Cumi would be able to look to Judah for protection. It is not good for such a pretty, young girl to be in charge here all alone—without the master of the house nearby."

Benjamin seized the opportunity to further his argument: "All the more reason for taking Cumi home with us! It is not safe here for her, as Tamar said."

This time Jacob waved his staff at them and stated emphatically, "I will argue this matter no further. We must depart. Cumi must remain."

Tamar, who was still standing beside Benjamin, felt the lad's body stiffen. She gave him a nudge and whispered in his ear, "Perhaps you should go bid Cumi farewell. You do not want to anger your father—especially if you expect him to accept Cumi as a daughter-in-law some day."

As Benjamin swaggered off toward Cumi, Jacob watched after him. Then he said to Tamar, "I shall be pleased to see some distance between those two. The idea of such a young lad fancying himself in love. And with a servant girl! Even saying he wishes her for his wife. I used to pride myself on Benjamin's good judgment, but I am sorely disappointed in him in this matter."

"Love does not always follow the path of good judgment," Tamar replied. She was thinking of herself as well as Benjamin when she said it.

"I see that you take my son's side against me," Jacob said with disapproval.

"Do you object to Cumi because she is a servant or because Benjamin is your favorite son?"

"For both reasons. Just look at them!" Jacob pointed his staff in their direction.

"He is merely comforting her, Father Jacob. Cumi is still deeply mourning Shelah's death."

Jacob ignored Tamar's statement and called, "Benjamin! Come! We must depart."

Cumi trailed behind Benjamin as he walked reluctantly back to join the caravan. She tried to compose herself to offer her farewells to each in turn. When Tamar bent down from her donkey to kiss her goodbye, Cumi did not understand her friend's words.

"Do not think for a moment you are rid of me," Tamar said in a low tone so only Cumi could hear. "I shall be back with you before you know it!"

"Do you say that just to comfort me in my loneliness," Cumi whispered back, "or because you think Master Judah will want you now to replace my mistress as his wife?"

Tamar smiled to acknowledge Cumi's quickness to understand. "Both," Tamar said.

As Jacob embraced Cumi, his words were even more difficult for the girl to comprehend. He said, "Do not water your cheeks with more tears, Cumi. Metal becomes stronger only when it goes through the fire. Your mettle has been tested, but you will prevail in strength and courage."

Cumi did not ask either of them for explanations. She wiped

her eyes and said to them, "I shall miss you all. God go with you to protect you on the road. Farewell."

Then she looked up to see Benjamin mounted on his beast and ready to go. She dared not speak to him or even look his way any longer. His face was too sad. She ran quickly back toward her tent because she knew she would never stop crying if she did not.

Benjamin was still sitting motionless upon his donkey, looking back toward Cumi's hasty retreat as the caravan began moving down the road ahead of him.

"Look at him," said Jacob over his shoulder to Tamar. "The silly pup scarcely has grown fuzz beneath his nose, and already he thinks he is a grown man, well schooled in the ways of the heart. Come, Benjamin! You lag behind us!"

"It seems to me," Tamar mused, "you once taught me some wisdom concerning age. Did you not say manhood was but a state of mind? I think Benjamin may be mature beyond his young years, even as you are far younger than your white hairs proclaim."

Jacob pretended not to hear her and did not reply. He knew his possessiveness was the real basis for his objection to his son's relationship with Cumi. He also knew he was judging the boy too harshly and being selfish himself. Even a man of God was not able to be prudent at all times.

No words were exchanged as the three jogged along together on the homeward road. They took no notice of the sun-warmed fields of grass nor of the scents that filled the air—fennel, thyme, and other odors beloved of sheep. Benjamin thought only of Cumi, while Jacob thought of Benjamin, and Tamar thought of Judah.

Cumi, meantime, lay within her tent, thinking of all of them. And of Shelah. His sudden and tragic death dominated her thoughts, no matter how hard she tried to focus on other matters. She knew she had to force herself to attend to her duties, now that even greater responsibilities rested on her shoulders. But all she could do was stare at a ring of colored glass beads and listen to the sound of a singing top engraved with a prayer. She hoped the prayer was a powerful one. These items were all she

202

had left to cling to as she asked God for strength and wept for grief and shame.

Judah's arrival was greeted with little ceremony. The servants had become accustomed to executing their tasks without him, especially Zed, the talkative head steward who had delusions of self-importance anyway. After the added prestige of ruling in the master's absence, Zed quite resented Judah's return. Women servants, likewise, were reluctant to welcome Judah home. They were very compassionate and loyal to their suffering mistress while she lived. Now that she was gone, they felt Judah's conduct had hastened the day of her death. Perhaps Shelah's as well. They feared and dreaded the return of their moody, stormy-tempered master.

Even amiable Cumi shared some of the others' feelings. Judah's arrival meant burial services and wailing mourners chanting the death rituals. Worst of all, it meant Cumi would have to answer questions she knew Judah would be asking about Shelah's death.

Nathan stood by Judah throughout the mourning days and was the one through whom Judah began to communicate with the others. Zed's resentment was increased as an outsider appeared to usurp some of his authority, even to the extreme of taking up residence with Judah inside the main tent. Everyone else was glad to have Jacob's faithful messenger at Judah's right hand. That meant they could continue going about their duties without the master's watchful eye upon them.

Cumi was thankful for the extra time to get herself under control before having to face Judah. She knew a confrontation was coming, but she was in no hurry for it. Nathan's responsibilities were extended to include some of her tasks. He brought Judah his meals and ran errands such as transporting clean and soiled laundry between the master's tent and hers. Nathan also entertained Judah and seemed to have a calming effect upon him. It was a much happier household, everyone said, than before Judah went away. He seemed more docile and less domineering. Had death not been the reason, everyone would have rejoiced over the change in Judah, the improvement of staff morale, and the smoother operations of the household.

Before many days had passed, however, Nathan began to long for his own family back within Jacob's tents, and he said so. Judah thought about asking Nathan to move his wife and children and to become a permanent replacement for the aging, cantankerous Zed. But Judah could not bring himself to ask anything of his father, especially parting with a valuable servant. He thought to himself, *If the day ever comes when I can find courage enough to go to Israel, confess all, and repent of my sins, perhaps then the gift of a servant would seem trivial in comparison to the greater gift of forgiveness.* Judah wanted very much to be reconciled to his father.

Judah was surprised to find that his days of mourning also were spent devoting a great deal of time to thinking about Tamar. He remembered taking her in his arms that one and only time he allowed his desire for her to surface. Her hold upon him seemed to extend beyond her legal right to seek a replacement husband. Tamar was deserving of a better future than having to remain a childless widow in Israel's house or being forced back to her heathen homeland. She crept into Judah's thoughts during long, lonely hours of peaceful days and nights that were such contrasts to those he had spent in Adullam.

Then there also was the unresolved matter of the covenant promise. Even if he did not receive the blessing—and he could not imagine that he ever would—Judah knew he wanted and needed a wife. Tamar needed a husband. Perhaps they needed each other and could move together beyond all the misery of their pasts. Shelah's death seemed like a final chapter that closed the book on Judah's past life. He needed a new beginning, and he wanted the next volume of his history to be better than the former one. Tamar might be the one to help him find the way to make that happen.

Judah had touched on these subjects, using Nathan as a sounding board. Judah did not go beyond mentioning Tamar's legal claim and an unnamed sin that alienated him from his father. He found Nathan both a willing listener and a wise counselor. The servant's own father died before a similar rift had been mended, and Nathan's guilt and regret remained after his father was gone.

"I am sad I must leave you, Master Judah," Nathan said on the day of his departure.

"Not as much as I regret seeing you go, Nathan. You have been of great comfort to me." Judah's need for a friend had been much better served by Nathan than by Hirah.

"Will you be coming unto your father to speak of the matters we discussed?" Nathan asked.

"Perhaps. In time. I must first face myself before I can face Israel. I still have many things to ponder and decide."

"I hope you will come soon. I know it is not my place to advise you in any way, but since you have shown me the honor of taking me into your confidence, I wonder if I might speak one last word in your ear."

"Of course, Nathan. Say on."

"Your father loves you very much, and he longs to enjoy your company again. Your brethren rarely have any dealings with him other than discussing flocks and matters of money and business. In his old age, he is lonely and would welcome a visit from you. He also has great affection for Tamar. I know it would give him great happiness to see you joined together in marriage with her before he dies."

"How is it you know so much about Israel's private feelings?"

"I observe. I listen. When my father died, your father offered me comfort. We had a conversation about fathers and sons and the importance of family closeness. He encouraged me to love my wife and children and to let them know how much. He said family ties often get knotted and tangled, but love and forgiveness are the tools which straighten out the kinks."

"That sounds like my father. He has a platitude for everything."

"It may surprise you to know your father has regrets, just as you do. He blames himself for many of his sons' transgressions. He said his own favoritism created their resentment of Joseph. He thinks the others would not avoid him and you would not have moved your family away from him if he had given you and your other brothers equal attention."

"He said that?" Judah could not imagine Israel being that open and personal with a servant.

"That and much more—things he needs to share with you himself. He is old, so I would caution you not to make the mistake I did and wait too long." Those were Nathan's final words before he mounted his kneeling camel and sped off to his home and loved ones.

When Nathan was gone, the duties of serving Judah once more fell to Cumi. Judah deliberately had avoided contact with her for a while. He wanted her as composed as possible when he questioned her about the death of his son. He knew Cumi did not want to face him. He also feared there might be tears, and too many of those already had been shed by the mourners.

When it could be put off no longer, Judah sent for Cumi. He determined to be as gentle with her as his lion nature allowed him to be.

"Cumi, sit down," he said to her when she came at his summons. "Now, do not look so alarmed, and do not tremble before me. I have never hurt you, have I?"

"No, Master."

"Well, I do not intend to start today. You have been a faithful servant, little Cumi, and as a daughter in my household." He sat himself before her and smiled as he patted her hand.

"And you as a father unto me," she said meekly to return the compliment.

Judah remembered Nathan's parting words about the importance of family ties, love, and forgiveness. He also was reminded that Cumi's own father was dead. Judah wanted to speak to her as he often wished Israel had spoken to him during days of his rebellious youth in Adullam:

"If I am as a father to you, you must trust and confide in me. I need for you to tell me all that came to pass on the day of my son's death—the whole account. It seems to be shrouded in some sort of mystery. You must believe that I will try to understand, and even forgive if that is necessary. But I must have the truth before we can put this matter to rest once and for all."

Cumi did not raise her eyes to look at Judah. She could not speak.

"Now, Cumi," Judah encouraged her, "I know it may be difficult to talk about this. It also is difficult for me. But it must be done. Let us have it over, shall we?"

Cumi took a breath and blurted out, "It was my fault, Master. I killed Shelah."

"What is this you say?"

"Shelah's death was my fault. There, I have made my confession. Now you can do with me whatever you will. I could not live another day with this great sin on my conscience, so I am glad you finally have asked me."

"Please slow down, and start from the beginning, Cumi. Did you push Shelah into the waters where he drowned?" The thought of this small girl doing harm to his son was preposterous.

"No, I did not push him, but it was my fault all the same." She wiped her eyes, forbidding herself to cry. She had said it over and over to herself all the way to Judah's tent: *No crying*!

"I beseech you, Cumi, begin at the start, and go to the end. Leave out nothing in between."

Cumi folded her hands in her lap to keep them from shaking. "If I must start at the first, then I must tell you Benjamin and I hold deep affection for each other. That is the reason for it all."

"My brother is also involved? Please explain yourself, Cumi."

"Benjamin and I wanted to be alone, away from Father Jacob's constant watching. We often would slip away from the camp and go to a place called Hidden Brook whenever we could. But Shelah found out. I think he . . . he was jealous."

"You mean jealous of Benjamin's attentions toward you?"

"Yes. That sounds like I praise my importance too highly I know, Master. But it is the truth. For some reason unknown to me, both Benjamin and Shelah found me to their liking."

"That is not hard for me to believe. Go on."

"Shelah started trying to . . . well, trying to get my eyes to turn from Benjamin to himself. Even when I explained that I loved only Benjamin and that we hoped one day to marry, Shelah could not be dissuaded. In fact, he threatened to tell Father Jacob of our secret meetings and to cause much trouble for Benjamin and me."

207

Judah could not picture his immature son either with romantic notions or with the capacity to do any of the things Cumi described. But Cumi was not one to lie.

When Judah did not protest, Cumi went on. "Shelah and Benjamin quarreled, and I became frightened. I decided to pay no attention to either of them for a while, lest more trouble result."

"What does all this have to do with Shelah's death?"

"Both Shelah and Benjamin knew I was going to the brook. I told Father Jacob I went to pick mulberries there. He is quite partial to mulberries, and . . ."

"Please, Cumi, do not wander from the subject." Judah was getting impatient.

"I said where I was going in front of Benjamin because I wanted him to hear. Even though I wanted no harm to befall him, I did long to be alone with him just one more time. To explain that I was not angry with him and only ignoring him because of Shelah's threats. That was sinful of me, I know, but I did not want to arouse Father Jacob's anger; yet, I needed to speak alone with . . ."

"Cumi, I understand all you say. Now, how did Shelah die?"

"I am coming to that, Master. What I did not know was that Shelah overheard me say where I was going. He was listening outside the guest tent where Father Jacob and Benjamin and I were. Shelah followed me to the brook. Benjamin saw him ride after me and misunderstood the whole thing. Benjamin thought I had arranged a meeting with Shelah. That is why he did not follow us right away. He was angry at first, but then he became curious to see if I truly could turn my affections so quickly. Later, he arrived at the hidden brook after . . . after . . ."

Judah grasped Cumi by the shoulders. She had covered her face with her hands at the remembrance of the awful day. She seemed unable to continue.

"Cumi, you must go on. I need to know what happened to Shelah at the brook." Judah tried to restrain himself from harshness, but her story seemed never to answer his one question.

"I know it is wrong to speak with disrespect of the dead, but . . . but Shelah behaved quite shamefully."

"Did my son attack you?"

"He . . . tried. I pushed him away and called him names. But he continued to come at me. He said I was not a woman as was Tamar, but only a child . . ."

"He said he had been with Tamar?" Judah's voice lost all former restraint.

Cumi was sorry she had reported that part. "I did not believe him, Master. He was saying so many outrageous things. I think Shelah was trying to play the part of a man to impress me with stories of his many romantic conquests. Nothing he was saying seemed the least believable."

"Romantic conquests? That sickly child? If Tamar seduced my son, she will pay for it. But now I am getting off the subject. Never mind that part. Pray, go on."

"When I continued to refuse him, Shelah ran after me and tried to pull at my garments. I could find no place to hide, so I . . . I climbed the mulberry tree."

"And?"

"And Shelah came up after me. I was so frightened! I could not move when I reached the largest limb that extended out over the waters. Shelah reached for me, and whether he jumped or fell, I shall never know. All I know is he hit the waters with a terrible splash."

"Was he killed instantly? Was that all?"

"He . . . oh, he . . . Please, Master, do not make me say more—not now."

"Cumi, this is the very part I want most to hear. Did he strike his head? Did he take his own life? What happened next?"

"This is the most terrible part. He called up to me, still in the mulberry tree. He said if I did not give him my favors, he would go under the water and never come up again. I thought he was just trying to trick me, so I kept refusing him. Then he went under. He stayed under for a long while, and I became more frightened. At last, he came up for air. He said that time was only to test me, but the next time he meant to carry out his threat. He went under again, after jumping up high in the air, and he plunged down very forcefully beside the large rock in the brook.

209

Oh, Master, I thought surely he would come up as before. I should have gone down to help him!"

"He did not come up the second time?"

Cumi was crying, despite all her efforts to keep control. "No! I thought perhaps he was swimming away under the waters—or that he was up to another trick. Even when his body came to the surface, I still could not move. I thought it was a prank to entice me to come down to him! Then, when I finally realized he was not coming up again, I froze to the spot, unable to move."

Instinctively, Judah reached for Cumi and held her in his strong arms. Her head was buried on his chest as she wailed and sobbed. Tears dripped from her eyes to soak Judah's robes, and he had tears in his eyes as well. Finally, he said, "There, there, Cumi. Do not cry; do not cry."

Judah laid Cumi upon his couch and fetched a dipper of water from a nearby pail. He soaked a cloth in part of the water and poured the rest into a cup. He bathed her eyes and cheeks and gave her the cup to drink. She could not hold the cup with her trembling hands, and she was still sniffing and gasping too hard to swallow. But after a few moments, with Judah's steady hand guiding the cup, she become less emotional and was able to take a few sips.

"Better now?" Judah asked.

Cumi nodded, but it was obvious she would have difficulty saying anything more.

"For my sake, Cumi, can you tell me the rest? Please?"

"I just kept sitting there in the tree, Master. I tried to move, but I could not! I kept holding to the branch and staring down at Shelah, bobbing, face down in the waters, up and down."

The picture painted by Cumi's words crushed Judah's heart. He did not know whether to feel sorrow for his dead son, compassion for bewildered Cumi, or loathing of himself for taking off to Adullam. So many emotions were racing through his brain, he felt that he needed the session to end quickly, while he still could contain himself.

"Is there anything more you can tell me, Cumi?" he asked in a tremulous voice.

"I was paralyzed, Master. Oh, if only I had gone to Shelah, I might have saved him. But I did nothing! Absolutely nothing but hang onto a tree limb. I not only caused your son's death, but also did nothing to prevent it!"

Judah did not speak right away. "It was not your fault," he said when he could. "Do not blame yourself, for that will do no good for Shelah now."

"How can you say that to me? I could not even move when Benjamin arrived. Benjamin tried to revive Shelah, he really tried, but I just stayed up in that tree like a frightened animal. Benjamin had to carry me down, or I would be there yet!"

"Fear makes us do strange things like that sometimes, Cumi. I understand. I lay no blame to your account. Thank you for telling me all this."

"Benjamin would not let me tell Father Jacob. Oh, I wanted to! I wanted to confess long ago, but Benjamin was afraid I would be sent away. Now you say you do not blame me. Master, how can you be so forgiving?"

"Perhaps because I have much to be forgiven for myself. My fears have driven me to deeds I deeply regret, Cumi. You only stood by and did nothing. I am guilty of actively causing . . . It is no matter. I can understand your feelings because I share the sin." His thoughts drifted to Joseph.

"You? How can you have part in this? You were not even there."

"Even so, I hold myself accountable. I should have stayed here after Shuah's death to be with my son. I abandoned him—as I abandoned so many others who deserved better from me."

"No, Master. I am the one responsible, not you."

Judah raised his voice. "It is *my* fault, Cumi! At least, it is not yours. Shelah also must share the blame for what he tried to do to you. He had difficulty breathing. Going under the water for so long could have caused his lungs to burst. You said there was a large rock there. He might have struck his head. I am content to believe it was an accident and forget about blame-placing."

Cumi blinked up at him, hardly believing her ears. "You do not wish to punish me? I will not be sent away?"

"Of course not. Do not ever speak of this matter again. Ever! Do you understand?"

211

She nodded her head, but she did not understand. She watched Judah's face begin to change before her eyes. His voice took on the old anger of former days. She dared not say more to him, for she had the feeling he might begin to shout and vent rage such as she had not heard in a long time. *He blames himself,* Cumi thought. That was not a good sign. If the old patterns were returning, that meant others soon would begin to suffer pain right along with Judah.

"Master?" Cumi wanted to say something comforting, but she did not know what.

"It is better that Shelah is at peace with his mother, rather than alive and here with a father such as I. I never knew how to show my family the love they needed from me. Now it is too late, they are gone, and that is the end to it. They all are better off dead."

Cumi reached out a hand to touch Judah's sleeve, but he pushed her hand aside and shouted, "Do not touch me! Leave me now. Go!"

Cumi walked back to her tent, confused by Judah's sudden mood change. Things seemed to move in circles. With each tragedy, her master's reaction seemed worse than before. Why did he push away people he needed most? Would he be incriminating others again now that he was heaping incrimination upon himself? She wanted to flee to Benjamin, to get away to a safe place, but if ever her master needed the same understanding he had given her—albeit briefly—it was now.

Thirteen

Days were passing slowly, much too slowly for one as impatient and impulsive as Tamar. Settled once more in her comfortable dwelling among Jacob's kinsmen, Tamar counted the days until she could confirm her suspicions about carrying Judah's child. She thought of nothing else, but she would not speak of it until it was a certainty.

Her companions were Father Jacob, old Eliezer and young Benjamin, but her association with them brought fresh and stronger criticism from the women in camp. Only the very old and the very young, not a single contemporary, befriended her, so her time was spent dreaming of and preparing for a better future. She did not intend to live confined like this for the rest of her life.

Tamar continued to sit at the feet of her teachers, Jacob and Eliezer, soaking up knowledge she hoped to pass on to her son. Her child would not receive all his instruction from the male guardians of wisdom. No, she would be a teacher—the first among her country's women ever to dare seek such a role. She intended to share precious moments other women would never have with their sons—imparting knowledge and making discoveries about ideas and truths, the scientific world and the living God, the beauty of nature and the spiritual delights of artistic endeavors.

She was becoming more proficient on the harp, and she continued to write words and music that sprang from her creative mind. By the evening campfires, she entertained and amazed her male companions with her compositions. Eliezer was so impressed that he gave the harp to her as a gift. Father Jacob could not keep her supplied with enough reading and writing materials, so his gifts to her became rare purchases from merchants who traveled to distant lands. With Benjamin, Tamar kept hope alive, sharing youthful, romantic dreams of one day making a family with those they loved but were, for now, unable to touch. They enjoyed long walks and conversations, and Tamar, without realizing it at first, did her practice teaching with Benjamin, her first pupil.

Tamar also fulfilled her desire to learn to paint pictures. Her first attempts were more appropriate for the dung heap than for exhibiting or including in Father Jacob's art collection. The old men were of little help in this area because their gnarled and shaking hands were unsuited to holding paint brushes steady. But Benjamin shared her new adventure into the world of self-taught experimentation with colors and designs. On lazy days, the two of them would pack a picnic lunch and take art supplies out to the hillside, there to recreate their poor substitutes for nature's artistry. Tamar also realized her dream of becoming a portrait painter by including figures of servant girls carrying their water jugs and shepherds in her landscapes. Reluctantly, Eliezer indulged her whim and sat for her attempts to capture him on her canvas, but she never was able to get his eyes right. Sitting in one position for any length of time always resulted in the old man nodding off to sleep.

Father Jacob kept his promise to inquire about Tamar's prospects of bringing her case before the council fathers. He made discreet inquiries among those he trusted to keep a confidence because neither he nor Tamar wanted Judah forced into a union against his will. They hoped that deliberations could be made in a private, rather than in a public, session. If the decision went against Tamar, privacy would save face for all concerned and avoid the embarrassment of a public hearing. If preliminary prospects looked promising, it was thought that even the possibility of a favorable verdict might nudge Judah to take action voluntarily for the sake of his pride. Tamar's case was so unique that decision-makers were scratching their heads over it. No word had come to Father Jacob yet, and Tamar was forced to continue to hope and wait.

There also was a waiting period necessary because of Judah's time of mourning. And waiting to know if she carried his child. And waiting to hear news from Judah's camp about his future plans, if any existed. It seemed to Tamar that her entire life revolved around waiting for things. Waiting was not what she did best. She much preferred action to inaction, but all her past attempts to take action had resulted in unforeseen and unhappy consequences—all but one.

After his visit with Judah, Nathan gave Jacob a report that had been a singular bright spot of encouragement. But thereafter, other reports of Judah had not been as good. Shepherds and servants at the public watering places brought news home to their wives who gossiped among themselves as they washed and mended clothes or stretched animal hides to dry. That was not a very reliable source of information, because third- and fourth-hand accounts often were embellished or exaggerated. However, when Nathan's messages began to add credibility to the gossip, it was taken more seriously. His travels to outlying areas brought back eyewitness, first-hand accounts.

Jacob was becoming very worried about Judah, and he said so at the close of the evening meal as he sat with Benjamin and Tamar.

"Nathan tells me Judah has become deeply depressed," Jacob said. "His only contact with anyone is Cumi. There is talk that he is so disturbed that he may do something drastic—either to himself or to others."

"What reason is given for such strange behavior?" asked Benjamin.

"He is sorely vexed, and his servants are fearful for the health of his mind," Jacob replied.

Benjamin, whose thoughts were never far from one person, said quickly, "That gives me great concern for Cumi, Father! If Judah is acting drastically, what evil might come to her?"

Tamar waved away the notion. "You two! You are worse than the gossiping women in the camp. Benjamin, you know Judah would never harm Cumi. And, Father Jacob, you surely must realize how understandable it is for Judah to be distraught. To lose an entire family is no matter to be taken lightly. He needs time to grieve and mourn. Then he will come to himself again." Her words were more optimistic than the secret doubts and fears the report brought to her mind.

215

Jacob was leading up to a different turn in the discussion: "Judah's complete reliance upon Cumi should put a stop to your foolish ideas about marrying that girl, Benjamin. Judah would not consent now to parting with her to come here any more than I would allow you to go live there."

Benjamin countered, "I can do many things you ask of me, Father, but giving up hopes of marrying Cumi is not one of them."

Undaunted, Jacob continued, "When the time comes for you to marry, my son, you must be willing to be joined with the proper damsel. Cumi has been your first and only romance, an impulsive fancy of your youth. As you grow older, you will come to seek God's will in the matter."

Tamar knew Father Jacob's will was more likely the point. He was scattering seeds into Benjamin's mind, going tiptoe around the same idea he had tried to plant in hers about uniting his two favorites. She spoke up to protect herself as well as Benjamin from such a fate: "When Judah and I are wed, he no longer will have to rely upon Cumi. I gladly shall relieve her of that service."

Jacob was visibly displeased. "You both live in a world of dreams. Soon you will have to awaken and face reality. It is prayer time. You two rebels would be well advised to join me in seeking the Lord's wisdom, not your own, regarding your futures."

"Father," Benjamin proposed, "perhaps we should journey to visit Judah and see about him."

"That seems a worthy idea," Tamar chimed in. "If Judah is truly ill or distressed . . ."

Throwing up both hands into the air, Jacob interrupted to say emphatically, "I have never seen the likes of you! You both think and speak of nothing but impossibilities! Judah has made it very clear the last thing he wants is interference from visitors. Now—to our prayers!"

And so it went. Benjamin and Tamar with their wills at odds with Jacob's will. All three of them certain they knew God's will was not that of the opposition.

When the first month was passed, Tamar's hope of pregnancy seemed confirmed. She wanted to leap for joy, to tell the world—especially the busybodies who sat in the women's quarters—"I am with child! I am the chosen handmaiden of the Lord!" Then those who had scorned her would realize they had to bow down and worship the fruit of her womb.

Tamar concealed her joy and held her tongue. She decided to wait yet another full moon for confirmation, lest all the upsetting trips, deaths, and intrigues had affected her emotions and caused her body to function off schedule. With the passing of the second month, Tamar scarcely could contain herself. But she still did not want to reveal her secret and then find disappointment and ridicule were all she had to show for her efforts. She would wait one more full moon, that there be no possible doubt. She had heard of women who so longed for children that their bodies played tricks on them. She did not want to be numbered among them. When Judah was told, there must be no mistake, no more shattered dreams.

So for three months she waited—even as she had waited for three years in her widowhood. She remembered how Jacob had waited and toiled much longer to obtain his Rachel. She knew news of fatherhood would bring Judah out of any depression or vexation that might still be lingering after so many deaths.

Other signs began to manifest themselves—the firmness of her breasts, the sickness she felt as the smell of the morning meal floated up to her nostrils, the weariness and faintness that came with the least provocation.

Unsuspecting Jacob had begun to make fun of her ravenous appetite and the naps she began to take in the heat of the day.

"Our Tamar is getting lazy and fat," he said to Eliezer.

"It comes from sitting here for my daily lessons instead of doing any strenuous work," Tamar joked in response. "Perhaps I should be put to work with your field hands before I begin to resemble my teachers, who are known to sit idly here with me in the shade to stuff their faces."

Tamar wanted to tell Jacob right then and there, but she restrained herself. She wanted Judah to be the first to know. Now that there was no doubt, she would make her plans to go to him. She felt certain any anger Judah might have toward her for tricking him would be overcome by the glorious gift of the healthy child she would bear him.

Tamar was in the process of gathering her belongings and trying to decide upon a plausible excuse to explain her departure when she became aware of another presence nearby. She looked up to see Leah standing at her tent doorway.

"Well," Tamar said. "Do enter, I pray you, Leah. I hope I can be as hospitable as you were to me when I last paid you a visit."

"There is no need for sarcastic little speeches, Tamar. My visit will be brief and to the point," Leah announced.

Tamar went on with her packing as she said, "I am most thankful for that favor. What do you want of me?"

"The truth, Tamar. It is being noised abroad that you are with child."

Tamar dropped the pack bundle and slumped to a cushion. How could anyone possibly know? She had spoken to no one. It must be one of Leah's tricks, a mere coincidence, nothing more. She would not give Leah any satisfaction until getting more information.

"I am not amazed at anything being noised abroad among the gossips of this household," Tamar said, trying to remain aloof. "I have been called everything else by those who follow your instructions to slander me, so it is no surprise that you think this of me."

"Is it true?"

"Do not tell me you want the truth? I thought lies were more to your liking."

Leah started to raise her hand to Tamar as she shouted, "You impudent wretch!"

Tamar grasped Leah's hand before it fell. "Not again, Leah. Never again will you strike me. I have suffered your indignities, turned the other cheek, remained silent when you defamed my name, but no more! This time if you strike, I shall strike back."

Leah lowered her hand as well as her voice.

"There is no need for violence," Leah said with difficulty. For all of her height towering over Tamar, Leah could not hide how frightened she was. She knew she was risking her husband's an-

218

ger in this confrontation, but she had to know: "I merely come here to find out if you carry my husband's child."

Tamar threw back her head and laughed. "Father Jacob's child? You are more ridiculous in this moment than you have ever been before. Leah, well you know your husband is an old man. His time of seed has long passed."

"I have heard of a man's strength returning in old age—when the proper stimulating herbs are eaten, or when a younger woman's charms entice him."

"You poor woman," said Tamar. "Are you so blind that you think your husband's inattention to you means he must be giving his favors to another? Your accusations are absurd!"

Leah was steadfast in her determination to get an answer from Tamar. "I will endure your bad manners because you seem to feel I have injured you in the past. Very well. Now we are even. Just tell me what I want to know, or must I go to Jacob for the truth?"

Fear seized Tamar. To have Jacob's suspicions aroused would ruin everything. Judah must be first to know. Too quickly Tamar protested: "No! Do not go to Father Jacob!"

"Ah-ha!," Leah chortled triumphantly. "So he is the father, but he does not yet know."

"You jump to unfounded conclusions, Leah. I meant only that there is no need to upset your husband with this foolishness. Do you really wish to incur his wrath—indicting him as you do me?"

Tamar had a point. If the rumors were untrue, going to Jacob would make him even more withdrawn, as Leah well knew. She did not want to hear him scold her.

"Then let us settle the matter between us. Are you with child?" Leah asked again.

"Leah, what in God's world would make you think that?"

"Have I not borne six sons and a daughter?" Leah asked indignantly. "I know the signs. I began to suspect as you grew larger each day."

Tamar touched her abdomen jutting out beneath her loose-flowing robes. Judah's child was a strong one, and Leah was right. It had grown more quickly within her body than was usual. Even Father Jacob had noticed. Tamar, herself, began to suspect twins, for it was well known that God's double blessing occurred in the family of Israel.

"Many women put weight upon their bodies. That does not mean anything except that I have been eating more lately." Tamar sneered.

"I well imagine that you have been. To nourish two?"

"Leah, stop all this nonsense. You have no proof against me."

"I have had you watched, Tamar. The sickness of the dawn can mean nothing else."

"You have people spying upon me?" Tamar howled. "Well, if your spies are so all-wise, let them also tell you just when it was that I have lain with your husband. How can I bear his child if I have not been with him?"

"That is precisely why I do you the favor of inquiring of you. There has been no such report. Either you have your affairs in broad daylight or in secret seclusion away from Jacob's tent and yours. You are sly, Tamar. I put nothing past you."

"You have had our tents watched each night? Someone is losing a lot of sleep needlessly."

"Since I do not have absolute proof of the deed—only evidence which becomes increasingly more apparent each day—I await an explanation. I do not wish to accuse you unjustly."

"You are unbelievable! When have unjust accusations against me ever stopped your mouth?"

"Since they may well involve my husband. You were with him at Judah's household. It seems you follow after him, like an eager puppy, wherever he goes. You came to me, feigning humility, bowing, and asking forgiveness. Then your next act was to straddle a donkey and chase after Jacob like the brazen slut you are!"

"You drove me away, Leah. I could endure your abuses no longer. I went to Father Jacob for his protection. And to mourn with the bereaved in Judah's house. Have you forgotten that my mother-in-law had died? I was there to offer comfort."

"It is your method of offering comfort I want to know about."

"You have a foul mind. And a disgusting mouth to match it."

"Rail against me if you wish, Tamar, but I will prove to you my heart can be merciful. I will take the child and raise it as my own."

Tamar was speechless for a time. Then she asked, "Why would you propose such a thing?"

"To save Jacob's reputation. I can claim that the child is mine. The townspeople know Jacob to be a righteous man. Perhaps they will believe God sent us a child in our old age, as was the case for our ancestors, Abraham and Sarah."

Tamar laughed again at the absurdity. Then she shook her head in derision and said, "Leah, I do believe you are quite mad. Did it ever occur to you that your husband's reputation might be brought equally low by falsehood?"

Leah tried another approach: "Tamar, if you care for Jacob—if you want the gossip to stop—then do this thing I ask. It will raise my standing in my husband's eyes if I show you mercy, and it will please him if I sacrifice myself to save him from ridicule."

"Oh," mused Tamar. "Now I finally see what this is about. You offer to be a sacrificial lamb for Father Jacob. You wish to win his favor."

"Exactly."

"Well, I am sorry to disappoint you, Leah, but the child is not Father Jacob's." The words were out before Tamar realized what she had said. She had admitted that Leah's suspicions were accompanied by grounds for censure. In her efforts to exonerate Father Jacob, she had condemned herself. She cursed her stupidity, a slip of the lip that cast her into the snare of her enemy.

"Then you *are* with child!" Leah gloated, pointing an accusing finger at Tamar. "I knew it! And by whoredom! This is even better. Since you are unmarried, you are guilty of breaking the law. Now we will see who is favored in Jacob's eyes. You shall burn, Tamar. You shall burn!"

No effort was made to stop Leah as she bounded out the doorway, heading straight for Jacob's tent. Tamar pursed her lips and tried to think of a way to save herself and still keep the identity of her child's father a secret. This was not Adullam. Here among Jehovah's people, a harlot was stoned or burned to death. Relationships between men and women were restricted to

221

wedlock, and she clearly had broken the law. She was guilty and deserved the full penalty.

Fear gripped Tamar's heart. Suppose Judah wanted the penalty upon her head for deceiving him? Instead of joy, resentment might well be Judah's reaction. Just when her heart began to thrill with victory and expectation, her whole world collapsed around her. This was no time to just sit by and think or to devise more schemes. She needed help from the only one who could give it. She ran as fast as she could to Jacob's tent, bursting in as he stood listening to Leah's tales.

"Do not listen to her, Father Jacob! You must let me defend myself and explain," she cried.

In an accusing and arrogant tone, Leah blurted, "What defense is there for whoredom?"

"Leave us, Leah. I will hear what Tamar has to say," Jacob said with quivering lips.

"But, my husband . . ." Leah protested.

"Leave us, I say! And if you value your life, you will speak no word of this—to anyone!"

Jacob's words were final. Leah left, but not before casting haughty glances toward Tamar.

Tamar stood silently before Jacob. Then she threw herself at his feet and let out a plaintive moan: "You were right. Taking God's will into my own hands has become my great undoing!"

"Sit down, child, and tell me that Leah's words are unfounded."

"Would that I could, but I cannot."

"Then . . . then you are with child?"

Tamar nodded but could speak no words.

"Who is the father?" Jacob asked.

"I did not want to say . . . not until . . . Oh, what a willful, wretched woman I am!"

"Tamar, this is a grave situation. But I cannot possibly help you unless you tell me the truth, the whole of it." Jacob looked like he was going to cry.

"I carry Judah's child."

"Judah's? How can that be?"

222

"I followed him to Adullam—before I came to you at Judah's camp to mourn for Shuah."

Jacob looked puzzled. "Well, if he came in unto you in Adullam, Tamar, why has he not taken you to wife, according to the laws of God?"

"Because he does not know."

"He does not know you are with child?"

"He does not even know he has lain with me. Oh, Father Jacob, it is confusing, I know. It seemed a marvelous, sensible idea at the time. But now, I see what a fool I have been . . ."

"Tamar, once again, I ask you: Tell me the whole truth, not a snatch here and there."

Tamar related the events that took place by the wall on the Adullam road. She left nothing out. She told of disguising herself, taking his gifts, and playing the harlot to conceal her identity from Judah. When she stopped speaking, Tamar stared at Jacob for his reaction.

"Incredible," was all Jacob said.

"Incredible that I claim to be a child of the true God, then turn my back on His laws to seek the ways of sin?" she asked, prompting him. "If that is your assessment, I could not agree with you more."

"No, Tamar. I meant it was incredible how we both followed a similar pattern, down to smallest details. We both usurped the covenant promise without a rightful claim. You wore the shroud of a temptress, I the sheepskins and robes of my brother, Esau. We both are guilty of resorting to disguises and deceiving a loved one to win a blessing from God!"

"Does that mean that you understand?"

"I can understand your sin because I practiced the same evil, but that, in no way, excuses or alters the situation. There always is a price to be paid." Jacob's eyes seemed very hurt and tired.

"I know, I know. You warned me. Eliezer gave me similar warnings. You both told me to be patient and to wait for God's timing, but I was so afraid . . ."

"Afraid the Creator of the Universe was incapable of working out plans for your life without assistance from you?"

"I suppose that is true also. I see it all so clearly now—now that it is too late to undo. Oh, Father Jacob, what must I do? What is to become of me?"

"Judah must be told, of course."

"Suppose he brings me before the people?"

"You know what will happen. The harlot is . . . is put to death." He squeezed his eyes shut.

"Will the Lord take the covenant blessing from me? This, above all, cannot be!"

"I know not, my daughter. In my case, God's will prevailed in spite of my shameful deed. We only can hope it will be the same for you—that God yet may find you a fit vessel for service. But we cannot, must not, try to work the matter out ourselves. We must pray as we have never prayed before. In this moment, you do not want justice, Tamar. You must pray for *mercy*!"

"I have ruined everything," Tamar lamented. "All my plans and dreams were in vain. Look at the time and effort I have wasted—all for nothing!"

"You have learned a hard and bitter lesson, Tamar. If you only had been patient! But it does no good to speak further. We cannot change what is over and done."

"Promise me one thing, Father Jacob." She grasped his arm and made him look at her.

Jacob was too vexed and sad and uncertain to agree to anything, but her pleading eyes compelled him to ask, "What is it you think I can promise you?"

"If Judah will not have me, if he wants me put to death, you must convince him to wait until after my child is born. Perhaps some day Judah will love his child—but even if he cannot, my babe must live! An innocent infant should not suffer for my sins."

"Tamar, all I can promise is that I shall pray and seek the Lord's guidance. Frequently, the innocent suffer for deeds of the guilty. My partiality led to losing my blessed Joseph. Perhaps your innocent child will have to pay for your folly as well. I do not know. I do not know."

Tamar rose and turned away to fight the tears she felt stinging her eyes. "A just God should not punish a sinless child!" she shouted defiantly.

"Do not blame God for *your* mistakes, Tamar! You conceived

224

your child in sin and willful disobedience. Whatever happens now is not to be laid to God's charge."

His words cut like a knife to Tamar's heart. She ran back to throw her arms about Jacob's neck and held on like a frightened child. Jacob stroked her head and embraced her with all his strength, trying to find words of comfort and reassurance to ease the pain he shared with her.

"Tamar," he said at last, "I know the misery you feel. Your love for Judah is as great as mine was for Rachel. Such love can drive us to do wrong things. We are alike in so many, many ways."

At those words, she looked up into his face. "If that is so, then I must believe God will forgive me, as He forgave you. I must cling to that as my only hope!" Then she pulled back from him to say, "But then, I have never seen angels or heard God's voice. I am not the anointed prophet you are. How can I possibly think it would be the same for me?"

There was pity in Jacob's voice as he said, "God is no respecter of persons, Tamar. His forgiveness is assured to you the moment you ask for it. It is Judah's forgiveness that is in question here. He is such a proud man. He will be wild with rage when he learns he has been tricked and outsmarted by a woman."

Resting her head on Jacob's knees, Tamar opined, "Then God must show us a way to make him forgive me, to make him understand."

Jacob bowed his head, and Tamar could tell he was praying silently. She felt the atmosphere charged with an unseen and powerful force, an electrifying magnificence that seemed to fill the room with a spiritual presence unlike anything she had ever known before. It made her tremble.

When Jacob finally raised his head, he said, "Here is what must be done, Tamar. Nathan will be sent to Judah to tell him that you are with child . . ."

"No! Judah cannot be told in such a manner! I must be the one to go do it," she objected.

Jacob's voice rose, commanding respect for his authority: "You must cease to argue and listen in silence. If you refuse, or if you think you can deal with this situation in a better way by yourself, then I wash my hands of this and leave you to whatever fate you prefer to devise!"

Shaken by the forcefulness of the proclamation, Tamar said meekly, "I place my hand upon my mouth and do yield. I see that my willfulness is not changed so easily, even now."

Jacob was encouraged by Tamar's response, so we went on. "As your father-in-law, Judah will have the final say in determining any judgment or punishment coming to you. He will be compelled to come here and speak to me first, knowing that I have been as a father to you."

"What will you say unto him?"

"I will not press him one way or another. Judah's rebellious temperament demands that he be the one to decide. The more I would plead for you, the more he would lean to the contrary."

"And then?"

"The matter will rest entirely in Judah's hands. Only the Lord God can change Judah's hard heart—not you or I or any human being on this earth."

"You will say nothing on my behalf? Nothing at all?" It seemed a totally illogical risk.

As if reading her thoughts, Jacob said, "The ways of God are not the ways of man. What seems least to make sense in human judgment often is the very thing the Lord has ordained."

"That," Tamar said with conviction, "has been true enough for me. The things I have done so far have seemed reasonable solutions to my problems. They all have ended in failure."

"Tamar, you said Judah gave you certain pledges. Do you still have them?"

"Yes. His staff, his ring, and three golden bracelets. They are all I have—treasures by which to remember him. They are hidden within my tent."

"Keep them ready for the appointed time. I will tell you later what you must do."

Tamar hesitated before saying, "I will not oppose you in anything you command me, but I must ask, if you will tell me: Why must Judah come here?"

"If you go to him, I cannot help you. By having Nathan deliver the news first, Judah will have time for the shock and heat of his anger to subside. Above all, you must not confront Judah before adequate preparations are made. Too many memories linger at Judah's home to cloud the issue and create barriers. Here, where I am in charge, Judah will be more objective."

"I see. And I venture a journey on a jogging donkey would not be good for me in my state anyway." Tamar sighed and resigned herself to the difficult task of making no further plans of her own. She looked down at the largeness of her body. "I think I must carry more than one baby next to my heart. Or this grandchild of yours is a giant. I have grown immense so quickly."

"Twins have been known to grace my family. I am a twin, as are my sons, Simeon and Levi. Another bond of similarity between us," Jacob said, trying to smile.

"It would seem we share many such similarities, the worst of them being we both are masters of deceit."

"Yes, my daughter, but that is but a perversion of God's gifts. He gives us blessings of wisdom and wit. It is only when we do not use the gifts in concert with His will that we lapse into sin and use our wits to deceive. Then the blessing is transformed into a curse."

"Do you think I shall ever learn how to know God's will, as you do?"

"Of course. Just do the opposite of what makes sense in that obstinate brain of yours." He was trying to use humor to ease the tension. Although he would never tell her so, Jacob secretly could not help but admire Tamar's slyness in her conquest of his son. She, a woman, had done what no man could do in making Judah bow to her will.

"Father Jacob, do you think Judah will ever forgive me for deceiving him?"

"We both know he will resent being duped. But when he learns that he will have a child to replace those he has lost, when he recognizes he is not guiltless in creating this life, he must accuse himself as well as you. He is not without a conscience, and that is what we must depend upon."

"Even if Judah does not decree my death sentence, I hold lit-

227

tle hope that he will want me for his wife—not after what I have done."

"He might do so—for the child's sake. Who can know Judah's mind? It already carries the weight of much unspoken guilt. He may not want to cause more deaths added to all the others."

Tamar rose to leave, and then remembered another difficulty to be faced. "What of Leah and the other women? Will they not spread the news of my condition? I shall bring disgrace to your house. Oh, Father Jacob, I never meant to hurt you, of all people in the world!"

"Like a pebble thrown into a brook, the stone of sin creates ever-widening circles before it reaches its depths. I shall command silence from the women, but if the news becomes known, we shall bear the shame as we have borne other sorrows. Now, no more questions. I am weary."

She went to kiss him before leaving, looked into his sad eyes, and said, "I am so unworthy, I do not see why you even bother to try and help me."

"My mother helped me escape when my life was in danger. My brother Esau sought to kill me for my deceit in taking his blessing. Someone must help those who cannot help themselves."

"Your history seems to be repeating itself in me, does it not?" Tamar said.

"Yes, but remember who controls history—your destiny and mine. We both must be in constant prayer about this matter."

"I am so ashamed. I have avoided my private prayers for so long, I am afraid I do not know how to entreat the Lord any more."

"When one has sinned, it seems difficult to seek God's face. I remember that feeling. But I have learned such is the very time one *must* pray. When you feel far from the Lord, Tamar, do not be confused about who has moved away. Do not deny yourself the joy of restored communion with a loving, forgiving God who desires that you should come to Him."

"I no longer have illusions of seeking the covenant blessing," Tamar said with a desolate sigh or resignation. "I know my sin has made me unworthy of that. But I would like to seek restored communion with the Lord. If ever anyone needed prayer, it is I."

Worry lines faded from Jacob's face, and a smile came to his lips. "Tamar, my hopes for you are now revived! A humble confession of unworthiness is one's first step back to God's paths of righteousness. If you keep this new, repentant heart and submissive attitude, then the Lord yet may fulfill His purposes through you."

Tamar fell to her knees. With contrite tears and supplications, she threw herself into a prayer such as she never had prayed before. With Jacob beside her, they knelt together there for a very long time.

Fourteen

Judah lost no time in joining Nathan on the return trip to Jacob's tents. After receiving the news of Tamar's pregnancy and his father's request for an audience to decide her fate, Judah growled in his beard, threw together a few belongings, and departed immediately.

Nathan was used to delivering messages, even very personal ones, with the dispassionate objectivity Jacob expected. Nathan was trusted because he did not betray confidences nor discuss contents of messages with anyone except his master. But Jacob had made exceptions when it came to Judah. The first time was when Jacob had Nathan befriend and reside with Judah after Shelah's death. The second time was now. Jacob told Nathan more about Tamar's situation than the messenger let on. Nathan also knew more than Judah was told in Jacob's message. Nathan's mission was to have personal conversations and to subdue Judah's rage before he met with Jacob.

"The paths between your tents and your father's are much traveled of late," Nathan said as they rode along. It was difficult to think of small talk or pleasantries with Judah so distressed.

"Only since Tamar came back," Judah returned. His mind could not be diverted from the purpose of the journey. "When did the shameful news about my daughter-in-law come to light?"

"I do not know exactly, Master Judah. Just recently, I believe."

Judah's lips were drawn into a firm, even line as he spoke. "Is there much talk about it? I mean, has the scandal spread unto the townspeople?"

"I think not. Tamar remains in her tent and seldom ventures beyond my master's property. I have never known her to enter the town. And Master Jacob forbade the few who know of her situation to speak of it."

"That, at least, is a mercy. That wretched she-devil would destroy us all. Do you know, Nathan, Tamar even tried to seduce me?" Judah wondered why being with Nathan seemed to loosen his tongue. Past months of seclusion may have made him eager for conversation.

"She seduced you?" the messenger repeated. That was hard for Nathan to believe.

"Yes. At least, she tried. She returned seeking to marry Shelah, but she practiced her wiles on me. Her husbands barely cold in their tombs and she was back to devour my household."

"And you turned her away?"

"I never would give my manhood to such a woman! She is an enticing temptress who may offer momentary pleasure, but only long-lasting grief or successive deaths follow afterward."

"I thought Tamar was intended for Shelah. Why would she desire you?"

"She wanted everyone . . . anyone! She is a spider waiting for the next foolish victim to fall into her poisonous web."

"That is a very different picture than what I have observed. Many men have tried to seek her favors with no sign of encouragement from her. They have told me so."

"It must be that my family is the only one she is determined to destroy. If not by death, then by shame and disgrace. No more! She will cast spells and work her evil practices no more."

"Will you bring her before the council?"

"Oh, Nathan, I do not know. At first hearing of the news, I wanted Tamar to burn. But a public execution would destroy my father's good name. I do not wish to bring shame upon him, but Tamar must be made to pay for her sins!"

"It is wise of you to come and discuss the matter with Master Jacob before making your decision. You are right to say he would be hurt, for he loves Tamar dearly, as his own daughter."

"I know. I know. But she cannot hide behind him in this matter. She has gone too far."

"Will you allow her to offer an explanation before you decide her fate?"

"Explanation? What explanation other than harlotry? And

231

to think I once considered taking her as my wife." Then Judah added quickly, "Only to save Shelah from her grasp, of course."

"That was most noble of you, Master Judah." Nathan paused—as if a new idea had come to him—before he stated what Jacob wanted him to propose: "What a perfect solution! What a hero you would be to resolve this matter by taking Tamar as your wife now!"

"Are you completely mad?"

"I meant only that it would save the family honor."

"It would save the miserable hide of an Ishtar!"

"Very well. I just was trying to think of a less drastic solution than an open trial and the spectacle of a public burning. If Tamar's sin becomes common knowledge, it will mean disgrace for us all. The townsfolk will screech their scorns and curses after you and your father wherever you go. Will you both not become known as harborers of a harlot?"

"I will do my best to prevent that by sending Tamar back to the Baal country from which she came. Why should I wish to sacrifice myself to save a common whore?"

Nathan did not respond to Judah's rhetorical question. Before saying more, he would allow Judah to meditate upon the ugly consequences of any legal recourse against Tamar. They rode along in silence for a long time before the conversation continued.

"Nathan!" Judah cried. "You, yourself, said Tamar would be labeled a harlot. The fact that she is unmarried and with child proves that she seeks to lie with those other than my family. Has she named the father of the child?"

"If she has, I was not given the information to include in my message to you."

"Think, Nathan! Who has been in her company?"

"Only your father, Eliezer, and Benjamin. Surely, you cannot believe any of them have been intimate with Tamar?"

"No. Too old and too young. It must be someone else." Judah thought for a moment and then let out a shrieking wail.

"What is it?" Nathan asked in alarm.

Judah was remembering Cumi's words. She said Shelah spoke of being with Tamar. Judah had dismissed the thought because Cumi said Shelah only bragged of romantic exploits to impress her. But what if it were true? If Tamar had defiled his youngest son, there would be no need for a trial. He would kill her himself!

"Master Judah, what made you cry out?" Nathan asked again.

"I think I know who has fathered Tamar's child."

Judah did not say more. They had arrived at their destination.

As Nathan led their beasts away, Judah paused before going directly to his father. He needed to compose himself. His eyes wandered about the familiar sights as a flood of childhood memories returned. There was the sprawling house of hair in which his father dwelt. Over there, the women's quarters where he had grown up. Yonder, the tree of wisdom where he sat with Eliezer for his lessons or played beneath the spreading branches. Farther away, the tents where his brothers and their families resided. In between, the servants' quarters, the stables, the warehouses and storage bins. Something within him stirred with a nostalgic yearning to return to happier times. But with those sentiments also came the old guilt that seemed to deepen at his return. He knew it was better to dwell by himself in loneliness than to be here with those who would be constant reminders of his past sin.

Judah forced himself to face his father. He ducked his head under the flap that hung over the entrance to Jacob's tent and called out to announce himself.

"Come in, Judah. Peace unto you, my son," Jacob said, arising from a stool beside his table. "I am glad you have come."

Jacob embraced his son's tense and rigid shoulders and gestured toward another table-side stool. Judah did not move as he said crisply, "I prefer to stand, if you do not mind, Israel."

"As you wish," Jacob said as he resumed his seat and placed his lame leg upon the stool which Judah had refused.

"Let us get to the point at once," Judah said abruptly. "Who is the father of Tamar's child?"

"That," Jacob drawled slowly, "you will have to inquire at Tamar's mouth."

"She has not told you?"

"She does not want his name to be ridiculed. She bears her shame alone."

Judah scoffed, "Come now, Israel! You would make of our street whore a noble protector of her companion? I know you never can see evil in your darling, but you cannot expect me to believe she thinks of anyone but herself."

"Believe what you will, Judah, but the truth is this—she still loves the father of her child and would do anything to avoid hurting him."

"You know for a fact that the father is living?"

"Yes, he is very much alive."

"If that is true, it gives me some relief. I was afraid she had seduced Shelah before he died."

"I think a calculation of the time period of Shelah's tragic accident will disprove your hasty suspicion. Benjamin and I were within your tents at that time. Tamar arrived to join us *after* Shelah's death. Tamar's child was conceived while you were away, residing in Adullam."

"She must be made to confess his name. He stands as guilty as she is."

"As you say, Judah. I know that you, as Tamar's father-in-law, must administer judgment upon her for the deed. Shall I send for her that you may examine her now?"

"No! I have no wish to see Tamar. Let us first discuss what is to be done with her."

"The decision, as I have said, is yours to make."

"If justice is to be served, the law requires that she be put to death!"

Without looking at his son, Jacob said, almost absent-mindedly, "It always amazes me how accusers can be so sensitive to the sins of others. I often wonder if the man who puts the torch to a convicted harlot or throws a stone to bloody her head is himself without sin."

For a brief instant, Judah's mind flashed back to the Adullam road and the awful night he had debased himself ravaging a harlot. His father's words achieved their desired effect.

In a much calmer tone now, Judah said, "I think I shall sit

234

down after all." He placed a cushion upon the floor and wiped his brow with his sleeve. "I am more weary from my journey than I thought."

Passing Judah a cup of wine and a wet towel to wipe his face, Jacob said, "Now, what was it you were saying, my son?"

"I say Tamar is thrice guilty if she will not speak the name of her consort, marry him, nor leave this place immediately before her shame contaminates the entire family."

"I think Tamar would prefer to die rather than return to her heathen homeland. The possibility of her marrying her child's father, however, still may be an option—once he has been told of her condition and if he should be willing. Tamar is not at all certain he will be."

"The man does not know he is father to Tamar's unborn child?"

"Not as yet. Tamar wanted the entire matter left to your wise counsel, Judah."

"If my judgment were the only consideration, then I would say she should be burned. She has committed one abomination upon another to besmirch her mourning garments."

"As you say, Judah. How is it you want the trial conducted? Will you have the townspeople come to drag Tamar from her tent, bind her, and parade her through the streets to the place of judgment and then shout and applaud as she slowly burns to death?"

Judah knew his father's proposal was made as vividly unbecoming as possible. But why was he being so agreeable—offering no protests or pleas for mercy for Tamar? Why would Tamar want Judah's involvement in her sordid affair? Something very suspicious was going on here.

"You play upon me as the shepherd upon his lute," Judah said. "You think I do not see through you? You were hoping I would not want Tamar subjected to torment, but you are wrong, Israel. I should like her to suffer so severely that she would welcome the flames to her flesh. I would like to hear her screams as crowds taunted and condemned her with stones and torches raised high against her . . ."

Jacob no longer could hide his feelings. His drooping head

and two, small tears that ran from his thick-lidded eyes spoke the meaning of words he could not utter.

Making a sweeping gesture as if erasing his outburst, Judah said, "No, Israel, I repent of my words. It must not be in the way of a public display for all the world to see. That was my anger speaking just now. There must be a more reasonable way to dispose of this abomination."

Lifting his head, Jacob asked, "What, then, would you have done with her?"

"Could she not be put to death quietly—a private council and secret execution?"

"Judah, you know word could not be kept from spreading throughout the countryside. It would be an even greater shame to appear to hide and cover the transgression than to have an honest confession and open execution."

Judah thought for a while before responding. "Very well. Let no blood be spilled. I am weary of death and destruction. Tamar must be sent away, never to return here again. Let her go and take her offspring of sin with her."

Jacob's face brightened slightly as he nodded. "Banishment is a kinder fate than death, as you say, Judah. That, indeed, would be merciful of you. But who would care for her or provide for her and her child? None of her own people will take her back again. They said so when she left to return to you for her pledge of a husband. No one would marry a woman with a bastard child."

"That is Tamar's concern, not yours or mine. Let her give the child away and beg in the streets. Let the father of the child do his duty as a man. I only know I do not want to lay eyes upon her ever again!"

"You do not wish to have her brought before you here that you may question her?"

Suddenly Judah remembered Tamar had not identified her secret lover. In spite of his father's assurance that it was not Shelah, a nagging doubt still remained. Tamar might have lied to Israel. Before Tamar was sent away, Judah needed to defy her brazen refusal to answer that one question, not only because he was curious, but also because another name—any name other than Shelah's—would put that matter to rest. If it should be Shelah's child, how could it be rejected? How could he banish his own grandchild to be born unnamed and unloved? He did not wish to send his flesh and blood to die from neglect and poverty. That would be only more guilt than he carried already.

"Let Tamar be brought forward," Judah said at last. "I would have the harlot name her partner in crime, the man who should be given the opportunity to right this wrong, take Tamar away, and save us all from further dealings with her." To himself, Judah thought, *If no man can be named, it could be because the father lies dead in his grave.*

Jacob removed a bell from his table, arose, and limped to the curtained doorway. He rang the bell and spoke to the servant who appeared at the summons. Then the servant ran in the direction of Tamar's tent, and Jacob returned to his seat at the table.

"Judah, I think you still believe Shelah is the guilty father. Am I right?" asked Jacob.

"Do not call my son guilty!" Judah roared. "Should he be the one named, he had to have been beguiled and defenseless before the truly guilty one. If Tamar played the temptress to my weakling boy, there will be no further talk of mercy for her."

"I think you place too much blame on one side, Judah. God gives man the capacity to resist even the strongest temptation. Tamar was not alone in her guilt, but Shelah shared none with her."

"You have only Tamar's word—the word of a slut—on that, Israel. What of Tamar's obsession with our lineage for the sake of the covenant blessing? That would drive her to any lengths to worm her way into my family. She is not above seducing anyone, even a helpless boy."

There was an authoritative, unequivocal quality in Jacob's tone as he said, "I tell you in all truth, Judah, Shelah did not sire Tamar's child."

Judah did not know whether to be more relieved or outraged: "Then why has the man not been told? Why have you not demanded that he step forward to claim his offspring? What kind of man should be allowed to hide behind a woman's skirts to deny his duty?"

237

"A very weak and cowardly man perhaps?"

"Israel, if we can get Tamar to name and marry this man, then all will be well. There will be no scandal, no execution. And all of us will be free of this vile atrocity once and for all!"

"You speak in great wisdom, my son. That does seem the best of all possible solutions. We must insist that Tamar name the man and arrange for her wedding with him as soon as possible."

Jacob had no sooner uttered the words than the servant reappeared in the doorway. In one of his hands he carried a gold-knobbed walking staff. In the other, he carried a pillow draped with a harlot's veil that lay beneath a signet ring and three golden bracelets. He placed the items at Judah's feet and bowed.

The servant said, "Tamar has instructed me to bring these to Master Judah and to say that these pledges would speak for her." Then he bowed again and left.

At the sight of the objects, Judah's face blanched, drained of all color, and became ghostly white. Then it changed to a fiery red. The color rushed to the roots of his hair and seemed to blaze from his very eyes. He rose to his full height and stared down at the familiar pledges, too dumbfounded to speak.

Jacob asked, "What troubles you, my son?"

When Judah could find voice enough, he asked breathlessly, "These things were in Tamar's possession?"

"Yes," Jacob answered. "Tamar has said they belong to the man who got her with child. She said he who can discern whose they are also can name the guilty man."

To Judah's memory came the familiar, penetrating eyes of the woman by the wall, the one who sang her love song by the gate and offered stolen moments of love. Then his mind flashed back to the raw, unbridled passion that unleashed great cruelty and everlasting shame. There was no escaping the truth: He was the man! He was the man!

After a long silence, Judah spoke: "I see, Israel, that you plot with Tamar against me. You abet her in laying a second snare for me. First, I was lured on the Adullam road, and, now and here, another entrapment. Why, you even make me set my own sentence: 'Let the man step forward to do his duty and marry

238

Tamar, that there be no scandal.' How you must gloat at my utter stupidity!"

"It is not as you think, Judah . . ."

"I can understand how Tamar would resort to such loathsome trickery, but you—you, Israel? How could a loving father stoop to conspire with her against me?"

"I had nothing to do with Tamar's despicable conduct in Adullam. She is guilty, and there is no denying that. My only part in all this came afterward—when she confessed her sin to me and asked for my prayers. She knows she has wronged you and deeply regrets her transgressions. Every word I spoke to you on her behalf has been the truth. She awaits your judgment to determine her fate. My concern now is to try and bring some good from all this evil."

There was a taunting sneer in Judah's voice as he said, "Oh, I congratulate you, Israel. You and Tamar are both to be commended for your success. I have no defense against either of you! I deserve this. It is just retribution for a fool's inexcusable folly!"

"Do not speak so cynically," Jacob pleaded. "You have much cause for anger toward Tamar. But I pray you will find mercy enough in your heart to forgive her—for you, likewise, have much for which to seek forgiveness."

"Forgive her? There is nothing to forgive, is there? You have just said I am as guilty as is she. More so! In this moment, she stands more righteous, more justified than I." Judah threw up his hands in a gesture of helpless defeat.

"None of us can undo the past," Jacob said sorrowfully. "But we still may choose to create a better future. Go to Tamar, Judah. Tamar loves you more than you may ever realize. It was her deep love for you that goaded her to have you, at any cost. Now she pays that cost in the great pain of regret for deceiving you. She has changed, Judah. She will make you a good wife."

Judah gazed at his father in amazement. Slowly, his dismay turned to scorn, and he began to laugh, almost hysterically, as he said, "You would have me go to her, would you? You would send me forth to abide more trickery? Have I not yet endured enough that you wish me to seek further torments she has planned? Israel, you make me to laugh!"

"My son, it is time to forget the past—both yours and Tamar's. God can bless your union with grace and happiness if you will close this sad chapter. Do so, before there is more suffering."

"Oh, I am to forget now, is that it? Forget that Tamar brought death to my sons and brought fear to my wife's terrified heart before she died? Shall I also forget that Tamar laid in wait for me as a harlot and now will bear me a child conceived in sin?"

"Yes," answered Jacob emphatically. "I ask you to forget everything—both what you know to be true and whatever distorted truth you may harbor in your tormented imagination. Forget that you played the drunken lecher and defiled yourself with one you took for a harlot. Forget you ran off to a sinful land when you should have been home giving comfort to your motherless son. Think of a better future for yourself than any of those past mistakes."

Judah began to pace restlessly as he responded: "Even if I could forget all that, as you say, before many days Tamar's child would force me to remember."

"It is *your* child also, Judah!"

Judah grimaced at the words. "I can bear no more, Israel. I am weary. I will go now to my brother's tent and ask Reuben if I am still welcome there to stay this night as his guest."

"And Tamar? What have you decided regarding Tamar?"

"What choice have I? You and she have won. I concede the defeat."

Jacob did not try to stop Judah as he left without a kiss or word of farewell. The old man merely watched his son walk away weary, heavy shouldered, and distraught. He also saw Tamar waiting nearby under the tree of wisdom. He saw her draw near to Judah with cautious steps and open her arms to him. When Judah stopped and reluctantly turned to face her, Jacob could watch no more. He went to his feeble knees in prayer.

"Judah!" Tamar called softly, coming up behind him. "Judah, please stop, I pray you, for I would speak a word with you."

"I have nothing to say unto you," he replied without looking at her.

"Judah, turn not from me. If not for my sake, hear me for the sake of your child that I carry next to my heart."

Slowly, he turned to meet her eyes, those devastating eyes. "For that hold upon me, you will pay dearly, Tamar."

Lowering her eyes in shame, she said, "As well I should. I already have suffered, and I am prepared to take whatever more you deem to be my just punishment for unforgivable acts against you. But you must believe me, I never intended to hurt you or cause you pain."

"You could not hurt me, Tamar. You have taken from me all that is capable of feeling anything."

"Will you at least listen to my reasons . . . ?"

"I care not what selfishness motivated you to deceive me, Tamar. The deed is done."

"Yes, it was selfishness—a selfish desire to partake of the promised covenant with you, Judah, but it was more than that. My greatest selfishness was my loving you and wanting you so desperately that I would do anything to have you—even for one, stolen moment."

"Was it love to debase yourself before me?"

"It was my mistake to think so. And I would do it all again if it could win even your slightest affection for me."

"And would you go so far as to debase me again as well?"

"For that I beg your forgiveness. I never realized . . ."

"Enough, Tamar. I bear you no malice. My father has shown me I cannot condemn you without also condemning myself. I was the more sinful one. I deserve to go to the burning stake—not you."

"Oh, Judah, I regret that you learned about the baby from Father Jacob's lips. I wanted so much to come to you myself and beg you to forgive me—not for giving myself unto you, not for carrying your child, but for resorting to pretense and guile. It was wrong of me. I know that now, and I am truly, truly sorry. Please believe me!"

"I believe you should be thankful you did not come to me before now. Were I not here on the sacred ground where my father dwells, I might have destroyed you at the hearing!"

"I can understand that, Judah. I thought I was so wise in trying to outwit you. Now I see how utterly stupid it was. Tell me, what can I do to atone for my sin?"

241

"That is between you and God. I seek no retribution. Just stay away from me. That is all I will ask of you."

"What . . . what of your child?"

"I will not destroy the fruit of my loins, Tamar. I cannot make an innocent child suffer for the sins we both committed against Jehovah that night."

"Then my life is spared until I bring forth our son?"

"Your life—for what it is worth—will not be required at my hand. I said I might have destroyed you, had you come to me earlier with this confession. That would have been my reaction in the heat of rage. I am not outraged now, Tamar. The time of my anger is spent."

"What would you have me do?"

"Do? Why, you must marry me, of course," he said lightly. "I am duty-bound to wed you now, to honor the child, for the sake of my father's honor. Not for my own, for I have none. Certainly not to save what may be left of yours. Marrying you will be the punishment due me for my sin. You will come to live within my tents, Tamar. But do not seek to be unto me a wife."

"I do not understand, Judah."

"Do you think—after that debauchery in the darkness of a secluded street—that I could ever come to you in the sacred marriage act? The beauty of married love has been forever destroyed between us, Tamar. I do not want to look upon you and be reminded of myself that night."

She tried to reach for his hand, but he drew away. "Judah," she whispered tenderly, "that night, neither of us acted as we should. I know the way you behaved toward me was brought on by your grief over losing Shuah . . . and the evil influence of the Adullamites. You are no more like that than I am really a harlot. I swear to you, that night was the only time I ever was with a man other than my husbands."

"Even if I believed you, it would make no difference. I never can touch you again. Never!"

Tamar bit her lip to keep it from quivering. "If that is my punishment, I will bear it most gladly. To be your wife—even in name only, for the sake of our child—is so much more than I deserve. Thank you, Judah."

242

"You owe no thanks to me. You owe me *nothing*. That is just what I shall expect from you after we go through another deception together—the pretense of a marriage. That will be the final indignity you will hurl upon me, Tamar. Then there will be nothing left you can take from me."

"I can endure that. Perhaps with time, if I try hard to please you in every way, perhaps I can prove myself to you and earn the love and respect I have shattered."

He laughed. "Do not even try, for it will do you no good."

She was overcome with pity for him and incrimination for herself. The mighty lion was defeated. He seemed so lifeless, so lost. And she was responsible.

"Oh, Judah!" she cried. "My beloved, what have I done to you?"

"Why, you have opened my eyes!" Judah replied, walking in circles to pour out his stored-up feelings. "You have shown me myself and how senseless I am. Do you know, Tamar, I actually was thinking I was in love with you? I entertained all kinds of silly whims—like coming to you, pledging my devotion, and asking for your hand. Can you imagine anything so ridiculous? There I was in Adullam, feeling sorry for your plight in losing two husbands and thinking I could make it all up to you. I remembered how I had loved you, even while you lived in my household as my daughter-in-law, and how jealous I was of my two sons for having you. I remembered how lovely you were that night you came back for Shelah, and how I desired you for myself. I have no such foolish notions now—nor will I ever have again."

"You loved me and wanted me, Judah?" Tamar repeated, scarcely believing what she had heard. "Oh, there were times when I thought so, but I never was sure. There were just as many times when you rejected me and blamed me for things I had not done. You made me believe the only way I could ever have your love was to steal it."

"It grieves me to admit it, but since I do not ever again expect to have a conversation with you like this one, I will say it—I loved you! Why do you think I wanted you sent away? I did not trust myself near you. I did not want to betray Shuah, and if you had stayed . . . I would have . . . Oh, Tamar, why did you have to do this to me? To us?" Judah moaned.

"I could not believe you would ever want me. I wanted you more than anything in the world, but I felt my longings were hopeless. I felt unworthy of you."

"That is a lie! How can you say unworthy of me? You must have thought me nothing more than a debased whoremonger, good for nothing but a liaison with a wayside temptress."

"No! I thought only that it would take the festival crowd and mountain wine and lurid orgies to make your forget your virtue and to weaken your resistance to me."

"Could you not give me credit for even one decent emotion? Yes, I was weakened in Adullam, and I shall not soon recover from that weakness. You drained all strength from me."

"Is there nothing I can do or say to redeem myself in your eyes?"

"Not unless you can give back respect for myself, which I have lost. I traded that for trinkets and a walking staff, remember? Be content, Tamar. You have what you set out to obtain."

"No, I have it not!" she cried. "I still want your love."

"I have none to give. Just pray the child you carry is the son you wanted from me. If you bear a daughter, there is no second chance!"

Tamar knew he hurt her only because she had hurt him, wounded his pride. She held back tears she knew would fall later and said, "As you wish, Judah. I am content to do your bidding."

It was the same whispering, submissive spirit Judah remembered on the Adullam road. He loved her. He hated her. He could not bear to be in her presence any longer.

Walking away, Judah said, "I am weary. No more talk. I wish I had been the one to die."

As she watched him go, she recalled Eliezer's prophetic warning given to a willful, impatient woman: "You may get what you want, Tamar, and then lose all that you might have had."

Fifteen

"Israel, I beseech you, do not ask this of me," Judah begged. "I want only to take the burden you thrust upon me and be gone from here!"

"Judah, hear me. A semblance of propriety must be brought to bear upon this undignified situation."

"And you think it dignified to make a mockery of sacred marriage? You would prepare a wedding feast and call my brothers to celebrate the glad occasion when I must marry Tamar? I suppose you wish to adorn the bride in a virgin's girdle and veil as well?"

"Speak reasonably, my son. Of course I would not suggest such a thing. I only ask that you abide by the tradition of our sacred rites and that your relatives be present to witness the union. If ever a marriage needed God's blessing, it is this one. You and Tamar have brought enough dishonor to this family. I have never asked anything of you, even though there is much you owe me. Please do this one honorable thing, for my sake."

Judah knew his father spoke truthfully about a debt being owed. When Judah sold Joseph into slavery, Israel lost his godly, favored son and paid for it through years of grief and pain. Now Israel was enslaving Judah, and the cost would be lost pride and painful years married to Tamar. Judah had wanted to leave immediately the morning after a sleepless night within the tent of his eldest brother, Reuben. But his father had sent for him and informed him that he must remain until arrangements were made for a proper wedding. To Judah, there was nothing proper about it. It was hypocrisy and sacrilege. Worse, suffering through it did not settle the debt owed his father.

"I can just see the smug faces of all the relatives as they throw myrtle garlands with one hand and laugh us to scorn behind the other!" Judah complained.

"Not so, Judah. There are few who even know that Tamar carries your child—and they will respect your honoring the sacred rites of marriage, late as it may be to observe them."

Judah shrugged in surrender, knowing the futility of further argument. He would have to submit to this final degradation, telling himself it was but further evidence of God's continuing punishment for his grievous sins.

Tamar also was displeased with the thought of Jacob's huge family witnessing her marriage and making her a target for more ridicule. She did take comfort, however, in knowing that Father Jacob's blessing would be pronounced as she and Judah clasped hands upon his knees at the ceremony. Many prayers and blessings would be needed on her wedding day—and beyond.

Two days later, there was a quick and quiet ceremony. The marriage feast which followed was unlike those that customarily accompanied a gala event. The servants remarked that the atmosphere seemed more in keeping with a funeral procession than a wedding party.

Adults at the ceremony extended the expected courtesies without undue displays of emotion. Leah and the other women obeyed Jacob's command to be civil and to keep silent, lest one word of gossip bring his wrath upon them. They did allow themselves the secret pleasure of frowning with contempt at Tamar when they caught her eye and when Jacob was not looking.

Only the children, oblivious to anything but excitement on a festival day, thoroughly enjoyed themselves. They laughed, danced, and sang as they scattered flowers everywhere. Several of Jacob's older grandchildren decorated the cart that would take the bride and groom homeward to Judah's tents. Then they formed a procession, carrying cymbals and tambourines to parade past the wedding pair. They chanted their blessings and threw blossoms into the bride's lap.

Tamar received the flowers with glistening eyes. She forced a smile to her lips, but the tears in her eyes were not those joyous ones that ordinarily bespoke happy occasions. Tamar sensed the rigidity of Judah's body beside her and thought, *Oh, my darling, I know how painful this is for you. Would that I could ease the pain, even as I have brought it upon you.*

Judah did not look at Tamar, nor at his father. Mostly, he searched the faces of the brothers he had avoided so long—first by running off to shepherd flocks in Adullam, later by moving his own family away from theirs when he no longer could stand being reminded of their mutual guilt. It had been many years since all the brothers were gathered together in one place. Judah was the one always conspicuous by his absence at family gatherings and celebrations. Now, he was the conspicuous honor guest, and he knew his brothers shared his distaste for it. Judah was the brothers' condemnation personified, a goad to remember what they preferred to ignore.

It amazed Judah that his brothers seemed so carefree and serene. Their faces did not bear any marks of deep remorse for the conspiracy against Joseph. They married, produced families, tended their flocks, and forgot shameful deeds of long ago. Judah longed for such forgetfulness.

Judah's half-brothers—Dan, Asher, Gad, and Naphtali—all were standing together, laughing at an obscene joke Asher was telling. Nearby stood Simeon and Levi, the boisterous twins who always were together, usually to cause trouble of some kind.

Moving his eyes from the troublemakers, Judah glanced toward a sprawling tree that cast its shade upon two more, Issachar and Zebulum. They—along with Reuben, the twins, and Judah—were Leah's six sons, all true brothers. But Judah felt no bond of brotherhood with these men. The only one he could stomach was Reuben, perhaps because the eldest was not party to the selling of Joseph. Oh, he was part of the cover-up lies told to Israel, but Judah always felt that Reuben was capable of feeling regret. Joseph and Benjamin were Rachel's sons. Judah was kinder and closer to Benjamin, the motherless, lonely one who suffered the other brothers' disdain, as had Joseph before him. Judah tried to give Benjamin what had been denied Joseph, his older brother.

While other brothers kept themselves apart from the wedding couple, Reuben sat beside Judah, trying to be supportive and jovial in spite of sideways smirks from his siblings. The women sat in little clusters, holding their infants and keeping the toddlers away from the center of things. As usual, Benjamin was seated at his father's right hand. It was an honored position, but he would have preferred to be allowed to romp and frolic with the other young people. Leah, Bilhah, and Zilpha assumed less favored positions at Jacob's left as he hosted the spreading feast.

Reuben tried to think of something to say to jolt Judah from his somber mood: "Only for you, brother Judah, would I dress in these soft-flowing wedding garments. I am out of character in this disgusting, fancy attire. I much prefer my shepherd's apron and leather leg straps."

"I am sorry this has been inflicted upon you," Judah replied, staring straight ahead with absolutely no expression on his face. "But I am certain you could not be as uncomfortable as I."

"But you, at least, look pretty with your hair slicked back with oil and your beard neatly trimmed. Careful, or someone will be mistaking you for the bride," he teased.

Reuben was tall and similarly built to Judah. Many said they favored each other, but Reuben's complexion was ruddier and his face fleshier. He had a pugnacious expression and the rugged appearance of one acquainted with harsh outdoor life. Both belied his gentle, amiable nature.

"Have a piece of mutton," Reuben offered, holding a fleshy piece of meat in his powerful hand and extending it to Judah.

"No, Reuben. I am not hungry. In fact, I feel tired and ill. Will you make my apologies to our father? I think I shall go lie down in your tent for a while."

"Judah, you cannot do that. You are the guest of honor!"

"I am a reluctant guest, and nothing here should be honored—least of all, me. I can stand this mockery no longer!" With that, Judah rose to walk toward Reuben's tent.

Judah knew a new tent awaited him—a bridal chamber strewn with flowers and furnished with a bed bedecked with perfumed linen. Such it had been when he first took Shuah to the marriage bed to partake of what nature contrived for wedded bliss. Such it was for Tamar when she first gave her virginity to Judah's firstborn son. Such it could never be again—for either of them.

Judah dismissed the absurdity of sharing a bridal chamber

with Tamar. There had been too many frauds already. As soon after the celebration as possible, he planned to leave for home.

Becoming alarmed at seeing Judah's sudden departure, Tamar moved herself closer to Reuben to inquire, "Where is Judah going? What is wrong?"

Reuben patted the anxious hand upon his arm and said, "Do not fret, Tamar. Judah goes to rest for a while. I venture all the food and excitements have been too much for our bridegroom."

"Reuben, I need to speak with you—alone, away from this crowd."

"But we cannot leave the wedding feast. First Judah, then you and I? Father will be livid."

"I will go first—toward your tent. The others will believe that Judah and I have slipped away alone for a romantic moment or something. Wait a while, and then tell Father Jacob you have something to attend to—anything. Then follow me straightaway. I will wait for you yonder behind the tent of your wives."

Without awaiting Reuben's reply, Tamar slipped quietly away. Reuben watched her follow the path Judah had taken, but then she detoured, cautiously and unnoticed, behind the other tent. He made his excuses and followed. He found her outside the tent, seated on the ground. Her head was bent upon her raised knees, and Reuben could tell she was deeply disturbed.

"Tamar!" he called to her in a hushed tone. "You must not sit here on the dirt of the ground. You will spoil your wedding garment."

"I already have done so—long before now."

Reuben sat beside her. "I know of the matter concerning you and Judah. You must be patient with my brother. He is still hurt and grief-stricken from so many tragic deaths. And he thinks you and Father have made a fool of him. It is no wonder he is behaving strangely."

Tamar lifted her eyes in disbelief. "Did Judah tell you about . . . ?"

"Yes, I know that you carry his child and all the things that happened in Adullam."

"I am surprised he would speak of it to anyone. His usual

249

pattern is to run away somewhere by himself to nurse his sorrows in solitude."

"He had to speak to someone after his session with Father. When he came to my tent, he was in great agony. He greatly needed a supportive friend. I had to pry, to wrest information out of him at first, but soon it all came pouring out."

"Oh, Reuben, I am so glad you want to be Judah's friend. All the other brothers shun him. Is it because of me?"

"No, Tamar. Surely you noticed my brothers' lack of hospitality before today."

"I know. That always has puzzled me."

"Judah has ethics. They do not. They never like to be around anyone who reminds them of their own wickedness. They barely tolerate me, and I am hardly a righteous man."

"Reuben, the reason I wanted to speak with you was to ask your help. Can you tell me what I can do for Judah? I want to make up to him for all the sorrows I have caused him. I do not know where to begin. I thought you might know a way to break down the wall he hides behind."

"Love him, Tamar. Pray for him. Someday Judah will change."

"I am not so sure. He seems so withdrawn. He says he will never touch me again."

"Judah is searching now. He tries to find himself. He will one day."

"There is more troubling Judah than just what I did to him. There is some secret thing from Judah's past. I think it involves the other brothers—except you. That is why he confides in you."

"Would that were true. No, I am not guiltless."

"Will you tell me of this thing that torments my husband?"

"It would serve no purpose."

"But it would. If I knew Judah's source of grief and depression, I could help him bear it."

"Judah would not want me to tell you. When he is ready, he must be the one to do so."

"Why can you not tell me?" Tamar persisted. "Do you fear I would not keep the secret?"

"Not that. It is just that no one knows, save the ten oldest brethren. The matter must be kept hidden from our father, for to hear it would devastate him and send him to his grave."

"And you think I, being close to Father Jacob, would reveal it unto him?"

"No. It is a secret pact we brothers made when we were shepherds together. We all swore in blood never to tell anyone else. I cannot break my solemn promise. Can you understand?"

"Not really," she sighed. "My marriage seems of more importance than some silly agreement made by a group of rowdy shepherds. Coping with me for a wife will be trying enough for Judah without this dark secret continuing to plague him as well. If you cared for him, as I do, I believe you would want me to share the weight Judah carries on his shoulders."

"Perhaps," Reuben said slowly, "I may be able to tell you some day, Tamar, when our father lies in his tomb. But while he lives, I am honor-bound to keep my covenant."

"But surely you and Judah have spoken of this monster of a secret. You said he has need to unburden himself. He cannot continue to keep the trouble locked inside. It might be that I could become his confidant, as you are. Knowing the cause may point to the cure. Even if he will not allow me to be a wife, I should like to be his friend. That may be my only way ever to reach him."

"I understand what you say, Tamar, and I can see that your love for him compels you to want to help him. But it would only make matters worse if Judah learned I had betrayed his confidence by speaking to you against his wishes. He would hate me for it."

Seeing the futility of pressing Reuben further, she said, "Then you must make a blood covenant with me and swear that you will come to visit us often. Judah needs someone's friendship. If not mine, then yours."

"I give you my oath. There is no need to cut ourselves and draw blood to seal it, is there? Is my word good enough—so your beautiful wedding robes will not be spattered?"

Tamar smiled. "I will take you at your word, Reuben. But please let me know if you think of anything I can do or say to make things easier for Judah."

"I shall. Now, come. We will be missed," Reuben said, extending his hand to help her up.

As they walked back, Reuben thought how changed Tamar seemed—so soft and almost helpless somehow. She was not the same brazen, inconsiderate, and willful girl who pushed her way into the family as he remembered her from long ago. Reuben heard love for his brother in her voice, and he saw compassion in her eyes. Forceful determination remained, but it seemed to focus on Judah, not on her own ambitions. Marrying Tamar might be Judah's saving grace.

Reuben stopped to take a different route back to the feast so they would not return together. Before they parted, he said, "Commit all this to the Lord, Tamar. He will show you the way to win Judah's love and conquer any monsters that may exist. But do not try to push Judah too soon. Let him commune with his own heart for a while. Be patient and wait."

Tamar had to laugh. "You are not the first to give me that advice," she said. "Thank you, Reuben, for being my friend as well as Judah's."

She thought about Reuben's words later as she sat upon the flower-decorated cart which took her toward her new home with Judah. He did not sit with her, but upon his donkey, riding in silence ahead of the cart. It was not the kind of wedding day she would have chosen, but, for now, it was the next best thing.

Surrounding Tamar in the cart were all the wedding gifts Jacob had commanded every guest to bring. The gifts from Judah's brothers were both given and received with such reluctance that Tamar knew she would need to pack them away from Judah's sight once they arrived home.

Everything at the wedding had been done for one reason only—to please Father Jacob. He directed the entire drama from start to finish, giving all participants their roles to play, the lines to be spoken, and the attitudes to convey. It all was both comical and tragic.

Tamar wondered if Father Jacob really had hopes for this marriage to succeed. He talked and acted like he did and brought the only semblance of sincerity to what, otherwise, would have been a total travesty and sham.

Nevertheless, some of Jacob's wedding arrangements were obviously contrived and overdone. Even a man of his faith could not have believed the bride and bridegroom actually would occupy the lovely bridal chamber he had his handmaidens prepare. Tamar had seen it the day before the wedding, and it wounded her deeply. The adorned and perfumed marriage bed was an appropriate symbol for her entire relationship with Judah—a beautifully orchestrated dream, but one that remained empty.

In spite of all the pretense, however, there were brief moments she could treasure. Father Jacob's wedding gifts included things he knew would please her and help her survive as she marked time until her unborn child was born and her husband's rage and shame subsided. There were more reading and writing materials and vast arrays of art supplies. The most generous gift of all was the treasured painting she always had admired. He said he had planned to will it to her when he died, but giving it to her now meant she could remember him fondly in life as well as in death.

She also would remember the private conversations, the times of prayer, and the words of encouragement she received in quiet moments she shared with her adopted father before the wedding. Somehow, they both knew it might be the last of such times together. She drew strength from those moments with her dearest, truest friend. She knew she would have to draw upon that strength many times more as she faced an uncertain future with a husband who seemed to have absolutely no use for her.

Tamar raised her head to look at her husband. His back was to her as the cart jostled along behind him. She refused to accept his back being turned away from her as an ill omen. She began to pray for him. Even though she could not see his face, she knew it was as sad and empty as her heart.

Then her spirits brightened as she began to think of words to a love song she would compose and play upon the harp Eliezer had given her. She would sing it to Judah one day.

Silently, Tamar sent Judah a message that arose in her thoughts: *You do not wish to be near me, to speak to me, or even to look at me now, Judah. But someday you will love me as I love you. I shall wait.*

Sixteen

Within the tents of Judah of Canaan, the passing of time brought many changes. None of them were for the better. As if human problems and strained relations between husband and wife were not causing enough distress, nature's physical and environmental problems began providing an ominous background of foreboding. The dreaded word on everyone's lips was *famine*.

Canaan's well being was conditioned by rain. Usually, it fell twice in the year—the first rains in late autumn and the latter rains in the early part of the year. The land was poor in springs, and little could be done with river water in terms of cultivating crops. All life depended on rain.

When the rains did not come, there was cause for alarm. Instead of moisture-bearing west winds, the desert winds began to blow away all hope of a harvest. The results were aridity, crop failure, and starvation. This lack of rainfall had serious, far-reaching effects and reached beyond Canaan to the lands roundabout. Even in mighty Egypt, the yearly rising of the Nile River had failed, and croplands went unwatered.

Such a natural catastrophe was met at first with amazement, then with some hand-wringing, and finally with great lamentations. People were beginning to speak of hunger.

Tamar was not as concerned about the crop failure's threat of famine as she was about Judah's worsening condition. It was more than just his predictably strange behavior—avoiding her, taking his meals alone, and walking out of his way to keep from crossing her path. It was an all-consuming depression, recurring black periods when he would remain for days within his tent and allow no one to come near him except Cumi.

"It seems much like the same sickness my mistress had," said Cumi, shaking her head sadly.

Cumi and Tamar had grown close, while Judah remained alone and locked inside himself.

"Say it not!" Tamar protested. "Shuah was sickly, and Judah is strong. Shuah was near madness with grief over the loss of her sons. Something else ails Judah."

Cumi asked, "Could not the same grief and loss cause Master Judah to be ill?"

"Oh, Cumi, I do not know. Does he ever speak when you take him his meals? Does he give you any idea what is wrong? Does he ever ask about me?"

Cumi shook her head. "He hardly speaks at all. Or eats anything, for that matter."

"I am going to send for Reuben."

"How can he help?"

"Reuben knows the cause of Judah's secret grief. It is more than deaths of loved ones, Cumi. It is more than being forced to marry me against his will. I must find out what it is!"

"But you should not fret so, Tamar. You must stay sound in mind and body for the sake of your unborn child."

"I think my babe is strong enough for himself. Did you ever see such as this?" Tamar pulled her loose-fitting robe close about her from the back to reveal the bulge in front, the sign of her advanced stage of pregnancy. "I think I shall bear a full-grown man, not an infant! I pray this child may bring gladness to Judah's heart and make him well again."

Cumi's eyes brightened as she smiled, "I cannot wait, Tamar! Do not forget you have promised that I may help you tend the baby."

"I will not forget. Would that you also could tend me when I labor to bring forth this child."

"But, Tamar, I have never . . ."

"I know. Old Bella is the midwife. But I trust her not, Cumi."

"I shall stay close by you. She will not harm you or her master's child."

"I am not afraid the toothless one will harm me. I just do not like her, that is all. And I am certain she has no love for me. She resents my being the master's new wife."

"What will you name the child, Tamar?"

"Judah has not said. Give me his supper tray, Cumi. That will give me an excuse to go to him—to inquire as to a name for his son."

"Or daughter?" Cumi reminded Tamar.

"Do not even think it! Now, give me the food. You go and send forth a messenger unto Reuben. Tell him to say Judah is ill and sorely needs Reuben's attendance."

"Very well," Cumi sighed.

"What is it? What makes your face draw up like a sun-dried raisin?"

"I was just thinking how I wished Benjamin were the one being sent for."

"No, Cumi! No word of this must reach Benjamin or Father Jacob. Whatever troubles Judah is to be kept from Benjamin's ears. He would beg his father to come here, and Reuben says Father Jacob must be spared any knowledge of this. Only Reuben must come—alone. Be certain to tell the messenger to speak only to Reuben."

Tamar sent Cumi to commission the messenger before she approached Judah's tent. She found him sitting alone in the darkening shadows of dusk, staring at nothing.

"I have brought your supper, my husband," she said from the doorway.

"Why have you come here?" Judah asked in a listless voice.

"To bring your supper, as I said."

"Where is Cumi?"

"Busy with another task. Here is a delicious, savory stew, hot from the boiling pot. And fresh bread from the oven, and . . ."

"Leave it. I am not hungry now."

Tamar placed the tray on Judah's table and seated herself across from him. He turned his head away from her.

"The bringing of your meal was only one reason. There is a matter I would discuss with you, Judah, if you will hear me."

"We have nothing to say to each other."

"It is about a name for your child . . ."

"There will be no child."

Tamar's brows came together in a frown. "What say you?"

"The child will die—as all my other children."

256

"But Judah, your three sons were all sickly," she said, placing her hand to her abdomen. "I promise you, this child is strong as a team of oxen. Why, already he kicks with such force . . ."

"Go away, Tamar!" He gave a gesture of dismissal, both for the food and Tamar.

She knelt at his knees. "My darling, what is the matter that distresses you so? Tell me."

"If you wish the child you carry to live, you must get yourself away from here—and do it quickly!" Judah buried his face in his hands.

Gently, Tamar pried the fingers from his face to look into his hollow, expressionless eyes and to say, "I do not understand, Judah. What are you saying?"

"Do you not know? Have you not heard of the approaching famine? Even nature is cursing me and all those anywhere near me. Everything and everyone I touch must die. Your only hope for your child is to have it born in some other place away from me. Not here!"

"Judah, how can you blame yourself for the famine? It is the lack of rain, nothing more."

"Think what you will, Tamar. But to ignore my warning is to risk losing your child."

"Our child," she corrected him. "Judah, like it or not, I am your wife. I will not leave you, no matter what evil befalls us. I do not for a moment believe you have anything to do with delayed rains or crop failures—or the tragic deaths in your first family. How can you possibly take any blame for such things?"

"Because I weary of blaming others. I used to blame the death curse on you. Then Shuah. I finally have come to realize there is no one more guilty than I. I dispute with the truth no longer. Soon everything I possess will be destroyed forever."

"You babble nonsense, Judah. Others have lost family members to death by sickness or accident. Yours are not the only crops that are being destroyed. Every farmer and vineyard owner throughout Canaan suffers from the drought."

"You see? You see how widespread is the evil curse upon me? God is angry with me, Tamar. All of my family and neighbors will fall under the wrath of God if they are anywhere near me. My punishment is to see everyone fall, one by one, before I am last to be taken. I should have ended my life long ago and spared any further destruction."

"Judah, why is it you think God is angry with you? What drains the life and strength from you and causes you to heap responsibility upon your own head?"

Judah closed his eyes, as if to shut out having to think of the answer. "Even if I wanted to tell you, Tamar, I would not."

"Why, Judah? Why?"

"Because, even for all the grief you have caused me, I still do not wish you dead. I thought I proved that to you when I would not have you burned."

"Dead? You think I will die at the hearing?" Tamar might have laughed at the idea, but she could not. Judah was too serious. Deadly serious.

"You want proof, Tamar? I told Shuah of my sin. Straightaway, she died. No sooner had I confessed, than she died in my arms. To speak of it is to pronounce a death sentence upon the hearer. Is that what you want for yourself and your child, Tamar?"

"Judah, you must not think this way. Nothing could be so unspeakable!"

"When one takes for himself that which has been divinely ordained for another, that is to rob God. God will not allow such a one to go unpunished. Oh, I go too far with my unguarded tongue! I will speak no more. Go from hence, Tamar!"

"Not yet, Judah. You seem to think you have taken something God ordained for another. Did not your father do the selfsame thing? He took the birthright and blessing from his brother, Esau. He tricked and deceived his way to obtain them, but God forgave him his sin."

"My father did no deed such as I have done. Esau was unfit, unworthy of God's blessing. God will never forgive my sin against His most righteous servant. That is all there is to be said about the matter, and you waste your time to ask me anything more."

"Again you speak in riddles," Tamar said with a sigh of desperation.

"You must leave here for another reason, Tamar. You came to this family seeking part in the promised covenant to Israel and his descendants. Neither I nor any of my offspring will have a part in what you seek. My father will give the blessing to one who is righteous before the Lord. So, you see, there is no reason for you to remain here. Go, I tell you, before you suffer the doom that is surely to come!"

"Judah I do not believe in any impending doom destined to fall because of your past sins. Even if I did, I would not leave you. I have put away all thoughts about the covenant blessing."

Judah raised his eyes to look at her in surprise. This did not sound like Tamar at all.

"I grant you," she continued, "my strongest desire at one time was to bear a son of the covenant. I was willing to risk anything for that obsession. I hurt myself and others and did sinful things I deeply regret. But now my only desire is to be unto you a good wife. A good wife stands beside her husband—regardless of God's wrath, doom, famine, or some imagined guilt that may bring death in its wake."

"I do not believe you, Tamar. You would not put me above the God-inheritance!"

"I already have. How can I make you believe me? I love you with all my heart!"

Judah stood to his feet and forced himself to raise his voice: "Then you are a worse fool than I thought! You will be damned by God—along with me and the rest of them. Are you too blind to see that you waste love on a doomed man, one who cannot love you in return?"

"Then I shall pray for enough love for both of us. I will not leave you nor stop loving you, Judah. Do you hear me?"

He did not answer. He walked away from her, out into the open air. It was similar to another time when he walked out into the night, carrying Tamar, kicking and screaming at him. He rejected her advances and denied her love then. He had to do so now, but he wanted no screaming or quarreling. He lacked the energy. He had no more fight in him.

Tamar followed him and placed a hand to his shoulder to say, "Judah I am guilty of many sins against you. Can you not see

259

that I want to atone for them? I want to give you many children. I want to be your wife and make you happy again. That is all I care about in the world."

He brushed aside her hand and said, "I told you, Tamar, that you waste time dreaming of any such life. There is nothing good within me, so I lack the capacity for love. If you are determined to remain here to have your child, I will not prevent you—but the blood will be upon your own hands. I have warned you! Now, please do not come near me—ever again!"

"Always you reject me, Judah. But for once in my life, I have the patience to wait. I shall wait for you to love me until your beard is gray and flowing to the ground!" She trailed after him as he started moving away. "Do you attend unto my words, Judah?"

Turning to her for what he hoped would be the last time, he murmured, "You attend unto this, Tamar. I wish to die here where lies my true family—Shuah and my three dead sons. But if you insist on remaining and do not stay away from my presence, I shall be the one forced to leave this place."

"Judah, what are you saying? You think you are going to die?"

"Very soon. First, I should like to see my son . . . I mean, your child . . . but if not . . ."

His words made Tamar freeze in her steps. "No, Judah! I will not come to you again if it upsets you this much. But please speak no more of death!"

Tamar walked away from him, confused and hurt as she always was when they came together. He said he wanted to see his son. That was her only hope now of bringing him from his dark mood of despair. That and Reuben.

She stood still in the twilight, trying to piece together the strange things Judah had said. Something about robbing God and his taking something ordained for another. Who was the injured person, and what had Judah taken from him? And why could Judah not repent for it and return whatever it was?

The dust was blowing around her. It was dry and coming from the direction of the barren grain fields in the distance. She began to wonder if Judah's ramblings could have any foundation. Surely, it was only the sickness in his mind that made the coincidence of a famine seem like God's retribution. If the famine came, they all would die, as Judah predicted. But her child must not die!

Cumi found Tamar standing alone, dazed and glassy-eyed, in the midst of the camp. There were no tears, but Tamar's face looked like she had been crying.

"Tamar, what is it?" Cumi asked, placing an arm about her.

"It is Judah. I fear he truly is losing all reason."

"Come inside and tell me what has come to pass," Cumi said, taking her arm.

Cumi led Tamar back to the tent they shared. Tamar had not wanted a dwelling of her own, especially with the baby coming, and Cumi was delighted to have Tamar's company to ease the loneliness she felt since Benjamin left. The young women took familiar places across from each other as they often did when chatting into the late hours of the night.

"Oh, Cumi. I am so worried about Judah," Tamar moaned. "He believes he is going to die."

"I know," Cumi responded sadly.

"You knew this about Judah and told me not of it?"

"I did not want you more concerned than you already were. It reminds me so much of the way Mistress Shuah behaved before . . ." The girl's eyes began to blink tears at the painful memory.

"Cumi, was there something that brought joy to Shuah's heart when her spirit was turning toward thoughts of death?"

"All she ever desired was Master Judah's love. He gave it not to her."

Tamar bit her lip in deep thought. "But Judah will not have my love. That cannot be the answer for him. Have you sent the musicians unto him, as I have asked?"

"Yes, Tamar. But he turned them away. He wants no one with him."

"He will see Reuben," Tamar said in momentary triumph. "Have I not told you that, before the wedding, Judah lodged with Reuben and unburdened his heart to him?"

"The messenger is on his way to fetch Reuben even now. I do

hope that you are right and that he can bring Master Judah from this deep despair."

"Oh, we must pray that is so. Do you know, Cumi, my husband believes even the famine in the land is his own doing?"

"I know."

"What else do you know that you have kept from me, you tight-lipped, little imp?"

"I know his mind is more sad than anyone else's in the world. He no longer goes to his fields or has a care for anything. The servants are left to manage farms, vineyards, flocks, and herds. He no longer even comes forth for evening prayers as before."

"I knew of that much. Judah thinks God will not hear his prayers. Do you think we ever sin so greatly that God no longer hears us?"

"No, I think God is a loving Father who delights to forgive all wayward children."

"I once thought so too, Cumi. I, myself, have felt the weight of my sins lifted. But now . . . ?"

"You must not think otherwise. Master Judah tries to punish himself. I sometimes think he wants calamities heaped upon his head—just so he may feel chastised."

"Do you believe the deaths and the famine really might be God's punishment of Judah?"

"No, Tamar. And neither do you. You know our God of love does not send such sorrow. But I do believe He uses sorrow to bring us to ourselves and to draw us back to Him."

"Then why should Judah, a man well schooled by his father in tenets of our faith, think so?"

"He is deceived and confused. Oh, I think in marrying a woman prone to sickness, Master Judah was destined to bring forth sick children. I believe his rejection of Shuah brought her sooner to death's door, but the master is not in control of God's universe. Created beings cannot take responsibility for every wicked thing that occurs in a wicked world."

"You speak with exceeding wisdom beyond your years, little one. I tried to control the world, and look where it got me."

"But you carry Master Judah's child. Is that not the very blessing you most longed for?"

"Yes, but not like this. I wanted it for selfish reasons and plotted for it in sinful ways. I never would have schemed to get my way, had I known it might have hastened Judah's death!"

"Even if . . . even if Master Judah should die, you still will bear the child of the covenant."

"If that remark was meant to cheer me, it does not. And that hope, like everything else, has died. Father Jacob probably will pass the blessing to Benjamin. Judah has not proven himself worthy. Both Judah and Father Jacob have said so. But I shall not pine away about any of that. If Benjamin inherits the blessing, and if he takes you to wife, *you* shall become mother of the holy one. That will give me great joy, for you are far more deserving than I."

Shocked, Cumi shook her head forcefully. "No, Tamar! If Benjamin inherits the blessing, he must not marry me. One named to that noble calling should not take a servant girl to wed!"

"Dear girl," Tamar said, "I believe God works His will through simple, humble things. The great and mighty do not seek God nor think they need Him. So weak things are chosen to confound the prideful, and only God is glorified. I should not be surprised to find the Messiah born in a very humble place among lowly but devout people—such as you, Cumi."

"Do you truly think I yet may become Benjamin's bride?"

"If that is God's will. But do not make the mistake I did. Do not seek it or do anything to try to make it happen. Let the Lord work out your life's plan in His own way and time."

"How different you sound, Tamar! I can remember being told I must plan to make Father Jacob like me, work to win his approval so he would release Benjamin, and . . ."

"Praise Jehovah you were too wise to listen to the foolish woman who told you that! Just by being the sweet person you are, you have fared far better. Working out your own plan and using limited, human wisdom can result in achieving your goal and forfeiting your happiness."

Yawns of exhaustion soon demanded the conversation stop and surrender itself to sleep. That night Cumi's hands clasped her colored beads, and Tamar's hands lay upon her unborn child.

What they touched symbolized the hopes that, at least for now, seemed to exceed their grasps.

In the days that followed, Tamar tried to keep herself busy and her mind diverted from the crisis situations mounting around her. She helped Cumi with the cooking and baking and then sat to sew the tiny garments they were making. There were soft linen swaddling cloths, lamb's wool for blankets, and embroidered smocks and shawls. When Tamar tired of the needlework, she would take up her harp and sing as Cumi continued to create designs upon a beautifully woven coverlet.

Suddenly, Tamar put down the harp and stopped her song. In the distance she saw what she had awaited so anxiously.

"Reuben!" Tamar cried, almost tripping over both Cumi and the coverlet in her haste to rise. Movement was difficult for Tamar, but she was able to reach Reuben before he dismounted his donkey. She extended her arms wide in a welcoming greeting.

"Peace to you, Tamar," Reuben said. "I regret I could not come sooner. With the famine so sore in the land, we have been beset by bands of robbers. This was my first chance to get away."

"Robbers? You mean thieving of your flocks?"

"And of our foodstuffs as well. Father Jacob shares all he can with our hungry neighbors, but still many are starving all about us."

"We have escaped that trouble here, but it is about the only calamity we have been spared."

Tamar walked Reuben to a shady awning where Cumi awaited them with water for the traveler's feet. Then, without being bidden, she disappeared again to prepare refreshments.

"How is my brother?" Reuben asked, removing his sandals.

"Worse than I have ever seen him, Reuben. You must bring him out of this depression before it is too late. He keeps speaking of dying."

"I will do what I can, Tamar."

Cumi was back to extend a wine cup to Reuben. He hesitated and asked, "Are you sure you have enough? After the failure of the grape harvest, I should not wish to deplete your supply."

"Go on," Tamar encouraged her guest. "Judah has much laid up in store."

"I suppose living here, away from the townspeople, you do not have so many hungry neighbors wishing to take your provisions."

"Nor do we have as many mouths to feed in our household as does Father Jacob," Tamar said. "Do you think the famine will last much longer?"

Reuben cast his eyes skyward. "It lasts as long as we are without rain. Never have the heavens appeared less likely to bless us with any."

"What can we do if no rainfall comes?" It was a question Tamar had been asking herself.

"We will eat the meat and drink the milk of our herds. After that . . ." Reuben could not let himself add to Tamar's burdens, so he added, ". . . but it will not come to that, I am sure. Father has heard that in Egypt there is food aplenty. If the situation worsens, we always can go there to buy."

Tamar relaxed a little. "I am comforted by your words. Judah is too weak to guard his provisions, and the few womenfolk here have only menservants to depend upon."

"I should not worry. Judah has trained his men well. I will inspect things for you before I go and give any necessary instructions to the hirelings. Now, tell me of Judah's illness."

"He wants to die and fully expects to do so. He sits alone in his tent. He does not eat or speak to anyone. I think it is to escape the great guilt you have acknowledged to me. All I know is the few things he said about having robbed God and taken something that was not rightfully his."

"That makes sense to me. It fits the theory I assumed was the problem."

"It makes no sense to me, Reuben! And I have no theory whatever. You must tell me the cause of this secret guilt. You said one day you could, and if you do not speak now, another opportunity may not come before it is too late."

The grave expression on Tamar's face stressed the urgency of the situation, so Reuben thought for a moment and then said with a sigh, "I did not want to tell you against Judah's wishes and because of my blood oath. But if he is as ill as you say, and if

265

you think it could do some good, I suppose breaking an oath is less drastic than refusing to help you. Very well, Tamar."

Reuben recounted the history of shepherd brothers on a hillside, sparing no small part of the tale. He told of the brothers' envy of Joseph's godliness and his special place in Jacob's heart. He revealed how the brothers conspired to rid themselves of the spy in their midst, for Joseph always ran to their father with accounts of their many transgressions.

"There was great rivalry between Joseph and Judah for our father's blessing. Judah was especially jealous because he admired the boy's unblemished character, his spiritual gifts, and his close walk with God. Joseph was not the wild stallion that Judah was in his youth."

Tamar interrupted to ask fearfully, "What did Judah do unto his brother?"

"He sold him. To a band of merchants bound for Egypt."

"He sold him into slavery?"

"Judah was not alone in the crime. The other brothers wanted him killed."

"And you, Reuben? Did you agree to all this?"

"No, but I was not there to protest on the day this all happened. I had tried to protect the lad, but I could not stand against the whole lot of them against me. I was able to convince them to place Joseph in a deep pit. I planned to come back later and draw him out, but while I was away, Judah had Midianites take Joseph away in chains."

"No wonder Judah looks to you for friendship. You are not as guilty as he and the others."

"I am guilty of agreeing with them to deceive our father. Had I been much of a man, I would have refused or exposed the deed long ago. We spattered blood upon Joseph's coat, took it to Father, and told him Joseph was slain by a wild animal."

"And for this Judah suffers such agony? He did not slay the lad. Why is he so haunted by a deed that all the other brothers seem able to forget?"

"Judah feels he has usurped the blessing falsely. He knew Joseph was more deserving than he was. And to be enslaved in Egypt would mean torture or even death to an innocent who did

266

not warrant either. To confess the sin to Father was unthinkable. To accept Father's blessing under false pretenses was even more so. That is the dilemma with which Judah lives. I suppose in his mind, he is better off dead than accepting an undeserved blessing by deceit."

Tamar was putting it all together in her mind. Then she said, "The third time! The pattern was repeated three times. Father Jacob usurped the blessing by deceit. I did the same when I played the harlot. Now Judah also. Every one of us guilty of the same crime."

Reuben frowned and said, "It will not comfort Judah's heart to know others share a similar guilt. He told me before the wedding feast that he had thwarted the will of God. That is a heavy load for a man to carry for the rest of his life."

Tamar grasped Reuben's hand in both of hers to say, "Father Jacob is forgiving. He would accept Judah's repentance because he followed the same sly and deceitful paths to the blessing himself. He forgave me. Why can Judah not go to him and confess all? Even if denied the blessing, Judah would be free of the torment to his conscience."

"Except for two things, Tamar. If Judah exposes himself, he cannot do so without breaking his oath and exposing his brothers also. That would make Judah responsible for causing them to be alienated from our father. Secondly, Father's heart might fail him at the hearing, and Judah does not want responsibility for another death."

"So Judah believes his own death is the only solution? Oh, Reuben, what can be done? Some other way must be found to save my husband!"

"I have been thinking on that all the way here. So far, I have no answer, Tamar. But I shall speak to Judah and try to help him if I can."

"Then make haste to do so! Go to him at once!"

Tamar walked with Reuben until they neared Judah's tent. There she left him, along with all her hopes for the future—Judah's future as well as her own.

267

Seventeen

Reuben's efforts to revive Judah's spirits went unrewarded. Judah received his brother's company politely, but with something beyond restraint. It was as if Judah existed in some other world, a detached state of consciousness that could best be described as a breathing dead man.

"He is beyond my reach," Reuben said to Tamar after a few days. "Give him a strong and healthy child, Tamar. It seems to be his dying wish and his only reason for holding onto life."

Tamar received the report with greater strength than she thought herself capable of possessing. She was determined to keep herself well for the sake of her unborn child, for her time of deliverance was near. She also had assumed Judah's responsibility for managing the household, directing the servants, and making decisions. That required a calm, unemotional state of mind.

"It seems I am in a dilemma here," she said. "Certainly, I want to hasten the day I bring this child into the world and fulfill Judah's wish, but, you tell me once I do so, I remove the very thing that forces my husband to continue wanting to live."

"It may not be as bad as that," Reuben countered. "Seeing the baby may bring Judah back to us. I have impressed on him how much a child needs a father and how unfair it would be to leave this household unprotected without a patriarch."

"It is unbelievable how we talk as though living or dying could be a simple matter of Judah's choice. But in his case, that does seem to be the way it is."

"Not really, Tamar. God yet may intervene, so you must release Judah and place him in the care of One who loves him more than you do. I wish I did not have to leave you, but I do not think I can be of further use here, and I am greatly needed back home in this time of tribulation."

"The famine grows worse—even as Judah's condition does—but I am determined to fight the fear that seems to be my greater enemy just now."

"Afraid? You, Tamar? No, I perceive no sign of fear in you."

"Do not be deceived. It is more than fear of losing Judah or enduring the famine. I am even afraid of my time of bearing. There is no one here with any concern for me except Cumi. The old midwife despises me. I shudder to think of that woman putting her hand to my child. And I most fear how I will behave once you are no longer here to lean upon. The bravest woman needs a man's strength to supplement her own. Knowing I must stand alone makes me worry, lest I will crumble and fall apart."

"You forget—the Lord will be your strength as you face each challenge ahead. You are quite a woman, Tamar."

"Thank you for that, Reuben."

"I believe you have food enough for another month or so, but you need to keep a watchful eye on the servants. They are beginning to grumble about rationing their portions. I left specific instructions about that and about posting a guard by the storehouse and what to do if robbers come to call."

Tamar smiled her thanks for Reuben's assistance before she said, "The servants are having a difficult time. Always before, this has been a house of plenty where no limitations were placed on anything they wanted or needed."

"We all may profit from this experience. The famine makes us grateful for what we ordinarily take for granted."

Nodding in agreement, Tamar thought of Judah and said, "You are right, Reuben. Even sickness makes us thankful for good health."

Before Reuben mounted his donkey to leave, he embraced Tamar as she leaned her head against his chest. He said, "Entrust all this to the Lord, my sister. Remember, you do not hold the future in your hands, so you must commit your future into the hands of Him who does."

"That sounds like something Father Jacob must have taught you. Or a phrase from one of old Eliezer's religious models. Whatever the source, I will make it my inspirational motto to sustain me in the days ahead." Then Tamar waved and said, "Thank you for coming, Reuben. I appreciate all your help and comfort. Farewell, and God go with you."

Tamar would need more than comforting words to sustain her after Reuben was gone. Her authority was not accepted graciously by the servants, especially Zed, who assumed he, as head steward, would be in charge. In the past, whenever his master was away or when illness removed Judah from the scene, Zed enjoyed being a decision-maker who barked commands to the others.

Zed did not balk at taking orders from Cumi, not only because they were delivered in her amiable, soft-spoken way, but also because he knew anything she requested came directly from Judah. He was not so disposed when it came to anything suggested by Tamar. He resented being told what to do by a woman, especially one so recently elevated to the position of mistress.

The most serious of Zed's confrontations with Tamar concerned following Reuben's instructions about posting a guard at the storehouse where food provisions were kept. Since thieves had never been a problem before, Zed saw no reason to take such a precaution now.

Tamar suspected that Zed was becoming lax about the matter, so she decided to conduct her own nightly inspection tour. She had an inventory list, and the first time two bags of grain were missing, she gave Zed a stern warning. That made him only more resentful and less inclined to do what she said. The second night, Zed wished he had been more obedient.

Without knowing exactly why, whether from a premonition of impending danger or from becoming more wary after the first theft, Tamar took in her hand a harvesting sickle as she tiptoed cautiously toward the storehouse. She was startled by noises coming from inside and even more surprised to see an unfamiliar cart, half-filled with foodstuffs, standing outside the storehouse. The sound of voices murmuring in whispers told her people were in there helping themselves to what was left between Judah's household and starvation. They were hauling away a cartload of food!

Tamar peered in the doorway and observed two shadowy figures. One held aloft a lighted lamp while the other was lifting a side of dried mutton onto his shoulders. Without stopping to call for help or thinking of the peril to herself, she reacted instinctively, rushing in to slash at the intruders with the sickle waving wildly over her head.

"How dare you invade the house of Judah!" she shouted. "You shall not take food from my baby's mouth!"

The first blow of the sickle hit the topmost of standing wine barrels which overturned and crashed into others nearby. That sent a chain reaction of more containers falling and rolling with such a great clamor that it caused the man with the mutton to drop his loot upon his foot. The second man had the lamp knocked from his hand as he turned to see a crazed woman charging at him, wielding the blade in front of his face.

The robbers ran for the door with Tamar at their heels. She was still shouting and slashing at them from behind. Another blow clapped the mutton robber's shoulder and drew blood, but it did not stop him from running as fast as he could hobble on his sore foot. He was screaming with fright and trying to catch up to his companion who had disappeared into the night.

By now, the crashing of the barrels and the shrieks from both pursuer and pursued had awakened the entire camp. Servants came running from all directions as Tamar shouted, "Stop the thieves! Stop them! Do not let them get away!"

One sleep-dazed servant was successful in making a diving tackle that brought down one of the robbers, the one with the foot damaged by the falling side of mutton. It was a fleeting victory because the thief scrambled to his feet and ran away after first landing a wild punch to the servant's nose. Once the robbers were routed, all stood around in their sleeping attire staring at Tamar. She stood by the half-filled cart, holding her sickle overhead in a gesture of protective triumph.

Even Judah had roused from his tent and shuffled out to see what the commotion meant. The effect of realizing how his abdication of responsibility had placed his household in jeopardy jarred Judah from inertia. He rallied long enough to join the servants who were praising Tamar's unusual show of courage in a time of danger. He also discharged Zed from his position as head steward. Joel, a younger and more reliable steward, was given the honor and commanded to obey Tamar's orders from that night forward. Tamar had no more trouble with the servants.

Back in the tent with Cumi, Tamar was breathing heavily, still in shock and quivering long after the harrowing experience. Cumi did not know whether to applaud or chide Tamar.

"How could you dare, in your condition, go in there alone to confront those robbers?" Cumi asked. "You could have been killed or lost the baby! Why did you not go for help?"

"I do not know, Cumi," Tamar said honestly. "I had no time to stop and think. I just reacted, wanting only to protect my child and to defend Judah's property from marauders invading our food supply."

Cumi placed a cup of wine into Tamar's trembling hand and said, "I suppose you know you are a heroine now. All the camp is buzzing with respect and amazement at your show of strength."

Tamar gave a little laugh. "It is all quite amusing, really. The idea of the mighty Judah having his lion's den protected by a mad woman in an advanced state of pregnancy. No more robbers will dare invade us, knowing they have to contend with such a formidable foe."

Cumi tried to laugh too, but she was still quaking with fright over what could have happened. "I only hope you do not try to repeat tonight's performance ever again," she said.

"I think there is little fear of that. Judah instructed Joel to have a warning bell placed by the storehouse and to have a watchman patrol the property from now on."

"Where did you get the strength to run at them armed with a sickle?" Cumi wanted to know.

"Reuben said the Lord would be my strength in these trying times. The irony is I had just complained to him about how fearful I was of falling apart without him here to help us. I venture the Lord provides whatever strength is needed in a crisis, for nothing in my frail woman's body could have performed such a feat."

The days and nights that followed were uneventful and seemed to revert to the slow and slower marking of time amid fewer and fewer hopes for improvement. There was no prospect of rain. Food became scarcer. Judah's lapse back to depression seemed more grim than before.

Each passing day brought Tamar nearer the paradoxical time of destiny's twins—birth and death. She almost wished time would stop altogether. A period of famine was not a good choice for bringing into the world another hungry mouth to feed.

A few weeks later, Tamar awoke with a start. "Cumi!" she cried anxiously. "Cumi, arise! The time of my child's birth is near!" Tamar sat upright upon the bed mat and threw off the coverlet to point. "The signs of birth here tell me this will be a long and difficult day!"

"I shall go to tell Bella," Cumi said, scrambling to her feet.

"And Judah!" Tamar added.

"Of course."

"And Father Jacob. Send a messenger unto him. Oh, I know he perhaps may be unable to come here, but I should like for him to know just the same."

"You wish to have the messenger say only that your time of deliverance is at hand?"

"Yes. No. Oh, I do not know! Father Jacob has troubles enough of his own, but I suddenly feel that I need him. I flutter inside like a silly, scared little girl."

Cumi nodded her understanding. "I should think bringing forth your firstborn is reason enough for such feelings, Tamar. I go at once!"

"Cumi!" Tamar called again as her companion reached the door. "Hasten to return to me. I do not want to be alone with only Bella at my side today."

Bounding out the door, Cumi called her agreement to follow all Tamar's instructions. Her first stop was Bella's tent. The midwife was still sleeping and reluctant to arise. The old woman grumbled at Cumi, but she finally was prodded into motion at Cumi's insistence. Next, Cumi summoned the messenger, who, likewise, was too sleepy to comprehend until the message was repeated three times. Her last stop was Judah's tent. There Cumi found Judah dressed and standing in the center of the room. She imagined he had not been to bed all night because his eyes were red and glazed with sleeplessness. His evening meal tray from the night before remained, untouched, on his table.

"Good news, Master!" Cumi sang out joyfully. "This day will bring gladness to delight your heart! Tamar will bear your child today!"

Judah did not move or speak. Cumi repeated her words, but the second attempt still evoked no response. Slowly, she turned to leave.

"Cumi," he said in a weak voice. "Bring the babe to me that my eyes may behold . . ."

She did not wait for him to struggle for the words. She said, "I shall indeed, Master."

In spite of all the messages and preparations made by numerous sleepy people, that day was not an occasion for glad rejoicing. Tamar's time of travail lasted through the entire day, all through the night, and to the next morning. The labor was hard, and Tamar's enmity with Bella only made the pain more unbearable. Bella was neither gentle nor comforting. Tamar was both bitter and resentful.

"Can you not do something for her?" Cumi cried when the dawn of the second day brought no end to Tamar's groans and shrieks of pain.

"I gave her herbs and wine," Bella responded carelessly. She was seated across the room, frequently nodding off for naps, to await Tamar's progress. "Would that I could get some rest from all her wailing."

"You will be wailing yourself if I tell Master Judah of your lack of concern for his wife and child!" Cumi said sharply. She surprised herself with such harsh words, for that was most unlike her usual way of speaking. To correct herself, Cumi said less forcefully, "Please, Bella."

Cumi's words moved Bella to rise and go to Tamar once more. "Bear down!" the midwife commanded Tamar. Then she shoved a piece of dried sheep hide between Tamar's teeth and grunted, "Bite on this!"

Tamar's forehead and robes were wet with perspiration. She spit out the sheep hide and gasped, "I am bearing down, you old fool! Dear God in Heaven, help me!"

274

Seeing the agony on Cumi's face, Bella said, "I can do nothing until the head appears." To Tamar, she said, "You do your part, and I will do mine."

Cumi was ready to protest again when Bella took another good look. "Ah," she said with her great, toothless mouth gaping. "I see something at last. But it is not the head! It is an arm!"

Tamar screamed, "Cumi! Do not let this hag draw forth my child by his arm!"

"Do not be foolish," Bella groused. She unraveled a thread from her head shawl.

"Why are you doing that?" Cumi asked. She had never attended a birthing before, but she was certain Bella's gesture had nothing to do with helping Tamar or her baby.

Bella did not answer as she tied the red thread around the baby's protruding wrist. Then Bella busied herself feeling and probing and pushing until the hand disappeared inside again. Cumi thought she might be sick at any moment. Never could she be around pain or blood for long without becoming ill herself.

"I placed the scarlet thread upon the hand because it came forth first. It is a sign," said Bella.

Tamar was writhing in pangs of anguish, but she found strength enough to shout, "Never mind your signs and sorcery, you lazy, old woman! Get on with this ordeal before I die at your hands!"

Bella growled several times as she placed her hands over Tamar's abdomen and pushed with all her might. Cumi was certain Tamar's screams could be heard by all the servants throughout the camp and by all the field hands a mile away as they dug for roots to supplement the food supply.

"What are you doing now?" Cumi asked, wide-eyed and open-mouthed.

"Be silent, or get you hence!" Bella returned. "You want this over, do you not?"

Cumi remained silent and watched. It seemed that Bella was turning and twisting with one hand and probing and clutching with the other. Cumi thought Bella was being unnecessarily harsh with one in so delicate a condition, but the old woman seemed to know what she was doing.

275

An instant later, Bella was ordering Tamar to push harder and harder still. At last, with a long, loud groan from Tamar and a tug followed by a chortle of triumph from Bella, a baby was held aloft in the midwife's bloody hands.

"This is not the one!" Bella cackled as she examined the baby. "This is not the same one!"

Through clenched teeth and gasping for breath, Tamar asked weakly, "What do you mean?"

"See? There is no scarlet thread upon the wrist." With one hand, Bella held the newborn by the ankles, and, with the other, she soundly thumped the soles of two, tiny feet until the baby cried.

"Forget the insane talk of thread! Is it a boy? Is it strong and well?" Tamar inquired.

Bella did not answer. She was involved with her own tasks and had no time for chatter. Then, handing the squalling infant to Cumi, she gave detailed instructions for cleansing, wiping, anointing with oils, and wrapping as she pointed out materials she had laid out on a nearby table. Neither of them was paying the least attention to Tamar's continuous flood of questions.

"Cumi! You tell me! Is it my boy? Will one of you answer me? I pray you, hear me!"

"You have your boy," Cumi said with her face beaming.

"And here comes another!" shouted Bella. "Bear down again, Tamar."

"What? Oh, oh, oh!" yowled Tamar. "I thought this was all over!"

"Twins!" squealed Cumi in delight. "Tamar, you have given birth to twins!"

"Both boys," said Bella a few minutes later as she held up a second baby. It was the one with the scarlet thread tied around his wrist. "How is it you allowed your brother to break forth before you?" Bella asked the infant. "You should have been the firstborn, but the other has pushed past you to take your place."

"Oh, let me see them," Tamar begged. "Which is he who follows the tradition of Father Jacob and his lineage to push aside a brother and assume the blessing of a firstborn?"

"In time. In time," said Bella as she laid both babies at

Tamar's feet. "There is more work for me to complete here, so lie back and be silent."

Cumi felt herself grow faint as she watched Bella at her tasks. "What is that?" Cumi asked.

"Stupid girl! Ask me no more questions," Bella said sharply as more groans of pain came from Tamar. "Here, Cumi. Hold this basin for me. And hold it still."

When at last the ordeal was over and cleaning up tasks were completed, Bella and Cumi each laid a small, swaddle-wrapped son in the waiting arms of the new mother. Tamar—thirsty, hungry, exhausted, and still experiencing after-pains—felt happier than ever before in her life. *God's double blessing,* she thought as she gave each of her sons a tired but contented smile.

"Dear boys," Tamar said holding her sons close to the warmth of her breasts, "now your father will surely love me. You are the two sons I can give him to replace the ones he gave me."

Cumi smiled along with Tamar and boasted, "Indeed, they are fine, beautiful boys."

Still looking sour, Bella sneered, "Just look at the two of you. Why, you are both crying like the babies there. I am going to bed!" She began packing up her supplies.

Before Bella reached the door, Tamar called out to her, "Thank you, Bella. God bless you."

Bella waved her hand in the air for lack of an appropriate reply. "You had a bad time of it," was all she could think to say before she was gone.

Both Cumi and Tamar uttered cooing sounds to the babies, looked at each other, and burst into giggles. Then they would start the routine again and do it over—always concluding with the giggles. They could not help themselves. They were savoring the delicious aftermath of exhilaration that comes only with experiencing the miracle of birth.

"It has been a very long time since laughter and joy came to this household," Cumi said. Then she remembered Tamar had not eaten. "Oh, I must go fetch you some bread and broth. You must be famished." Cumi said.

"First, Cumi, you must do something else for me," Tamar said. "You must make a thank offering to God. But do not let the other servants see. They would be most unhappy about slaying a lamb for a sacrifice when all the land cries out in hunger."

"Master Judah asked me to bring the newborn to him, that he might behold with his eyes the fruit of his loins. Shall I also take the twins unto his tent now?"

"Will he not come here to see them?" Tamar asked hopefully.

"I think not."

"Go again unto him, Cumi. Bid him come here to see his sons. This moment must be shared between us. He must come unto me!" There was the sound of the old, willful Tamar in her voice.

"Very well, I shall try, Tamar. I can say carrying two babies in my arms frightens me, for that would be the truth. Perhaps he also would want to participate in the thank offering rites."

Cumi left to run the errands, but was back immediately, before she had completed any. "Tamar!" she cried. "There is a great host approaching! I think it to be all of Judah's brethren, for I could make out a few of them in the distance."

"Why should they all be coming here? I sent only for Father Jacob. Surely they cannot think we have food enough to share with them."

"I will go inquire of the matter and bring you word."

"And Cumi, do not forget to entreat Judah to come unto me."

Cumi nodded and left Tamar to nuzzle her sons and to wonder about the scarlet thread's meaning, if one existed. She had abandoned hope of the covenant blessing, but it did seem almost providential that one of her sons moved aside the other for the honored place of firstborn. She looked at that son and said, "Have you also chosen to be the *grabber*—even as your grandfather and father before you? I must compose and teach you a song that will remind you of the suffering that goes with such a choice."

When Cumi returned, she brought Tamar a tray of food, but the former joy was not upon her face. Her eyes were cast down to the floor.

"What is it, Cumi? Judah will not come to me?"

"No, Tamar. He asks that his sons be brought forth to him. And there is more sad news. The famine has become so severe that our visitors are stopping here only briefly. The brothers are

278

on their way to Egypt to purchase food, lest all of Father Jacob's household starve to death. They come to inquire of our needs and to see if Master Judah will accompany them."

"But Judah is too ill to travel!" The very idea seemed madness to Tamar.

"But I do have something to report that will please you. Tamar, Father Jacob has come. He and Reuben are even now within the master's tent."

"Bid Father Jacob to come unto me, Cumi. Take the babes to Judah, and tell Father Jacob how my heart yearns to see him."

"I am already here," came a voice from the doorway. "Let me see my grandsons!" Jacob hobbled to Tamar's side and opened his mouth in awe. "Tamar! You have brought forth the double blessing unto us, for these babes are strong before the Lord. Just look at them!"

"I am glad you approve of my children. Now kiss their mother who deserves greater praise for laboring to bring them into the world. You should know I do not deal in half-measures!"

Jacob kissed Tamar's forehead and clasped her hand. "What does Judah say of his sons?"

"He has not come unto me. He wants the babes brought forth to him." There was an edge of bitterness in Tamar's voice. "Here, Cumi. Take them and go!"

When Cumi disappeared with a white bundle in each arm, Jacob turned to his despondent daughter-in-law. "Do not grieve, Tamar. Judah will come to love you one day for this. It is the finest gift in the world when a wife gives sons to her husband."

"I only hope you speak words of prophecy. Judah has shown no indication of ever loving me since the day of our wedding. My greatest fear is that he will despise his sons, as he despises me for the way in which they were conceived."

"My daughter, you must forget the past and think pleasant thoughts. You must remain strong and happy so that in nourishing your young, you feed them no guile."

"Father Jacob, will you remain here with me—when the others go to Egypt to buy food? I think I need you now more than I have ever needed anyone."

"I had thought to do just that."

"You had?"

"I do not wish Benjamin to take such a long and dangerous journey. So I planned for the two of us to stay here with you while the others went forth."

Tamar clasped Jacob about the neck. "Oh, Father Jacob! How good you are to me—to perceive my need before I even make it known unto you." Then she thought of the selfishness of her request. "But what of your own wives and servants? Will not your household be defenseless with you and all your sons away? I can just imagine how Leah carped to think of you being here with me!"

"You forget I have many menservants well trained to guard my house. They are quite used to managing things under Eliezer's watchful eyes. Besides, I did not come only for your sake, Tamar, but for mine as well. I have missed your company. And Benjamin has plagued me to bring him to visit Cumi. Though I like not his strong attraction for her, I came to silence his mouth."

"You are a generous, wonderful man. Always thinking of others."

"How has it gone between you and Judah?"

"He is sick unto death, Father Jacob. He will be unable to ride to Egypt."

"Such a change might be good for him. To get away, to see new sights and the wonders of Egypt, all that could take his mind off present troubles and bring him back a new man."

Before Tamar could respond, another voice was at the doorway calling, "May I come in?"

"Reuben!" Tamar exclaimed. "Come in, by all means. I am delighted to see you."

"You have given me two, exceptional nephews," Reuben said, kissing Tamar's hands. "I have seen them just now—within Judah's tent. Cumi brought them to Judah while I was there."

Tamar grasped Reuben's arm. "What did Judah say? Was he pleased?"

"I am sure he was."

"But he did not show it, I am sure. He is such a shell of the man he once was. He shows no enthusiasm for anything any more."

Quickly, Reuben defended his words: "I did not say that, Tamar. I did not stay long enough to observe Judah's reaction. I left immediately, so that he might be alone to get acquainted with his sons. That is a special time—when a man holds his children for the first time."

Jacob spoke up: "Tamar concerns herself overmuch without cause. Judah will be coming here for a long visit with you very soon. It may take him a while longer to allow wounds of the past to heal, but he will turn his affections toward you and be with you soon. You will see."

Reuben held up a hand to signal Jacob. "I think not, Father. Judah plans to leave with us immediately. He sent servants to prepare his beasts for departure for Egypt, that we may lose no travel time while there is the safety of daylight."

Tamar was appalled. "But Judah is too ill to travel! Such a journey would bring only harm to one so weak and unwell. He has been at death's door. You must not take him with you!"

Reuben decided to be blunt, to spare Tamar nothing, and to speak the truth: "Judah says he will not leave his newborn sons in want. He goes to buy bread for his household. He says he wants to do one final act of mercy before . . ."

"Before he dies," Tamar finished the sentence. "Always he thinks only of dying!"

Jacob placed a comforting hand upon Tamar's shoulder to restrain her. "This may be better than you think, Tamar. I told you it would do Judah good to get away from this place and to divert his mind from his sad memories. And it proves that Judah still cares for you. Whether he admits it or not, he goes to provide food for your needs too, does he not?"

Although she did not want to admit it, Tamar heard wisdom in those words. A journey would get Judah out of the dismal solitude of his lonely tent and force him back into the world of activity. She remembered another crisis that had brought him out—when the robbers came. Her man of action took charge that night, but when the danger was over, he retreated again. Perhaps this journey was God's way of getting Judah to function and eat and live again. Judah had said he would die after seeing his offspring. That time had come. Tamar could not impose the death sentence on her husband by insisting that he remain. This was another test of whether she would be willful or submissive.

"Do you think he will, at least, come to bid me farewell?" Tamar asked meekly.

Reuben shook his head. "We must make haste, Tamar. The others already are back upon their beasts and ready to go."

"Oh, Reuben," Tamar said with pleading in her eyes, "take care of Judah. He trusts you and confides in you. You must help him come to himself and stay his hand should he speak more of destroying himself to escape his guilt and misery. Please, bring him back safely to me."

"I will remain at Judah's side and watch over him for you, Tamar. I give you my oath."

When Reuben was gone, Jacob embraced Tamar and said, "Do not fret, my dear Tamar. In spite of the famine, I have renewed hope for joyous days ahead. Judah has not been close with his brothers for many years. Bound together in this cause, they may resolve their differences and repair the rifts to restore family unity. Once those problems are resolved, Judah may be able to cope with other problems here as well."

"What differences among the brothers?" Tamar was uncertain how much Jacob knew of the true reason for all Judah's guilt.

Jacob's eyes clouded over as he said, "I have never known the exact cause for the ill will between Judah and the others. But enmity between them began right after I lost Joseph. I have not pursued the matter further with any of them because . . . because I was afraid the truth might be as painful for me as the pain Judah bears."

Tamar thought Jehovah must have given Jacob discernment to perceive more than he knew from facts and evidence. She wondered if he even believed the tale about a wild animal or any of the other explanations his lying sons brought to him. She also wondered if Jacob kept silent to save himself from greater sorrow or to spare the brothers themselves.

Cumi returned with the twins, and Benjamin followed behind her. They both had very broad smiles, but Benjamin's face changed as he approached his father.

"Why may I not go with my brothers to Egypt?" Benjamin whined. "Even now they are mounting their donkeys. I would so like to see the wondrous sights of Egypt with them."

Jacob put a protective arm about his youngest. "Some day you may travel the world, my boy, but you are too young for such a journey now."

"Too young! Always too young! When will you realize I have grown to manhood?"

Jacob's eyes were severe as he replied, "It takes more than years to make one a man."

Tamar saw the gulf between old and young becoming wider with every word, so she spoke up to intervene: "Benjamin, you are greatly needed here. Cumi and I will be defenseless women left alone when the men leave. Will you not consent to stay here as the man of the household?"

Jacob followed Tamar's lead by adding, "Yes, verily, Tamar is right. I am too old and lame to oversee Judah's house. Can we not depend upon you for that task—if you think yourself old enough for such authority? I do not know, Tamar. It is a heavy responsibility . . ."

"Wait!" Benjamin broke in. "I . . . I suppose I am needed here. There are ten riding to Egypt, but none left here to protect the women and newborn children. There might well be robbers."

Tamar cast a knowing glance toward Jacob as she took her sons again from Cumi. Then she said, "Thank you, Benjamin. Robbers have appeared already. For the sake of these little ones, I shall feel much safer with you here to protect us."

"I too thank you," said Cumi shyly. She was not the least interested in seeing Benjamin depart with the others.

"Come, Cumi," Benjamin said in a commanding voice. "You must show me about the camp and acquaint me with all that I shall oversee. You must tell me of any problems that need my attention."

Tamar and Jacob held their laughter until the two were gone.

"The lad takes his responsibility quite seriously," chuckled an amused Jacob.

"They do make a fine pair. Have you changed your mind about Cumi as a prospective bride for Benjamin?" Tamar asked.

"It is much too soon to talk of that. Besides, we have more important matters to consider—the famine, Judah's health, and these little boys here."

"And Judah's attitude toward me. Oh, Father Jacob, he will not allow me to be a wife unto him. Nor will he even speak to me."

"Did I not tell you to think only beautiful thoughts? Your milk must be pure and wholesome for my grandsons. Your sour mood could curdle it and make them spit it back in your face." Then Jacob remembered something Tamar said earlier. "Tamar, you spoke of robbers?"

"That is a tale to tell you after supper. I will set it to music and play it for you on my harp for your evening's entertainment. It will greatly amuse you."

Jacob could not believe there was anything amusing about robbers, but he let the matter go to return his attention to the babies in Tamar's arms. One tiny arm waved in the air. Another son's mouth gaped open in a wide yawn. Tamar explained the significance of the thread on the hand of the second born.

"Do you think Bella is to be believed? Could it be a sign that the firstborn has triumphed over his brother?" Tamar asked.

"It well could be," Jacob replied. "My mother said it was a similar sign from God when I emerged from the womb grabbing the heel of my brother. What are your sons to be called?"

"Judah has not said, but I should like to call the firstborn Pharez. And the other Zerah."

"So be it." Jacob placed a hand upon each little head and pronounced a blessing.

Eighteen

Jacob's sons were awed by the sights that awaited them in Egypt. They arrived in the capital city on a festal day to witness throngs of people crowding the Street of the Sun. There was to be a parade, and Pharaoh himself was to appear at the end of the procession.

Even if Judah had not decided to put aside his melancholy and suicidal thoughts to seek food for his family, he would have been impressed by the city—golden monuments of all sizes and shapes, great houses magnificently constructed of malachite and azure, and tall buildings for commerce with lotus garlands adorning their stately, white columns. Such splendid architecture completely captivated the tent-dwellers who had never beheld such spectacular artistry before.

There also were fair booths and flowers everywhere. The air was filled with mingled aromas of fragrant blossoms and pungent wares from the booths and markets along the streets. There were more people in one place than the brothers had ever seen, all standing beneath multi-colored banners flapping in the breeze. Gold seemed to flash from everywhere to reflect the light of the glaring sun overhead. The glint of gold sparkled from the paint of gilded columns, from high balustrades and windows, and even from the bejeweled dress and neckwear of the citizens.

Greeting the expected procession were women striking tambourines and boys jumping so high that their youth-locks bounced unceasingly. As the wide city gates opened, streams of carriages passed through, each drawn by high-prancing horses decorated with tall plumes upon their heads. Hosts of scribes were assuming obsequious postures to record with their reeds everything that was happening.

Judah shaded his eyes to admire in the distance the colorful mountains of Thebes. Fresh air, regular meals, and forced companionship during the journey to Egypt had produced marked improvements in Judah's health. Still not fully recovered, he was wan and weak, but he fought to overcome such weakness to complete his task and to delay the course of events he felt were inevitable. As long as he was here, he decided to enjoy whatever pleasures were left in his life.

"What are they celebrating?" Judah asked Reuben.

"Such festivals usually come at sowing and harvest times, but, with the famine throughout the land, I cannot imagine why they would be rejoicing now," Reuben replied.

Gad pointed to venders and market booths laden with food and said, "Why should they not rejoice, my brother? Look you there. There—where the rest of our brethren are standing to stuff their mouths at that booth. Here they seem to have victuals aplenty. Have a sample of some of the delicious morsels I just purchased from there."

Judah noticed that more people were drinking than eating. Everywhere both voices and goblets were raised in drunken disorder. It reminded him of Adullam. Disgusted, Judah said, "Even their women seem to drink to excess. Not to mention exposing their bodies as they do it."

Gad bristled. "Now, do not start moralizing, brother Judah. I have heard that drinking is part of their religion. There is a shrine called the Place of Drunkenness to honor the goddess of drunkenness."

Judah whispered to Reuben. "I am glad our father is not here to behold this idolatry."

Laughing and shouting, Simeon and Levi walked up to them. The twins had been exploring on their own, and they obviously were excited about something.

"You will not believe the sight we have just witnessed. Come and see it," Simeon urged.

Levi added, "It is part of the celebration. A troupe of entertainers displays a procession of women carrying long phallic emblems. They make them to stand erect by means of strings."

"Next they are to bring forth a ram to mate publicly with a virgin," Simeon laughed. "Make haste, for we do not want to miss such a sight."

Judah winced and said, "What possible enjoyment can you two derive from such spectacles?"

"There he goes," moaned Gad. "I knew a journey with Judah would be no pleasure."

Levi joined in to mock Judah: "Have you no respect for the Egyptians' religion? They commemorate the rigid readiness of the male. Is not erection and procreation a matter of dear life itself? Or do you prefer to worship at the shrine of impotence?"

Simeon nudged Gad and Levi away and said, "Come on. The rest of our brethren await to go with us. They are not so holy that they scorn a good time, as do our prudish brothers."

As the others hurried away, Reuben placed an arm about Judah. "They are to be pitied. But their behavior should not surprise you, Judah. To sport and debauch and indulge their baser natures are old habits with them. You know that."

"Yet it pains me to see them disregard our father's religion so flagrantly," Judah said. "I wonder how they heard of such depraved events. None of our tribe speaks their language."

Reuben was the most studious of the brothers, except for Joseph. From Eliezer, he had learned about Egypt, so Reuben had a ready reply to most of Judah's questions: "There are many interpreters who delight to instruct visitors. This is a learned place, full of culture and knowledge from many lands. To speak many languages is not uncommon here."

Judah remarked, "But in this place I fear the wisdom far exceeds the righteousness. Let us go to the main street for the parade. I want to see Pharaoh when he passes by."

"He also is an Egyptian god," Reuben said as they made their way through the crowded street. "The people here love him devotedly."

"Would that our people loved our God as much. Would that I had such unfailing devotion."

"Judah, stop torturing yourself. We both have performed sinful acts with women outside the boundaries of God's law—you with Tamar and I with Bilhah. We both repented and are now lawfully married men who no longer condone fornication and adultery, as our brothers do. Why can you not realize God has forgiven you, and you have no right to be less forgiving of yourself?"

"Perhaps the sin of this place only makes mine more evident. Not that I need so great a reminder. Whether in Egypt, Adullam, or Canaan, I cannot escape myself."

Reuben sighed as he said, "I was taking heart that you had improved in spirit. Do not fall back into the dark shadows from which you have just emerged."

"I have not arisen from the shadows, Reuben. They trail behind me wherever I go. This journey was for one purpose only—to feed the hungry. Then I want to find peace, and that means I must stop having to live with myself."

Reuben wanted to say more, but now was not the time. He pointed to the flashing gold of Pharaoh's chariot approaching in the distance and went on with the lesson: "Pharaoh comes at mid-day, in honor of the sun god. Eliezer once said the priests take purificatory baths and incense themselves at the palace before they follow the Pharaoh to make their sacrifices. Then they repeat the rites before the people of the land. With drink and dance, the people believe they can enter an age of peace and prosperity, a new beginning."

Judah said, "An easier religion than ours if drink and dance are all one needs to find peace."

In the parade, palace guards preceded Pharaoh. They wore leather leaves over their apron kilts and feathers in their helmets as they carried colored streamers atop gilded poles. As the sun reached its zenith, a cry burst forth, guards raised their spears, and Pharaoh descended upon the crowd. The people became wild, throwing themselves upon the ground, waving banners, tossing flowers, or holding young children overhead. Judah turned his eyes as women ripped open their garments to offer their breasts in both hands unto the monarch. It reminded him of seductive Mai.

What did impress Judah was Pharaoh himself. He stood in a high, glittering chariot that blinded the eyes in the mid-day sun, and he drove his magnificent, white stallions in a cloud of fire and smoke. He wore a jeweled collar on his white linen garment and a crown decorated with a formidable, rearing cobra, another symbol of the Egyptian sun god.

Pharaoh was accompanied by attendants—soldiers, body-guards, archers, and shield-bearers of many different races. To their living god and his attendants the crowd sang songs of adoration, applauded, and cheered in a frenzied uproar of jubilation. Next came another chariot driven by a young boy to whom the crowds shouted, "Hail, child of mighty Pharaoh, our future hope and glory!" In a third chariot sat Pharaoh's chief wife, the first lady of the land, who was lauded as their "mother of god." She wore a huge headdress in the form of a vulture with its wings hanging down to her shoulders. She was followed by princesses, ladies of the court, and Pharaoh's friends.

A jovial stranger standing beside the brothers began to speak to them in their own language. He welcomed them and seemed anxious to assist them by answering their questions.

Reuben asked the stranger, "Can you tell me where we must go to buy food? My brothers and I are here to purchase as much as we can to feed our starving households in Canaan. How is it we go about approaching the mighty Pharaoh?"

Laughing, the stranger explained they did not go to Pharaoh himself, but to the governor of the land who had the granaries in Menfe and who determined who was permitted to buy. He gave them directions to the place, but he was unable to understand why the sojourners would not want to wait until all the feasting and festivities were over.

The rest of the brothers had rejoined Reuben and Judah and overheard the conversation with the stranger. They agreed with the stranger that there was no reason to be hurrying off to Menfe before they had partaken of all the city's hospitality.

"I wish to stay a while," said Simeon, eyeing a lovely Egyptian girl who passed by in a scanty, clinging tunic. "Why can we not enjoy the festival first, and then attend to our business on the morrow?"

Reuben replied sternly, "If I know you, you would not have money enough to buy food on the morrow. No, we must take our leave right away."

Because Reuben was in charge as eldest, the others grumbled but obeyed. The mounted their beasts and headed for the governor's distribution center. As they rode along, Reuben continued to answer their questions and to serve as their tour guide and spokesman.

"Notice the garments they wear here," Reuben said, pointing to Egyptians they passed on their way. "They are very practical. The sun is so severe that they wear white to offset the sun's burning rays. To keep cool, they make garments spun from flax so fine that their bodies are visible underneath. Some wear nothing at all."

Levi asked, "Is it true the people here also wear wigs upon their heads?"

"Quite true," Reuben replied. "Both men and women often shave their heads and wear artificial hair."

Judah wanted to know, "Why do the women have black painted lines about their eyes?"

Reuben laughed. "To make themselves beautiful, of course."

"I prefer to see women fully clothed, with their own hair on their heads, and without thick, black streaks around their eyes," Judah commented.

Reuben continued, "Egyptians enjoy art work—not only on their buildings and tombs, but also on themselves. They sometimes tattoo pictures on their bodies."

Dan became interested in the conversation and suggested that Reuben tell them about the religions of the area. He was confused by all the images and monuments to so many deities.

"Egyptians worship everything," Reuben said. "Besides Pharaoh and the sun, there is Osiris, god of the underworld; Herus, god of ancient kingdoms; Isis, goddess of fertility; and hosts of others, including all sorts of beasts—cobra, cow, hawk. They even think the great Nile River is a god. They worship almost all created things, just not the true Creator."

"Even as many Canaanites worship their idols to Baal and Ishtar," said Gad. "I am not surprised that they worship the sun. It beats down with such fury, it seems god-like to me."

"Do not complain," Reuben scolded. "Be thankful God has brought us to this place. Look about you and see the great storehouses and corn bins. There are also underground pits for stor-

290

ing grain. Someone must have known a famine was coming and made provision in advance."

Asher asked, "What does our great and wise teacher have to tell us about Menfe, this place to which we must travel?"

Reuben ignored the sneer in Asher's voice and replied, "It is a metropolis of tombs near On, the city of temples and worship of the sun god. It is a great seat of learning with a university."

"I think I prefer sitting under the tree of wisdom, listening to old Eliezer," said Judah. "There is something ominous about all these great buildings and the pagan symbols and images that adorn them."

When the brothers entered the walled city of Menfe, they made their way down narrow streets toward the great distribution hall. They were tired and bedraggled from their ride in the blazing sun. Perspiration had caked road dirt to their skin, and hot winds had blown sand into their eyes to turn them red. Judah, who had been weak at the start of the journey, was now almost unconscious, drooping upon his beast. The only one not grumbling was Reuben as he instructed them to dismount and then led them to sign the register and wait to be called before the governor.

Naphtali spoke for all the complainers when he said, "I see no reason for this long delay. Why must we sit here and wait? We have money. Let us buy and move on."

Reuben explained, "The kind stranger told me the custom is to come before the governor. He personally attends to all transactions among those from other lands who come here to buy."

"But why?" several brothers asked in chorus.

Their answer did not come from Reuben. A large Egyptian guard, who spoke the language of Canaan, stood before them and said, "Adon, our just and wise governor, must be sure that false men do not take precious grain when there is no need. You must wait here for him to call you."

Gad asked, "And how long do we wait before we can see this Adon?"

"That will be up to him," snapped the guard, taking the register, disappearing behind two ornately carved doors, and leaving the brothers to wait in the gleaming, marble anteroom.

Reuben noticed that Judah was about to collapse, so he laid him to rest upon a stone bench. Then he sent Asher to wet a piece of cloth in the bubbling fountain outside the entrance. The cooling water for Judah's head was long in coming. Asher's eyes were dazzled with the beauty of the garden surrounding the fountain. After leaving the dried brown foliage of Canaan, what he beheld was a striking contrast. He walked around, exploring the lush, green bounty of the place. There were fig trees, date palms, and plump fish swimming in a large pool. The Egyptian secret of obtaining water without rainfall was a marvel to see.

By the time Asher rejoined the others, the Egyptian guard also had returned. He spoke briefly with Reuben and then led them all to a door that was not the same one through which he had entered and exited before.

"Come, Asher! Stop dawdling!" Reuben called. "We are being taken to a rest house for the night. The governor will not see us until morning."

A buzz of discontent went up from the group until Reuben's commanding voice silenced them: "Peace! This delay may work to our advantage. We are a sorry-looking sight with grime and road dirt upon us. We will make a better impression upon the governor if we are rested and cleaned up and wearing garments that do not smell of sweat."

Simeon sneered, "Who wants to make an impression? We only wish to buy corn."

Reuben became more emphatic. "And we shall not be able to buy anything unless we follow the governor's orders. Now, come!"

The ten followed the guard out the door to a separate wing of the building. Reuben and Dan half carried Judah, who could barely stand. They seemed to be entering a private guest house.

"Wait!" Levi shouted when the guard ushered them into their luxuriant quarters. "We cannot afford expensive lodgings such as these!"

The guard half smiled as he said, "There is no charge. You are to be guests of the governor. If you should want anything, just knock upon the door, and one of the servants will come to do your bidding."

Before any further protest or questions could be formed, the guard disappeared. Then they heard the click of the sliding bolt upon the door after him.

Dan ran to the door and banged upon it, shouting, "Come back! Why have we been locked in here?"

It was a question in the minds of all of them. They were guilty of nothing amiss. All they had done since arriving was to sign the register. Why had they been placed under house arrest? Or was it arrest? They surely were in no pit or dungeon! Their eyes bulged in wonder at what they saw as they surveyed their quarters.

The main room in which they stood sprawled out into an apartment large enough for a group twice their size. There was a hall leading to a lavish lounge with flower-twined columns and plush furnishings. Sleeping chambers provided a separate room for each guest; a soft, sweet-smelling bed; and a well-provided toilet area with equipment, appointments, and items for personal use. Steps led down to a sunken pool for bathing. Elegant food, drink, and dainties were spread out upon a large table in the dining suite. Some foods were mysteries, and some items and inventions puzzled the brothers, who had no idea what they were nor how they were to be used.

It all was far too complicated and elaborate for simple, tent-dwelling foreigners. Every imaginable comfort seemed to be available in the sumptuous rooms in which they were to abide for the night. But what did it all mean?

Reuben went to one of the small apertures that permitted light to enter the room. He peered through a grated lattice work to see more guards pacing back and forth in the covered walkway outside. A Nubian slave stood by their door. The obvious conclusion was that this was the promised servant standing ready to do their bidding. Reuben knocked on the door.

When the huge black man entered, it was not difficult to make him understand that Judah was suffering from sun stroke and fatigue. The Nubian examined Judah, grunted what sounded like a solution to the problem, and went away. He soon returned with a foaming vile of medicine.

"Drink!" the slave commanded.

As if by magic, the drug revived Judah, who sat upright for the first time.

The black man was gone; the door was locked once again; and the brothers were left standing in the room with blank expressions on their faces. First, they looked at the bolted door. Then, they looked at each other and shrugged.

"This is all very strange," said Dan. "Very strange indeed."

Simeon mused, "I wonder if I knocked on that door, if the black man would bring me the Egyptian beauty I saw on the street today."

Levi gave a wicked smile and said to his twin, "If so, have him bring nine of her sisters, one for each of us."

Reuben held up both hands for attention. "Now hear me, my brothers! I do not understand what is happening to us now, nor can I predict what will happen on the morrow. But I can tell you what will and will not happen tonight. There will be no drunken orgy, and no strange women will be brought through that door. We will bathe, dine, retire for a night of much needed sleep, and arise refreshed in the morning, ready to approach the governor who holds our fate in his hands."

Judah, who was feeling much better, knew he should stand with Reuben against the others. Their faces and murmurings indicated trouble. "Reuben is right. We must present ourselves before the governor with the reputation of being upright men, not night brawlers and wanton fools!"

The majority, albeit unwillingly and reluctantly, finally yielded to the minority opinion. They all were so tired and hungry, that a quiet meal and good rest was beginning to take precedence over all other creature comforts.

Ten sons of Judah retired that night in a strange place in a foreign land. Their bellies were full of delectable food, and their minds were full of unanswered questions.

In the other wing of the massive building, long after the business of the day was concluded, a man sat upon a throne in the Hall of the Nourisher. He held the book of the registry and gazed at it in silence. Adon, the Egyptian name for the foreign governor of Egypt, was second in command, next to Pharaoh himself. He shielded his eyes so the few attendants, those still re-

294

maining with him at that late hour, could not see the peculiar look on his face.

"Leave me!" the ruler commanded. "All leave me except Omar."

Magistrates, scribes, ministers, and guards filed silently from the room. When they were gone, Adon beckoned to Omar, the governor's interpreter and his closest friend.

"See here these names?" Adon asked, pointing to the register. "Reuben, Simeon, Levi, Judah, Dan . . . all the others listed as sons of Jacob from Hebron of Canaan?"

"Your brothers!" Omar gasped. "Oh, Adon-Joseph! Finally, they come!"

Omar knew that the reason the governor had instituted the registry was in the hope of one day seeing those names written in the book.

"I shall have an audience with them tomorrow," Adon said. "Tonight I must calm myself from my joyous excitement and think of a plan. How shall I greet them? How must this be done?"

"I doubt that your brothers will be so glad to see you. Remember, they are the ones who hated you, rent your garments, and threw you into a pit before they made you an Egyptian slave."

"That is of no importance now, Omar. Were it not for Judah selling me to the merchants, I never would have come here and risen to my position as Pharaoh's favorite. I owe a great deal of appreciation to my brethren."

"I think you give your brothers more credit than they are due," Omar said with concern.

"God ordained that this be so. He sent me dreams in my youth to show me my brothers would one day bow before me, and now it will come to pass! Oh, Omar, look at the results God has accomplished, not at the means by which the results occurred."

"Still, I would advise being cautious—until you are certain these men bear you no more malice nor intend to do you further harm."

"Some of their malice was well deserved. I was a young peacock in my youth, full of boasting and self-importance for my favored position and my power to interpret dreams. I took full

295

advantage of my honor as the favorite son and threw it up to my brothers at every chance."

"Come now, Adon-Joseph. I cannot believe you capable of being like that. You are the most kind, unselfish man I know—feeding those with money to buy and the poor as well."

"Perhaps my early years in an Egyptian prison taught me to behave with more compassion and to control my tattletale tongue."

Omar laughed. "You were a tale bearer also? I cannot believe it. Do you think your brothers will recognize you now? Even though your appearance may have changed, your speech surely will give you away as their tattletale little brother."

"You are right. There are certain things I must find out before I reveal my true identity to them. You must speak for me, Omar. You will be my interpreter at tomorrow's audience."

"But why?"

"See—Benjamin's name is not registered. I must learn whether that means my true brother is dead, or still with my father, if he is yet alive. I fear my brothers' hatred of me may have been turned upon Benjamin. I must know what kind of men they are before I know how I must deal with them. I easily can forgive their ill treatment of me, but if they have harmed others, I . . . I . . ."

Omar could tell that his friend was perplexed and dealing with a host of conflicted emotions—joyous anticipation at the expected reunion with his estranged kinsmen, curiosity about the past and present behaviors and motives of his brothers, doubts and dread about the best way to proceed, and concern for the welfare of his beloved father and younger brother.

"I think you were wise to delay meeting your brothers until morning." Omar said after a time of observing his lord in silence. "You shall need quiet to sort things out and to pray to your God for guidance. And I know you will want to discuss this weighty matter with your wife."

"Yes, Asenath always is such a blessed comfort and help to me. She knows how I have wished for her to meet my family and for my father, if he is still alive, to see my two sons. Oh, Omar, would it not be marvelous if I could bring all my family here and spare them from the famine in their land? I would like to share my bounty with them and have them nourished at my hand."

With a smile of admiration, Omar said, "I think you would take the whole world under your wing for protection, if you but could. Look at all you have done—not only for the Egyptians, but also for starving people from many other lands."

"Give the glory to God alone, Omar. He may have used me to work His wonders, but He just as easily might have chosen another. He gave me the power to interpret Pharaoh's dream foretelling the famine. He gave me the intelligence to know how to store up food against the days of adversity and how to feed His hungry people. The Lord, alone, is to be praised, not His servant."

"I am rightly chastised, Adon-Joseph. I know that yours is the only true God, above all the gods of Egypt. And I know He will be with you tomorrow when you meet with your brothers."

"Well said, Omar. Let us go home now, so that we both may pray for God to direct us when you serve as my interpreter and I interrogate the ten sons of Jacob."

Together they walked solemnly from the Hall of the Nourisher, passing the walls of painted murals of Egyptian life—scenes of sowing and threshing, workers ploughing with oxen and applying the sickle to the golden grain. Adon-Joseph paused at the picture of fat and thin cattle and read again the inscription it bore to interpret it: Pharaoh's dream of seven years of plenty would be followed by seven years of famine, but the God of Pharaoh's minister would deliver the people from want and sorrow.

Nineteen

At the time of the audience the next morning, Jacob's ten sons were apprehensive. Being locked up all night made them tremble at the thought of approaching the ruler who sat upon his great throne, high above their heads.

They had no way of knowing the governor, likewise, trembled, although for a very different reason. He held a handkerchief to his face as the ten men bowed their faces to the floor, the very thing foretold so many years before. From over the edge of the silk, the ruler cast his tear-glazed eyes to look at each in turn—the eldest, like a great tower; the broad-shouldered lion; the twins who did not dissemble their natively belligerent air; each one thereafter with a distinguishing characteristic to identify himself in the mind of the one on the throne.

A beckoning gesture from the governor brought the ten closer, where they again bowed to pay him homage. "Hail, Mighty Deliverer!" the brothers sang in chorus as they had rehearsed. They had decided that the paths of praise and obeisance would lead most quickly to the corn they needed along with the freedom they desired.

Adon's muffled voice spoke from behind the handkerchief: "Interpreter, ask them why so many have come at once to converge upon us. How can so many of the same family come here and leave their wives unprotected and their households in want? It seems more likely they would have sent an ambassador if they are truly sons of the same father. Inquire of them!"

While Omar translated the words, the eyes behind the handkerchief continued to search the faces before him. Was this the same hate-hungry wolf pack that attacked him and dabbled his colorful prince's coat in blood? Some showed signs of gray streaks in their hair and beards. This made Joseph shrink back a little, for it was hardly believable that his father, with sons this age, could still be alive. But for all his doubts and fears, there was mingled joyous exhilaration in recognition. They were his brothers, and he loved them still.

No sign of recognition came from the brothers, however. Never would they have imagined the aristocratic potentate upon the throne was anyone familiar. He seemed very austere and forbidding as he sat erect, wearing his impressive, brilliant garments and magnificent collar.

As spokesman for the group, Reuben replied to the governor's inquiry, "We are from Canaan here to buy food. Because of the terrible starvation in our land, every brother of this family came to take back all we can buy to meet the needs of our great household."

As the interpreter repeated the message, Joseph capitalized upon Reuben's slip of the tongue to pose his next question: "This, then, is your entire family—ten brothers?"

"No," Reuben corrected himself. "We were twelve brothers in all. But one is too young to travel and remained home with our father. The other—he is no longer with us."

Joseph was overcome with happiness to learn that his father still lived and that Benjamin was safe. But the test was not over. With feigned outrage, he stood to his feet to shout, "I perceive you change your story as you go along—saying first that every brother is before me, then that there are two more. I do not believe you are all brethren. You must lie, for you look not all alike!"

Reuben tried to explain that differences were due to being children of different mothers. He stressed that they all had the same father, Jacob of Canaan, so some were only half-brothers.

While Reuben's explanation was being interpreted, Joseph had to turn his face away. His eyes were filling with tears of joy, as he thought of the possibility of seeing his father again. The turning away only added to the uneasiness of his audience.

"If you are from Canaan," Joseph prodded, "tell me the route you took to arrive here."

Judah could see Reuben faltering, looking dismayed that he was not faring well in the interrogation thus far. To assist his brother, Judah spoke up: "We came down from Hebron to Gaza and then along the coast toward Egypt."

Joseph looked squarely into the eyes of his rival for the covenant blessing. The eyes did not have the same piercing hatred of long ago. They seemed tired eyes, full of sorrow and suffering. Joseph thought Judah had been either physically ill or mentally tormented, perhaps with guilt. Probably both, for the sickness of the spirit often causes the body to fall ill as well.

Playing his role most convincingly, Joseph cried out, "I still do not believe your words! The route you suggest is hard and fraught with robbers. Fierce dust storms are frequent. How is it you survived such a perilous journey in safety?"

"With our God's help we were brought safely to your door," Judah said through the words of the interpreter. "We had only one dust-abubu, of moderate severity."

Joseph pounded a fist upon his throne's armrest. "Interpreter, tell these men that they lie. My earlier suspicions have been confirmed. They are not true men!"

At the interpreter's words, the brothers began to protest at once and to buzz among themselves, unable to understand why they were being so unjustly accused.

"Silence!" commanded Joseph without waiting for interpretation. "Why do you suppose you were locked up last night? Only guests of honor or prisoners receive free lodging here!"

"Prisoners?" cried Reuben. "But why?"

Joseph's explanation was long, so it was broken down into manageable portions for the sake of the interpreter and to observe the brothers' reactions to each part. First, the governor repeated his first accusation—so many names together in the registry indicated that they could not be brothers. Ten heads of a combined household would not depart together, leaving none behind for defense. To that accusation, Reuben replied there were numerous servants to guard the women and children at home because their father, the family patriarch, was wealthy—blessed of Jehovah God, whom he served faithfully.

Second, Joseph said sons of so large a family—especially one with a father as blessed and as wealthy as Reuben claimed him to be—would not need to come begging. Reuben realized his boasting of his father's wealth was a mistake. The subtle ruler was convicting him with his own words. All Reuben could think to say was that they were not hungry for gold, but for bread.

Third, Joseph accused them of being spies. He said wicked kings of the east sent them to discover a way of invasion and plunder to take the fruits of his land by force. Reuben was totally stumped. He could think of no way to prove that they were not spies.

Once again, Judah came to Reuben's rescue. When he was granted permission to speak, Judah said, "Consider, merciful lord, that it rests with you to give evidence against us for being spies, rather than for us to disprove it. That is the custom in our land where justice is pronounced by a council of the city's learned fathers."

"Is your system of law in Canaan more just than mine?" Joseph countered.

Judah bowed before answering. "I mean not to defy you nor to question your reputation for justice. I only meant to remind you that you have no proof against us, for there is none."

Stroking his chin while Omar gave the needless interpretation, Joseph then said, "The strong-shouldered one speaks with a sly, but mighty, tongue. I will prove my justice equal to that of your learned council in Canaan. I shall put your story to a test. Since I am responsible for feeding the hungry of many lands, I cannot take a slightest chance against spies. Therefore, choose one among you to return to your home and bring me the alleged younger brother you claim to have. The rest will be kept my prisoners until the younger brother stands before me to disprove my suspicions."

Without pausing to think, Reuben blurted out a protest as his brothers gestured frantically, encouraging him to say the right thing. "My gracious lord, we have eleven households in want, including my father's with our ten. If only one of us is allowed to return with food, it will not be enough. That is the very reason we *all* came—to show the lord of Egypt we each need corn in plenteous amounts, not by the ephah, but by the homer!"

Judah thought of another argument, so he whispered it in Reuben's ear. "Another reason it would not be prudent to send one of our ten home," Reuben said as Judah's prompted, "is that a lone traveler is sure to be attacked by robbers. Then the food would fall into the wrong hands . . . the younger brother could not be brought before you . . . you would be keeping nine men imprisoned unjustly . . . and all eleven households would die in the famine." As he finished, Reuben nodded his approving thanks for Judah's help.

Joseph almost smiled to see his brothers working so hard to provide convincing arguments. It reminded him of being questioned by Eliezer in an exercise in logic. It was also amusing because they squirmed and fretted when there was no possibility of danger coming to them at his hand.

He said, "I wish to give you men benefit of every doubt. If you are not spies, but truly several households of the same family in want of food, it would be unmerciful of me to send it not. I should not want the deaths of the starving upon my head." Then with a nod of recognition to Judah for his obvious contribution, he added, "Nor would I want robbers to steal my provisions."

The brothers took heart at the interpreter's version of Joseph's words, but their moment of exultation was short-lived. Joseph continued, "Therefore, this do and live—for I also fear the same God you worship—select one among you to remain here as my prisoner. The rest may carry food home to the starving. But all shall return, including the youngest, in order to reclaim the prisoner."

A hushed silence filled the room. Not a brother could speak. Judah was the only one to find words: "Mighty ruler, you are merciful to devise such a plan, but how can we comply? Our father guards the youngest with his life and insists he take no perilous journey. The boy never leaves our aged father's side. That is the reason Benjamin—for that is his name—is not with us now. To tear the lad away would cause our father to die of grief."

"That is absurd!" cried Joseph before the interpretation was finished. "What father holds to a son like a mother holds a babe to her bosom?"

"A very old and pitiful man," Judah replied. "The lad is our father's only joy in his declining years since . . . since the loss of the other brother, one who held a favored place in his heart."

Joseph's memory flew back to being the favored son of that adored father. It wrenched his very heart, but he dared not show it. "If your father is a true man of God, he surely will not suffer another son to remain here in bondage. No! I shall not change my mind again. You must bring your youngest brother here to verify your story, or you prove yourselves to be spies!"

The brothers began to speak among themselves while Joseph leaned on his elbow and listened. He motioned the guards away when they moved forward to silence the tumult of the prisoners' voices. Joseph was learning things he wanted to know as the men bickered, complained, and suggested alternatives.

Reuben raised extended palms for silence and shouted, "Brothers! It does no good to speculate or try to devise ways to avoid this situation. We have no choice but to do as the governor commands. Our only decision now is the selection of the one to remain here while the rest take food to our families and try to find a way to explain this tragic situation to our father."

"I will stay," Judah said quickly. "My life is worth less than any other."

"No!" Reuben replied sharply. "You are the heir to the blessing. It must be another."

Judah was ready to say he wanted no part in the blessing, when Simeon broke into the conversation: "I will stay! I like it here in plenteous Egypt. Even as a prisoner, I shall live more sumptuously than at home as a free man."

"Care you so little about your family?" asked Dan, amazed at Simeon's willingness.

Simeon scowled. "I thought you wanted a volunteer. Well, I am he. I know that you will divide the food evenly with my wife and children as with your own."

Levi was shocked and a bit angry that his twin wanted to stay: "You are wrong if you think they will give you beauteous Egyptian maids to comfort you. They will not do so for a prisoner!"

Reuben signaled for attention once more: "Enough! For whatever reasons, unselfish or otherwise, we should appreciate Simeon's offer to remain. Since the rest of us do not protest Simeon's decision, it shall be according to his word."

"But I protest!" Judah said earnestly. "Can you not see this whole matter is further retribution, one more of God's punishments, for the sin against our brother, Joseph? I am the one who had him sold into Egyptian bondage. So I should be the one to be repaid in kind and be bound here. I do not wish to live, and my days of joy are over. I have brought misery and famine to our land, so you must leave me here if you ever wish to enjoy prosperity again."

Reuben clasped Judah by the shoulders: "You take too much blame upon yourself, brother Judah. If this is verily God's punishment, then we all share in it."

Joseph could bear to hear no more. His nose began to prickle as he sniffed into his handkerchief. To Omar he said, "Tell the brothers to remain here. I am unwell and must retire to compose myself."

The ten men watched in confusion as the mighty ruler broke down before them and left the high dais. Flanked on either side by lance-bearers, they stood too frightened to think of escaping.

"What happens now?" asked Issachar. "What is wrong with the governor?"

"Who can know?" Naphtali replied. "Perhaps he goes to his physician for medicine."

Asher said, "I do not understand this, Adon. Calling us spies and demanding a prisoner!"

"But," Judah said, "he spoke of believing in our God. Egyptians do not worship as we do."

Dan added, "He changes so quickly—setting us up with lodging and food, even providing medicine for Judah, and then becoming cross and cruel with us. Perhaps he, like Pharaoh, is a god, a two-faced god, who blesses one moment and curses the next."

"Quiet!" commanded Reuben. "The interpreter still stands near. Such words against the ruler can get us into more trouble still. We could pay for your foolish remarks with our lives."

Zebulon lowered his voice to a whisper: "Adon returns. Bow down, and be silent."

By the time Joseph returned to the hall, he was himself

again, but the handkerchief was still held to his face. In a voice thick with emotion, he asked, "Have you selected the prisoner?"

Simeon and Judah both stepped forward.

"There seems to be some dispute as to which of you will remain. Very well, I shall be the one to choose." With that, Joseph pointed his fan toward Simeon, who, except for a faint smile of triumph, looked straight ahead as though being imprisoned did not bother him at all.

With a gesture from Joseph and a command from the captain of the guard, soldiers advanced and bound Simeon before their eyes.

Judah called to Simeon as the guards led him away, "Courage, Simeon! I shall do all within my power to return and have you released. It is not meet that you should suffer for my sin."

Simeon's faint smile burst into a laugh: "You cannot always be the only one to suffer, Judah! I know how you love self-punishment and glory in playing the martyr, but I have won this cup of suffering. And I mean to drink it in enjoyment!"

Judah's face burned at the taunting, but he still hoped Simeon would be treated well. The prisoner flashed a toothy smile, lifted his bound hands in a farewell wave, and shouted, "Do not hurry back with Benjamin too soon, my brothers!"

Joseph returned his attention to the nine: "As for the rest of you, you are free to go and purchase provisions. I will not charge you the highest price, lest you say Pharaoh's minister exploited you. Besides the corn, you may buy wheat and barley, but I advise you not to risk trying to sow the corn. The drought will continue, and the seed would be wasted."

Under his breath, Asher said, "The man even predicts the weather for the coming year."

"I bid you farewell," Joseph continued. "Remember, you are still suspects. The long famine will bring you again to me, but be certain your younger brother comes back with you."

With a clap of his hands, Adon-Joseph broke off the audience and dismissed the brothers. He paused only long enough to whisper further instructions to his steward and to give a parting glance toward the ones who still had no idea who he was. Then he exited.

305

Moments later, the brothers followed the steward to another office in the building where they received vouchers for the food-stuffs to be purchased. So quickly were the measures of grain weighed and their animals loaded in a nearby courtyard, they were able to set off for home the same day.

They traveled a good distance from Menfe toward the frontier before approaching darkness forced them to stop and set up camp for the night. They had been given special provisions for their meals along the roadway. Legs of mutton, broth, bread, and dried fruits were packed in skins to keep them fresh. The travelers chose a campground that was a pleasant and convenient spot. There was a crooked palm tree for shade and shelter, a small hut that served as an inn, and a well nearby. It was obvious that others had camped here, for the earth was blackened from their fires.

"Was it not strange that extra food for us to eat as we traveled was included in the purchase price?" Judah asked.

"That was not the strangest thing to have happened on this trip, brother Judah," Reuben replied. "I suppose because of the plenty in Egypt, they could afford to be generous to us."

All the others chimed in to comment on the trip that defied explanation. Their spirits lifted as they spoke of bringing bread to their hungry families, but spirits fell again when they spoke of Simeon being imprisoned and problems associated with convincing their father to let Benjamin return to Egypt with them. They commented most about the strange behaviors of the governor who had entertained them like royalty and then called them spies. They agreed their father would not believe any of it, for it all seemed so far-fetched they could hardly believe it themselves.

Each brother had a different task to perform when they stopped for the night. Some unloaded the donkeys. Others drew water or built the fire. Judah's task was feeding the beasts, both those they rode and the pack animals. As he opened his feedbag, he let out a cry of alarm.

"What is it, Judah?" asked Reuben, who had taken an oath to always stand close by.

"Look at this!" Judah opened the feedbag wider. "My money is still within my sack!"

"Judah, did you not pay when the grain was measured?"

"Yes, I am certain I did. Oh, Reuben, my mind is now confused. I do not know for sure."

"Say nothing of this. It must have been an oversight. We cannot turn back now with the money. Remember the governor's words. The next time we see him, Benjamin must be with us."

"Do you not realize why God has done this to me?" Judah asked as the muscles of his face drew tight and he wobbled on unsteady feet.

"Must you always interpret every event in terms of your own, personal punishment?"

"Of course, I must. Consider how unexplainable this is. Does your heart not sink to think of the consequences? The governor will now think us thieves as well as spies."

Reuben slapped Judah on his broad shoulders, both as a playful gesture and in the hope of knocking some sense into him. "Think of it as a blessing of fortune, my brother! You get your grain gratis and should not complain."

"Not complain? Would you not complain if each day brought a new tragedy into you life?"

Reuben was becoming more and more provoked with Judah. "My brother, I have tried to be patient with you and sympathetic to your legitimate sufferings, but you are beginning to weary me with the way you take some kind of peculiar delight in making each day's event your personal tragedy. Did you not hear what Simeon said to you about wishing to be a martyr and loving self-punishment? He spoke for all of us. The brothers, and I count myself among them, are becoming increasingly agitated by your depressing behavior, somber face, and constant self-incrimination."

Judah was jolted by Reuben's harshness. "What are you saying, Reuben?"

"I am saying that you are an ass!" Reuben shouted. Then, seeing the look on Judah's face, he lowered his voice to continue. "Judah, you are not the only man in the world who has ever suffered or committed a sin. Others learn to get over the past, accept forgiveness, and try to make something of their lives. You just give up on yourself. You hide in your tent and force Tamar to

307

take on your responsibilities. You blame yourself for everything from deaths in your family to the famine. If you insist on feeding your guilty conscience and being depressed and planning your death, please do so without bringing down everyone else with you. Right now, I am beginning to feel contaminated by the infection your spread. I am depressed enough to die too!"

Judah did not know whether to be hurt, angry, defensive, or something else. He tried both hurt and anger: "I am happy to know how you feel. From now on, I will keep my troubles and my opinions about them to myself. I shall not burden you by speaking to you of them again."

"There you go!" Reuben cried in exasperation. "You cannot even accept helpful criticism without turning it into another reason to mope and feel sorry for yourself. You used to have the reputation for being a strong man. The lion they called you. But you have turned into a weakling. Instead of using your energies to fight and conquer, you want to lie down and die. That is being a coward, Judah!"

"What do you suggest I do?"

"For now, I suggest you get your mind off of yourself and start thinking about others. Force yourself to say something positive and cheerful for a change. Eat something. Get a good's night's rest, and face the long journey in the morning in an improved state of mind."

It was not as easy as that. Reuben did not know how often Judah had tried to turn off his mind and quiet the demon voices inside his head that seemed to have more control of him than he had strength of will.

Even though Judah intellectually agreed with Reuben and knew his brother was right, there was no way to explain why he could not follow the well-intentioned advice. Judah turned and walked away. He could not take the simplest parts of the advice. He ate little and slept less.

Through the night, Judah tossed to and fro and kept thinking of how displeased his father would be at this latest development. How did the money appear in his feedbag when he was certain he had given it for the food? His father was an honest business man and had taught his sons to be the same. Now Judah had more to confess to his father than just the selling of Joseph.

Then Judah's thoughts turned to Simeon. Why had the governor chosen him? Judah would have preferred to stay far away from his godly father and to avoid the day of reckoning over the matter of the covenant blessing. If he had been the one imprisoned, it might have been true atonement for his sins. He would have become a bond slave in Egypt, the same punishment he had inflicted on Joseph. That would have been a just settlement of the debt and given Judah some relief from his guilt. But he was thwarted even from that.

When Judah's restless mind raced to images of Tamar and his newborn sons, he desperately tried to stop himself from thinking, but it was impossible. He was glad to be bringing food to his house, but dreading to face his wife. He could not continue to avoid her, but he dared not allow himself to love her. He did not want his first family's fate to befall his second family as well. Why did he have to believe that was inevitable?

Long ago, Judah had decided the best solution for everyone would be for him to end his life. Reuben was right. That was the coward's way out. Why had he turned into such a weakling with all fight and strength drained from him?

Then, the most horrible thought of all jumped into Judah's tormented and confused mind. It was a staggering question that would haunt him for the rest of this and other sleepless nights.

The question was this: If he could not escape God's retribution in life, would it still continue with him forever after death?

Twenty

During the absence of the sojourners to Egypt, Tamar and Cumi tried to content themselves with whatever would help them forget the famine. Tamar's greatest joy was in motherhood. She nursed her young, played with them upon the bed mat or out under the trees, and sang to them as she created lullabies on her harp.

It was the first time Tamar had ever felt such love, such tenderness. Apart from her close relationship with Father Jacob, she never had given herself so devotedly to anyone before. The birth of the twins seemed to brighten the drab, barren, rainless days. That special happiness would have been complete if only she were permitted to share it with her husband. But Tamar was learning to take life one day at a time and be thankful for what she had.

Cumi's joy in having Benjamin so near was overshadowed by Father Jacob's protectiveness. He made it impossible for them to be alone. He often held to Benjamin's hand in Cumi's presence, much to the lad's chagrin. Benjamin had suggested several times that Cumi slip away after dark to meet him, but Cumi always refused.

"I must win your father's respect if he is ever to want me for a daughter-in-law," Cumi said. "If he finds us conspiring against his will, that respect—and our relationship—will be lost forever."

So the young lovers had spoken their love words mutely with their eyes across the supper pot, or whispered at the well, or visited with Tamar and the twins—always hoping for a stolen moment together that would not arouse suspicion.

"You would think a man his age would need to nap longer during the day!" Cumi complained to Tamar as they bathed the twins. It had been over a month since the brothers departed, but the passing weeks had not provided an opportunity for Cumi and Benjamin to pursue romance.

"Why do you wish Father Jacob to take a long nap?" Tamar questioned.

"So Benjamin and I might sit under the trees and talk—undisturbed!"

"Oh, I see. I am afraid I have been so busy with the little ones, I quite forgot about your love affair, Cumi. Perhaps I can entertain Father Jacob this afternoon."

"Oh, would you? I give you my thanks, Tamar."

"Father Jacob still will not speak of Benjamin's desire to marry you?"

"He avoids it like an illness. Each time Benjamin mentions the subject, Father Jacob either ignores him or brings up names of other suitable wives."

"Take heart, Cumi. I am sure it is not Father Jacob's dislike for you, but his reluctance to part with Benjamin, that is your problem."

"Be that as it may, Benjamin may be forced to marry another—for the sake of his manhood."

"Cumi, I do not mean to sound cruel, but Father Jacob will not live much longer. Let him have Benjamin for now. Then you can have him for the rest of your life."

"I had not thought of it in that way, Tamar. I have never been so impatient before."

"Love does strange things to change us, both inside and out." Tamar thought of her overwhelming love for her babies as she kissed one on a plump cheek.

"It has changed you, that is true enough. I suppose if you can wait for Judah to love you, I can wait for Benjamin," Cumi sighed. "But I would much prefer to have Father Jacob hold our sons on his knee, as he does yours."

Cumi started drying and oiling the bodies of the twins before passing them off to Tamar for their wrapping in fresh linen. Both tiny mouths opened wide in howls of protest.

"The boys are hungry," Tamar said as she pulled her robe from her shoulders.

"Wait!" Cumi commanded. "You have not drunk your goat's milk yet."

Tamar shrugged and took the cup Cumi offered. "It seems ridiculous, does it not?" she laughed. "Would it not be easier just to give the goat's milk directly to the twins?"

"You know it would not," Cumi chided. "Now drink!"

Tamar examined the cup before drinking it. "This milk looks peculiar. It has a strange taste also. I imagine the herds are finding only poor vegetation to eat, and that is affecting their milk supply. I do not suggest you try to make cheese with this watery stuff."

"Our dwindling food supply is becoming tasteless also," Cumi lamented. "I do hope the brothers return soon from Egypt. Some of the servants are wanting us to move to a place that is not plagued with drought and famine."

Tamar settled the two babies, one upon each breast. She tried not to think of Cumi's concern for the food supply as she watched the sucking mouths, taking the nourishment of her own body. Instead of drought and famine, she pondered instead the wonder of how marvelously God had created his creatures. She had to believe He would provide what was needed for her sons.

Cumi was standing by, ready to assist, until she heard her name being called.

"Go on along," Tamar said. "I can manage here."

Cumi was gone only a brief while before she rushed back to Tamar. "Good news!" she cried. "The brothers are returning. One of the servants spied them in the distance."

"Jehovah be praised!" Tamar exclaimed, struggling to rise without dropping the infants in her haste. "We are saved from the famine!"

"I must go tell Father Jacob and Benjamin. Then I will return to adorn your sons for their reunion with their father." Cumi whisked herself away to spread the good tidings.

When the travelers drew near the camp, it was not noticed immediately that only nine had returned. A welcoming party of four assembled to greet the men and their precious cargo. Each carrying a baby, Tamar and Cumi joined Jacob and Benjamin in their waving and rejoicing.

Benjamin's keen and youthful eyes were first to discern: "Father, there are only nine returning. One of the brothers is missing."

"No! Say it is not so. Not again," Jacob mumbled. Even with his dimmed vision, the old man blinked and knew immediately. "It is Simeon. He is not with them."

"How can you be sure, Father?" Benjamin asked.

"My eyes may be failing, but I know the house of Israel. It is Simeon who comes not."

"Father Jacob is right," said Tamar, shielding her eyes with her one free hand.

"Perhaps he comes after them—a far ways behind," suggested Cumi hopefully.

"Or perhaps some harm befell him on the road," Jacob proposed through clenched teeth. "Or his brothers have sold him—for bread. It would not surprise me."

Only Tamar caught the deeper meaning of Jacob's words. She concluded that Jacob truly did know the house of Israel—and the sins of Israel's sons as well.

Reuben was first to reach the assembled group and embrace his father with traditional greetings. Jacob did not smile or return courtesies. He went to the point: "Where is Simeon?"

"He lives and has not been harmed, by my oath," Reuben said. "Are you not glad to see us safely back with sacks filled to the brim?"

Jacob still did not smile. "Of course, I am glad. I thank God for your return. Now, where is my missing son?"

Reuben could see that his father was not to be put off and would speak of nothing else. "Let us all get out of this wretched sun, and you shall be told all that has come to pass."

Servants brought water basins as the family group squatted or sat in a circular fashion inside Judah's sprawling tent. The women were not permitted to enter, but Tamar and Cumi sat under the awning outside to hear Reuben's report of the journey. Tamar's great curiosity about it almost made her forget that Judah had not even looked at her when he arrived. She thought for a moment he was going to reach for one of his sons—the one Cumi carried—but he changed his mind and went in with the others. Tamar thought he looked stronger and healthier than when he left.

"Now," came the commanding voice of the patriarch from within the tent, "I am ready to hear all you have to report about your trip to Egypt, but kindly start with Simeon's whereabouts."

Reuben began to relate the events that led to Simeon's imprisonment. He stressed the contradictory behavior of the strange governor who locked them up, but treated them well with fine food and medicine for Judah, only to mistreat them with false accusations of being liars and spies. "What remains now," Reuben concluded, "is for us to prove our innocence when we return to Egypt. Then Simeon will be free to return home."

Jacob did not believe anything he had heard. He said, "This appears to be another fabricated tale like the one you told me the last time you came home to say I had lost a son."

"No, Israel," Judah said. "I swear to you, every word from Reuben's mouth is truth."

Because Judah had been less deceitful with him than his other sons, Jacob decided to stay open-minded and at least listen: "Then tell me, Judah, what evil you and your brothers did to merit being called liars and spies. Tell me also why you must go back before the governor and what proof you plan to offer to contradict the accusations. Finally, I am hard pressed to understand why such proof will make the prison doors suddenly swing open to release Simeon."

"I know it all sounds utterly preposterous," Judah said. "We could not understand what was happening to us while we lived it. We did nothing amiss. The governor simply did not believe so many of us together could be brothers of one family, so he assumed we were there for a devious purpose. He put us to a test by holding Simeon ransom until we return to prove our identity. Then he said Simeon would be released, unharmed, at once."

"If you could not prove your heritage then and there, how do you plan to go about it later?"

The brothers began to look at each other, none of them wanting to be the one to respond to that question. All eyes went back and forth between Reuben and Judah. Reuben pointed to Judah,

314

and all the others encouraged him. They knew Judah's word would be most apt to be believed.

"This is the hardest and least understandable part of all," Judah began. "When the governor questioned us, he asked if we ten were all of our father's sons. We told him the youngest remained at home with you. Then he accused us of changing our story, and he demanded the youngest be brought before him as proof of our truthfulness."

Benjamin let out a yelp of delight. "I am to go on a trip to Egypt! Gladly will I go, for I am curious to see this curious governor!"

Jacob pointed toward the doorway. "You are dismissed, Benjamin. A boy does not interject his foolish prattle in a counsel of the men. Excused!"

Benjamin did not hesitate to obey his father's stern order. His expression changed from eager delight to sullen disappointment, but he scrambled to his feet and joined Tamar and Cumi outside the tent door to eavesdrop with them.

"It would seem," Jacob began with the utmost calm in his rasping voice, "that you men are not content unless you continually are depleting me of my sons, one by one. First Joseph, then Simeon, and now you would take away the youngest as well. Pray, tell me, how many more shall fall—or am I to be left completely childless?"

Judah rose to his feet. "It is not as you think, Israel. We all know how dearly you love Benjamin, so you must not think it was our idea to separate him from you. I begged the governor not to require this as the test. I told him how it would grieve your heart to allow Benjamin to go."

Still speaking with composure, Jacob said, "First, I do not know why I should *not* think you might wish to separate me from my children. Second, if the whole lot of you have an itch to return to Egypt, I willingly give you my leave to go. Take unto the giver of grain any proof you wish to reclaim Simeon, but do not ask for my youngest son to go with you. It is out of the question."

Levi, who had been totally lost without his twin, leapt to his feet and shouted, "How can you allow Simeon to remain a prisoner in a strange land forever?"

315

Jacob raised his hands and eyes upward, as though in an attitude of prayer, and spoke to an unseen presence above him: "Lord of Heaven! They accuse me of having no heart for Leah's child and Levi's twin. They act as if I had gone to Egypt and given him away. Send me strength to bear the added sorrow of having their own sins cast upon me!"

Reuben moved closer to his father to sit at his feet and say, "The grain we bring from Egypt will not last forever. The governor predicted even greater famine will consume our land. We must return to Egypt to buy more food when what we bring now is gone."

Jacob nodded in agreement, but his attitude did not change. "Quite true, Reuben. If the famine continues, I do not forbid you to go again to Egypt. I only forbid you to take Benjamin."

Dan spoke up: "But the governor said we would not see his face if we came back without Benjamin. This unpredictable ruler is a hard and formidable man whose word is law. If we disobey his command, we all could end up in prison—or pay for disobedience with our lives."

Jacob threw up his hands. "How can I believe these wild tales? Why should a stranger in a foreign land be so overly concerned with this family? Explain to me why he needs to see Benjamin before he will sell you grain. Egyptians are known for their abominations, and it may be that the governor wants a handsome, young boy for his own pleasures. Or perhaps he wants a strong lad to help build his tombs and altars. Or to use as a human sacrifice to some false god. Even if Benjamin survived the hazardous journey, who knows what evils might ensnare my youngest?"

The brothers fell silent. They could offer their father neither assurance of Benjamin's total safety nor assurance of the governor's completely benevolent intentions.

After a while, Judah remembered something that might have great bearing on the argument: "Israel, the ruler of Egypt is a believer in our God. He said so himself. Would a man of God commit heathen abominations with Benjamin? Would God's servant, one devoted to feeding the hungry, wish to injure an innocent youth? Other than holding Simeon for ransom, this man did

316

nothing to harm any of us. Rather, he was kind and generous and most hospitable to us. Simeon so enjoyed the ruler's accommodations, he gladly volunteered to remain as the man's guest."

Jacob thumped his staff upon the floor and bent over in mocking laughter. When he finally could speak, he said, "Now you really make me to laugh! No wonder the governor called you liars! You tell me Simeon *wished* to be imprisoned? You expect me to believe an Egyptian, in a the land of idol worship, is one who believes in Jehovah? Now, you go too far!"

Judah said quietly, "Can God not reveal himself to anyone—even an Egyptian?"

Before Jacob could answer, Levi went to kneel before his father and plead, "I humbly beg you, Father, let us take Benjamin that we may free Simeon. Then you will have your full number of sons with you as before."

"Ha!" Jacob exclaimed. "Full number? And where is Joseph? I always have held you accountable for the disaster that befell him—and now you want me to entrust Benjamin to your care? If you could not protect Joseph from harm on a peaceful hillside, how shall you protect Benjamin on a dangerous journey to a heathen land?"

Reuben noted Judah's sagging shoulders and knew what Jacob's words were doing to the already guilt-ridden man. Reuben's heated emotions began to gush forth like an overturned pot of boiling water: "Father, hear me! The past is past. Do not torture us further with remembrance of our former failures. Rather, let us prove ourselves reformed with this last chance. Yet, do not entrust Benjamin unto us all, but only to me. If I do not bring him back, then slay my two sons. In the presence of these witnesses, I pledge that you may, with your own hands, strangle my beloved sons before my eyes if I do not keep this oath to return to you both Simeon and Benjamin."

Touched by Reuben's speech but still undaunted, Jacob said, "I am no avenging angel to kill your sons! That would not bring back Benjamin should he be lost! With Joseph and Simeon gone, I cannot risk losing all I have left. To lose him would bring my gray hairs in sorrow to the grave."

Except for Reuben and Judah, the brothers looked at each

317

other knowingly and compressed their lips. The old jealousy and resentment welled up inside them. Jacob's favoritism that once enraged them enough to want to kill the favorite seemed a rekindled reincarnation when their father called Benjamin *all I have left*.

"And what, then, of Simeon?" Levi demanded.

"I shall mourn for him and pray for his deliverance," Jacob replied.

Putting his hands to his hips, Asher cried, "You speak of praying, but you do not heed our prayers that you would do the right thing—to release one of the other sons *you have left*.! Why is Benjamin so favored that he is of greater value to you than Simeon?"

Issachar's protest was loudest: "When food runs out, shall we all sit here and *pray* rather than taking Benjamin to Egypt to get food for our bellies? Is Simeon to you but a worthless dog? You speak so piously of God, but some devil has given you a most selfish heart!"

A collective gasp went up from the other brothers. Never was a son to speak against his father in such a disrespectful manner. Such dishonor was punishable under the law, whether one agreed or disagreed with a father's judgment.

Jacob did not scold or strike Issachar, the least of expected punishments for such an outburst. He merely folded his hands and said quietly, "Disburse. Discussion is ended. You are excused."

In dead silence, the men started rising and preparing to leave as a stable servant rushed in, shouting in excitement, "Master! Master!" He bowed before Judah.

"What is it?" Judah asked.

"See—the money! In every man's sacks! We were unloading the feedbags, that the animals might rest unburdened. We found the money taken to buy grain in Egypt still within each one."

Jacob rose and steadied himself upon his staff. "Ah, now it comes to light. You cheated the lord of Egypt and did not pay for his grain. That is the real reason Simeon has been imprisoned, is it not?"

Astonished looks on his sons' faces defied Jacob's conclusion. They all spoke at once:

"What? Our money returned? It must be some curse or Egyptian black magic," one said.

"But we all saw our money fairly counted out against the weights," a second protested.

"Oh, this cannot be! Some error has occurred!" cried another.

Judah took his servant by the shoulders and looked him in the eyes. "You say *all* the money we took with us remains in the sacks—not just mine?"

The servant nodded. "Come and see."

All rushed to follow the servant to the stalls—all, that is, except Reuben. He turned to have a final word with his father.

"We did pay for the grain, Father," Reuben said emphatically. "You must believe it. Do you think us shrewd enough to steal all those burdens of grain from under the Egyptian guards' noses and get away with it?"

Jacob thought for a moment. "I do not want to misjudge you. It does seem improbable that the guards could be so easily fooled. Nor does it seem likely that this great amount could be an oversight on their part. But how do you explain the money being returned?"

Reuben said, "We told you the ruler is strange. This may be a test—to prove our honesty or to make sure we return to him. Or maybe Judah is right, and he is a God-fearing, generous man who delights in doing secret kindnesses. I do not know why, but, despite trickery and accusations, I feel this man cares about us. He seemed genuinely concerned about your welfare and about the hunger of our families. At one point, he became overcome with tears and had to leave the hall. I know not what all this means, but I do know you can believe your sons are not thieves!"

Jacob's face was drawn and weary. "This is too much for me in one day. I must rest and try to sort it all out and pray on it."

Reuben encircled his arm about his father and said, "Before I leave you, you must tell me you believe us. Our reports of the events in Egypt were true. We did not steal money nor do anything that would dishonor you. You must trust me, for, on my oath before God, I swear I speak truth."

Jacob said, "I would like to believe you, my son. Tomorrow we will return to take food to my household. Maybe then, when we are settled and calm, we can speak further of this problem. Now, I am too overcome by it all to speak or think clearly. You must leave me now to my rest."

Two of the eavesdroppers who listened at the doorway, Benjamin and Cumi, had followed after the brothers as they ran to the stalls to investigate the money situation. Tamar, however, remained behind. She waited to talk to Father Jacob. As Reuben came out, Tamar whispered to him, "I will add my words to plead your case." Then she ducked her head to enter Judah's tent.

"My honored and beloved father, may I have a brief word with you?" Tamar asked.

"Not now, I pray you, Tamar. I must go to the guest tent and lie down. My head spins with the news my sons bring to me."

She took his arm. "Come and lie here on Judah's couch. I will rub your head to sooth it. And, if it would please you after we talk, I will fetch my harp and play you a restful tune, as I do when I sing the twins to sleep."

Jacob allowed her to help his feeble body down to recline upon the couch. He was too tired to walk to the guest tent anyway.

"Where are my grandsons?" Jacob asked.

"With Cumi and Benjamin—each with a babe in a sling upon their backs."

"Ah, that is soothing indeed," the old man sighed as Tamar's soft hands stroked his brow. "Did you hear all that Reuben and the others said concerning what transpired in Egypt?"

"You know very well I was listening at the door."

"What think you of the strange tales they bring to me? But wait. You said you had a matter you wished to speak to me about. That first."

"The matters are one and the same," Tamar said. "I believe Reuben and Judah. For all of their other faults, I have not known either of them to be liars. And no one could make up such tales as they told. What could be their purpose in wishing to deceive you?"

"I have no answer to that, Tamar. My sons have deceived me before, and that makes it more difficult for me to believe them."

"Always you think the worst. Perhaps Reuben was right to suggest you give them a second chance to prove themselves reformed."

Jacob lifted his head up slightly to look at Tamar. "Did you not hear the terrible things my sons shouted at me?"

"Judah and Reuben did not do so. They are the ones I believe. And even those who railed upon you in anger did not dispute the report nor give any different versions of it."

"Even if the report is accurate, you cannot think I should let them take Benjamin away. You do not agree with that absurdity, do you?"

Tamar tried to keep her voice low and her demeanor calm. She knew Jacob was in no state to debate with her. She decided to be objective and to restrict herself to reviewing facts and asking questions. That, she surmised, would allow Jacob to arrive at his own conclusions.

"If the rains do not come and the famine continues," Tamar said slowly, "we soon shall need more grain. If Benjamin is not permitted to accompany the brothers on their return to Egypt, will we not be hungering as before?"

"Oh, I do not know. Perhaps Issachar may be right to say my reluctance to believe them and to give Benjamin up to them is bound up in selfishness."

"It is easy to cling tightly to a dear one and to love him selfishly, but it is very hard to love someone with arms open to let him go," Tamar said, thinking of her own situation with Judah.

Jacob did not miss Tamar's unspoken message, the analogy that compared her love for Judah to his for Benjamin. She let him ponder her words in silence before she continued:

"I certainly shall dread your departure back to your own tents," Tamar said to continue her comparison even further. "You see how selfish I am to want to have you here with me? I do not wish to share you—even with your wives."

Jacob smiled, thinking how much more pleasant her company was than that of any of his wives. "You are a comfort always, Tamar. My head feels much better now. You know how to lift my spirits and to cause me to smile."

That compliment was an encouragement for her to go on: "Have you considered the strangeness of all the money being returned to the brothers? Do you think it could be some sort of a sign from the Lord?"

"If my sons speak truth, then there is, verily, something mysterious about it. Perhaps it is a sign, Tamar. Perhaps I am being put to the test. God may be requiring my beloved son, even as my Grandfather Abraham was required to sacrifice his son on God's altar."

"But remember," Tamar said taking his hand, "you have told me how the Lord stayed Abraham's hand and how Isaac was spared. The test was Abraham's willingness to release Isaac to God's care. When Abraham withheld nothing, he proved he loved his God more than anything else, even more than the son of his old age. He passed the test, and the son was given back to the father."

Jacob sat up to face Tamar. "Always Jehovah speaks to me through you, my daughter. If I must give Benjamin up, if that is my test . . . But all this is speculation! I have no assurance whatever that this is the will of God."

Tamar could see he was wavering. The battle of his will against the will of the Lord. She would not press him.

"It would seem," Tamar proposed, "you are in the midst of another wrestling match. I know you will pray about all this, and that the Lord will reveal to you the right thing to do, for always you want God's will above your own. I shall, likewise, remain in prayer concerning the matter. If the famine lifts not, then that would seem to me to be yet another sign that . . ."

"I shall not be swayed by a woman!" Jacob said defiantly. "My sons first, now you—all of you prevailing upon me to send my little one into danger. How could that possibly be God's will?"

"Because it is so totally in opposition to your own desires, perhaps? Is that not what you instructed me when I wished to plot and scheme and place my stubborn, selfish will above God's better plan? You, yourself, taught me God wants nothing between us and our wholehearted devotion to Him. You said He al-

322

ways tests us with that which is closest to our hearts—to see if we love Him more than all else."

"Leave me, Tamar! I wish to sleep and to talk no more." He had nothing more he could say.

Tamar rose and departed, but, looking back as she went past the door flap, she caught sight of Jacob's upcast eyes and his lips inaudibly moving.

Twenty-one

The drought continued to oppress the land. Fruit vines were withering, animals were dying, and corn bins were getting low. In Judah's tents and those of his father's family, it had not taken long to deplete the provisions which were obtained without price. Sacks from Egypt were not as plentiful as the number of mouths they had to feed.

When no word came concerning plans to deal with the scarcity, Judah took it upon himself to prevail once more upon his father. He saddled his beast and headed toward the households of Israel' encampment. He gave no warning nor any farewells.

News of Judah's departure came to Tamar from the lips of the gray-bearded stable keeper. He told her she was left in charge and would be assisted by the new head steward, Joel, until the master's return. There was no mention of when that might be. Tamar was displeased.

"Oh, Cumi," she said later. "I had hoped that the passing of time, the birth of the twins, or the journey to Egypt would change Judah's attitude toward me. Nothing changes. He is still distant and wants me not—neither for his wife nor for anything else. He never will."

"You are the one always trying to instill in me the virtues of patience and hope," Cumi said with a comforting smile. "Perhaps you should take your own advice."

"He left for Father Jacob's tents today without a word. I did not expect a farewell kiss, but I would have thought he might speak to me or see his sons before going. When he openly hated me, I could accept it. But now that he just ignores me like I do not exist, I simply cannot bear it."

In a effort to cheer her, Cumi said, "Is not being ignored an improvement over being hated? He seems to be moving in a more positive direction, Tamar."

"My presence here is a continual thorn in his side. He leaves on any pretext."

"Tamar, if he goes to Father Jacob, you know it is to speak of the famine. That shows you he wants to provide food for your mouth. I think Master Judah greatly improved since returning from Egypt. At least, he no longer sits alone in his tent all day moping and speaking of dying."

"But neither does he enjoy living!" Tamar argued. "How can he go so long without a woman to love?"

"I know only that he wants to be punished. Perhaps not taking you in his arms is the greatest punishment he can inflict upon himself."

"Would that I could believe you, Cumi. But I have begun to think Judah never will be completely whole again until he is free of me. He has too many reminders of his past sins, and I am the worst reminder of all!"

"If the brothers go again to Egypt, perhaps a second trip will bring him back even more improved. Then all your fretting will have been for naught."

"I shall wait until he comes back, Cumi. But if Judah shows no signs of changing, then I shall have to leave."

"Leave? Where would you go? Unto Father Jacob?"

"No. There are too many in his household who would despise me more than Judah does. I do not intend to live the rest of my life where I am shunned and unwanted."

"Are you truly serious, Tamar?" Cumi was becoming concerned.

"I have considered returning to my kinsmen. The only question is whether or not to take my sons. It will tear my heart out to leave them, but I fear to bring them up in a wicked, heathen environment. I am considering leaving them with Judah—if he will have them."

Cumi's mouth was open, disbelieving what she had heard. "Think what you are saying, Tamar! This is much too drastic a decision to be made without a great deal of thought."

"I said I would wait for Judah's return. I tell you of this now for the twins' sake. I want them raised in a loving home with a happy family. When I am gone, would you care for my sons?"

"With all my heart, Tamar. If it should come to that. But it must not!"

Tamar laid out for Cumi the plan she had devised over a period of many lonely, loveless nights: "If you and Benjamin marry, perhaps you could live here or close to Judah—so he could see the boys from time to time. You would be a good mother, and Benjamin would be a better father than Judah has proven to be. I know there would be love in your home. I would like you to discuss this with Benjamin. He may not want his first children to be his nephews. If he is unwilling, I shall have to think of other plans—some next best thing."

When the magnitude of what Tamar was saying finally was perceived as a serious request, Cumi said, "Tamar, you obviously have been thinking of this a great deal. I will speak to Benjamin, of course, and you know how much we both love the twins. But whether I ever can marry Benjamin or not, I would not shirk any responsibility you give me, least of all to those darling babies. However, the whole thing seems to me a very flawed plan—for everyone involved. You belong here, not among your pagan kinsmen. Master Judah and the twins need you, even though they may not know it now. It is absurd to think Benjamin and I ever could take your places! I shall pray for Master Judah's rapid recovery because your children should not be denied the joy of being with their very own parents."

Judah was completely in the dark about any of Tamar's feelings, much less her plans for the future. He lived too far from reality to be aware of anything outside his own misery. The twins did bring an occasional smile to his lips, but it was a fleeting moment in an existence otherwise devoid of purpose and happiness. When things were going well, he merely went through the motions of living. During a crisis, however, he suddenly would lay aside his inertia, come alive, and take action. He had done so when the robbers invaded and when the famine prompted a first trip to Egypt. Now, with another critical food shortage in the offing and with Simeon in bondage for what he thought should be his own punishment, it was crisis time again. Judah meant to see that a second journey to Egypt included Benjamin.

When Judah dismounted at Jacob's stables, he was surprised to be met by Benjamin. From him, Judah learned two things. First, he would have to delay his visit with his father because Leah was in the patriarchal tent raving about something Judah preferred not to hear. Second, the other brothers were all away, slaying from their flocks so they might have something to eat.

"It has come to that, has it?" Judah asked. "All the corn from Egypt is consumed?"

"Yes," said Benjamin. "We have neither seed corn nor bake stuff. There is much sickness. Many of the little ones have no milk either, for most of the herds have gone dry."

"Verily, that is the way of a famine. Without the rain, the grass dies. Then the hungering animals fail to produce."

"Even in mating, the animals are lacking," said Benjamin. "The he-cows and he-asses no longer cover the she-animals that new life may begin."

Judah was astounded. "How is it you know of such things among the he and she animals?"

"Oh, Judah," Benjamin said with disgust, "do you think I am still a suckling child? When will my family learn I am now grown up? Look you here! I have begun a beard."

Judah saw a fine, reddish growth on the lad's chin. "Ah, now I see how grown up you are."

"I think I am ripe to take unto myself my own she-animal. Is it not the custom to do so?"

"But our father still refuses to give you leave to marry?"

"Still. Will you speak to him, Judah? I have tried, to no avail. I think you must have heard I wish to wed Cumi. I know she always has cared for your household, but I thought now that you have Tamar, perhaps you would consent to give Cumi to me. Would you?"

"We will see. I have another matter to discuss with Israel today. If things go as I hope, then the subject of releasing you to marry may seem much less of a dire sacrifice than my proposal."

"The journey to Egypt to buy more provisions!" Benjamin whooped in delighted excitement.

"You knew I came today to speak of returning to Egypt?" Judah wanted to know.

"It is all I think about—and all that the brothers think of as well. It is the reason I have been staying with Reuben and avoiding Father. We are showing him our displeasure at his refusal to send me with the others to buy more Egyptian grain."

"You mean to tell me you are refusing to take your favored place at Israel's right hand?"

"It is the first time I have ever denied him, and quite lonely for me. But something had to be done to persuade Father. We all will starve to death if he does not relent and allow me to go."

"Is your absence the reason my mother is now within Israel's tent?"

"Yes. Leah is overjoyed that Father has no one else at his side, now that Tamar and I are absent from him. Leah keeps trying to obtain the favored position, but she is so annoying that her presence usually causes a great argument to erupt."

"Is it not a drastic measure you take, Benjamin? You will regret it sorely if anything happens to Israel while you keep yourself apart from him."

"Reuben says Father soon will tire of Leah's company and so yearn to see me again that he will, at last, yield his stubborn will and permit me to go. Now that you are here to add your voice to our protests, Father surely must listen to reason."

"I sincerely will try my best to convince him," Judah promised.

"You are a fine one to speak of separation from Father as a drastic measure. You have lived away from him for many years now. Are you also trying to prove some point?"

"No! An entirely different situation," Judah said loudly and defensively.

"Judah, is your sharp tone a symptom of your poor health? Are you any improved at all?"

"I have not been ill, little brother. You should not listen to gossip that flies between my tents and these. If I seem unwell to you, remember I have buried a wife and three sons."

"But now you have a more beautiful wife and two healthier sons."

"Impudent one, be silent! The famine seems to make you

quick-tongued and dull-witted. Ah! I see Leah is leaving Israel's tent, so I must go now and conduct my business."

"May I ask you one thing more before you go? I need to ask your advice."

"What troubles you, Beni?" Judah was glad to change the subject from his health.

"The other brothers and their children dislike me—because I am Father's favorite. They do not understand that I like it no better. I do not brag that Father calls me his only true son and gives me gifts they do not receive. I try to be friends, but they all refuse me—except for Reuben."

Judah let out a long sigh. "I will tell you a strange truth. There is wrong here on two sides. Even though you are innocent, you suffer for the faults of those on both sides. Israel's favoritism causes resentment when he does not treat all his children as equals. The brothers are also at fault because they and their children become jealous of you. They are most unjust to despise you when it is Israel's partiality that places you in the middle of a dispute you have not caused."

"I know that part, Judah. What puzzles me is why they do not speak to me, or even to each other in my presence. If I am around, they fall silent—as if they are afraid of me. Why is that?"

"They fear they may say or do something to offend Israel's favorite. They think you could cause trouble for them if you spoke against them to our father."

"But I never would! I have heard them speak of how they disliked the brother who was killed. They said Joseph was a tale bearer. I would not be as he was!"

Judah swallowed hard at the mention of Joseph's name and cursed the memory that never ceased its torment. He said sadly, "They have no assurance of that. And they distrust you because you are different from them." To himself, he thought, *You are not hard and cruel as they are.*

"I think if I go to Egypt, they may get to know me better and trust me more. Then if I marry, we will be alike. That will prove I am truly grown up and a separate person from my father. I will be as one of them. Going to Egypt and marrying Cumi are my solutions. Am I not right, Judah?"

Judah marveled at the simplistic solutions a youthful imagination could find for complexities of life. He was anxious to leave for his talk with his father, so all he responded was, "Perhaps."

As Judah started moving away, Benjamin trailed along. "There is one thing more."

"What is that?" Judah was irked that he seemed unable to bring this conversation to an end.

"You are the only one who can solve my greater problem," Benjamin said with the look of doom upon his face. "Our brothers also grumble against me because they think I shall be Father's heir. They say Father will pass over you for the covenant blessing and that I shall receive the God-inheritance. I do not want it, Judah! Please promise me you will take it! If you do not and if it falls to me, then Father will never let me marry Cumi. He thinks a humble servant girl would be unworthy to marry the bearer of the blessing."

This was the last thing Judah wanted to discuss with Benjamin, but he had to say something to allay the lad's confusion and fears. "The time of the pronouncement of the blessing has not yet come, Benjamin. When it does, it will not be your decision or mine, or even Israel's. It will be as ordained by Jehovah. I am undeserving of it, so I seek it no more than you do. You must not distress yourself about something that neither of us can control. Jehovah will also ordain the woman to bear the next son of the covenant. You and I must trust a greater Wisdom than ours in this matter. Now I must go speak to Israel. If he will not release you to travel to Egypt, the blessing will be irrelevant and no cause for worry anyway. We all shall be dead."

Judah left an astonished Benjamin to contemplate his last statement. Although it was said with the ironic tone of a jest, the underlying seriousness of it held a weighty truth.

When Judah reached Jacob's tent, it was a relief to find Leah gone and the patriarch free to talk. It was not a comfort to find the old man looking so drawn and sad as he described the loneliness imposed by his other sons' alienation. Even Eliezer's company was denied because the famine brought with it a spreading epidemic that made his old friend ill and near death.

"Perhaps Eliezer needs healing herbs to give him strength,"

Judah suggested. "The special kind I was given to revive me while I was ill in Egypt."

When Jacob ignored the obvious allusion to Egypt and wished to speak of other things, Judah tried again: "Israel, before Eliezer fell ill, did he study the signs to determine when the drought might end?"

Jacob moved uncomfortably upon his stool, unable to avoid the direct question. "He said the great river of Egypt will not water the banks because it has not rained in the land of the Moors. It does not rain there because no downpours come here in Canaan, due to the sea making no clouds. It is like a circular pattern perpetuating itself with no ending in view."

"And how do your provisions hold out?" Judah probed.

"We have begun to eat the meat of our flocks. But so many animals die, their carcasses bring flies and pestilence. That has led to much sickness to add to the woes of hunger."

"And what shall come next?"

"How shall I predict the future? I continue to pray to Jehovah for deliverance."

"And if the Lord opens the way of deliverance, will you then accept it? Or will you continue to sit here on your backsides, lifting no finger against the want that consumes your children?"

"Very well, Judah. I know why you are here and what you are thinking—that to send Benjamin back to Egypt is the way of deliverance. But I am not certain that is God's will."

"Has the Lord revealed to you an alternative course to save us?"

"How dare you question me! You, who claim the destruction of our land is God's punishment upon you! Are you not the one to find the remedy?"

"Quite right, Israel. If I bring this evil upon us, I must—before I die—do what is needful so the innocent suffer not with me. When I return to Egypt and remain there, the famine will lift. However, I cannot go unless Benjamin goes also. The Egyptian ruler has decreed it."

Jacob fiercely shook his head at Judah and said, "Such nonsense and folly you prattle! Your concept of God is a false one. Whatever guilty sin tortures your mind, God does not require

331

you to be an exile in a foreign land as your penance. Nor does He send a famine to us to chastise you. He requires of a sinner one thing only—a contrite heart that seeks forgiveness."

"There is no forgiveness for me," Judah said flatly.

Before more was said, Reuben burst in. In his arms he carried the limp body of a tiny child. With heavy strides, he marched over to his father and deposited the child at Jacob's feet.

"This," Reuben bellowed as he gestured toward the unmoving child, "is the price I must pay for your obstinate perverseness! Behold what you have done! You have killed my child!"

Judah lunged forward to restrain Reuben's hands that were fast approaching Jacob's throat. Judah squeezed Reuben's convulsing body in a tight bear hug until he could force the enraged man backward onto a nearby stool. When Judah released his hold, Reuben was on his feet again, arms flailing and fists pounding at Judah's face and chest. He fought and raved as a wild maniac.

The brothers' raucous struggle continued across the room, knocking over furniture, lamps, and cutlery in its wake. The two men finally landed simultaneously upon Jacob's great bed, where they rolled and grunted as Reuben continued to strike and Judah tried to do two things at once—defend himself from the blows and restrain his heavier brother from inflicting any more damage either to property or to himself.

Jacob stared at his sons in disbelief and fright, sending forth little whimpering cries that went both unheard and unheeded. Not knowing what else to do, Jacob hobbled over to the thrashing bodies, raised his staff high and aimlessly in the air, and let it fall on the head of the person who was on top at the time. The head was Reuben's. Stunned from the blow, he loosened his hold upon Judah long enough for the younger brother to get the advantage and roll to the top.

Sitting astride Reuben's chest and holding both of his arms pinned back, Judah shouted, "What it this, Reuben? Why do you charge at Israel like an untamed animal and strike me without due cause?"

Huffing and gasping for breath, Reuben stammered, "I . . . I apologize, Judah, for turning my rage upon you . . . I am myself again. You may take your buttocks from my chest so I can breathe."

Judah was hesitant, but, slowly and cautiously, he removed himself and allowed Reuben to rise. Judah's eyes were still upon his brother's hands, and he remained in a defensive pose until he was certain those hands would not attack again.

Reuben staggered over to stand by the child's body and to point an accusing finger toward Jacob. "This is the cause of my anger! Because of you, Father, my youngest child, my only daughter, is dead. Is this the further recompense you require? Because I ask that your youngest go with us to Egypt, my youngest must pay for it with her life?"

Judah said, "Pray, explain your words, Reuben. What are you saying?"

"Because of Father's delay and refusal to release Benjamin to us, the famine worsens. Wells go dry, food from Egypt runs out, and we have to eat from our flocks and herds. Now that wormy meat has become polluted. My little Mahala, who ate broth made with the polluted meat, is gone! More become sick each day—both in my family and others as well. Fever, retching, cramps and dehydration attack one after the other. My outraged brothers stand ready to take Benjamin by force, but I convinced them to allow me to beseech you one last time. When I came back from the slaying of the flocks, I found Mahala as you see her now. I would prefer that we go to Egypt with your blessing, Father. But even without it, we shall go. And Benjamin rides with us!"

When he finished his oration, Reuben picked up the child and carried her out of the tent. He left his father and brother standing in silence, watching him go.

Judah was the one to break the silence after Reuben left. "It would seem you must wrestle an angel again, Israel. But this time, I do not think you can prevail. You must submit."

Jacob dropped back upon his stool and lowered his head to rest on his table. His body shook as Judah stood helplessly over him, uncertain what to do next.

When Jacob raised his head, he said, "Would that your words had not the ring of truth to them! I indeed have wrestled, and now comes the dawn of realization upon me. I have been the youthful rebel in my old age. Reuben also spoke truth. My love for my child has cost him his child."

"But you can prevent more deaths!" Judah shouted. "Relent and give us your blessing as we go and bring back food. Do not force your children to rise up against you and steal Benjamin away in the night. Do you not want to behold his face and embrace him before we go?"

Jacob nodded mutely. He looked so full of sorrow, Judah wanted to comfort, not chide, him.

"Do not be concerned for Benjamin's welfare," Judah said. "He will be restored to you, even as your father, Isaac, was spared for your grandfather Abraham's willingness to give him up."

"Those were the very words Tamar spoke to me. Can I continue to fight against the lot of you? Can I doubt that God speaks to me from so many mouths?"

Judah went to his knees beside his father and said, "I, Judah, will go bail for Benjamin. If he goes down at my side, I will protect him, both on the road and in Egypt, that he not so much as strike his foot against a stone. I will protect him from heathen evils. I will be surety for him. By this raised right hand, I swear it. Of this hand shall you require him if he returns not to you."

Jacob's eyes were red and smarting with tears as he said lovingly, "Oh, Judah, my son, my son. Heir to the blessing, only unto you could I entrust the care of my heart's beloved."

"I am unworthy of your blessing, but I will take your favored son that our people die not of starvation."

"I shall make a covenant with you, Judah. If I do this thing, you must return with Benjamin to protect him on the homeward road. There must be no further talk of your remaining in Egypt."

"But I have told you—the curse of the land is bound up in God's curse upon me."

"Judah, I listened to God's word to me through your mouth. Now you must hear it through mine. I yet have hope that you will prove worthy of the God-inheritance, and, verily, your actions in this moment give me much encouragement. You gave me your pledge to protect Benjamin, so it must be from the time he leaves my side until you set him again here before my eyes."

Judah made no further protest. His decision to withdraw from his kindred and exile himself in Egypt could be delayed until he fulfilled the bargain. It was little that his father asked. Because he had won the victory of Jacob's submissiveness, it was enough. He would not argue for more.

"Very well," Judah agreed. "I will stay at Benjamin's side—both going and coming. And I will place him in your arms at our return."

"God grant it according to your words, my son."

"Thank you, Israel, for this you do. I know the anguish of your soul's decision."

"But still another fear comes upon me," Jacob said, taking Judah's arm for support. "If the money in the sacks came by devious means, then you shall be more suspect than before."

"I am sure it was the doing of the Egyptian governor, Israel. He was, as I have told you, a man who fears God and who was most generous to us."

"Nevertheless," Jacob continued, "you must do this: Take of the offerings our ill-bearing trees will afford—the last of the dried fruit I was saving, some spices and honey, almonds, and myrrh. Place them in our best vessels. And take double money in your hands. And also the money that was found in your sacks. Peradventure the governor will believe it all was an oversight and, by these gifts, will know you are not thieves, but true and honest men."

"It will do no harm to our cause to take presents to the ruler. Your suggestion is wise."

Before Judah rose to depart, he did something he had not done in a long time. He bent over and kissed the old man's cheek. A flood of tender feelings came over Judah, and he did not think it would be difficult to be close to his father ever again.

Judah moved toward the tent door to go tell the others of his father's decision, to send Benjamin to embrace Israel, and to offer what comfort he could to the grieving Reuben. Then he recalled that his household would also need to be informed of his whereabouts, now that plans were finalized.

335

"Israel, will you send Nathan to tell Tamar I shall not return home, but I go with my brothers to Egypt?" Judah asked.

"Yes, verily, I shall do that. Is there any other message you wish me to send to your wife?"

Judah paused to think for a moment. He left Tamar and his children without farewells or pleasantries. Perhaps he should send some message of regret for that or words of encouragement to sustain his family before he again left so abruptly on a long journey. There was every chance his promises to Israel could not be kept. There were dangers ahead to face. He might not see anyone within his tents ever again. But what did he have to say?

At last, Judah spoke: "No. That is all."

His son already was outside when Jacob called him back in again. "Judah! A final word!" Jacob seemed almost unwilling for him to go.

Jacob laid his hands on Judah's head and said, "Receive my blessing as you take your brother before the Egyptian ruler. God Almighty give you mercy before that man, that he may send back Simeon and Benjamin. And may the Lord watch between us while we are absent from each other."

After Judah was gone, Jacob sat alone in his tent. Giving words to the worst of his secret fears, he said aloud, "And if I be bereaved of my children, I am bereaved."

Twenty-two

In the light of early dawn the next morning, the brothers set forth on their second journey to Egypt. All the wives, children, and servants of Jacob's great family stood scattered about for the departure of the ten travelers. In the midst of them stood the family's patriarch.

All eyes were upon Jacob, for the entire audience had come to see how he would react as he took leave from Benjamin, his dearest possession. Rumors filled the camp about Jacob's sudden reversal. Some said it was the brothers' alienation and refusal to speak to their father. Some said it was the loneliness Jacob felt without Benjamin. A still grieving Reuben said it had taken his daughter's death to move the intractable Jacob. Others remarked that Jacob simply had come to his senses about a worsening famine, and his own belly had caused him to become reasonable.

Speculation ceased when Jacob raised his hand to speak his final words to the sojourners: "You leave in the same strength as before—one less and one more. Know that it was Judah and his God-words unto me that brought this thing to pass. Judah, you gave your bond for Benjamin, pledging that I might require him at your hand. But you are released from that oath. What man can give a bond for God? No, I see now that this, verily, is God's will, and in that will alone will I put my trust for Benjamin's safe return."

All eyes turned to Judah. Then they moved back to Jacob as he continued his address.

"I see consternation on your faces, but know that Israel girds himself up to be God's man—one who will give any sacrifice unto his Lord. I build upon the Rock of the Shepherd to grant me back the pledge I entrust, in faith, to Him. Hear all of you! Jehovah is no monster-god as those of other lands! He does not mock human

337

hearts nor forsake His word to turn away from those who dili-gently seek Him. He is glorified in moments such as these when a man throws himself completely upon the Lord's mercy."

Jacob moved toward Benjamin, who sat upon his donkey, and summoned the lad to come down. It was a long while before Jacob could stop holding, kissing, and whispering in his son's ear. At last, Jacob removed a golden chain from his own neck and placed it over Benjamin's.

"A token of remembrance," Jacob said softly.

"But Father, I have no gift for you to remember me by until I return," Benjamin protested.

"No matter, my son. I carry your image in my heart of hearts."

"Father, tell old Eliezer I shall bring him healing medicines from Egypt to restore his health."

"He will be pleased," Jacob said. Then he set Benjamin be-fore them all, directly in front of himself with his hands on his son's shoulders, to say, "I now will pronounce the benediction."

All heads bowed, and some fell to their knees to observe the rite in a posture of worship.

Jacob raised his trembling voice to pray: "Gracious Lord, only as a loan to be returned do I give my son to you. And yet, be it not according to my will, but Yours alone. Be merciful, Mighty One, to all my sons, and prosper their journey. Give them wisdom before the lord of Egypt that they may bring us bread from his hand in this time of tribulation. Amen."

All offered an audible *amen* in such a loud chorus that few heard Jacob as he turned to Reuben and said, "I am sorry I did not come to myself sooner to prevent the sad and needless loss of your daughter. I hope you can forgive me. I will watch over your sons and wives for you."

Turning to Judah, Jacob said, "God go with you. Even though I trust in Him and release you from your pledge, I know you will look after Benjamin and take care of the little son of death."

Jacob's voice was breaking, so he waved to the others and turned away toward his dwelling. He did not want the women to see his tears.

Judah wondered at his father's words as the caravan set forth and moved beyond Jacob's tents. Did calling Benjamin *little son of death* refer to Rachel's death at the boy's birth, or was it Israel's fear for Benjamin's life on this hazardous journey, despite all his proclamations of faith?

Throughout the journey, Benjamin was treated royally. Not only the protective Judah, but also the other brothers, considered the youngest among them the most important member of their party. This was partly out of fear of Jacob's reaction if they returned without bringing back the favorite son. It also was because he was the evidence required to convince Egypt's governor that they were not spies. Benjamin, who previously had been shunned by his older brothers, was enjoying both the trip itself and all the extra attentions.

There was a third motive for seeing to Benjamin's welfare. Judah and Reuben had discussed their accountability to God for their crimes against Joseph. They opined that they did not want further accountability added to the debt by allowing a second brother to fall in harm's way.

The result of all the attention was overindulgence. Benjamin received choicest bits of the food they had scraped together for their journey. He was the first to drink from the water skin. Someone always was inquiring as to his comfort and needs. Although the brothers took turns standing guard each night, Benjamin was the only one who ever slept soundly. The others kept rousing and peering from half-opened eyes to see if Benjamin was still there.

As Reuben made his bed for the night near Judah and Benjamin, he laughed, "The boy will be spoiled so that even Father, the greatest of his spoilers, will not want him back."

Judah agreed: "With all of us giving our cloaks unto him that he not take a chill, he is more apt to suffocate than to freeze tonight."

Reuben pointed to the sleeping Benjamin and said, "He does seem to be pleased with his first adventure away from home and his nine brothers hovering over him to do his bidding."

"And it is long overdue," Judah stated. "He told me how unfriendly his brothers have been to him because he is the favorite.

Poor boy—motherless, unadopted by Israel's other wives, and then forced to be under his father's nose all the time! He hates that, as any lad would. He wants his brethren to accept him as a man. He even wants to be a lover, for he speaks of marriage."

"Marriage? I well can imagine Father's reaction to that!"

"Things may change, now that the bird spreads his wings with us and flies from Israel's nest."

"But Judah, we have yet to return the bird safely to that nest. There still is the matter of the unexplained money in our sacks—and a two-faced governor to deal with before we can fly home."

"For some reason, I do not fear the governor, and I believe all will go well."

"That is the first optimistic statement I have heard from your mouth in a long time, Judah. I am glad you left your gloomy disposition back home. Does all go well for you and Tamar?"

"There never can be a life for us as husband and wife, if that is your question."

"Can you never forgive Tamar for her sin of deceiving you? Especially since that deception brought forth to you those superb, twin lion cubs?"

"I forgave Tamar long ago. It is myself I cannot forgive. I can never lie with her again."

"Your refusal wrongs her. She is your wife! You must forget what happened in Adullam."

"Reuben, can you forget that you have lain with Bilhah, our father's concubine? Since she is mother to your brothers, that is the sin of incest and contrary to Jehovah's law. Now imagine having to marry her. Could you ever look at Dan and Naphtali without being reminded that you violated their mother? Could you then bed Bilhah in the sacred ways of holy, married love?"

"Your comparison is unjust. Bilhah is my *father's* wife. Tamar is *your* wife, mother of *your* sons, legally entitled to *your* bed. My act of wantonness was a sin committed in the heat of youthful passion. I do not let my past transgressions go on ruining my life forever, as you do."

"We are different men, Reuben. I was forced to marry Tamar

for the sake of the family honor. I do not have to pretend our marriage is anything more than a convenience for my sons."

"But Tamar loves you! Even if you deny it, I believe you still love her. Any man would!"

"I do not wish to discuss the subject any longer." With that, Judah turned his back on Reuben and pretended to sleep as he stared blankly into the campfire.

At dawn on the final traveling day, the brothers adorned themselves in their best attire. As usual, Benjamin was given special attention so he would make a good appearance before the governor. He wore a brightly colored tunic and aba with ornate fringes and draperies—a surprise gift from Jacob that Judah had been instructed to pack and bring along. Judah even oiled the boy's unruly thatch of hair until it resembled a shiny helmet.

"Now," Judah said, stepping back to admire his handiwork, "you are a sight to behold, little brother. The governor will be so taken with you, he probably will sell us grain at half-price."

Benjamin held out his arms and looked down at himself. "I have never had such a fine coat!"

Another young boy in a fine coat. Judah tried not to think of Joseph as he said, "Hurry and mount. We can reach the governor's office by noon if we do not tarry."

Eager expectation was mingled with fearful dread as Jacob's sons rode to the official building where vouchers were issued and grain was delivered to foreign trade. The unexpected awaited them when they went to register as before. Upon seeing their names, the guard called for soldiers.

"You will be escorted to the governor's home," the guard said, closing the registry book.

Reuben asked, "Why are we being sent to the lord's house?"

"My instructions were to send you there as soon as you arrived today," was the reply.

Benjamin spoke up excitedly, "How did the governor know we were coming?"

Judah restrained Benjamin with a firm grasp and barked, "Hold your tongue!"

The guard smiled at the boy and winked as he said, "The lord of Egypt is all-wise and knows all things." Then he gestured to the officer in charge. The officer escorted his charges back to the courtyard where the brothers' donkeys were tied.

As they rode on their beasts under military escort, each brother offered a theory to explain this latest complication. They were riding to their doom, to enslavement as personal house servants, or to enjoy a good laugh with the governor who was playing tricks on them again.

In the midst of all the conjecture, Judah began to fear for Benjamin's safety. He leaned toward Reuben and said, "If things go ill, you and the others keep the guards from me while I flee with Benjamin. I gave Israel my word to protect the lad with my life."

Benjamin's sharp ears had picked up Judah's remark, and he quickly protested. "No, Judah. I want to see the ruler who wants so much to see me. I am adorned and anointed, and I will not hear of us trying to run away."

"You will hear a loud swat to your backsides if you do not keep silent!" Judah admonished.

Soon they arrived at a gracious villa in the best quarter of town. Never had any of them seen such elegance! At the gate, they were led around a lotus pond to the entrance of the house. A man approached from a terrace and stood beneath a spreading palm. He paused and bowed.

"Greetings. I am the house steward. If you will please follow me, I will have footbaths prepared for you before you dine with the lord in his chambers."

Puzzled glances were exchanged among the brothers. Benjamin let out a low whistling sound from pursed lips. Immediately, he slapped his own hand over his mouth when he caught Judah's glaring eye. He wanted to ask how the steward spoke their language, but he did not dare.

At a courtyard, servants began unloading the donkeys and carried into the house the gifts Judah told them were brought for the governor. Reuben got the steward's attention and tried to explain the oversight of the money being found in their sacks.

"We have brought double money for the governor this time," Reuben said, "for we are honest men. We do not know how this happened, but we hope the governor is not angry with us."

The steward smiled and said, "Calm yourself, my friend. Everything is in order. No money of ours is missing. Your God must have given the blessing to you. The treasure you found in your sacks has nothing to do with the just transaction of business you conducted on your first journey. Now, kindly follow me. Come see who awaits you inside."

As the curious group entered, they beheld a welcome sight—Simeon! He was unattended, unbound, sitting at a footbath, well dressed in Egyptian attire, and looking quite content. He had not wasted away as a prisoner, as Levi had predicted. Rather, he had put on considerable weight. The brothers all crowded around him, shouted joyous greetings, and pounded him on the back.

"Are you well?" cried Levi, embracing his twin several times. "But I can see that you are! What has come to pass since we left you?"

Simeon told them he had lived in luxury and comfort. With an air of dignity, he bid them to sit down and refresh their feet. Then he offered them drinks and tasty morsels from a tray nearby.

"Do you have the run of this place that you take over in such manner?" asked Levi.

"No," Simeon replied with a laugh. "This is my first day at Adon's home. I reside in the gracious rooms at the office building. You remember—the ones we all shared when we first came. I was told earlier today that lookouts spied your caravan coming, so I was sent here to greet you. I must say you took long enough to return—not that I have minded being a hostage at all."

"The delay was in convincing Father to release Benjamin for the journey," said Reuben.

The brothers continued to chat and exchange news. Simeon wanted to know of the famine and his family's welfare. His brothers wanted information about Simeon's life in Egypt. But the conversation halted when the steward reappeared to lead them to the dining chamber. A meal was laid out upon long tables, magnificent with flowers and fruit arrangements and tableware such as was never seen in Canaan. Their gifts for the governor were arranged attractively on a buffet.

The steward announced the arrival of their host, who entered with an impressive train of dignitaries behind him. The brothers bowed along with the servants to welcome him.

"Greetings," Adon-Joseph said. "Arise, men of Canaan, that I may introduce you to my guests. Oh, do not look so amazed that I now speak to you in your own tongue. Using an interpreter became so annoying to me, I decided to learn your language since we last met."

The ruler pretended to take no notice of the brothers' startled reaction to his rapid and flawless mastery of their native idiom. He proceeded to overwhelm them even more. As he introduced each by name, he seated them at the table according to their ages, from eldest Reuben to youngest Benjamin.

When Joseph came to Benjamin, he paused before showing the lad to his seat. Placing an arm about him, Joseph said tenderly, "And you are Benjamin. God be gracious to you, my lad." The ruler swallowed hard and drew out his handkerchief. "Begin to eat," he commanded over his shoulder, "and I shall rejoin you in a moment." His next words were lost as he quickly departed.

"Again he leaves us," Dan whispered. "The sickness that sends him from the room is upon him once more."

Servants began to serve the guests at the table. It was arranged in an open triangle, with the ruler's place at the apex. On the right were the Egyptian notables. On the left, the Canaanites, with Benjamin's seat at the governor's left hand. The arrangement unnerved Judah, who was at the far end of the table. He feared Benjamin's jabbering mouth would say the wrong thing.

When Joseph returned, he had washed his face and renewed his spirits. He began introducing the Egyptian dignitaries to Jacob's sons. Then he acknowledged the gifts on the buffet and said, "I am most pleased with the fine presents from your father. I gather he is still alive and well?"

All brothers' heads nodded in unison, for they were now beyond words. They already were stunned into silence by the lavish array of foods—fruits, breads, cakes, vegetables, pastries, and spun-sugar ornaments the hungry Canaanites never saw or tasted before. Beside each chair was a dainty washing stand and

344

basin. Aproned servants, cup-bearers, and wine stewards kept beakers full, while other attendants brought forth main dishes. There were platters of veal, mutton, fish, fowl, and game. Joseph sent forth some of each with his compliments, but the largest piles of the choicest selections were given to the boy at his left. To Egyptians, that indicated highest favor.

Embarrassed, Benjamin looked toward Judah with a distress signal of apology. He could not eat half of what was on his plate. Joseph did not seem to mind that the high pile of food was not consumed. Instead, he began to question the boy about his home, his father, and his interests. Joseph's manner was so pleasant, the apprehensive Canaanites began to relax and eat. Benjamin's embarrassment disappeared, and he avoided Judah's eyes to speak up boldly to the ruler.

"Would my lord answer a question which has greatly puzzled me?" Benjamin asked.

"Ask what you will," replied a smiling Joseph.

"You amaze me with your ability to know our names and to seat us in the order of our birth. You called our names as my father says all the world will one day know them—because we are a chosen people of our God. How is it you seem to recognize us as our very own father does?"

Joseph lifted a silver cup adorned with cuneiform inscriptions and said, "My cup here is a very special one. I not only drink from it, but also divine from it things I want to know."

"Is it magic?" Benjamin asked with his eyes almost popping from his head. Divination and magic and other kinds of occult sorcery were strictly forbidden by his religion. Israelites believed that only God was their source of supernatural wisdom and that all else was demonic idolatry. Even though Benjamin was a bit frightened by the cup, he also was extremely curious.

Joseph, who also abhorred all such pagan practices, evaded giving a direct answer in order to maintain his cover story. Instead, he offered an ambiguous response: "You might say that. As I hold this cup, I also can discern many other things. I see your homeland, for instance. Your father's tents and his four wives. No, only three remain, for one has died."

Benjamin's mouth dropped open. "That is my mother!" he cried.

"I also see," Joseph continued, "two brothers, the sons of that true wife, but one vanishes."

"My brother, Joseph! He was killed!" Benjamin was becoming excited. "What else?"

"No," Joseph said softly. "The older brother was not killed. He was placed in a dark pit that resembled a grave. But the pit was not his grave. The brother was drawn out, and he yet lives!"

Benjamin was aghast. His mouth was ready to cry out, but he could not. He was too dazed and bewildered. Before the youth could find voice to ask more questions, the ruler put the cup down on the table and stood to his feet.

"I regret that I must leave you now," Joseph said to the whole group. "I must return to the office building to see to the wants of other hungry travelers such as you."

Joseph washed his hands at his basin as a servant poured water over them. The Egyptian nobles were doing the same as they prepared to leave with him. The Canaanites sat motionless.

Then Joseph said, "I bid you farewell and God's protection on your homeward journey. You will spend the night as my guests, of course, and on the morrow take your leave with the grain you have come to purchase. All of you, including Simeon, are free to go and no longer under any suspicion. I know now that you are not spies, and I am greatly relieved to say so. I apologize for frightening you and for inconveniencing Simeon. Take with you my fondest greetings to your father and my thanks for his generous gifts."

As the Egyptians followed Joseph from the room, they left behind a confused group of brothers on the left side of the table.

The next morning, the brothers were no less confused, but they definitely were in better spirits. Their animals were laden with grain as they took the homeward road toward their hungry families. Some of them were more than jovial. They were boastful and bursting with pride.

"Imagine!" Asher said with his head reared back. "We have Benjamin and Simeon safely with us to delight our father. We have full grain sacks, and we are honorably acquitted of all charges of espionage. Why did we have any fear?"

"So honorably acquitted," Dan added, "we even broke bread with the ruler and his court! When he saw his error in falsely accusing us, he had to go to far lengths to right the wrong."

"Quite right," Issachar said. "The former abuse made us most deserving of the banquet!"

Disgusted with them, Judah growled, "We were not abused, and we deserved nothing!"

"What insect bites at your insides?" Simeon jeered.

"Brother Judah is back in his usual color of mind—black!" called out Levi.

"The whole lot of you sicken me," Judah said. "When you are found innocent in one instance, straightaway you think yourselves blameless in all. Do you think being cleared of the ruler's charges now makes you so free of all guilt that you boast of deserving great honors?"

"Judah," Reuben implored, "do not dampen their spirits. We have reason to rejoice."

"But not to gloat with arrogant pride!" Judah returned.

Reuben held up a hand to Judah: "Nevertheless, let us have no quarrel."

Judah shrugged, indicating that he would say no more. He turned his attention to Benjamin, who had become very quiet. "What ails our youngest brother—sadness to leave mighty Egypt?"

"No," Benjamin replied. "I was thinking of the ruler and his divining cup."

"Pay no attention to such evil," Judah warned. "Many such feats of magic are known in Egypt, but those practices are fakes, ungodly rites of false religions. Take no part in them!"

Benjamin turned to face Judah as they rode along. "It was not the cup, but the ruler who amazed me. He described our homeland. He knew all about me. And Joseph! He said our brother was not slain by an animal, but that he still lives. Can that be?"

"All things are possible with our God, Benjamin. Perhaps the Almighty saw fit to restore Joseph's life. If He did so, He

347

would need no divining cup or witchcraft or any other evil means."

Reuben overheard Judah's words and leaned over to whisper, "What think you, Judah?"

Judah whispered back, "That Joseph may yet be alive. When I sold him, were the traders not bound for Egypt? Perhaps Joseph is still in bonds or a slave waiting upon some wealthy heathen. I mean to find out. When I have restored Benjamin to Israel, I will return to Egypt and ask the governor to assist me in discovering Joseph's whereabouts."

"And then?" Reuben asked.

"Then I will seek Joseph, release him if I can, or buy him back. I even would take his place as a slave if I can arrange such a bargain with his master."

"But Judah, you cannot be serious!"

"Quiet! The others will hear. Can you not understand, Reuben, that I cannot have another moment's peace as long as I fear Joseph is alive and in bonds? If he has served the better part of his life enslaved because of me, the least I can do is exchange what is left of my life for his."

Completely oblivious to Judah's conversation with Reuben, the others had begun to sing, so cheerful was their mood. They had not gone an hour's journey, however, before the harmony turned to sharp discord. Advancing from the rear was a band of Egyptian soldiers. They were led by the governor's steward in a steed-drawn chariot followed by several wagons full of armed men.

The army descended upon Jacob's sons, shouting noisily as they overtook them and formed a circle about the astonished men. The steward ordered them to dismount. They obeyed. Benjamin let out a cry of alarm at the sight of the drawn bows and upraised lances. Judah placed a hand of protection on the youth's shoulder before facing the grim-looking steward. Could this be the same man who, only the day before, had shown them such kindness?

"Wherefore have you rewarded evil for good?" the steward shouted. "Why have you stolen my master's silver cup?"

A rumble of protest arose as the brothers looked to Reuben

348

to defend them to the steward: "Good steward, if you speak of the ruler's wine cup, we have it not."

Judah protested, "More false accusations? Must it all start again? Why is the ruler of Egypt always looking for reasons to indict us—first as spies and now as thieves? Our father is a wealthy man, and we can have all the silver cups—or gold ones—that we wish. Why should we steal his?"

The steward raised his voice: "There is no false accusation this time. The silver cup, the one from which my master drinks and divines, was used yesterday at the banquet. You men were left alone in that room after the ruler and his company withdrew. It is clear that one of you must have taken it. But most suspicion falls upon the boy there. He was last to touch it."

Judah tightened his hold upon Benjamin's shaking shoulders and said, "To defend this lad with words is senseless. Our defense rests with a lack of evidence. The burden of proof clearly is yours, so search now our belongings. You will not find a cup, silver or otherwise, nor even a napkin from your master's table among our things!"

As the guards began to search, Judah continued his tirade: "We are not vagabond thieves! To steal from the provider-of-grain would be utter stupidity on our part."

"I quite agree," was the steward's flippant reply. "Because Egyptians are fair and moderate people, we do not seek to punish the innocent. Only the one in whose belongings the cup is found shall be arrested. The rest of you will be free to go."

"Then you soon shall see the dust rise up in your face as all of us get back on our donkeys and ride swiftly homeward," Judah said smugly.

"Here it is!" went up a cry from one of the searchers. "Found within the sack of the youngest, even as our master predicted."

All eyes immediately turned to Benjamin, then back to the silver cup in the guard's hand.

"Benjamin!" Judah shouted. "Defend yourself! Open your mouth and tell us how you came by this silver cup!

"He must have taken it!" Zebulon accused. "Did you not all see how his eyes grew large yesterday when the ruler showed it to him?"

"We are shamed!" cried Asher shaking a fist. "Shamed by our youngest! Did he not cry out when he saw the soldiers approach? He knew why they came after us. He cried out from guilt!"

"Be silent, you idiots!" Judah yelled to Zebulon and Asher. "Do you wish to make matters worse yet? We have not heard Benjamin's explanation. Speak, lad!"

Tears began to form in Benjamin's eyes. "I know nothing. I did not steal nor even touch the cup before we left the table."

Judah was beside himself, unable to know what to think. He said to Benjamin, "Do not weep. It will make you appear more guilty still. We will solve this mystery, never fear."

In the midst of the frenzy, some wailing brothers began to tear their clothing, a sign of complete remorse. Others were shouting curses at Benjamin.

"Cease this hot-headed display!" commanded the steward. "I told you only the thief must return to face my master. The rest of you may go safely on your way."

The shouting gave place to sighs of relief as Judah said, "I shall go back with the lad. I have sworn to protect him and must not leave his side."

"Very well," the steward agreed.

"We all shall return with him," Reuben commanded. "There is something amiss here. We must all stand with Benjamin at his judgment and not leave him in the lurch."

Now the brothers' anger turned upon Reuben. They hotly contested his proposal and argued that some of them had to return with the grain for the sake of their starving families. Simeon objected that he already had spent enough time as a prisoner in Egypt. Issachar complained that they all should not have to suffer "for the wicked brat's thievery."

Reuben was not swayed by their arguments. He railed, "You are all too quick to judge your brother! How can you just go on your way and leave him behind? I am more shamed by your cowardice than by any charges against Benjamin. Are you men? Have you considered how it will go with you if you return to our father without his beloved? I think you will fare better to put efforts toward clearing him than to make explanations for deserting him in a foreign land!"

The men murmured among themselves, considering Reuben's words. They faced a dilemma. To go back with Benjamin could mean their own punishment also, not to mention the certain starvation of their loved ones. To show cowardice, to abandon their brother, and then to find a way of explaining it all to their father were equally unacceptable alternatives.

"I leave it with your consciences," Reuben said. "Judah and I stand with Benjamin. Who stands with us?"

Reluctantly, Gad moved to join the three, saying, "I, for one, would prefer Egyptian bondage to facing Father with a tale of another lost son. Joseph's blood on my hands is quite enough. I do not want to have Benjamin's there also."

"Our father would surely die at the hearing," Levi agreed.

"Perhaps seeing all of us standing up for Benjamin will convince the ruler of our courage—if not our innocence. It is worth a try to make a good impression," Dan said without conviction.

Simeon heaved a long sigh. "I have, after all, become accustomed to life in Egypt."

One by one, the other brothers consented to return with the suspect, some more willingly than others. The most reluctant finally relented, more from shame of being the only ones to hold out against the others than for any genuine concern for Benjamin's welfare.

"Be it according to your words," the steward said when the decision was final. He ushered the lot of them into a wagon while the soldiers tied their donkeys behind it.

So it was that the brothers went back to the city from which they just had come. This time as they journeyed, there were no prideful boasts nor joyous songs. There was not even any talking, for none of them dared discuss the situation or question a tearful Benjamin again. He had guilt and dread written all over his face.

They rode in silence and hoped their father's prayers for their welfare had reached Heaven.

Twenty-three

It surprised the brothers to learn that once again they were going to the governor's house instead of to the office building. Judah and Reuben were not as surprised as the rest, for nothing seemed out of the realm of possibility after two experiences with the changeable governor of Egypt. They were deep in thought, trying to devise a credible defense to clear Benjamin. It seemed hopeless, for the cup in Benjamin's belongings defied any explanation.

At the villa, they were escorted to a private chamber to await the governor's coming. The wait was deliberately painful and long. Adon-Joseph wanted it just that way.

Benjamin was first to break the silence. "I am afraid," he said with his lips quivering.

"Put your faith in God. All will be well," Reuben said as convincingly as he could.

The one who wished to be thought of as grown up and ready for marriage was a little boy again as he moaned, "Did you not hear? The one found with the silver cup would be punished. Will I die? Will I have to be a servant here in Egypt and never see my father or Cumi again?"

Judah stopped pacing the floor to say, "Instead of using this time to fret, try to think how that cursed cup got into your sack. Who was the one who filled it up with grain?"

"How should I know?" Benjamin wailed. "I was not even around at the time it was filled."

Judah stroked his beard. "This Egyptian ruler seems to enjoy playing with us as if we were dolls on strings. I think this is one more of his schemes. He has invented yet another plan to get us back here to testify before him. I think he enjoys the argument of our debates. Before we can plan your defense, Benjamin, you must tell us truthfully whether or not you are guilty. If you are, we must seek mercy. If you are innocent, we must demand justice."

Benjamin pouted, "I give you my oath on Father's head, I did nothing! You were beside me as we left the banquet hall. Did you see me with any cup? Where could I have hidden it? Did you see me put it in my grain sack before we departed for home? Judah, I cannot make a single move without your eyes upon me, so you, of all people, should know I am innocent."

Murmurs of disbelief arose from several of the brothers. They said it was better to depend upon the governor's mercy to overlook a silly child's impulsive prank than to attempt a defense when none existed. They reasoned that the ruler liked Benjamin and might forgive him now that the cup was back where it belonged.

"But I did not take it!" Benjamin sniffed.

"Then dry your eyes," Judah said sternly. "You must appear as guiltless as you say you are. The rest of you men keep silence when the ruler arrives. Your unbridled tongues will not help me as I plead Benjamin's case."

"Who made you our spokesman in Reuben's place?" Simeon demanded with a sneer.

Reuben waved his hand with a sigh of relief. "I give Judah leave. Father appointed Judah Benjamin's guardian on this trip, so it is Judah's responsibility to protect his charge."

"What will you say for me, Judah?" Benjamin asked, swallowing and fighting his tears.

"The truth," Judah said. "God will honor nothing else, and your destiny rests now in His hands. Pray that the Lord will give me the right words to say."

Judah was aware of his brothers' snide glances. He knew they must think him a hypocrite.

A gong sounded to announce the ruler's arrival. The accused and his brothers flung themselves down before the chair upon which Adon-Joseph seated himself. They remained with their foreheads touching the marbled floor for what seemed an eternity before the ruler spoke:

"Did you think without my cup I could not divine who had

stolen from me? Arise! Stand up as men, and confess your awful deed!"

Judah stepped forward and looked into the ruler's eyes. Quietly, he rent his garments before the assembly, bowed his head, and spoke so softly no one believed it was Judah, the lion, speaking.

Judah fell to his knees and said, "What can be answered to the mighty one of Egypt to satisfy the charge against Jacob's sons? We are guilty in the sense that your cup was found among us, but how your property came to be in one of our sacks, we cannot say. You who are wise and just in all your dealings, you who feed the starving and who have been wondrously generous to us in our need, only you have the power to solve this mystery. You say your divining cup can tell you all things. Pray, seek from it to find the culprit in this cause, for we have not the answer for you."

"A pretty speech," the ruler said. "And well I might look into the cup. Do you not fear that if the truth revealed there convicts you, you shall be worse off than if you confess here and now?"

"No, gracious lord," Judah replied. "We trust in God and your mercy. You told us you know our God and honor Him. He will not let you unjustly punish the undeserving. Only one thing I ask. If you truly honor our God, pray to Him before you use any form of divination."

"You speak for yourself I know, but are your brothers agreed with you in this decision?"

"Yes, we are united," Judah said solemnly as he acknowledged the nods of the others.

"But the cup was found in only one grain sack. How is it you all stand before me when Benjamin was the one who possessed the convicting evidence?" the governor asked Judah.

"If he be pronounced guilty, then we all take his punishment upon ourselves. In this way, you may know our sincerity to believe in Benjamin's innocence and our faith in God to prove it."

"You impress me with the courage and conviction with which you speak, but I am not one to inflict punishment upon all for the crime of one. If the lad has wronged me, he alone will remain here in my custody. The rest may go in peace to your father."

Adon-Joseph clapped his palms together and commanded that the silver cup be brought forth. Before it reached his hands, Judah was compelled to speak again.

"You must know that the matter of the silver cup is all of my doing!" Judah blurted out.

A gasp went up from the others in the room. The brothers did not know whether Judah was the actual thief or he was taking Benjamin's blame upon himself to save the boy.

Judah continued, "It is not that I stole anything from you, but all the miseries upon my brethren, the misery of the famine, every misery to this present one, are naught else but God's punishment for *my* sin. The Lord has seen my iniquity and has brought woe upon us all."

Reuben could contain himself no longer. He stepped forward, grasped Judah arm, and raised him from his knees. Making Judah face him, Reuben said through clenched teeth, "What you are saying has no bearing on this situation. Do not do this!"

Judah pulled away and replied, "No, Reuben. I have kept my sin covered too long. I will now openly confess it and beg the ruler not to give my sentence to another."

Adon-Joseph shielded his eyes as he studied Judah's face. "What is this great evil of which you speak?" he asked.

Ruben stepped in front of Judah to reply. "Mighty ruler, Judah cannot take all blame upon himself. I and my brothers share in the guilt he wants to confess. It is an irrelevant matter."

Judah shoved Reuben aside to move even closer. "Will my lord hear all my heart and not let my brother prevent me until I have explained to you the whole of it?"

When Adon-Joseph gave Judah the floor, a transformation took place. The despondent man, the one who had withdrawn into himself and shut all others away, became open and full of words. He began by explaining the great love his father had for Benjamin and how difficult it was for Jacob to release his favored son to come to Egypt. Judah's voice became husky as he continued:

"Thus I preface my oration, so you will understand how dear this lad is to our father. The reason for that closeness is to make

355

up the loss of Joseph, our brother who is no longer among us. Joseph was our father's favorite, and I despised him for it. Joseph was to receive my father's blessing, and I envied him for it. I wanted the blessing so much, I became Joseph's rival for it."

"At some point," Adon-Joseph said, "I assume you will connect this story to the matter of the stolen cup."

"Yes, if you will have patience with me, mighty one." Judah cleared his throat, trying to think how to say it all more quickly. "I thought the inheritor of the blessing would be transformed into a righteous man. My folly was believing that if I took Joseph's place, I would become my father's favorite and possess the spiritual grace that rested upon Joseph."

The governor's handkerchief was dabbing at his eyes, for he knew what would be spoken next. He saw before him a repentant man who truly regretted his sin against his brother.

Judah said, "I see by your tears, my lord, you understand my foolish plight. How you must pity me for thinking I could change my lustful ways by usurping another's God-inheritance or by obtaining a blessing by deceit. Heeding the devils in my soul brought nothing but destruction—first I destroyed Joseph; then my wife and sons lay rotting in their graves; then God sent famine to devastate the land and to strike all who come near me. This latest misfortune must not destroy Benjamin, for if he is not returned to Israel's bosom, my father surely will be destroyed as well."

"Good ruler, may I speak now?" Reuben interrupted. When Adon-Joseph nodded, Reuben brought up words from his anguished heart: "I cannot stand by and hear Judah blame himself for only his part in a larger conspiracy. Judah did not slay our brother, Joseph, but these other ruffians before you intended to do just that. Judah sold Joseph into slavery. As regrettable as that is, it is not to be compared with the greater malice they would have inflicted. My brothers hear me break my blood oath to remain silent, but I can keep silence no more. We lied to our father and told him Joseph was dead. We all, except Benjamin, are guilty for the loss of one brother. Do not take another from our father! The youngest is innocent and must not be the one punished for our guilt."

Some brothers were red with anger. Some turned pale and cringed with downcast eyes as Reuben and Judah openly resurrected their buried past. Judah fell upon his knees once more.

"Did Adon not give me leave to tell my story to completion?" Judah protested. "I became surety for Benjamin and swore to my father I would bear blame forever if I did not return his youngest to him. Let me now be his ransom. I will remain here as the lowliest of your servants to serve Benjamin's sentence. Send Benjamin home safely to my father. If you do not, my father surely will die! Let me, who sold one brother, now for God's dear sake, buy back another!"

With the divining cup in one hand and the handkerchief in the other, Adon-Joseph slowly rose and walked forward. All plainly could see the tears on his face. In the language of the Egyptians, he cried out, "All of you, leave me! Only the accused Canaanites shall remain!"

When the room emptied of servants and attendants, Joseph lifted the cup to look into it. Immediately, Judah fell prostrate on his face and wept. The other brothers followed Judah's lead and bowed themselves to the floor. They dared not look as the sentence was pronounced.

"Hear now the message from Jehovah, the one true God! He speaks to me and through me without divination!" Joseph hurled the silver cup aside and resumed his prophecy. "There was a sheaf standing in the field, and, lo, eleven sheaves bowed round about, making obeisance to the standing sheaf. The interpretation of that dream is fulfilled now as you bow down before me here. The Lord also reveals to me the guilty party who placed the vessel in Benjamin's sack. He is in this room. All others are guiltless of the crime. The blame rests upon . . . Joseph, son of Jacob!"

The familiar words from the past rang in every ear. The pronouncing of the verdict caused every bowed head to pop up and look in astonishment at Joseph.

With outstretched arms, the governor of Egypt cried out, "I am Joseph, your brother! Arise and draw near to me that I may embrace you—every one!"

No one made a move. The brothers were troubled, amazed,

doubtful, relieved, and dazed all at once. They did not know whether to run to him or from him.

"Do not remain as statues," Joseph ordered with a laugh. "Stand up, and come here to me!"

Benjamin was first to move. He ran into Joseph's open arms, shouting, "I thought so! I thought you were my true brother—by the way you acted yesterday at the table. How else could you know so much about all of us? You never could, for all the divining cups in the world!"

"My little brother! Dearest Benjamin!" Joseph called out as he wept upon the boy's neck.

With Benjamin still holding to his waist, Joseph stepped in front of the stone-faced brothers to kiss each one. When he came to Judah, Joseph said, "A most moving and powerful speech, Judah. I should have been likely to release Benjamin had he been guilty of a thousand crimes."

Judah turned away from Joseph's open arms. "Do not kiss me, I pray you. I praise Jehovah for your safety, but I am unworthy of your smallest favors. I am so sorry, so terribly sorry for what I did to you." Judah covered his bowed head in his hands and walked away to face the wall.

For the moment, Joseph left Judah alone and turned to the others. Some stood open-mouthed, some held clinched fists upon their heaving chests, some seemed transfixed, but all of them wore faces colored with fright. They did not make a move to approach their lost brother.

"Do not be afraid of me," Joseph chuckled. "I will play no more tricks upon you, I give my word. I see you have suffered enough. I want only for you to forget the past and let me hold you close to my heart—now and always. Stand not away from me! Come!"

Slowly, one after the other, they inched closer. They approached him cautiously at first; then they were all upon him—shouting, crying, touching, embracing, and kissing his cheeks.

"Reuben, you tower of strength!" Joseph said as he felt massive, crushing arms almost take his breath away. "You were most persuasive—both times you argued your case before me."

"I cannot believe it! I cannot believe it!" Reuben kept repeating. "Then the cup, the money in our sacks, calling us spies, all those false accusations . . . Were they . . . ? Were you . . . ?"

"All my doing, I admit it," Joseph confessed. "It was partly to assure you would return to me, partly as a test to see what you were made of—before I decided what to do about you."

"But why did you not reveal yourself to us from the start?" asked an offended Zebulon.

"So the story our grandchildren tell will be more exciting," Joseph smiled. "I almost told you several times. I longed to—each time you made me weep! But you needed a few moments of anguish to test your mettle before our reunion. I thought you might still want to toss me in a pit!"

"You gave us more than a few moments of anguish," complained Levi. "I think we are more than repaid for our evil against you. Your torturous pranks had all of us afraid for our lives!"

Joseph was quick to correct Levi's misunderstanding. "Think not that I played deceitful games to frighten you or for revenge. I felt God leading me in each instance. I think He wanted you to repent of your past sins voluntarily—and not from any forced confession from me."

Simeon's brow was wrinkled into tense lines. "But why did you not tell your identity unto me while I was with you here and my brothers were back home? Why did I have to stay locked up instead of at your side? Why did you choose me as your prisoner instead of Judah? And how did you rise from a bond slave to become the mighty governor of all Egypt?"

Joseph shook his head. "Too many questions to answer at once, Simeon. All will be made clear to you later. The servants will show you to your quarters now, so you can rest before we dine together. I have a great celebration planned. I want you to meet my wife and my sons, and then we shall talk all through the night. Go now, and I will rejoin you soon."

When all the final pleasantries were exchanged and the last handclasps were given, ten of the brothers were moved toward the huge doors to follow the servants awaiting them in the hall. They left, all talking excitedly among themselves, marveling

359

that the youthful dreamer of dreams had become the compassionate food provider, the strange ruler who played dual roles—the benevolent hero and the devious villain—in this human drama of reconciliation.

When they were gone, Joseph turned his attention to the brother who was left behind. Judah was still standing dazed and motionless with his face to the wall.

When Joseph walked over to place an arm about Judah's shoulder, he felt his brother's tense body go rigid. "Be not angry with yourself, Judah, that you sold me hither. It was ordained that God would send me to this place before you, to feed the hungering and to preserve life."

"Do not soil your hands to touch me," Judah said, moving a step away. "Let me leave this place now as you celebrate reunion with the other brothers. I do not want to have to look into your eyes to see my shame written there."

With greatest tenderness, Joseph turned Judah around and forced him to look into his eyes. "Behold!" Joseph cried. "You do not see your shame or my retribution in these eyes, but only love and forgiveness. Let the past be blotted out from memory. Let us start afresh from this moment."

Brushing past Joseph, Judah cried out in anguish, "How can you look upon me with gentle eyes after the evil I have done unto you?"

"I perceive that you already have suffered quite enough without my added chastisement. Sin always brings its own punishment, for we never escape from ourselves." When Judah made no response, Joseph added, "Come and sit with me here, Judah."

Judah allowed himself to be led to a couch in a far corner of the room. He sat beside Joseph, but he still could not look at him. Judah's shoulders remained slumped and his head was bowed.

Joseph rubbed the hunched and tense shoulders as he spoke: "Let me assure you, I cannot be angry with you, Judah, when it was God's intent that I be transported to Egypt. You did not act from pure motives, I grant you, when you sold me and hid the deed from our father. But can you not see that I was destined to be brought here to save people from famine as the ruler of Egypt?"

360

"A ruler of Egypt," Judah repeated. "We indeed bowed the knee to you, even as you foretold we would when you interpreted your dream to us long ago."

"Then can you not see that God brought good from that which you did unto me? The Lord has made me second only to Pharaoh and lord of all the land. This never would have come to pass if you had not thought of the way to get me here with the tradesmen bound for Egypt. God put the plan in your mind. You actually saved my life, for the others surely would have killed me."

"None of that matters. It still does not excuse . . ."

"I did not say anything you did was excusable. But your deeds certainly are understandable and forgivable. Judah, you are very like our father. He also deceived his father, Isaac, to obtain God's blessing. He became alienated from his brother, Esau, in the process, but they became reconciled. You and I must become reconciled brothers as well."

Judah finally lifted his head and looked at Joseph. "Such goodness and mercy! I cannot understand it, nor can I accept forgiveness or rewards from your hands. I am undeserving and must pay for my sins, Joseph. At one time, I wanted to die for those sins. But that could in no way right a single wrong. May I stay here, as your servant, and try to repay you in some small measure with the toil of my hands and the sweat of my brow?"

Joseph gave a little laugh of admiration for Judah's sincerity. "No, my brother. You must stop trying to pay for deeds of the past. You have my forgiveness and God's. Now you must forgive yourself."

Judah rose and began to pace, as he always did in times of agitation. "How can you say God will forgive me? He will not hear me, though I cry at the top of my voice unto Him. He is far from me and has brought me great sorrows to show His displeasure with me!"

"If you feel your are estranged from communion with God, the fault is in you, not Him. The Lord loves you and wants you near, but He waits patiently for you to approach, for He does not force Himself upon his children. The sorrows you have suffered

361

are not God's punishments, but a means of drawing you to Himself—for healing of the hurts."

"I do not understand your words," Judah said as he sat down again. He felt he was hearing the voice of the Lord speaking through Joseph, and he wanted very much to understand.

To illustrate the welcoming arms of God, Joseph spread his arms toward Judah and said, "You must perceive God as a loving Father, not as a revengeful tyrant. He does not want your death, Judah. He wants your life! What good to God are you as a bond servant in servitude to perform some kind of self-imposed penance? Rather than punishment and death, seek to live a more noble life than ever before! That is how to make atonement."

"But I feel it is too late for that. Your words are wasted on me, Joseph."

"I thank God it is never too late, and nothing He contrives is ever wasted. But we shall have more time to talk of this later. In fact, I think we shall have a great deal of time together. I want you and all the others to bring your wives and little ones here to live. I can provide good grazing for your flocks in the land of Goshen nearby. I do not want you perishing in the remaining years of famine. I want you all with me, nourished by me, with all the wealth of Egypt to be yours. We shall be together as a family once more."

Judah shook his head in wonderment. "Such a man you are! Well I know why you were our father's favorite—and now Pharaoh's favorite. Always I have been jealous of your wisdom and godly virtues."

"Envy me no more, Judah. All who desire it may receive wisdom from God. All who desire to do so may walk close to Him. I am no more special to the Lord than you are, but the Lord devises different plans for each of us. We are no longer rivals for a birthright blessing, Judah. We both will partake of different shares of the blessing of Israel."

Judah's brows raised in curiosity as he asked, "What do you mean?"

"God has revealed to me in a dream that you, Judah, will be the channel of His promise to send forth the Messiah. Indeed, from your descendants will come the Christ!"

Judah wanted to laugh in derision, but he could not laugh at God's prophet. Still, Joseph's words made no sense. "Not so, Joseph!" he protested. "God cannot use a life as wretched as mine for so blessed an honor. You are the one for that."

"Poor, doubting Judah! You did not believe in the dreams of my youth. Yet they came to pass. Now you put no faith in the dreams of my maturity. They also shall come to pass, whether or not you believe them. This is not my plan, but God's. He already has given me my life's purpose—to feed the hungry and to teach His ways in a land of idolatry."

"But I tell you, I am not worthy!"

"If God depended upon human worthiness to achieve His purposes, nothing would ever be accomplished! Who in this world is sinless? God is the one who is worthy—and able to work through the most sinful of flesh. Lives are never praiseworthy outside of God's will, but the humility I see in you now is the very attitude required. God can use such a life as yours."

Judah turned his head away again. "But that simply cannot be! I have been immoral—selfish and greedy. I have violated God's law to sin against Him and hurt others . . ."

"God can forgive each sin you name," Joseph said with an offhanded shrug of unconcern.

"But . . ." Judah searched for words to make Joseph understand. "I have taken unto myself a heathen wife, a Canaanite. Since Shuah's death, I have remarried. I know the Lord would not use such a one to mother the family of Messiah!"

"How can you know that? Are you a judge to proclaim what the Almighty can and cannot do? Are you wiser than God Himself? I too have married a heathen—the daughter of the priest of a pagan god. But while I have lived in this kingdom of wickedness, I have maintained my childhood's faith. God has guided my every step. I have a home founded upon the true faith. Can your wife not learn to be a believer in Jehovah—the same way as my wife has done?"

"Oh, Tamar is a believer in the true God. I did not mean to infer . . ."

"Tamar? Yes, that is the name revealed to me in my dream.

363

Well, Judah, that confirms it. She is the one God has chosen for the honor—whether or not you find fault with His choice."

Judah was dumbfounded. His father and Tamar herself always believed the covenant promise was to be her destiny, but that was before Adullam. As painful as it was to confess, Judah had to tell Joseph about Adullam. That insurmountable barrier still remained between Judah and Tamar. And between Judah and his God.

Judah tried to keep his voice from trembling as he said, "At the risk of continuing to argue with God and you, His prophet, I must tell you something deplorable, Joseph. Our sons, mine and Tamar's, were conceived in lust and harlotry . . . before we married . . ."

"I know that," Joseph said with no apparent apprehension.

"You know what?"

"In my dream about you and Tamar, God told me you would have twin sons—just as your father and grandfather before you. Although they would be conceived in deception and sin, God was not to be thwarted thereby. He said the one destined to perpetuate the covenant would race past his brother to be the firstborn blessing-bearer. God said He would give you a birth sign, that you might know whom to bless when it was the child's time to receive his inheritance."

"The scarlet thread!" Judah gasped. "My servant told me my firstborn moved aside his brother whose wrist was entwined with a scarlet thread!"

"Yes, that was what I saw in my dream. The Lord knew you would be hard to convince, for you are a stubborn and fierce lion of a man, my brother. Like our father, you wrestle against the Lord's angel—but you will prevail as did he. God's prophecy to you is that from your loins will come the Christ, the Lion of the Tribe of Judah, for thus shall He be called. Do you now believe? Do you finally see that God is not limited by human limitations?"

"I have no more words of argument, yet my head reels at all this. I want to put faith in your words, Joseph, for I know you always speak truth. I want very much to believe . . ."

"Then just do so, Judah! No wonder God had to send dreams

to me and signs to you. Never have I known anyone harder to convince and so unwilling to let God bestow a blessing than you!"

Judah bowed his head as a flood of warmth suddenly came over him. It seemed to awaken a dormant, almost forgotten, spiritual awareness remembered as a spark, faint and promising long ago. Now it was a rekindled fire, burning with heat and light deep inside him.

With tears of joy and relief streaming from his eyes, Judah said, "Be it now unto me according to the will of the Lord. I shall seek no more to die, but if God grants me His merciful grace, I shall live my life, ever dedicated to His highest purposes."

Joseph embraced his brother and held him close. The rigid resistance was gone, and Judah's broad shoulders no longer drooped. His head was held up, and his face seemed aglow with new joy and peace. Judah did not look the same. He did not feel the same. He was not the same.

Joseph said, "How my heart rejoices at your words, Judah! You were sent here for this very hour to be reconciled to me and to the Lord. All that remains now is for you to renew your vows to Jehovah."

"Will you . . . Will you pray with me, Joseph? It has been a very long time since I did that."

"Indeed, we shall pray together. I have an altar built nearby, and it awaits us even now. Come, we must pray before we join the others."

As they left the room, arm in arm, Judah said quietly, "We are no longer rivals, Joseph. By God's unexplainable providence, we are brothers!"

Twenty-four

For several days, Joseph kept his brothers with him in Egypt before he consented for them to leave. There was the urgency of the famine and the desire to send glad tidings home to Jacob, but there also was a need for healing and reconciliation among the brothers.

Joseph and Judah became very close during those days. Joseph served as Judah's mentor, counselor, role model, friend, and spiritual guide. As they sat together for meals or for long hours under the evening stars to discuss the ways of God, such a change came over Judah that even the other brothers noticed he looked and acted both healthier and happier.

When Reuben asked him about it, Judah said, "I am at peace. I feel as though I have been reborn, and now I shall begin to live. Such a weight has been lifted from my shoulders, I feel as light as a bird's feather."

Judah's jovial mood was a welcome change from his former dark periods of depression and outbursts of temper. He was more pleasant to be around. The new Judah also began to create a regenerate atmosphere among the others. There was, in the presence of the godly Joseph and the reborn Judah, a desire on the part of all the other brothers to rededicate themselves to the God of their fathers. It was an unlikely setting for a spiritual revival, but one seemed to take place within the home of the ruler of a land known for its immorality and idolatry.

Perhaps the greatest influence upon Joseph's Canaanite guests was the home life observed and enjoyed at the governor's villa. Love and kindness dominated the atmosphere where Joseph and his wife, Asenath, were bringing up their two aristocratic sons, Manasseh and Ephraim. Even servants and visitors spoke no harsh words. It seemed that Joseph's dwelling was more of a sanctuary or temple of worship than a home. The atmosphere bespoke warmth and compassion and other virtues known only to those in a right relationship with their Creator and their fellow human creatures.

Simeon and Levi could not comprehend the quiet politeness, such a contrast to the sharp words, arguments, and backbiting gossip that existed in their own households. However, what really impressed the twins were evidences of Joseph's great wealth and power. A little of their old jealousy could not be denied when they saw their brother's material blessings and the reverent honor he received as a beloved and popular ruler in his adopted land.

Judah heard the twins discussing how unusual it was that Joseph was rich and influential, and yet he remained generous, humble and approachable. When Levi said that a lesser man would fall prey to greed and pride, Judah's comment was, "Perhaps that is why God did not choose any of the rest of us for Joseph's position."

When time came for the homeward journey, Joseph's generosity exceeded every brother's expectations. They were not only provided greater numbers of grain sacks than before, but also given wagons from Joseph's royal stores, mules, drivers, and armed guards for protection of the great caravan as it traveled the dangerous roads. There was a special purpose for the wagons:

"Take these," Joseph told them, "that you may return again with your wives, children, and servants. Bring my father unto me with all his vast households, and I will prepare a new place for all to live and flourish in Goshen. The wagons will carry all your goods and belongings, that nothing be left behind when you leave Hebron." Then he prayed, blessed them, and sent them off.

It was a most impressive caravan that departed. Besides hauling the anticipated grain sacks, the royal wagons carried luxurious specialty foods of Egypt, huge barrels of finest wines, and gifts for all members of Jacob's entire family. Joseph's subjects, who had heard of the governor's happy reunion with his brothers, turned out to wave their farewells and to throw bouquets.

"This reminds me of the Pharaoh's parade we observed on

our first day in the capital city," Reuben remarked. "Setting aside their strange religion, Egyptians are good, friendly people."

Benjamin received thorough enjoyment from the crowd's attentions at the farewell party. He wore the new Egyptian garments Joseph had given him and felt most important. He was tempted to accept Joseph's invitation to remain until the others returned, but he was anxious to see Cumi.

Benjamin exclaimed, "What stories I will have to tell Cumi about my trick-playing brother, the governor! And how our father's eyes will grow wide when he sees this great wagon train Joseph sends to fetch him to Egypt!"

"And will Father be surprised to hear that Joseph lives!" Reuben added.

Judah opined, "Surprised? That is not the word for it. I fear he will fall upon his back in shock when we bring him the news."

Judah's words gave Reuben pause. He nodded agreement and said, "We must think of a way to tell him so that his heart does not faint at the telling. It must be done tactfully, to be sure."

"And we have another thorny matter to discuss with Israel," said Judah. "Confession must be made of our guilt long ago. There is no delaying it now that a living Joseph cancels out the fable told to him about a wild beast and a bloody coat."

The other brothers were dismayed at Judah's words. Dan spoke up to suggest, "We can tell Father the merchants delivered Joseph from the paws of the beast and brought him to Egypt without our knowledge."

Judah was appalled. "Would you add yet another sin to our charge by lying again? And what other lie would you tell when Joseph and Israel meet? Shall we ask Joseph to conspire with us to deceive our father again? I think not, Dan. We must make a total and truthful confession."

"Will you speak for us, Judah?" asked Reuben, who had no desire to assume the role of spokesman for this confrontation. "You have the powers of oratory and persuasion."

"What is required is a gentle tongue," Judah countered. "That I have not."

Benjamin sang out, "I know who can do it gently—Tamar!

She gains Father's ear when no one else can. Would not a woman best take the sting from the telling?"

There was agreement with Benjamin's suggestion, not so much because it had great merit, but because all were relieved to pass the task to another. Who could find the best way to say, "Father, we sold your favorite son for money and then lied and let you suffer all these years"?

"Judah, will you ask Tamar to break the news to Father?" Dan asked hopefully.

Judah's reply was, "Tamar may prepare his heart, if that is your will, but we all must face Israel thereafter to beg his forgiveness. Only cowards hide behind a woman's skirts."

All were hoping that the move to Egypt and the joy of hearing Joseph was not dead would overshadow any long-term anger when truth-telling time arrived.

Leaving Egypt's plenteous bounty was made even harder as the caravan moved each day nearer home. The way became rougher and the landscape more dismal. The parched earth and fields cried out for moisture to the glassy sky, but only soaring vultures were to be seen above.

On the last night of camp before arriving home, the brothers met around the campfire to hold council. There were the issues of breaking the news to Jacob and planning how the move to Egypt would be implemented. It was decided for all to go first to Judah's camp and set servants to the task of packing for the return trip. Tamar would be sent immediately to talk with Jacob and to see that his households were preparing for the move. She would take escorts and ample provisions for their hungry families. After the brothers had rested at Judah's and packed the wagons with his supplies, they would go to Jacob's, confess to their father, and all move toward Egypt together.

Judah, more than anyone else, was anxious to make the move. It was not just because of the famine in Canaan or the better grazing lands Joseph had promised. It was in Egypt that Judah found himself—or found God again, to be more exact. He interpreted the transplanting of his roots as a new beginning, the start of a better and more productive life. Too many sad memories were in Canaan. He wanted to leave them behind and start over.

Judah spent a lot of time sorting things out and making decisions as he traveled the road toward home. He decided to give Hirah all his holdings in Adullam. Hirah had been a faithful steward for many years, and he longed to be promoted from hireling to master. Besides, it would be too troublesome and time-consuming to herd all the flocks from there, if any flocks still existed. Of course, all the hired shepherds were welcome to move to Goshen on their own, if they wished. Judah thought it best to leave the choice up to Hirah—just as long as he promised to leave Mai behind if he decided to make the move.

Judah's thoughts also turned to Tamar. Waves of regret and shame swept over him when he remembered what his unspeakable behavior must have done to her. Her only wedding gifts from him had been his isolation, his avoidance, and his thoughtlessness. During his dark periods, it had never occurred to him that she might be hurt or resentful when forced to assume his responsibilities with no word of appreciation for it. After observing how loving Joseph was to his Asenath, Judah concluded that he had been a dismal failure at being a husband.

He had repeated the pattern twice—once with Shuah, then again with Tamar. He had never shown love to either of them. Shuah had died for want of his love. But what of Tamar—the strong and resolute one who always connived and wormed her way into getting what she was after? Could even the most independent of women live without affection and fulfillment as a wife? Judah wanted to love her. Actually, he did love her. He just did not know how to tell her or show it. Perhaps if he took home some of the God-love he received in Egypt, he could share that with her.

As the royal caravan inched its way along the dusty road, Judah's heart began to pound as he saw familiar sights that indicated he was almost there. He raised himself half off his donkey to look into the distance. Surely, he would soon see the striped tents of his compound any time now.

There—on a rock, high above the final slope—he caught sight of a figure. Perhaps it was a servant sent as a lookout to

370

keep watch for those who would bring food for their gnawing hunger. The figure began to fling arms in the air in a welcoming gesture of recognition. It was a woman. No, a young girl. She descended the crest, running barefoot with the sun picking up the glitter of bright-colored beads about her neck. It was Cumi!

Digging his heels into his donkey's side, Judah raced ahead of the other mounted riders and the slow-moving wagons until he met the oncoming figure. He flung himself off his beast and went the last few yards between them on the run with outstretched arms. He caught Cumi about the waist and started swinging her around until she was too dizzy to stand when he stopped.

"Oh, Master!" Cumi panted when he held out a hand to steady her upon her feet. "I have watched every day from that rock, hoping to see you returning. God has heard my prayers. I am so glad you finally are here!"

"And I am glad to see you," Judah said as he walked with her and held his donkey's reins in his hand. "But not as glad as Benjamin will be when he gets here, I am sure. How is my family? Are my sons well and strong? Tell me the news, Cumi."

Cumi did not answer directly. "Oh, what marvelous wagons coming yonder. Were they purchased in Egypt to bring home the food?"

"Of wagons and Egypt later. First, tell me of Tamar and the twins."

Cumi's eyes, as usual, were brimming with tears. She would have cried anyway for the great happiness of seeing the brothers return with grain, but Judah's inquiry only added to the overflow of emotions which typified her sensitive nature. She looked at Judah's face and observed a more healthy and amiable change for the better. It was not just the brightness of his face. It was his concern for his family and the way he had greeted her so playfully that seemed totally out of character for one with Judah's usual solemn and melancholy moods.

"You must be in much better health, Master," Cumi said. "I can tell the trip and the food in Egypt have agreed with you. I see it in your face and hear it in the sound of your voice."

Judah stopped walking and faced Cumi squarely to ask, "What is the trouble? Do not dance around the question or talk in

371

circles before coming to the point. When you do that, I know something is wrong. Now, out with it! The famine? Sickness? What?"

"It is not famine or sickness, although both have been our companions since you left. It is that you arrive not a moment too soon. Even now, Tamar has packed her belongings and is prepared to leave on the morrow."

"Leaving? For where? Why?"

"I know it is not my place to say anything, but Tamar is my dearest friend. It is for her sake I must tell you—so you will prevent her. She thinks you will overcome your sadness and become happy again only when she is gone. She thinks that her presence is a burden to you and that you will never regain your strength of mind and spirit until she leaves your household."

"And my sons? Does she plan to take them away also?"

"She leaves them with me. Well, with you, really, but she was not certain you want much to do with them. She hopes, in time, they will bring you joy and you will grow to love them."

"How can she think all this nonsense? What mother can walk away from her children?"

"Oh, Tamar loves the twins more than life itself! It will be agony for her to leave them. But she said she is leaving you the small part of herself that you could love."

"Where does she plan to go?"

Cumi's eyes were spilling large tears as she answered. "She is returning to the land of her fathers and does not want the twins brought up in such a bad place. Oh, Master, you know Tamar despises it there. She will not be welcome in this time of famine when food is scarce enough without another to share the rations. I am afraid she will starve to death. Prevent her! God has sent you back in time, so you must prevent her!"

"Do not cry, Cumi. I will do what I can to stop her from this madness. But I must know why she wants to do this. Does she wish to leave because I have treated her so ill? Is that it?"

Cumi nodded, then added quickly, "Oh, she understands that your sickness is to blame for the way you avoid her. But she says she cannot continue to live where she is unwanted and unloved. She says she has always been selfish and taken things she

372

wanted. She thinks leaving you is the most unselfish, sacrificial thing she has ever done. She says it will make you happy to see her go."

"Where is Tamar now?"

"Within our tent. I came here praying you would return before she set out. You do not really want to be rid of her, do you, Master?"

"That is absurd."

Judah wanted to ask a hundred more questions, but the wagons and donkeys had caught up with them, and several of his brothers were dismounting. Benjamin spied Cumi and came running toward them. It would be impossible to get more information from the girl now.

Cumi stood holding her breath as Benjamin ran to her. Their arms encircled each other as the older brothers, greatly amused, looked on. To see young lovers so rapturously happy and Benjamin kissing away the tears on Cumi's cheeks gave each man a sudden longing for his own wife and a fond embrace. But none of them was as moved as Judah, who quickly sprang back upon his donkey.

"I am going on ahead," Judah called to the others. "Cumi will direct you to your lodgings and get servants to assist you with the unloading. If you need anything, just ask Cumi—that is, when she can break away!"

As the men's laughter grew louder, Benjamin turned red with embarrassment and Cumi buried her face in her apron.

Judah knew that Tamar was within the tent because he heard her singing and playing her harp even before he reached the door. There were tears in her voice.

Judah imagined she was singing to his sons a sad song of farewell. He did not enter immediately. He had to think what to say to her. He spied several bundles packed and standing by the doorway. They were the same bundles she had carried with her when she first returned to Judah's tents to claim her promise from him. Hiding behind the door flap, Judah peered in, unseen, to observe what Tamar was doing now that the music had stopped.

Tamar's back was to the doorway. She reached to give a push

373

to two small hammocks that were hanging from ropes attached to posts above. She made soft, motherly sounds to quiet the babies who had begun to fuss when she stopped singing.

"Oh, I see," Tamar said to her sons. "You want another song, do you? I am afraid I have no more songs to sing. I have taught Cumi all I have written, so she will have to provide your entertainment from now on."

The mild fussing turned to loud squalls, so Tamar pulled down her robes to the waist to bare her shoulders and back, clearly visible to her unseen visitor at the tent door. She reached for the babies and began to nurse them. The crying ceased as they made sucking noises of contentment.

"Oh, my dearest boys," Tamar said. "How I shall miss these precious moments with you! I have made arrangements for a very good wet nurse, however, so do not worry about keeping your little bellies full, not for one moment! And when your father returns, he will bring grain from faraway Egypt, and he will tell you marvelous stories about what he did there. You must be very good to him and love him very much. You are my only hope to bring a smile to his face, and I know you will. He will teach you to be fine, strong men and . . ." Her voice broke into quiet sobs.

Judah could take no more. He wanted to rush in and forbid her to walk out of his life, but he could not enter and interrupt while the babies were at Tamar's breasts. He withdrew a few yards from her tent and began to pace. He tried to envision life without Tamar. Never before that instant had he ever thought he needed anyone in his life as much. He wanted no wet nurse feeding his sons nor Cumi singing to them! He thought of Tamar far away and miserable and alone, turned out from her father's house for want of enough food. He saw her begging in the streets, destitute, perhaps even starving to death, while he and his sons lived in the luxury and bounty of Egypt. He had no idea what he could say or how he could say it, but he had to do something.

She was placing the babies back in their bed slings and adjusting her robes when Judah finally was able to go back to the tent door and quietly call her name.

Tamar turned part way around and saw him standing at the door. He was looking down at her with what appeared to be tenderness in his eyes. At first, she imagined herself to be dreaming. She blinked, but he stood there still.

"Judah?" she questioned. It was not so much that he had changed in appearance, nor the fact that she had heard no servants shouting to announce the returning caravan from Egypt. It was her own misgivings about the reality of his presence in the same room with her, actually wanting to speak to her. "Is it truly you?" she asked.

"Yes. We returned just now. All safe—every one, including Simeon and Benjamin."

"Praise God!" Tamar breathed. She closed her eyes for a moment. When she opened them she saw him draw closer to look first at her and then at his sons. A smile was on his lips and the tenderness had not left his eyes.

Judah fumbled for words. "I was here before, but I did not wish to disturb . . ." He felt clumsy and embarrassed for not announcing his presence earlier.

"It is no matter," Tamar said. "The twins are finished feeding and going to sleep now."

Judah thought how beautiful she was as he searched for words to tell her the things he was feeling. But all he could do was look at the babies and say, "I . . . I have never thanked you."

"Thanked me? For what?"

"For my two strong and handsome sons." Why could he compliment them, not her?

"I should as well thank you," Tamar said. "They are beautiful, are they not?" As Tamar rose to glance down upon the sleeping faces, she was aware that Judah was at her side. They stood in silence, neither knowing what to say next.

"Well, Judah," Tamar said as casually as she could, wondering at this strange reunion after such a long time of physical and emotional separation. "You must be tired. I will get you . . ."

"No, I pray you, sit down. I must speak with you, Tamar." He grasped her arm, but quickly released it again, not wishing to be presumptuous or forward. "The others will be here soon. I rode ahead."

Tamar studied Judah's face as she sat with him. Nowhere in

his eyes could she read the meaning of his presence there nor his changed demeanor.

Judah cleared his throat. This was more difficult than addressing the Egyptian governor. He was right to tell his brothers he was not a man of gentle tongue, but this was no time for logic or arguments to persuade Tamar. Yet, she seemed to hold his life in her hands, as Joseph had.

"Cumi met our caravan and said you plan to . . . to go away," Judah said lamely.

"I think it best—for everyone," she replied, placing her hands in her lap and resting her back on a floor cushion.

"Of course, I shall not forbid you, if . . . if it is your desire to leave, but . . . but do you think it wise to go away . . . from the twins? They are at such an early age."

Tamar swallowed hard, thinking for a moment he was going to say something else. "I have made arrangements for their care." When Judah did not say anything more, she asked, "When did you see Cumi?"

"Just now. On the hillside. She watched for our return and met us down the road."

"How did you fare in Egypt?" Tamar asked, unsure of the conversation's exact direction.

"Very well. You will not believe all that occurred. I hardly know where to begin."

"At the beginning, of course," she said, drawing her knees up and settling herself to listen.

Judah gave a disjointed account of the story. It was difficult to speak of other things when his heart was so full of emotion, but it also was easier than groping for feelings he could not express. Perhaps starting with an objective report of the journey would help, giving him more time to lead up to the more important things he hoped he would find words to say later. He told Tamar of the governor's tricks, their being arrested for the cup in Benjamin's sack, Joseph revealing himself, and the surprise reunion of the estranged brothers. When he got to his conversion experience, he became emotionally tense, and ineptly ill at ease. He did not tell that part well. It was so hard to be open enough with Tamar to express deep feelings about God or spiritual things or, most especially, love. They never before had conversed quietly, only in fits of rage.

When Judah paused, he looked into Tamar's eyes and thought he saw understanding there for the unspoken parts of his story. Perhaps she knew him better than he knew himself. He wondered how she felt toward him and if he had killed all the love she once professed for him. Could he bring himself to ask her forgiveness? If he could, would she grant it? Or was it too late?

Tamar's outward appearance belied her heart, pounding for joy. She wanted to shout to Judah that he no longer had any reason to continue punishing himself. Now that he knew his brother was alive and well, Judah could put away his guilt and his moods of dark depression and angry rage. Perhaps now he could be the husband she wanted and loved. She spoke none of this to Judah. She waited to hear from him before she said the wrong words and spoiled everything.

The last of Judah's story involved the move to Egypt and the brothers' wanting Tamar to break the news to Jacob about Joseph. Judah told her, "They feel your gentle, woman's touch is needed to soften the blow that surely will fall when we must stand before him and confess our guilt. But this is only a request to you, Tamar, not a command. You may refuse if you desire, for it is not your place to have to prepare the way for our confession."

"I gladly will do what I can for you and your brothers," Tamar said. "The confession may not be as difficult as you think. Father Jacob never believed the wild beast tale. He always has suspected something else, and this is a much happier ending than he ever could have imagined."

When Judah said nothing more, Tamar did not know where she stood with him. He made no mention of wanting her to go with them all to Egypt. Was she included in any of his future plans? Was she still his wife, or was she merely a convenient messenger? She had to know.

"Judah, I had planned to be gone from here by tomorrow's dawn, rather than to delay my departure any longer. Each day I am with the twins, leaving them becomes more difficult. But I can take your message to Father Jacob first . . . before I go away . . . and you see my face no more."

377

"Tamar!" Judah started to protest her decision to leave, but words stuck in his throat. She had every reason to leave him, and if he had made it impossible for her to live with him after all he had done to hurt her, he could not blame her. He shifted direction to say, "Reuben told me that you knew all along of my shameful deeds—how I sold Joseph because of my jealousy and deceived Israel. I am glad I did not have to give you the details of that sin as I reported to you of Egypt."

"Judah, I would not have condemned you, had you told me yourself, because I am not without sin. I still live with a deception worse than yours—my memories of a harlot in Adullam."

"That is over and forgotten. If there is any blame there, I share it with you. I treated you more shamefully than you treated me."

Tamar thought Judah's words were the closest he had ever come to an apology. She looked at him in amazement and said, "You are changed. You are not the same man who left here."

"I do not feel the same, Tamar. My brother, Joseph, is the reason. He taught me many things. There is such a spiritual atmosphere within his home. It is unexplainable! By God's grace, I would like my household to be as his."

"I am glad to hear it. I hope your household will be as you say."

"That will be in Egypt, of course, in the land of Goshen where all the sons of Israel will reside. Joseph says we will live off the fat of the land and never fear hunger again."

"For that I also rejoice. I am thankful I shall not be concerned that my sons will lack bread in the days to come."

The stilted politeness of their conversation had reached the limits of endurance for both of them. Neither Judah nor Tamar could bring themselves to say what they really felt. Each waited for the other to give some indication, some opening that would broach the topic on both minds.

"You sound as if you do not plan to be part of the household in Egypt. Are you still quite determined to leave me?" Judah asked with a lump in his throat.

"I have caused you such pain, Judah. You were forced

378

against your will to take me as your wife. I will not hold you to that, or anything else, any longer."

"Tamar, tell me truly, do you want us to go separate ways? Has it been so unbearable?"

She looked up at him in surprise. "Unbearable? For you, yes. But not for me."

"It has not been so for me, Tamar!" Judah said emphatically. "I was not myself. My mind was so distracted that I did not think clearly. I wanted to die! I thought the only way to save you and my sons and to save the land from famine was to destroy myself—before I brought destruction upon you and everyone else. That seems so foolish now, but that was my state of mind."

"I know. I truly understand, Judah," she said gently.

"If I ask you to stay with me, will you? I mean, will you want to stay?"

"Only if you desire it."

"I make you no command. Tell me first, what is it *you* desire?"

"Only to please you. That is a wife's first duty to her husband."

Judah pounded his fist in frustration. "We have tiptoed around the edges too long. I shall speak clearly. I think . . . I think our sons should be nourished by their mother, not by a wet nurse!"

Tamar let out a disappointed sigh. "Oh, I see. It is only for the welfare of the twins that you want me to stay with your household."

"I did not mean that."

"Then, pray, what exactly did you mean?"

"I mean . . . What is your feeling for me, right now, Tamar?"

Tamar thrust out her jaw. The question had been put to her, so she would answer: "I love you, Judah. I have always loved you, and I always will. Why else would I be willing to give up my dearest treasures, my only sons, when I depart?"

Now it was Judah who sighed in disappointment. He completely overlooked her pledge of love and heard only her last few words. "Then you still plan to depart?" he cried.

379

"Judah, in the name of truth, pray tell me what you want me to do! Do you love me or not?"

Judah felt blood rush to his face. He could not speak. A slant of light had seized her hair and turned it to flame. Her eyes still flashed and sparkled from the emotion of her last words. All Judah could do was sit there, in awe of her beauty, captivated by her, desiring her, needing her.

"I judge by your silence," Tamar said, "that your feelings for me are unchanged. How foolish of me to think you could forgive me! Such pride I have for thinking you could care for me!"

Judah grasped her hand to say, "You speak the words I had in mind to say to you! I did not think you could forgive me or care for me any longer. Wait! Just now, did I hear you say that you loved me?"

"Must I say so again before you will believe it?"

"I am so overcome with feelings, but so very poor at expressing them." He took both of her hands and pressed them to his lips. "Dear Tamar, my heart is full, but my head is still distracted. I am not yet the man I want to be, a man you can respect. When I offer you my love, I must be more of a man than I am now. I cannot promise you I can be a husband to you, not the kind I want to be—a godly one, like Joseph. But if you can be patient with me and willing to wait . . ."

"Willing to wait?" she interrupted. "Why, I have become very accustomed to waiting."

"Then, can you stay with me and give me time to grow as a man? It is asking a great deal of you, I know, when you could find so many better husbands . . ."

"Judah . . ."

"I shall try hard to make up to you for the heartaches you have borne because of me . . ."

"Judah!"

"It is no easy task for a rough lion to be gentled, but I think I can change if only . . ."

"Judah, attend unto me! I will stay!"

Judah's mouth flew open in surprise. "You will stay?" he repeated.

As he saw the vigorous nodding of her head, he fell speechless again: "I have no words!"

"Then say no more. I am content," Tamar said, believing the words would come later.

As a baby whimpered, they both turned to look at their children, and Judah said, "Joseph has seen a vision from God. He prophesied that I will inherit the blessing after all, and that our firstborn will receive it after me. He said you were to be mother of the covenant promise."

Tamar clasped her hands to her breast. "He said that?"

"Yes," Judah replied. "And Joseph's dreams are not to be doubted. God's will seems to prevail—in spite of all our sinful, misguided efforts to thwart it."

Hearing the approaching caravan and the voices of his brothers outside, Judah led Tamar to the tent door, pointed, and said, "Look you there, Tamar—Benjamin and Cumi. They are so happy. You should have seen them upon the hillside. He all but devoured her!"

Tamar smiled and waved to greet the travelers. She said, "Father Jacob will give Cumi and Benjamin his blessing and consent for them to marry. I just know it. Stranger miracles than that have happened." Then, softly under her breath, she added, "to me this day."

As they stepped outside, Judah said, "When Israel gets to Egypt and sees Joseph's sons, he will forget that Benjamin is his favorite. In the blinking of an eye, he will release Benjamin to marry, as you say. I am no prophet like Joseph, but that is my prediction."

"Why do you profess such confidence about it?" Tamar asked him.

"Because Ephraim, Joseph's younger son, looks for all the world like Rachel. I think Israel will have a new favorite very soon."

"Your description of Egypt tells me life there will be beautiful and marvelous—for all of Father Jacob's hungering families."

"It will be so for you and me also, Tamar. A new and better life—as long as we keep our trust in God and seek His will."

Closing her eyes and sucking in her breath, Tamar exclaimed, "And we shall see our son anointed as the one chosen to be heir to the covenant blessing!" Tamar had to say it aloud to make it be true. The thing she most desired, her whole purpose in life, had been worked out by the Lord—once she stopped trying to scheme and plot to work it out herself.

Without realizing it, Judah had slipped his arm about Tamar's waist as they stood watching the men unloading the wagons. From that great bounty would come the food they would eat for their evening meal. It would be the first decent supper the household had enjoyed in so long that Judah thought a celebration feast was in order. He asked Tamar what she thought.

Tamar did not hear Judah. It was not because of the noisy travelers' voices, nor the loud commotion of the unloading process, nor the rejoicing shouts of the servants. It was Judah's arm around her. He was touching her! She wanted to reach up to kiss her husband. She wanted to say something clever like, "Show unto me the way Benjamin all but devoured Cumi on the hillside."

Instead, Tamar just stood there, thinking how much better things might have gone if she had not been so stubbornly willful and impatient. By trying so desperately hard to win, she had lost so much. She had created many obstructing barriers that had to be removed. Judah still seemed to be groping his way through a cloudy veil of mist in search of himself. It might take him a very long time to recover from wounds that needed healing, especially the blows to Judah's pride and self-respect that resulted from Tamar's shameful trickery on the road to Adullam.

But a new road lay ahead. Upon that road, Tamar might have to settle for her next best thing. She smiled. She could wait. She had faith that, in God's own time, the barriers would fall, the veil would lift, the wounds would heal, and she could obtain all her heart's desires.

The End
and
The Beginning

382